Mystic Creek

Mystic Creek

The Trilogy

Slade Belgard

Copyright© Case Number 1-3129447201

All rights reserved, Published in the United States by
Belgard Literary Creations

Cover design by
Charlotte Smith McDaniel

Illustration by
Juanita Dew Patrum

Library of Congress Control Number: 2016933602

Printed by CreateSpace, Charleston, SC

Belgard, Slade
Mystic Creek: a novel / Slade Belgard

ISBN-13: 978-0692639597
ISBN-10: 0692639594

PRINTED IN THE UNITED STATES OF AMERICA

First Edition

For Mom

Chapter 1

*"How dear to this heart are the scenes to my childhood,
when fond recollections present them to view."*
~ **Samuel Woodworth**

Who doesn't love the sizzling aroma of fresh cooked crispy bacon? The country cured scent tantalizes your sense of smell, the taste buds drool, the belly rumbles, and you can't take your willing eyes off of it as it disappears into your mouth. Does anything taste better?

When Jake Willoughby smells bacon he travels back in time, some forty plus years, to his dear mother's loving, warm and inviting kitchen, and the best bacon he had ever eaten; the very best food he had ever eaten came from that kitchen. Jake's mother, Mina, loved to cook, and his family loved to eat. Gathering around the dinner table was their grateful and joyful together time.

Sometimes he smiles, other times the tears flow uncontrollably. He is reminded of his beautiful family, his humble upbringing, and the very best of days. He is reminded of how much he misses them all and how much he would love to sit around the breakfast table right now with each and every member of his family like they did when he was growing up on John's Island, South Carolina, planning the events of the forthcoming day, and most of all, to feel the love and refuge of family and home.

Given another opportunity, he would appreciate their company, their stories, their smiles and laughter, and would tell each one of them how much he loved and treasured them. He would express sincere regret for the poor choices he has made along the way, and he would ask his parents to forgive him for his selfish acts that may have led to any disappointment in him.

Jake longed for one more moment, just one more with his mom, dad, brothers and sister, and his favorite uncle, Hal, and his best pal Tommy. Jake had always felt robbed of time with his family and friends; they all left way too soon, leaving him completely alone. He never fully understood why. It felt to him like someone spilling wine on a Rembrandt, a priceless work of art completely ruined. The abrupt halt of his youth is a total mystery.

We trek on with each new breath checking off each passing day with its forward passage to end. Though many years have passed, many suns have set, and many people have come and gone, the smallest of things can place us right back there again.

Sights, sounds, and smells tap the recall button, and immediately send us to a time and place that we cannot physically visit, yet there we are in all of its glory. The good or bad ruminating about a certain time, place, person, or event. Sometimes the visits can be so vibrant and perfectly visible, as if we are truly there in our physical body. The senses work in overdrive, emotions overwhelm us, and instantly the time and events are recreated when we flow back through the pages of our lives.

A happened chance lent Jake an opportunity to travel back in time, whether willing or not, while buying athletic shoes in a big box sporting goods store. Jake walked down a random aisle when a small display catches his attention. It stops him in his tracks, and Jake stares fondly at the neatly arranged baseballs on the shelf. They are all new and unspoiled. He reaches for one of the new baseballs, and brings it to his nose. For a quick millimeter of a second, Jake's life flashes by and he sees himself as a child again, just like those times when smelling bacon. However, his surroundings and lack of focus quash the nostalgic visit.

Jake enthusiastically strolls to the cash register, and purchases the little baseball, along with a pair of shoes and an energy bar. He is almost as excited about this baseball as he was nearly four decades earlier. Later that evening, while relaxing in his recliner and sipping on a cold beer, a fervent Jake slowly and carefully removes his new purchase from its package. In one huge hand he slowly turns the white ball and admires the fresh and flawless baseball, and notes each shiny red stich. He lifts it to his nostrils, and the prodigious power of the newly dyed leather enters Jake's body, captures his cognizance and holds him hostage.

Now, he gladly surrenders, and the journey back in time begins as Jake Willoughby travels through his existence in the rewind mode. He passes by all of the sights, sounds, smells, and all of the many days and nights that got him to this point in his life, sending him back to the beginning of his sharpest and most relevant of memories; the summer of 1968.

Nineteen sixty-eight; it was the year that introduced to the world many new iconic games, toys, television shows, as well as songs, movies, sculptures and junk food. Twister, Hot Wheels, *Mister Rogers' Neighborhood*, and *Hawaii Five–O* took over American living rooms. *The Graduate* filled movie houses, and consumed conversation. *Hey Jude* stayed in everyone's heads, and greatest of all, the Big Mac, one man's interpretation of a hamburger, was consumed by the world. At just 49¢ for a hamburger with special sauce, how could anyone go wrong?

The Green Bay Packers, Detroit Tigers, and Boston Celtics all won their respective championships, and the St. Louis Arch was added to the American landscape. The 8-track player echoed through all automobiles, and with a single dollar bill in your pocket you could get a gallon of gas, travel to the nearest golden arch, fill your rumbling belly, and drive home in time to watch the premier of CBS's weekly televised news magazine, *60 Minutes* on Sunday nights.

But it wasn't all fun, games and food. The war in Vietnam was at its bloodiest peak and the American culture had changed. Assassination was rampant, demonstrators rallied in violent protest, and The Cusabo Indian spirits of John's Island were awakened.

Jake had earlier memories too, of course, but this particular year was the most prominent one in his young life; one that followed him like a perpetual shadow lurking behind his every step, and haunting him nearly every day. It was the year when so many drastic changes and events took place, with a domino effect in his life. It was when things connected and disconnected at the same time. Riddles were created, solved, and not really solved at all. Things seemed distinct, yet obscure, all in the same moment and same frame.

Puberty came calling with it many vicissitudes. Unsuspecting Jake assumed it was a lot like the acid trips people were experimenting with at that time, but he was on no acid, no drugs at all; perhaps the Flintstone chewable vitamins.

Jake is courageous enough to sit down for the first time to try and solve the riddle within the riddle. He is ready to visit the beginning of a tragic path, to try and find the missing pieces, then place them all together in order to make sense, and to answer all the whys and why nots.

Jake had often wanted to revisit his life, and try to figure things out, but life itself got in the way, and he had always put it off for another day. Now is another day, and it is as good a time as any. Why not?

"Do you really want to go there Jake? Do you really want to face the demons? Maybe it's the only way to conquer them."

Taking a deep breath, and swallowing hard, he answered aloud. "Let's do this."

June 1968 ~ a magical time.

…Comfortably sitting on the soft, cool, green grass in the shade of the oak, and clutching his baseball in one hand while wearing his weather-beaten glove on the other, Jake, in his excitement, started recollecting a few days prior when the summer actually began as a distant lawnmower echoed across the Carolina blue sky.

In his first thirteen years of life, long and lanky Jake Willoughby spent many summer afternoons in the shade nestled against the exposed roots of this mighty live oak that sat on the south side of the yard of his John's Island home. The only difference in this day, and the others is the fact the he is now the proud owner of a new Major League

4

baseball, a real hardball, something he had been wanting for quite some time, and started to believe that he would never get. Sitting beneath the large tree, Jake closed his eyes to relish the moment. He put the new ball to his nose to savor the new smell before it was used, stained, and tattered.

Jake was not accustomed to anything new so this was a really big moment in his life. He started thinking about it, and realized that this was the very first thing that ever belonged to him before anyone else, besides his Superman suit, because he had always settled for seconds without complaints.

This was about the most elated and excited he had ever been about anything. He had spent weeks fantasizing about actually holding one, now he not only holds it, but it is HIS, all his and no one else's.

He can throw it, catch it, stare at it, smell it, and put it to sleep each night in his old hand-me-down fielder's glove given to him by his older brother, Ronnie. Maybe, just maybe, one day he'll get a new glove. In the meantime, the current glove was just fine.

It was very sentimental, and had several more diving catches left in it; one thing at a time. This is his ball, and it means the world to him. He is thrilled just to stare at it and hold it in his hands. Jake could not believe it, he was exhilarated beyond words. What a perfect day.

Chapter 2

"Misfortunes tell us what fortune is."
~ **Thomas Fuller**

It all began when Mina told Jake's dad, Wavy, aptly nicknamed because of his thick wavy red hair; she believed Jake wanted a new baseball. She explained how the old one was nearly unrecognizable and about three catches from losing its cover.

Mina's motherly intuition was spot on as she watched her son's eyes light up every time he saw the ball on display during the family's weekly trip to the Western Auto. She also witnessed Jake glued to the pictures of it in the weekly newspaper advertisements. This pulled on Mina's heartstrings, especially since Jake never once said anything about wanting it, because he knew it wasn't in the Willoughby family's budget. Jake never asked for anything, and knew going to Western Auto was usually to get something for the automobile, the house or yard but never anything personal, least of all, something as unimportant as a baseball.

Thinking back on it, Jake remembered being a good son. He never complained when he had to settle for hand-me-downs or second best, because that was their way of life and he never knew any difference. He always did as he was told, and was very respectful of everyone, especially elders. This is the way Mina and Wavy raised all of their children. Jake didn't know that there was any other way.

Jake pondered the reasoning behind such a wonderful gift. It was nowhere near Christmas or his birthday, and his grades in school were pretty average. Well, wait a minute. He did get promoted to the next grade; that had to be it.

One afternoon when his dad got home from work, Jake jumped into the backseat of the new gold Chevy Biscayne, at Wavy's urging. Mina got into the passenger seat, and Wavy grabbed the big wheel, as he fondly called it. It was always exciting to leave rural John's Island and head anywhere, but especially downtown Charleston, and even more so knowing that they were headed to the Western Auto on upper King Street. This store was loaded with goodies, but it was also home to a certain baseball that Jake had eyed from an earlier visit.

"How much longer?" Jake asked no less than a dozen times during the twenty minute ride to town.

As they pulled into the small, gravelly parking lot, Jake could barely compose himself. He was so excited that he was literally jumping and bouncing in the back seat.

Now that he was here, he could smell the newness of the horse's hide on the beautiful ball all the way out into the side parking lot. Jake launched himself from the car the second it stopped, and ran toward the front doors of the store despite his parent's plea to stop and wait for them. Only after nearly knocking down an older, hunch-backed gentleman using a cane did Mina make her voice loud enough to connect to Jake's good senses.

The older, squinty-eyed man with a long, gray, unkempt beard, and shabby sweater looked startled. He exposed an appalling mouthful of crooked, coffee stained teeth when he realized the young child's excitement meant no deliberate harm. He tilted his soiled, well-worn, brown fedora in acknowledgement, and said hello while leaving his rancid breath hanging in the still air, then mumbling to no one in particular as the old hunch-back man proceeded warily down the sidewalk. Dismayed by the time delay, and the spookiness of the old man, Jake impatiently waited his parent's arrival at the store's entrance, and kept looking anxiously in their direction.

Finally, they approached the shiny glass doors and Wavy, almost as excited as his son, quickly grabbed the door handle to allow the freckle-faced, shaggy haired Jake to enter. The doors opened to the dome of auto parts, and the overwhelming smell of fresh new rubber tires. It was much like releasing the gate on a rodeo bull, as Jake quickly arrived at the apex of his of baseball yearnings, or as close as he would ever get. Mina and Wavy were left at the front of the store grinning with enthusiasm. Like a bolt of lightning, the ball appeared right before Jake's big, brown eyes in magnificent glory pleading to go with him.

Jake breathlessly engrossed the long anticipated moment; he eyed every red stitch on the ball as if he were a new dad counting fingers and toes on this fresh extension of himself. The milky white ball was flawless, it was perfect. Almost too perfect to play with, but that is the whole purpose of having it is to play with it., pretending to be Mickey Mantle, Tom Seaver, Pete Rose or Johnny Bench. Not to have it sitting on a shelf collecting dust, and serving no function at all except to please the new owner.

"Man, oh man, the guys are going to be so jealous of me," Jake said aloud. "I can't wait to get it home, and show it off."

Jake was a good, thoughtful kid. Always kind to others and he was very well-mannered and polite. He always did his chores in a timely manner, and was constantly concerned and compassionate about other people. He was taught to always be very courteous towards others. He was honest, obedient, did well and behaved in school, and he had above average intelligence when applied. He was also pretty good with the pencil on all levels; penmanship, creative writing and sketching. He was extremely observant for a young boy; he looked at and took in everything and everyone around him with great attentiveness and curiosity.

Physically, he was a good head taller than everyone else his age. His long legs gave him more speed than his friends, which they all loathed when it came to games and contest, because Jake always won. He was usually a team captain, or always the first picked for a team at selection time. Jake had a handsome face with pronounced features. He had dark chestnut brown hair and eyes, both of which appeared black at most times.

The young man had a small mask of freckles that sprinkled from cheek to cheek across his small nose, a girl's nose, he had been told by his older brother Kenny. The attractive nose highlighted his broad toothy

8

smile, which gave sparkle to his large, endearing eyes that were accentuated by his long, dark lashes, and thick arched brows. Most people considered Jake very handsome, and often complimented him, something he never gave much consideration to. He figured he was just an average, normal kid, but that would change drastically in just a few short weeks.

Chapter 3

"Home, the spot of earth supremely blest,
a dearer, sweeter spot than all the rest."
~ **Robert Montgomery**

In 1961, Wavy Willoughby decided that he missed the rural life style of his upbringing, and would like the same for his sons. Not wanting the secluded, away from everything farm life, and having fallen very much in love with Charleston, he and Mina both shared the desire to stay put. The only area in the low country that Wavy showed any interest in was John's Island; named after Saint John Parrish of Barbados, the first settlers on the island.

In the early sixties there were a few new neighborhoods, some of them startup homes, sprouting up in the area that were actually affordable, after the couple put their savings into it. Wavy knew that he could always add on to the modest home as needed. He and his family were excited about their new home on the island, and its perfect location, with close proximity to several beaches, rivers, and downtown Charleston.

The Willoughby's lived in a new subdivision called Oak Crest, near the south end of Maybank Highway, on what was once a thriving rice plantation, and over the generations it also served as a cotton, cabbage, and potato farm. It was located two miles past the intersection of Main Road, which turned into Bohicket Road at the crossing, and channeled through a tunnel of majestic live oaks. This area leads through Wadmalaw Island, and on to the coast of Seabrook and Kiawah Islands, and the Atlantic Ocean.

The Willoughby home was a three bedroom house with two baths, sitting on a one acre corner lot. It was tucked away and hidden in dense acreage of a wide variety of large hardwood trees that was once home to abundant wildlife. It was a modest wooden frame house with a carport, front porch, and a detached garage which sat in the middle of the wooded lot.

It was a beautiful place to call home with all of the magnificent live oak trees and a wide variety of other beautiful shade trees, plants, flowers, and shrubbery, most of which were planted by Wavy and Mina over the years. Adjacent to this he had a garden which was a 50 foot by 40 foot paradise of vegetables, consisting of a huge array of seasonal items like corn, cucumbers, assorted greens, a large variety of peppers, onions, squash, sunflowers, tomatoes, and even watermelon. Wavy loved gardening, and knew all the tricks of the trade having grown up on an abundant and profitable farm, and he religiously followed the Farmer's Almanac.

Mina had her flower garden near the house. She was very attentive to her garden as she loved flowers. It consisted of, depending on the seasons of course, roses, daffodils, petunias, forsythia, impatiens, marigolds, sunflowers and lilies. On a nearby trellis she grew yellow jessamine and hydrangeas, and in the center of her flower garden sat half of a whiskey barrel in which she grew scarlet sage, narcissus hawera, and black-eyed Susan. Nearby, in an old, rusty pail near a birdbath, she grew rosemary and basil.

A very handy Wavy added a bedroom, and a screened porch at the back of the house facing the magnificent South Carolina low country sunsets. He also had built a huge workshop where he enjoyed his wood work, tinkering, and quiet time with his thoughts, and fermenting scuppernong grapes in two huge oak barrels. There he spent countless hours building bookshelves, wall shelves, cabinets, small tables, bird houses, and anything else he happened to think about. Not to mention taste testing his "grape juice". He also built a small wooden storage shed behind the garage to house his tools and yard equipment.

John's Island is the largest island in South Carolina, and the fourth largest in the Southeastern United States. It was first inhabited by Nomadic tribes of Native Americans, such as The Stono, The Kiawah, The Bohicket, and Cusabo, meaning good water, Indians. Spanish explorers gave up on the island when they could not find any jewels, but English settlers realized it was perfect for agriculture. Indigo, tea, rice, and cotton became the main cash crops until the boll weevil came and took over.

After many years of experimenting, and hard labor, the islanders discovered that potatoes, cabbage, corn, onions, greens, and ultimately tomatoes would thrive on the island, as well as many species of trees, plants, animals, and birds; a truly magnificent place that Jake never appreciated until many years later after he had left it.

Many of the current John's Island residents are third and fourth generation farmers, several of which are close friends with the Willoughby's. Wavy and Mina enjoyed afternoon rides around the large island, and introducing themselves to everyone that they came across, even as far as knocking on doors. Everyone appreciated the respect and courtesy offered by Wavy and Mina.

Many of the old-timers often gifted the Willoughby's with anything they wanted to pick from their farms and gardens. Many residents let them dig up native plants and trees to set out in their own yard. Farmers, shrimpers, fishermen, mechanics, plumbers, carpenters, you name it, knew the Willoughby's and they knew they were part of a very friendly and helpful community.

In those days the island consisted of several small Mom and Pop stores and gas stations, a railroad depot, which included the post office, produce packing sheds and farms, but not much else. It seemed that there was a small store every mile or so along the two major roads, Main and Maybank Highway, on the island. To access the island you had to drive over either of two swing bridges that crossed the Stono and Ashley Rivers which formed the island.

Only a few of the thriving stores in the forties and fifties survived into the late sixties, but they too eventually died off like their proprietors. Then there came the invasion of the big box retailer on neighboring islands, and surrounding areas, putting a squeeze on the small businesses in their quiet, rural world.

Chapter 4

"Childhood knows the human heart."
~ **Edgar Allen Poe**

For many reasons, June of 1968 was a very special time in Jake Willoughby's life. First of all, he was on summer vacation, which meant no school or no homework, and meant fun and playing all day, every day, with his entire group of buddies and best friend, Tommy Stern. There were no deadlines or commitments and young Jake and his merry men loved this. They would ride their rickety, old bikes and spend hours exploring through the woods, which was an over grown, abandoned plantation and forgotten farm. They would ride their bikes on old trails in the woods, and create new ones. They would control their neighborhood streets with their rusty "warhorses" on wheels.

The rambunctious crew would ride to the historic Angel Oak by way of the dusty dirt road, just a mile or two away, that led to this five hundred year old live oak. They would climb on it as high as they could then surrender to its overwhelming size. Then they would hop on their bikes again, and head down the road to Church Creek, but only when an adult was present to ward off any mishaps.

Many times they would catch blue crabs with chicken necks tied to the end of piece of string, a net for retrieving, and a bucket in tow to hold their catch of the blue shelled delicacies. They were always cautious to stay on the firm, compacted banks, and not step in the pluff mud for surely they would be slurped up by the hungry muck. Every now and then one of the kids would get pinched by the defensive and doomed critters, and someone's mother, usually Mina, was always doctoring with the mercurochrome and bandages.

Once or twice, against their better judgment, they would sneak down on their bikes to the slippery banks of Church Creek without an adult. This was something Jake knew was wrong, but the oldest boy in the group, Johnny Moore, would call anyone chicken who didn't come along. Being called chicken in front of your friends was forbidden, and

Jake was going to never allow that to happen, so every time this was mentioned, Jake thought of another adventure that would interest his buddies more, to deter them from the treacherous mud.

Their bicycle journey often found them stopping at Staley's Corner Store in search of butter cookies, penny candy, and bubblegum, which they could afford by redeeming empty soda bottles they had collected by the roadside and grassy ditches. The Mary Janes, Squirrel Nut Zippers and butter cookies from a large glass jar would go down so much smoother with an ice cold Coke of their own; such a treat in middle of a hot summer day. The visit always included cheerful conversation from Anna Belle Staley, the black, gregarious proprietor, who seemed to constantly smile and always sent greetings home to the family.

"What a delightful person," Mina would always say about Anna Belle. "Remember Jake, she is a lady of color."

"I know, I know, they're colored people." Jake would respond.

The boys would often hang around outside of the store with some of the regulars beneath the shade of one of the large oaks, or sit on a huge stump and enjoy their snacks. They would watch others eat pickled pig feet, hot sausage, huge slices of bologna and cheddar cheese, unlike Jake, who was used to his meager sandwiches. The happy and loud older folk would wash down their lunch with a tall malt liquor named after an old west handgun. They spoke their own language so it was hard for Jake and his pals to decipher what they were talking about, but it must have been funny because it caused a lot of laughter, and knee slapping from the bloodshot eyed group.

In between the fun destinations the group would often look into the sky and count the C5A Galaxy military cargo and supply planes. These planes would travel in groups of three on their way to Vietnam to supply American troops with all the provisions needed to defeat North Vietnamese communist - Viet Cong, or as Ronnie and his pals would call them "Gooks", who were trying to take over South Vietnam, and were killing our young men by the droves.

The second and most important reason why this is a special time for young Jake is because his older brother Ronnie, the giver of the glove, the one who taught Jake how to catch and throw a baseball, is coming home. He will be on a thirty day leave before he goes to Vietnam. This was a bittersweet visit for Jake as he idolizes his older brother, and wanted to see him every possible moment because he knew, based on overheard adult conversation, that this could very well be the last time he saw his brother. This makes Jake depressed, so he really has to make it count.

The last day of the school year was indeed a special day. Jake could hardly stand the anticipation. It meant so many different things to him like Ronnie coming home, trips to Grandma's house, cutting long pants into shorts, and going barefoot. He would be outside for the entire three months, swimming in Green Hole, which was a large man-made pond, formally a sandpit that all the locals swam in. There would be bookmobiles, watermelon, and the daily jingle of ice cream trucks. Jake got even more excited thinking of all the things he would do after enjoying early morning cartoons, and *Captain Kangaroo* although he would never admit to anyone that he still watched these shows.

Jake would build forts in the woods, with all of his closest buddies, until they were called in for lunch. It was common to hear parents loudly calling each child that it was time to come home for whatever reason. Then they would prop up in front of the television and watch Roy Rogers and Gene Autry.

He started thinking of some of his more favorite things to do, like long bicycle rides to Angel Oak and Staley's Store to see if Anna Belle would give them free cookies and candy, which she often did. He would definitely play hide and seek with Kathy and Julie, which they had been doing for years, even though they were probably a little old for that now. But with the onslaught of hormones, Kathy started making that a lot more interesting as of late but Jake was a little slow in that department.

Jake would play with all the neighborhood kids, especially baseball and the game Pickle, which is when you try to tag out a runner before they can safely land on base. Jake loved to hang out with his best friend Tommy, the aforementioned girl's older brother, and a kid by the name of Johnny Moore. Thinking of all of this fun, and no school had Jake drooling on himself with anticipation. Wow, man, this all going to be so great. Most of all he would be with Ronnie, and hopefully his older brother would spend a lot of time with him.

Jake then thought no teachers, no homework, or the anxiety about whether or not he was dressed well enough not to be teased and picked on by classmates, which happened quite often since Jake wore his older brother's hand-me-downs.

Jake never told anyone about the bullying. He just assumed it was a way of life, and assumed there will always be mean kids in the world. A nearly six foot tall, Kenny, Jake's other older brother, who was born between Jake and Ronnie, occasionally walked up on the mistreatment and never had to say a word, and the harassment would stop instantly. Kenny asked Jake if it had taken place often. Jake lied and said no. Never the less, Kenny wanted to keep an eye on his younger brother. He himself often picked on Jake, but he wasn't going to allow anyone else to do it.

Two days after summer vacation began it was time for Ronnie to come home, after three months of boot camp at Parris Island. The excitement was thrilling for Jake. To Jake, Ronnie was perfect in every way He often watched his brother, and would emulate his every move, from the way he combed his thick, black hair, to the way he would walk and talk. He even emulated the way Ronnie slid his brown, leather belt through the khaki belt loops six inches at a time.

During his senior year in high school, Ronnie was drafted into the armed forces. He chose the Marine Corps because of its reputation as the toughest of all branches of service, not because of *Gomer Pyle,* as many would jest, but because he felt that he had something to prove. Uncle Hal was not aware that his nephew admired his military resume. Even if college were a possibility, the young patriot would have chosen the military.

Ronnie was small in stature, due to being born premature at only four pounds, and he always felt that he had to demonstrate to people that he was a tough man despite his limited height. The draft news distressed everyone, especially Mina, but also young Jake, who at first didn't realize exactly what this meant, or the danger involved. All Jake knew was that he would not see his hero brother as often because he would be far away. Jake didn't want to think about that at all.

After weeks of missing his brother, and overhearing constant whispers from family members in other rooms of the house attempting to not upset Jake, it all started to set in. The top stories on the national news each night didn't help matters either. This was not a good thing at all. This was the most awful thing that Jake had ever known. His bologna and cheese sandwich and butter cookies were doing cartwheels through rings of fire in his rumbling belly which made him feel sick, an unusual sick, a bad news something horrible is going to happen sick.

Jake was afraid for his brother, and was worried for his mother. Each night before bedtime he would kneel at his bed and pray for his brother's safe return and for his mother's peace of mind before climbing into the comfort of his safe bed. He and his brothers were taught early on by their mom to pray to God each night. Jake usually prayed after wrapping himself up in the warm coziness of his blanket, but the seriousness of the situation seemed to call for a more intimate and passionate show of humility. Now more than ever, Jake strongly wanted to be heard.

After the first long month of letter exchanging, the family was finally able to visit Ronnie at Parris Island at the U.S. Marine Corps Recruit Depot Eastern Region, near Beaufort, South Carolina. The enthusiastic family loaded up the Biscayne one chilly and cloudy Sunday morning in February, and took Highway 17 South towards Beaufort in the pouring down rain.

Jake was euphoric, and could not wait to see his brother. After an hour and half of riding in the rain, they finally reached their destination. The young teen was mesmerized at the entrance gate, something about

Parris Island, and the large Marine Corps globe and anchor logo that made Jake marvel in admiration. Everything was so intimidating and iconic at the same time. The reputation of the Marines Corps was bigger than life.

This place had been the training ground to many young soldiers and heroes, but most of all it was the place that prevented him from seeing *his* hero for the last few weeks, and it was the place that changed and disrupted all of their perfect lives.

The heavy pouring rain made it very difficult to see, let alone, drive in unfamiliar territory. They passed through the security gate, and had to stop to ask a young poncho wearing recruit directions to the visitors center because the rain had obscured the street signs. The radio was playing Gary Puckett singing about a young girl, whose name must have been "Susie Q", because she was the topic of the next song, and by the time they reached the correct destination, Susie was visiting the "Harper Valley PTA".

Mom, Dad, Kenny, Jake and the golden Chevy parked in front of a sad, gray, two story brick building sitting alone on the corner just off the puddle bearing sidewalk. It resembled something from an old black and white movie; eerie and alone on the corner bordered with large trees being pummeled by the merciless torrents like an old prison tower guarded by a fifteen foot bronze statue. *Iron Mike* had a Maxim machine gun slung over his right shoulder and a M1 1911 raised high in his left hand, which was to memorialize the Parris Island graduates who were killed during World War I.

The enthusiastic family had no umbrella, and braved the volley of raindrops from the parking lot to the building, which had only a small awning of shelter from the storm. Being younger and faster, Jake was the first to arrive at the main entrance, Kenny a close second, then Wavy who was holding his wife, and hovering over her to intercept as much rain as he could. Once the four drenched visitors were on the small cement slab everyone anxiously waited for their leader, Wavy, to open the door.

They were the only ones inside the huge building, other than a dark green fatigue wearing clerk at the gray metal desk to the left of the front entrance. He had on the same uniform as the action figure G.I. Joe in all the television commercials. This was the first soldier that Jake had seen in person, and it reminded him of his long ago toy soldiers come to life. Inside Jake was overwhelmed by all of the exhibits showcasing the history of the iconic Marine Corps. Many old uniforms and weapons over the years, including World Wars I and II, and the Korean conflict were sealed within glass cases throughout the building.

Then the front door opened with a blast of heavy rain, and with it a very unrecognizable soldier dressed all in one color, including a dripping rain poncho. Ronnie's face was gaunt and sporting new horn-rimmed glasses. As he removed the hood from his poncho, and a very distinct Marine fatigue cap, you could see that his hair was nearly shaved completely off. There was just a small patch, standing stiff like a cleaning brush, which stood on the very top of his head. His eyes appeared deep set and tired. Mina, once she recognized her son, nearly gasped at the changes, but caught herself from speaking it out loud.

Jake and Kenny both had to take second glances to make sure that this was indeed their brother. Wavy knew right away. No one really knew what he had endured the last four weeks, but they knew it had to be hell based on the changes to his once boyish good looks. His weekly letters never indicated the true extent of boot camp. Only years later would Jake know some of the brutality his brother faced, not only during training but during the war itself.

After entering the open area, Ronnie appeared as though he was looking around for permission to smile and to greet his loving family. Finally, not seeing anyone to ask, he broke loose smiling, and ran towards everyone. He gave his mom a big bear hug, his dad a firm hand shake, and gave Jake and Kenny a rub on the top of their heads.

This day Ronnie looked ten feet tall, as Jake admired his soldier brother from head to toe. Jake thought Ronnie's boots were especially cool looking with the fatigues appearing to be tucked within them.

After what seemed like a really short visit, the family said their goodbyes, and took to the road once again.

An unnerving, hollow and sickening feeling overcame young Jake. He felt sad, lonely, and disheartened. He had not felt this way before except when Ronnie first left over a month ago, but it was not quite this intense. He was miserable and did not like it. The future did not look bright at all. He desperately wanted to cry but mustered up the strength from somewhere to refrain from doing so. He literally felt like he would die, and at this moment he truly wouldn't had minded if he did.

Finally, another wretched month later, Ronnie's graduation day from boot camp finally came. What had seemed like an eternity to the entire Willoughby family was over. Ronnie's older sister, Diane, loaded her two children, Hutch and Sara, along with Kenny into her metallic blue 1967 Oldsmobile Bonneville. Jake rode in the Biscayne with Wavy, Mina and sat in the backseat between Uncle Hal and the neighbor girl Christine, who Jake thought smelled very nice. Christine Stern, wearing her famous pink and white polka dotted cotton sweater, obviously had some interest in Ronnie.

Ronnie's family and girlfriend arrived, parked, and sat in the old metal bleachers on a sunny spring Saturday morning. They impatiently watched as platoon after platoon perform its perfect marches across the enormous asphalt, which spread out in front of the massive Statue of The Corps proudest moment, the American flag raising at Iwo Jima, based on the famous photo from World War II. The sight was spine tingling, accompanied by the most awesome sound ever, echoing between the rows of large live oaks was the Marine Corps band perfectly playing their honored hymn.

Mina pointed out to Jake a young soldier, whom she believed was her second born son, although Jake was skeptical. From a distance it did not look very much like his brother, but based on what the first month did to his appearance Jake could only imagine what the second month would do. He stared intently trying to recognize his brother. Just to catch a small resemblance of any kind would make him feel so much better. The spring drafts raged the great flags carried by young soldiers who were fervent to put to test everything they had learned for the past three months. They were ready for war, in their minds anyway. These naive kids did not realize that most of their young beautiful lives would end before Christmas.

They all drove over to Hog Island for a picnic. The spot they found was surrounded by beautiful red and white azaleas, which were Mina's favorite, and shaded by colossal live oaks looking like something from an old horror movie draped in long hanging gray Spanish moss. The family and the new Marine took station at two large picnic tables, and quickly tore the lids off of buckets of the Colonel's famous and delicious chicken along with mashed potatoes and gravy, complimented with coleslaw, soft dinner rolls and chased down with ice cold sweet tea. With everyone smiling, the day just could not get any better. Well maybe some apple pie would make it better, but in their haste no one thought of dessert. Diane even forgot Ronnie's favorite, her banana pudding, which was left in her fridge back home on John's Island. Forgetting it upset Diane tremendously, but Ronnie just laughed it off. "It just wouldn't be the same if someone didn't forget something."

After one more month in Camp Lejuene, North Carolina, Ronnie would finally get to come home for a whole thirty days, a full month. Kodak Instamatics snapped photographs that would outlast anyone there that day. Their beautiful smiles would only be images on a piece of paper tucked away in a dusty, old shoe box sitting in the far corner, high on a shelf in a seldom used closet, in a now vacant, musty and cold bedroom, at the end of the long, quiet and dark hallway.

Wouldn't it be nice to travel back in time, and bring everyone back for just one last picnic? Melancholy Jake Willoughby is doing just that, the journey backwards that he had put off for so many years. To hear the laughter, see the smiles, and feel the warmth and sentiment made the trip worthwhile.

Chapter 5

"The night has a thousand eyes and the day but one;
yet the light of the bright world dies with the dying sun."
~ F.W. Bourdillion

In the late evening of June 5, 1968, Jake's elated family headed back
from the bus station with a grinning Ronnie in the backseat with his
overstuffed olive green duffel bag. Ronnie was thrilled as they pulled
into the gravelly driveway of home sweet home. He appreciated being
home again amongst the trees and flowers in the warm moonlight. At
that very same moment, on the opposite coastline, a prominent U.S.
Senator lay on the concrete floor of a hotel kitchen struggling for life,
while his blood flowed freely from bullet holes in his wounded head,
neck, and shoulder.
Jake was next door at Christine Stern's home. Yes, the pretty young
lady with the big, green eyes, anticipating Ronnie's return. Jake was
best friends with her only brother, Tommy, and often played with her
younger sisters, the three youngest of the four, for now that is. On any
other night Jake would have been at home in his own bed drifting off
to never, never land but not tonight. Tonight his beloved brother is
coming home and his family went to pick him up from the bus station
while Jake stayed with the neighbors and friends, the Sterns. While
Napoleon Solo respects the wishes of his UNCLE, Jake and friends are
still wide awake anticipating his hero's return.

Jake was watching television but not really paying much attention to
it. He had both ears focused on the driveway 100 yards away. The
greatest summer ever was about to unfold; Jake did not realize that it
would turn out to be the exact opposite.

Nearly a half century later Jake can still evoke the scent of his new
black Marine Corps sweatshirt that Ronnie had brought him from
Parris Island and can see, hear and feel the horror in the voice of the
television announcer as he interrupted regularly scheduled
programming to bring you a special bulletin report; Senator Robert F.

Kennedy had just been gunned down at the Ambassador Hotel in Los Angeles, moments after his acceptance speech for winning the California presidential primary.

The sweatshirt is long gone, the black leather ID wallet with the Marine Corps insignia incrusted in gold that Ronnie gave him now rested in the palm of his large adult hand. He looked at the wallet with affection as he slowly rubbed his thumb and fingers across smooth leather of one of his most treasured possessions. Much of the gold paint had cracked and peeled away, but enough traces remained that you knew it was the Marine Corps' emblem when you saw it. Jake slowly rubbed the wallet just as he did the baseball minutes earlier almost as if he expected a genie to appear and grant his wishes.

And so it begins; the best summer ever. Wednesday began with a joyful, lemon yellow sun resting in the magnificent blue sky as the crisp summer morning arrogantly pushed away the long bittersweet and sweaty night that would linger in the vaults of Jake's mind. Mina cooked for the boys the best breakfast any of them could remember. The kitchen, if not the entire home, has a smell that hovered in the air beckoning its flock to come feast on its banquet of edible delights. It comprised of creamy, buttery stone ground grits, fluffy scrambled eggs, fried smoked sausage, sugar-cured country ham, fresh stewed tomatoes, crispy toast, and piping hot coffee. The way only she could prepare it. They all ate like starving wolves. In between huge bites they would talk, laugh, talk and laugh some more. This was the happiest the entire family had been in quite a while.

Uncle Hal was there, a retired Marine himself, who now lived with his sister Mina, and her loving family on beautiful John Island, as he called it. Wavy was there after telling his employer that he would be in bit later. The dog and cat were nearby feeling the excitement, as well as the vast array of wild birds feeding in the many trees.

It just doesn't get any better than this Jake thought, wishing he could make these moments last forever, or at least turn into several hours so he could relish in its majestic mood. He laughed, smiled and glowed with his beautiful family.

…As he looked back, his smiles were drowned out by tears because he knew those precious moments would never again be replicated. They were ALL gone, and he was left alone with his memories, scents, tears and sounds and questions. It all swirled inside his head, even the great top 40 hits from that era spinning on the old record player, echoing and bouncing off of his skull.

After a couple of hours the three brothers headed over to the Stern's house, and Wavy left for work. Uncle Hal took his coffee and the newspaper outside to sit under the tall leaf filled sycamore in the front yard, and propped himself in a webbed folding lawn chair. Mina washed the dishes, smiling the entire time. Christine anxiously awaited Ronnie's arrival because she had plans for her man.

In the living room, across the scratchy television screen, was the news they all had been dreading. Bobby Kennedy, RFK, had died from the wounds he had received the night before. Over and over again the news showed the haunting image of him lying on the floor asking his wife Ethel how badly his wounds were. As the entire room stared in disbelief and sadness, Jake grew antsy. He and the giggly girls, Kathy and Julie, Christine's youngest sisters smiled at each other and walked outside with their brother Tommy into the warm splendor of summer.

Sensing the young ones boredom, Ronnie and Christine delayed their plans to include everyone, and decided they would all drive down to Green Hole to swim during one of the blistering days of summer. It was much safer place to cool off than the surrounding creeks. Ronnie had spent many hours cooling off in the huge pond after many laboring hours sweating it out at the nearby tomato packing sheds in previous summers. He and his best friend, Buddy Barfield, would dive off the deep end which looked like a cliff to Jake. They would take turns doing their best Johnny Weissmuller into the cool inviting water, but if Mina or Wavy had known this they would never be allowed to visit the pond again.

Everyone jumped into their cutoffs, threw a few snacks in a brown paper sack and piled into Buddy's '61 white Chevy Impala convertible. The entire group was singing "The Letter" by The Box

Tops, as they headed south down the tree lined Main Road. The singing and screams of delight surely can be heard still many summers later resonating through the tall pines and majestic oaks that speckle the terrain.

The splashing, swimming, and laughter made everyone forget the bad news of the morning. It helped Ronnie forget soon he would be heading to perhaps his own doom in a fairly unknown Asian country where young Americans went to die.

...In a few months, sitting on the edge of a hillside in sweltering heat, and surrounded by whirling bullets launched by an enemy whose entire existence seems to be to kill young American men, Ronnie would close his eyes, and see his entire family and all of his friends laughing, swimming and splashing each other in the huge pond.

He could hear the off-key singing, and feel the love massaging his now aching heart. He could smell the country ham, and taste his mother's comforting, creamy grits. He could feel the stinging in his palm as the horse hide pounded the cowhide of his Rawlings mitt. He could taste Christine's cherry flavored lipstick, and he could feel the warmth and security found in his mother's bosom. He could see the pride in his dad's teary blue eyes. He could hear his younger brothers laughing at a cartoon or yelling at each other, what a magnificent sound he thought; a sound that he once despised but now he cherished and longed to hear it again.

Isn't that was what it was all about, to be carefree, innocent, peaceful and loving? Isn't this what they, as young soldiers were fighting to protect in another country, a faraway land never before heard of? How would this affect his world on John's Island except to decrease the population? It made no sense. Still, as an American patriot, you do your part for the freedom, and protection of your country, your comrades, your family... but Vietnam?! What in the hell does Vietnam have to do with swimming in Green Hole?!

Chapter 6

"Boyhood is a summer sun."
~ **Edgar Allen Poe**

Summer time is nearly as magical as Christmas is to a thirteen year old. Days are longer, and full of pure endless fun which includes so much adventure and joy, day after day. It's your own tailor made vacation to do or not to do anything you want, and a very ideal time in a kid's life. Day dreams become reality and adding, subtracting, multiplying and dividing all become a distant memory. The confluence of laughter and screams of delight merge with the summer breeze and dances across the marsh grass as the fiddler crabs scramble to find their secretive homes.

In between activities, Jake sometimes finds himself just relaxing, and doing nothing for a few moments. While lying in the grass beneath his favorite tree, and looking far off into the horizon floating above in the blue sky, the white clouds offer dissimilar shapes and sizes often resembling dragons, Vikings, pirates, cowboys, and birds of prey. Prior to this summer, his busy mind would play out one fantasy after another with the characters in the sky. As he finds himself growing older, he is staring less at the clouds, and more at what lies beyond them, and all the wonderful things to do beneath them.

The days are long but not nearly long enough for the invigorated Jake, who has a million and one things to do. It's amazing how many activities children seem to pack into a single day. Yet, as we become adults, there is never enough time for just for a couple of activities, let alone any down time. So, where does time go? No, really, where does time go? When we no longer use something, or it expires we discard it. When the days are done where do they go, into our memory banks? Memories fade just like photos under constant light. Why can't we physically return for a visit whenever we like? Jake has obviously watched too many episodes of *Time Traveler*.

Ronnie and Jake walked to the end of the neighborhood to visit the Barfields. Buddy, who has been Ronnie's best friend for many years, wants to talk to Ronnie about the Marines. He has been served a draft notice recently and is quite interested in joining the Marine Corps. Mainly not to be outdone by the smallest guy in the neighborhood. As Ronnie spoke with Buddy and his mother, Jake was mesmerized by the television set which showed the flag-draped coffin of Bobby Kennedy, RFK, being lowered toward the tarmac as it arrived in Washington, D.C. Jake had only seen one flag-draped coffin before which belonged to Bobby's older brother Jack, the President of the United States, who had also been assassinated five years earlier. Even though he was only eight at the time, Jake distinctly remembers JFK's coffin being pulled by a horse drawn carriage mainly because everyone was so captivated by the death of the president.

After the short visit, Ronnie and Jake walked to Staley's Corner Store to grab a pickled egg, two Cokes and a pack of nabs for Jake, which he gobbled down quickly. Ronnie offered his little brother a bite of the egg but Jake could not muster up the courage to put a pickled egg in his mouth, and he looked away and cringed as Ronnie did just that. The worst part was fathoming how someone could eat one of the many pickled pigs feet that were sitting in the large jar next to the eggs. Thinking about all of those butchered feet in a jar of vinegar, it was all Jake could do to keep from gagging. He was going to forget about that. There sure was some odd food at Staley's, but as long as they kept cold Cokes and penny candy Jake was satisfied. He was spending a full day with his hero and can't remember being happier, pickled pig feet, eggs and all.

Mina returned home after dropping Wavy off at work so she could do some grocery shopping, and let the boys borrow the car to go to the movies, and maybe later on to the swimming hole they all dubbed Green Hole. Ronnie wanted to see a war movie. Maybe he assumed he would get some pointers on how to survive Vietnam. *The Dirty Dozen* was playing in town at The Gloria Theatre on King Street, which was built in the early 1920's, was a beautiful, stately building and the closet movie house to John's Island at the time. The three boys had been to many movies there over the years. When the Gloria Theatre opened, in addition to films it presented Vaudeville shows, concerts and dance contests. In its day it was definitely Charleston's premiere showplace and the closest thing the city ever had to a movie palace.

Entering under the brightly lit marquee, patrons found a spacious ticket area with a terrazzo floor, artwork, and posters of current and coming attractions. From there they proceeded down a long beautifully decorated vestibule and into the foyer where they waited for the uniformed ushers to guide them to their seats.

The foyer offered access to a smoking room and attractive lavatories, along with a stunning rockery containing a goldfish pool, stuffed birds, Spanish moss, and colored lights. The abundant beauty of the Gloria Theatre continued inside the auditorium, which was decorated with murals, highly detailed iron grillwork, and cast iron sculptures. But, the most visually stunning feature of the auditorium was the dome with its special lighting effects. At first a soft amber light pervades, gliding into yellow, and then to a bright daylight effect. After that the climax effects came, and then the sky fluxes which became daylight giving way to night. One gazes into the infinite depths of the firmament while stars twinkle most realistically and while fleecy clouds roll by traveling serenely in the sky. During World War II, Charleston saw a large increase in military personnel, and began allowing movie theatres to show films on Sundays.

After loading up with popcorn, candy, and sodas, and the fusty odor of a by gone era, the two sat down to watch *The Dirty Dozen*, led by Lee Marvin, a former Marine turned actor. Jake would probably not have cared to see this film except his brother wanted to see it so he was content. After the two hour movie they walked a couple blocks south down King Street passing many stores and shops. When they reached the corner of King and Society Streets Ronnie could not resist one of his favorite places in the entire world, Patrick's Deli, so they quickly entered and had lunch which included pastrami on toasted rye with Swiss cheese, and spicy brown mustard, sided with German potato salad, and washed down with sweet iced tea. Hey didn't we just see the dirty dozen kill a bunch of Germans? Now we're eating their potato salad? It's a strange world in which we live. Oh, look over there at the cute little Toyota.

Jake loved the sidewalks of Charleston. He enjoyed peering into the shop windows as he compiled a mental wish list for Christmas; window shopping as his mother called it. Even the sidewalks in Charleston were different from any other city. The scent, the energy, the unique shops, doors, windows and architecture always amazed Jake, and being startled by the trusting and hungry pigeons swooping in for a random crumb. The people seemed different too. This was a time when the city consisted mostly of natives born to the area, which Jake proudly boasted, having been born at the Medical University of South Carolina at a time now found only in newspaper clippings or vintage photographs.

When walking through the celebrated peninsula one could smell the ivy on the concrete walls that protected the historic property from outsiders. You can smell the old humid dankness, and antiquity of most of the large homes, and sometimes catch a sniff of whichever food someone inside the home may be in the mood for.

Later, as an adult, Jake found himself walking the shady south of Broad Street sidewalks of Charleston quite often. Sometimes just for an echo of yesteryear, and often trying to reflect the good and positive of his youth. In his creative and inquisitive mind he would wonder about the families that called these beautiful buildings home; the experiences that had taken place there and the many stories that could be told. He would often fantasize and make up stories, and daydream about being a part of this wonderful city a hundred years earlier.

It was a different world from the one he knew, and many times over the years found himself in some of these homes by way of friends and business acquaintances. One of Mina's dearest friends lived on Tradd Street, and would have all of them over several times through the years. Jake and Kenny even got to Trick or Treat a time or two in the historic neighborhood. Wavy still had friends there too from when he lived in one of the carriage houses off of Savage Street.

Many years later, Jake could close his eyes and feel the summer sun on his freckled cheeks in the middle of December. He could taste the pastrami and popcorn, and yes, even the German potato salad as the small Toyotas whizzed by. He could smell the pipe tobacco, and sweet perfume throughout the many years of his life. Adults forget what thirteen year olds visualize in their tender and innocent thoughts. Some things from Jake's youth were worth remembering.

Ronnie decided to take advantage of the vehicular freedom so he drove around the historic peninsula through all the alleyways and backroads and one way streets. They parked at White Pointe Gardens and strolled between the huge oaks then walked the entire length of the Battery staring out at the open ocean, Fort Sumter, and of course at the lovely, magnificent homes. Then they would drive across town to Hampton Park where they would grab some sodas and fresh roasted peanuts, half of which they fed to the friendly and hungry squirrels that made the vast park their home. Then they walked through the shade to visit the penny-eyed gator at the zoo which always fascinated Jake.

Young Jake and eighteen year old Ronnie reached the new golden Biscayne, and headed back to John's Island with certain reluctance. They both loved downtown Charleston and didn't care much for the rural location of their home. Getting to experience the city, even for just a small amount of time, was a joyous excursion. Returning to John's Island for Jake was like returning to a land of monsters and bogeymen, actually closer to that than one would think.

To Jake, the drive home was boring; Maybank Highway was lackluster other than the magnolias lined up in front of the Municipal Golf Course. As a kid, Jake took for granted the magnificent oaks that lined Maybank Highway, and what is known as Dead Man's curve, because he has seen them nearly every single day of his life. He took for granted the smell of pluff mud as they crossed the small bridge over Penny Creek, and the beautiful shore birds that made home in the edge of the nearby forest and fed daily on the various creek banks of the Stono River.

On an occasional Sunday you may be lucky enough to see the prized eight foot eastern diamondback rattlesnake that some proud local had killed, and hung from the gasoline tank so that all drivers could gawk at his huge trophy. It also served as a warning that more of the giants were crawling in the thick woods. The same woods that Jake and his pals played in all day. Wavy believed that was a chilling trophy because he had been bitten by one of the large monsters when he was a kid.

During the last three mile stretch of the two lane black top they passed by the eyesores on the island. There were dilapidated houses and mobile homes resting in front of the highway. Every other mile sat ghosts of what was once busy little stores for whomever lived in the now imploded homes to shop in for their various needs.

When they finally returned to the island it was near time for Mina to go and pickup Wavy, so they missed out on Green Hole that afternoon, but the next morning Ronnie rode with Wavy to work, and drove the car back home. Before he arrived back on the island he had breakfast at the Goody House in West Ashley which was one of his favorite places. Ronnie was checking off his list.

Jake, Kenny, and the Stern kids were all waiting for him when he got home. They loaded the car with lunches, a cooler, towels and themselves and off to the swimming hole they went. A beautiful sunny June day was in the works as they parked and walked up to the large manmade pond, and laid out their supplies and towels near the water. All of the guys were in awe as Christine removed her tee shirt and short, shorts, and revealed a beautiful near naked body with two small straps of material that some identified as a bikini. It was very small and emerald green, perfectly matching those large, spellbinding eyes.

Ronnie had to be riveted, if not drooling; the young woman had quite the figure. Jake could not help but stare at her boobs which 98% were revealed. He got busted by the beautiful young woman, and he quickly ran off with her brother, Tommy, to enlist some others to play chicken fights in the pond by riding piggy back on each other's shoulders, while trying to knock the riders into the water.

The remaining Stern girls, all adoring little bikinis wanted to participate. Jake was thrilled to have Kathy's near nakedness wrapped around him as they bullied the others. He could not believe how totally perfect Barbara looked in a bikini, and how huge her boobs were. His eyes became fixated, and he could only imagine that Kathy's boobs looked the same as they bounced off of the back of his head. He thought to himself, wow we should have been out here every day. He never before knew what these girls were hiding under their tops and sweaters.

After about an hour of frolicking and booby bouncing in the water they all sauntered off into the nearby trees leaving Ronnie and Christine to play in the pond after they had been watching the youngsters earlier and soaking in some rays. The edge of the woods was bordered by many plum trees and blackberry bushes. There they decided to pick from the trees some of the many red, ripe plums, eating one or two of the juicy fruit as they plucked away. The girls were busy bending over and picking blackberries, and quickly stuffing them into their hungry mouths. In the distance a battery operated transistor radio strained to belt out "Hello, I Love You" by The Doors. Jake was feeling the same sentiments at the moment.

Jake started thinking about his history with the girls. For the past several years, Jake often found himself playing house or doctor with Kathy and Julie, the two closest to his age. Kathy happened to be a little more educated in the house and doctor areas than Jake was.

He happily followed instructions and found himself confused on many occasions with lots of unanswered questions. Like the time they played hide and seek, and Kathy found him in the closet and went in and closed the door and kissed Jake on the mouth. *Red, ripe plums are good.* They were only like 10 or 11 at the time, Huh? You really have to wonder how a girl of her age would know such things, ah, the wonder of it all.

Jake had seen plenty of kissing in movies but wasn't too interested in it himself at that time. Just give him a bicycle or baseball and he was content. In just a few short weeks Jake would make Kathy's wish come true, just neither of them knew it yet. Well maybe Kathy did based on that mischievous grin that seemed permanently planted on her pretty little face as of late.

Chapter 7

"Give me the splendid silent sun with all his beams full-dazzling."
~ Walt Whitman

Saturdays are always the best with cartoons in the morning and good moods everywhere. Kenny enjoyed the Tasmanian devil, and often called Jake by that name. *The Bugs Bunny Road Runner Show* was a favorite of everyone including big brother Ronnie, whom Jake considered a grown man with no desire to watch cartoons. Jake believed eighteen was a grown man, and apparently so does the military.

How does Wiley Coyote continually survive the trauma that would certainly kill anyone or anything that was not on television? "It's a cartoon," or "it's just television," was often the response from anyone listening to Jake's question just a couple of years earlier. The world of make believe. Make believe? You mean as in where you make things up, anything, anything at all? Yes, anything at all. This is one reasons Jake has never outgrown his love for Looney Toons cartoons.

After the cartoons ended Tommy and Johnny came to fetch Jake so they could play Pickle. This was a fun game and one that Jake really enjoyed. Jake never knew where that phrase came from or if it really made any sense. Jake considered himself pretty good at this as he was rarely touched by glove or ball. He made it from base to base with the skills of a pro or so he thought. The ball was a ragged, gray mess with the seams coming apart and the inside of the ball visible to the world with all of its corkyness. Their worn down and tattered gloves were pretty much the same, hanging by a thread, and not very padded where it counted, which caused a lot of stinging in the palms when a ball landed in the center. Yet they never complained; they just played.

They were young, innocent and having the time of their lives. They didn't know or care that everything they had was all hand-me-downs. They didn't know or care how the rich lived. All they knew was they were having a blast and the day was theirs. To their knowledge they were not a hand me down. Each day was brand new day that belonged to each of them to share, to enjoy and to laugh as hard and as loud as they could until they were exhausted. Then they would lay their young heads on their pillows that no doubt once rested other tired, blissful heads and drifted off into never, never land only to awake to another glorious day that was all theirs to do with as they pleased. Summer vacation was a kid's paradise.

The first Sunday of summer vacation rolls around, and after another huge, tasty breakfast and reading about the antics of Charlie Brown, Nancy, Prince Valiant, Rick O' Shay, Lil' Abner and Dick Tracy. Ronnie, Kenny and Jake walk the one mile to the First Baptist Church of John's Island. At the time it was a fairly new building, odd in color, sort of pale pink Jake thought.

It was a two story square building, and much larger inside than one would think looking at it from the road. Just to the right and just slightly to the rear of the square, pink building stood the original church. An old, white frame building built in the 1920's was more in keeping with tradition with most of the buildings which stood on the island.

The newer church was built to replace the much older chapel on the property, which now housed the kindergarten class in which Jake and all of his pals had attended, and enjoyed making hand plasters and took naps on the thin floor mats in the middle of the day. It, like most buildings on John's Island, was shaded with large live oaks and sprinkled with tall pines and edged with camellias, azaleas, and perfumed gardenias with a couple of large magnolias always close by.

Amazing Grace sang by the choir echoed through the large, square building of worship and gave Ronnie chill bumps but to Jake, who couldn't keep his eyes open, it was the prelude to a nap and something his brother Kenny had been enjoying already for about ten minutes. The elderly, fine sartorial preacher pointed his long bony fingers at everyone in front of him and warned them all, including Ronnie, Kenny and Jake to fight the temptations of sin. He put a trenchant emphasizes on the word *sin*. Jake was wondering why the preacher was pointing and staring right at him – GEEZ! After the sermon, the boys dropped a dollar each which was half of Jake and Kenny's allowance in the offering plate.

"That dude was kind of scary," Kenny surmised after they shook the preacher man's hand.

"You should see my drill sergeants," Ronnie laughed as they quickly walked away from the churchyard.

Jake, now tired, hungry, and broke was anxious to get back home. The trio marched home down Maybank Highway looking very studious in their church clothes. Maybank Highway was a very quiet rural road and much less travelled in the sixties. The journey home included a stop at My Friend's Store, the largest, most modern and convenient store near home at the time but it lacked the welcoming down home feeling one got at Staley's Store, just up the road on the corner.

It was a long, low hanging modern building, half of which served as a breakfast and lunch diner, while the other side resembled a Seven-Eleven convenience store. The young men purchased a Coke and a pack of nabs for each along with a pack of chewing gum for them to share, which they would relish throughout the upcoming week. They felt blessed as they enjoyed the saunter, the company, and the purity of the warm summer Sunday.

Back at home Jake changed into cutoffs and tee shirt, no shoes or socks and jumped onto his old fragmented frame with wheels that somehow resembles a bicycle and headed out and about, while his mom's famous beef stew simmered on the stove top sending its enticing aroma to all senses of smell within the house.

Jake rolled up into the Stern's yard, dropped his bike near the carport, and banged on the screened backdoor. Jake suddenly had an interest in seeing the girls more than he cared to see their brother. After a couple of years Jake pretty much blended in with the five children and was always welcomed to walk right in at any time without knocking, but good manners has always been instilled into Jake's young mind, and remains with him to this day. His manners have always been one of his most redeeming qualities along with his southern charm which he developed and nurtured over the years.

As usual, the household of seven was embroiled in some sort of trivial argument. The noise was making its way deep into Jake's subconscious but it didn't seem to bother him at the time because it was not his family, just friends. After a while, Mr. Stern announced in a rather large booming voice that he hated arguing and it had to stop. He wanted peace and quiet after a long work week, and wanted only to enjoy his baseball game without constant interruptions and chaos.

Once the house was quiet, the head of the household, Mr. Stern, puffed on his Pall Mall and drank his lukewarm Schlitz, while he watched a Major League baseball game on the black and white television with a tin foil wrapped rabbit eared antenna. Thomas Stern, Sr. loved Major League baseball almost as much as he loved his beers, cigarettes and Mrs. Stern.

Mr. Stern was a man of medium build with a sun dried leathered face, and handsome features emphasized by his emerald eyes. He seemed to be vicariously living out his baseball fantasies by sitting in his old, stained, brownish armchair glued to the gray images of the games on television. Having a color television in those days was a luxury only afforded by the wealthy. The Willoughby's television set was larger than the neighbors but the image constantly scrolled up and down to the point of nausea, and required a patient and steady turn of the horizontal knob. It was also crowned with rabbit ears decorated in tin foil to halt this ridiculousness to no avail.

Jake felt a rumble in his belly, and the fabulous beef stew called him back home. Uncle Hal said grace and all at once everyone went to work scooping, pouring, passing, and finally eating. The feast consisted of chuck roast, short ribs, onions, potatoes, carrots, and mushrooms, and the savory ingredients were poured over white rice, and served with fresh speckled butterbeans, homemade buttermilk biscuits, iced sweet tea, and for dessert, homemade pineapple upside down cake, which was Wavy's favorite.

After eating, Jake's dad would lie down on his bed to read the Sunday morning paper. After reading and dozing off for a while he would break out his guitar, Old Nellie, and go back into the living room. Everyone gathered round to listen to his fingers pick the guitar, and sing a few tunes.

Jacob Todd Willoughby, Sr., known as Wavy, was a tall, quiet, and modest man with thick, wavy, red hair. He had many talents and gifts. Why this capable man never pursued any of his gifts no one knows for sure. Comfort and the good health of his family was satisfaction enough for this humble country boy. After his beautiful rendition of the Carter Family's "Wildwood Flower", Wavy jumped right into "Little Brown Jug" and "The Intoxicated Rat" without missing a beat. Then Ronnie had to spoil the jubilant mood with his request for "Lonely Tombs", a very sad and somber song about a man visiting his mother's gravesite.

For some odd reason Ronnie really loved this song; though it had a catchy chorus and melody it would bring tears to the eyes of everyone in the small room. Clear the throat dad; it's time to hear how Napoleon met his Waterloo, one of Jake's favorites. After nearly an hour of inexhaustible finger picking Wavy abruptly stood up without any notice, as he often did, and took his guitar back to his bedroom where he would lay down and nap for a spell. Wavy was a man of few words and certainly had no time for small talk. Everyone just sat there and looked at each other for a few seconds, and then each person in the room got up from their seats and went about their own business with not a word spoken.

Chapter 8

"A picture is a mute poem."
~ **Latin Proverb**

The unforgiving humidity and searing summer continued its inexorable march towards autumn. While the long adventurous days faded into the surreptitious accounts that no one had access to other than rely on that erratic, old memory bank hidden in the dusty alcoves of one's mind.

Ronnie was taking advantage of his final days of freedom by seeing Christine every chance he got. After the obligatory first few days with his little brother and family, he seemed more and more smitten with the green eyed beauty from the house next door. Jake soon realized that he had to settle for time with his buds, and only see his brother between his unexplained visits to the nearby woods. Just what were Ronnie and Christine doing running off into the woods every chance they got; picking pears, plums or maypops?

"Jake, throw the ball," Tommy yelled, breaking Jake's thought of his brother and Tommy's sister in the woods.

Pickle suddenly seemed mundane; Jake excused himself by stating he had an upset stomach. Feeling rejected by his brother, and more than a little jealous of Christine, Jake went home to contemplate and feel sorry for himself. Finally he found someone to ask about Ronnie and Christine. Kenny came bouncing into the living room with small transistor in hand listening to some old Doo Wop tune.

"What's going on in the woods that Ronnie and Christine have to be out there all the time?" Jake naively asked his older brother.

Kenny chuckled while staring at the television set "I guess they're making out."

"What does that mean?" Jake asked seriously.

"Kissing and stuff." Kenny stated as he shuffled down the hallway towards the bathroom. Jake just sat there scratching his big, dirty head.

A couple of hours later, as if he had telepathic powers, Ronnie invited Jake, Kenny and of course Tommy along to eat dinner with him and Christine. They all went to the Shoney's Big Boy on Savannah Highway and the Magnolia Drive-In Theatre just up the road from the busy restaurant. Jake was secretly wishing that the girls had been invited to come along. Loud music from the fifties blared across the parking lot as twilight entered the boys' day. Kenny, Jake, and Tommy played on the merry-go-round and swings in front of the big, white screen as the lovebirds snuggled closely, and giggled like a couple of children on a nearby bench.

As darkness settled in, everyone made their way to the concession building, and nervously waited in line fearful of missing the opening trailers of upcoming features. Jake, Tommy, and Kenny each handed Ronnie a dollar bill to help pay for their purchases. After the monetary transaction with the older lady at the register for the group's assortment of snacks and drinks, they all scrambled to the Biscayne and jumped in. Ronnie hung the heavy metal speaker onto the half rolled down window of his door so that the audio reverberated through the inside of the car for everyone's enjoyment.

Jake was thrilled. *How cool is this?* He thought to himself. He had not been to a drive-in movie in over a year, and had forgotten how much fun it was. About forty cars parked in rows and they all pointed at Clint Eastwood wearing a poncho, a flat hat, and a nasty looking cigar protruding from his unshaven face.

Jake believed he was unlike any other cowboy he had seen before. This was no Roy Rogers or Gene Autry or even Matt Dillon. Odd sort of fellow this Clint Eastwood, shooting down everyone he saw. Why is he so angry? Jake and Tommy chewed away on their giant dill pickles, Kenny finished his chili dog, and Ronnie and Christine fed each other hot buttered popcorn and tittered between bites.

The bright, Southern stars hovered above twinkling over the parking much like the headlights on the movie screen enhancing someone's enjoyment. *The fun we're going to have this summer, oh yeah!* The next night they were all going bowling at the Navy Base in North Charleston, or so they thought.

Just a few hours later, Jake's eyes opened to the sunny fresh day just like all the others before. Somewhere in the house someone was whistling the haunting tune from the movie they had just seen. He wiped away the sleep from his eyes, and focused on the Apollo spacecraft hanging from his ceiling. He could just picture himself as an astronaut suspended amongst the stars looking down at the small planet earth, and watching the world turn in its splendor as shadows replaced the brilliance of each new day.

This would be one of those days that Jake would visit in the future, over and over again, wishing it never happened. Wishing that he could change the events, and that he could delete it from any and all accounts, especially his own. Yet he couldn't change or do a darn thing about it. Unlike most other days it came and never left – EVER!

High from the heavens, the brilliant sun illuminated and glimmered on the nine cargo planes on their way to Vietnam. The heat and lack of rain wilted the last of the tomato plants in Mina's garden, as she filled her wicker basket with the red jewels. Jake was right behind her holding the basket as she plucked away at the dying plants. Mina was wearing her favorite outfit of the summer; light blue kulaks with large white polka dots now splotched with perspiration. It seemed to Jake she wore this outfit every day; maybe so, after all he wore the same cutoff jeans day after day.

Mina was preparing tomatoes to be canned later in the day but stopped long enough to make time to snap a few photos to remember Ronnie's visit home. She was hopeful this would not be his last visit but wanted to make sure that she had some pictures. Mina believed in picture taking, as her entire adult life was documented on photo paper.

They all dusted themselves off, grabbed the new Kodak Instamatic that Ronnie had purchased, and each took turns snapping away at every possible scenario.

Ronnie leaned on the gold Biscayne doing his best James Dean, while wearing his favorite cream colored chinos, penny loafers and a red, black and yellow plaid shirt; all that Jake would also wear one day. It made one nice photo and sat framed on a side table for many years. The small camera snapped away, forever freezing in time the picture takers, who took turns posing with Ronnie and snapping shots and faking smiles. Ronnie and Jake, then Ronnie and Mina, Ronnie, and Christine, Ronnie and Kenny, and then one of Ronnie, Mina, Kenny and Jake, with Mina's garden in the background

Just beyond the garden and the large weeping willow you could see young Tommy's house, and Tommy himself with his windblown blond hair ruffling back high in the air above his head running towards the group of picture takers eager to be in the photos.

No one knew it would be young Tommy's last photo. Christine did not know that she was taking her brother's final picture, nor did she even realize that he was in the photo when she pressed the shutter. Tommy approaches the group and realizes that the photo session was over and he missed out. He didn't want anyone to know that he was despondent over this; he began acting nonchalant while tossing the ragged community baseball in the air to have it come back down in his ragged old Rawlings cowhide with a loud smack.

Aversely, Jake ran to the old live oak where earlier he had been sitting and admiring his new baseball. He reached deep into the soft green grass that was covering both root and Jake's proudest possession and it was all HIS. Above his dusty head was a mighty roar. Again the second set of three cargo planes flew overhead making Ronnie's heart drop into his stomach.

Mina and Christine noticed his pallor, and felt sick themselves. After Jake stood straight with new baseball in hand, he noticed the last three cargo planes disappearing through the clouds and into the distance leaving long vapor trails and heartache behind. The giant planes faded from sight, yet left a trail where they had ventured, then they were gone; similar to ones very own existence. Zap and gone with a trail to the far side of nowhere. Ronnie would soon be on a similar plane that would also fade from this ideal and innocent place and time.

Jake felt downhearted. He saw the tears swelling in his mom's eyes, and the same for Christine. Kenny turned away not wanting to be seen crying because guys his age dare not cry. Jake admired the way Ronnie tried to comfort them as if it were nothing more than cardinals flying over in search of food. Jake was so in awe of his brother that he wanted to be just like him, in every aspect, even if it meant joining the Marines and flying off to Vietnam. No one was in the mood for anymore picture taking and as usual Tommy wasn't quick enough to get in on the action. Only a fuzzy, out of focus background shot to be lost over time in a dusty old shoe box.

Chapter 9

"He's miserable indeed that must lock up his miseries."
~ Thomas Fuller

Tommy's eyes grew nearly the size of Jake's new Major League baseball when he first laid eyes on it. "Oh my God, where did you get that? Whose is it? Is it really yours?" Tommy asked in rapid succession.

"Western Auto, mine, yes it really is, my dad, yesterday." Jake rapidly responded, proudly displaying his new ball firmly in his sweaty palm while giving assured answers.

"Toss it here," Tommy said, in a very animated and enthusiastic tone.

These words caught Jake by disbelief. What do you mean toss it here? He could hear himself inquire.

It is *HIS* ball and he didn't want to share it. The mere thought of someone else touching it sickened him somewhat, especially Tommy's filthy hands. Then he thought of grass stains, dirt and sweat covering the now clean and attractive white horse hide.

Jake was suddenly at a crossroad with no answer. Which way do I go? The look of consternation on Jake's face had to be on display because Tommy then said, "Please, I'll give it right back."

Jake apprehensively let go of the ball. He didn't toss it but handed it over with both hands. Carefully enclosing it with all fingers and thumbs has if it were a million dollar diamond or a piece of Grandma's brown cake, same thing to Jake. A perplexed Tommy admiringly gazed at the new ball as he turned it over and over in his dirty, sweaty palms. Jake was nearly ill at this point in what seemed like an eternity; those twenty seconds moved in slow motion to Jake as he was beginning to turn pale and he eventually recovered when Tommy mentioned pickle.

Jake was so ready to play and that is why he got the ball to begin with. It's just that owning something new and pristine, something you wanted forever was really hard to share, and watch it become tattered like the current ball. Jake wanted more time to relish the newness, the beauty and blissfulness of its perfect condition. Suck it up big boy, let's play ball.

The three barefoot and carefree summer vacationers commenced to play ball. Two misfires later, by a much uncoordinated Tommy, the perfection was gone, so was the Jake that had walked out on the right side of Tommy's carport. The dry June dust raised high above Jake's head as he slid into base and the ball popped off of the large thumb of Tommy's ragged old glove and rolled several yards into the backyard.

Johnny screamed, "OUT!!!!"

Jake looked back at him in complete disbelief, as he was a good four feet from Jake's left foot and the metal garbage can lid used for base. Had Tommy caught the throw from Johnny? Jake would have been safe since Tommy did not have his foot on the base and was late in tagging Jake.

Again, Johnny screamed, "OUT!!!"

After fetching the dirty ball Tommy agreed with the older Johnny, and claimed his best friend, owner of the new ball, out.

Jake was furious, "How can you say that you frigging idiots, are you blind?"

"You knocked the ball from my glove," Tommy screamed, trying to impress Johnny.

"You were nowhere near me with the ball you idiot," Jake demanded.

Mina must have heard the loud noise from next door as she called Jake to come home for lunch.

"I've got to go. Give me my ball," Jake shouted.

"No, we're still playing," Johnny said defiantly.

Jake was shocked that they would not return *HIS* ball to him, so he tried one more time with a little more firmness. "I said, give me back my ball."

The two bullies just stared and grinned at Jake. Now the taller and faster Jake was about to explode, as he angrily approached the two filthy liars. They hurriedly fled, with Tommy taking Johnny's lead to the bicycles lying nearby on the ground. Jake then dashed towards the thieves but they had a good lead and took off on their bikes. Tommy glanced back at Jake one last time; then came that moment in his life that Jake wished more than any other that he could erase.

Jake's black eyes seared through the dual emerald green pools on Tommy's face.

"I wish you were dead," Jake sneered.

Jake, resonating a very sinister snarl, that didn't sound at all like him at that particular moment in his life, nor was it something that he would ever say. Jake was a kind and gentle soul, but don't steal his baseball. For that minatory moment Jake did not look like himself either. He wasn't himself. Though he didn't show it, Jake was both startled and confused by the sound of the baritone growl that left his mouth, and it wasn't the high shrill thirteen year old in the midst of a changing voice. This was a low, deep from the bowels of some evil cave growl. In that split second, not only his voice but his entire demeanor changed to something very unrecognizable, and something downright scary.

The now frightened Tommy was flabbergasted, and quickly cut his eyes away from his best friend, whom he had just betrayed. The dusty, black haired, black eyed Jake, grinding his teeth with an absolute evil stare just stood there overcome with anger with clenched fist at the sides of his filthy cutoff jeans. Johnny, the head bully, carrying Jake's baseball lead the way as the two thieves hurriedly took to the street on their bikes, leaving a motionless Jake only watching their implausible departure.

The magnificent planet sun was never brighter as a furious trio of Galaxies tracing the powder blue sky with straggling white trails ripped through Jake's shadow. He didn't bother looking up and counting. He couldn't move, so he just stood there as the John's Island soil quivered beneath his dirty, bare feet. All of this mysterious rage was over a silly little baseball, but in the near distance a bird squawked loudly, heard by no one.

This is an image forever etched in Jake's mind. One that just sits there on a dusty shelf in his memory bank staring at his every move, like most shelved photos it becomes part of the landscape and taken for granted and never considered at until you stumble right on it. Then it steals your vision, and pierces your very heart and soul as you reminiscence and reflect on it. But, unlike a photo you cannot put it in a closet or a box out of sight. It's always there waiting for an opportunity to show itself. Hiding in the shadows waiting to pounce on the unsuspecting.

Unfortunately, for Jacob Todd Willoughby, it will forever sit in the darkness in the valley of shadows to taint his existence, and haunt his life with perpetual madness. No amount of time or space can erase the terrors of trauma inflicted in a young person, whether the mind is blemished or the evil be present.

Be warned when the crow cries… the horror begins now.

Chapter 10

"Oaks are in all respects the perfect image of manly character."
~ **William Shenstone**

The Angel Oak is no exclusion of character as it cast its enormous shadow on the earth that surrounds it. The sandy, dirt road leading to the magnificent tree was blistering hot that day as Johnny and Tommy road their bikes away from the red hot, angry Jake. The two thieves would seek the oak's sheltered sand in the dark shade to cool off their dirty toes. Jake would seek the shelter of his home, and the oscillating fan for refuge and his mother's soft, cooling voice and forgiving spirit. Everything was always alright if Mama was near.

As Johnny and Tommy cooled off, they gazed at the giant tree and its huge sprawling limbs that made it resemble some prehistoric monster. Tommy thought how he had hurt his friend, and of those final words that Jake spoke to him and how he had never seen Jake this way before or had he ever heard Jake speak in this manner. He knew that he brought it all on, but things just snowballed so quickly he couldn't really stop the events that lead to this very moment.

Tommy knew that he really messed up because Jake was his very best friend for the past two years, and they did everything together. Johnny was a new kid on the block that Tommy looked up to because he was older. Tommy wanted to impress the older, cooler kid but at what expense? Tommy needed to get back home and apologize to Jake, give his ball back to him, and make everything right. Tommy really was a good kid, and he felt truly horrible.

At that same moment, Johnny said, "Let's go to Church Creek and swim." What a great idea Tommy thought, as he pedaled away from one of Jake's and his favorite spots in the entire world. With great effort through heavy sand half way to the creek was the unmistakable stench of the pluff mud. It made its way into Tommy's nostrils and lungs and in his gut he knew that this was a mistake, and he should head home and make up with his real friend, Jake.

Tommy swiftly became ill; he felt he was going to lose his bologna and cheese sandwich all over his rickety bike, and it took everything he had to keep that from happening. He looked at Johnny who looked so cool with his long blond wavy hair blowing in the wind. Tommy also remembered that Johnny promised him his first cigarette; you only think you feel ill now. Tommy couldn't possibly wimp out because he would never live it down. The clear blue sky opened the water wide. What a beautiful place... to die.

...as the pendulum swings, the wrath is unveiled.

Chapter 11

"The hour of departure has arrived, and we go our ways –
I to die and you to live. Which is better, God only knows."
~ **Socrates**

Pluff mud has a sweet, pungent odor to it, as the Binya's describe it. Some say more like rotten eggs, but that depends on what side of Plum Island they happened to be on when they first took wind of the low country muck; also, whether or not they were near the North Charleston's factory and industrial air. Native Charlestonians, also known as Binyas to their Gullah neighbors, love their pluff mud. It wraps around the islands and feeds the shrimp, oysters, crabs and birds.

The brown-gray pluff mud of Church Creek or Bohicket Creek, as it was named many years prior for the Native American Cusabo tribe that lived along its muddy banks, was glistening in the summer sun as the tide was making its way in. Jake had heard much folklore, and legend about the ghost and spirits of the Cusabo tribe still hanging out along the creek banks and how they were angry about the way they were removed from their land. They are known as a vindictive, evil tribe waiting to wreak havoc upon all who enter their world.

Tommy and Johnny veered to the right on their bikes down a sloping path that lead below the Church Creek Bridge and down to the water where the awaiting pluff mud lies. The boys have been here before but not without older supervision. In less than an hour, the mud would not be visible at all; only the tops of the Spartina grass that grew high near the banks on the island would be seen.

The zealous tide rolled in the twine tied chicken necks that invited the blue crabs over for a bite, only to be snagged up by a swooping net but that was not the case today. Today the boys were only here to seek refuge under the bridge in fear that Jake and his mom or even worst,

Ronnie would find them and give them a good whipping for stealing Jake's new baseball.

Fiddler crabs scrambled as the boys tossed down their bikes and cautiously approached the mud. They knew the mud would suck up your feet, but because Ronnie or Wavy would call them back they never believed it would literally entomb you.

Nearby a boastful Egret proudly stretched its long neck, and plunges its head into the creek water in an attempt to snag some lunch. Overhead past the shadow of the bridge an occasional car whizzed by eerily shaking the bridge. The boys were safe they assumed, at least for a while until things calmed down. They could return home and act like nothing had happened, and hope that Jake would forget the whole thing when he found his ball on the back steps of his house.

What the two boys did not realize was Jake's baseball left the safe confines of the glove when their bikes met the ground. They had not noticed this for some time, while they were busy laughing about the way they left Jake standing alone with that pissed look on his face. Suddenly, Tommy did a double take when he saw the ball several feet away half submerged in the foul mud.

"Hey look," Tommy pointed to the runaway ball. Johnny at first was surprised to see it there, and then he chuckled. Tommy failed to see the humor because he was feeling extremely guilty for what he had just done to his best friend. Now it could all be over with quickly as the once white half of the ball baked in the sun. The tide was relentless in its attack and the boys were unaware of the quickly approaching current.

Tommy ran to get his friend's ball back and soon realized he was up above his ankles in pluff mud, and could not pull out his feet. The more that he moved the deeper and faster that he sank. Many things have been victim to the slimy killer. Tommy panicked and was frantically trying to escape the tenacious hold the mud had on him, only to sinker further into its murky depths. Johnny ran to his pal and tried to pull him free and felt as if he were going to yank Tommy's arms from his body. The ferocious water was rapidly rising to Tommy's chest as he screamed wildly at the top of his lungs. Tommy's green eyes were now absolute fear.

"HELP, HELP ME!!!!!!!"

Johnny now panicked as he saw his friend disappearing right before his eyes, and his own body quickly submerging into the mud. Johnny was a couple inches taller and a few pounds heavier than his endangered buddy, but he was also a little nearer to the long grass that he managed to pull onto and free himself from the eminent fate that waited. Both the boys were screaming until Johnny crawled to dry land where he stopped screaming and started panting. The only other sound was the gurgling water just behind him to his left. He watched in utter horror as the last strands of Tommy's blond wavy hair was covered by the water, gently floated for a second or two, then saw his friends finger tips on both hands struggled for air and finally sank below. The only traces to his existence, other than bike and glove, were the few bubbles that soon rode the brutal current into the embankment of the mystic creek and dissolve under the friable sky.

"TOMMY, TOMMY, TOMMY, HELP, HELP, SOMEBODY PLEASE HELP, OH GOD, PLEASE HELP, TOMMY!!!"

Chapter 12

"Where there is most light the shadows are heaviest."
~ **J.W. Goethe**

The resplendent summer sun raged in the middle of the tranquil blue sky, blistering with fierceness into the languid June day. The earth turned on its axis; a small speck of dust floating amongst the glorious worlds of the shared universe. People live and people die.

As the World Turns is wrapping up for the day, so Bob and Lisa Hughes will have to continue their argument tomorrow announced the famous baritone voice. Due to the extreme heat the electricity bill had been higher this past month so Mina, as always, sacrificed in order to help save money by turning off the air conditioner. The only source of any sort of cool air came from a small oscillating fan that Mina strategically placed in the far right side of the kitchen to circulate the warm air into her direction. It also helped shoo away the flies that Jake let in when he entered the house.

Mina knew right away that something was wrong with her youngest child. The infuriation was written all over his red cheeks and dusty face. HIS baseball had just been stolen from him by his supposedly best friend. It goes to show that you cannot trust anyone young Jake thought. This is like the worst thing that ever happened to him, which was nearly true, other than his left leg receiving third degree burns while his Uncle Hal burned leaves in the backyard early one January morning over two years ago.

Mina, still wearing her favorite blue kulaks, walked Jake's bologna and cheese sandwich and milk over to the table, as she pulled the chair out for the boy to sit after he had washed up at the sink. Mina sat opposite Jake and together they said the blessing for his lunch. Hearing his mama's soothing voice made the boy emotional. He quickly took a large bite out of the fresh sandwich and gulped down half of the glass of milk. He wiped tears from his eyes and then told his concerned mom what had just happened with Tommy and Johnny, and his beloved baseball, but left out the words he never again uttered to anyone.

What had he done to provoke such actions? Mina didn't understand it either, especially Tommy, who was always so nice.

"Boys will be boys," she said, as she patted Jake's shoulders.

She told him to relax on the couch and watch some television hoping he would doze off and forget about the entire incident.

"Maybe they were jealous of your new ball," Mina chimed in with motherly experience. "Try and take a nap, and by the time you wake up I'm sure they will have returned it."

Jake pondered what she said. Were they jealous of his new ball? That had to be it, were they also jealous of his speed? *Hateful brats, I'll get them back somehow.*

Jake knew his mom would be right as usual, and they'll bring his ball back.

"If they don't, I'll talk to Tommy's mom later today and we'll get your ball back," consoled the loving mother.

That's all Jake needed to hear, and the world was good again.

Mina was standing over the kitchen sink preparing her fresh batch of tomatoes for canning. The small fan was whirring with that awful monotonous sound, while he devoured the last bite of his bologna and cheese sandwich. Despite the fan's great effort, Mina was still sweating and the flies were still buzzing. Jake found the old fly swatter and went to work as hunter of flies, killer of many. Resembling a hungry panther, Jake studied the flies every move as he slowly moved in for the kill. Once a fly had landed, Jake swiftly pounded it with the mighty swatter, and more often than not he would get his target, ending its carcass exploding in millions of little pieces never again to be seen.

After ridding the kitchen of its nuisance, he was too wound up for a nap. Jake started plundering through the junk drawer, which was one of his favorite things to do. After a while he became uninterested and was wondering what Tommy's younger sisters were up to. Maybe some hide and seek… r*ed, ripe plums.*

An Ivory girl swung in the breeze on the scratchy television while Jake was standing in the doorway of the kitchen pondering his next move. He then heard a loud siren screaming in distress as it raced down Maybank Highway.

Out of absolutely nowhere Mina said, "Well, I sure hope that no one has drowned down at Church Creek," as she looked out of the window as if she were actually going to see something that was miles away.

Jake thought his mom's remark was kind of odd. Why would she say THAT of all things, even though it has happened before? He looked at the back of his blue polka dotted mom, who labored over the sink with a worried look on her face. She peered out of the large window that was guarded by a huge garden spider in the upper right corner, this bright sunny day.

Tommy's house was just beyond the large weeping willow in the backyard, but he wasn't there. A siren in the middle of a hot summer day must have given Mina ideas of a drowning. After a few moments, jaded Jake didn't think anything more about the siren, as he belched bologna. For many years to come Jake could hear Mina's alarmed voice make that fateful premonition about a Church Creek drowning over and over again, almost as much as he heard his own voice say *"I wish you were dead."*

The Guiding Light, one of Mina's favorite daytime dramas, was 15 minutes into its half-hour run on the gray scratchy screen, when it seemed the entire neighborhood erupted into sheer horror and screams of frantic panic.

A curious Jake wondered what in the world is going on. Did a cargo plane crash nearby? Some neighborhood kids were all running towards Tommy's house and a few of the neighborhood Moms followed, huffing and puffing and crying. Jake and Mina decided they had better follow suit because something very dreadful must have taken place. The screaming and crying became louder and louder. More and more people entered the Stern's carport, which was now spilling into the side yard, where just an hour ago Tommy stole Jake's baseball and raced off with Johnny Moore on their bikes to who knows where. Well, now everyone knows where. Johnny had run into his house caked and dripping in thick pluff mud, saltwater and tears. His bloodshot, terror stricken eyes and his new wet, muddy outfit had nearly scared his poor mother and younger sister to death. Johnny's mother ran down the street and broke the news to Tommy's mother.

Janet immediately became zombie like. Her eyes became lifeless, dark holes and her demeanor became solemn and grave as her movement turned slow and eerie almost like a robot. Christine, Kathy, and Julie all broke into shrill cries with hands over their faces as if to break the volume, or catch the vomit. Christine then noticed her mom's state of shock and grabbed her elbow with one hand, and put another hand around her waist and gently sat her into a nearby chair. Kathy looked up through a veil of tears and saw Jake, and instantly ran to him. She grabbed him and hugged him, and did not want to let go. Jake finally put his arms around the shaking girl hoping to console her and calm her down. The house soon became a tragic den of anguish and horror.

Jake immediately recalled his final words to his best friend, not even an hour ago and was nearly in a state of shock himself. He just stood there sort of light headed with a queasy stomach in complete disbelief. None of this could be real! He was sure that all this was just a nightmare. Tommy could not possibly be dead. He certainly did not wish his very best buddy in the whole wide world to be dead, not really. The screams, tears, sirens, and total chaos told him he was very much awake and that he, Jake Willoughby, was very much alive, but Tommy was probably not. Was he responsible? How can all this be? This was the best summer ever! What in the hell has happened?!

Kenny and a friend had just come in from a hard day's work at the tomato sheds, and saw his mom and brother in the middle of all the commotion at the Stern's house and stopped over. After hearing the news they immediately jumped back on their bikes, with wide eyes and dread in their bellies, and quickly headed to the frenzied scene of the alleged drowning. Police cars and the only island fire truck nearly blew the two teens from their bikes as they approached the bridge. The two lanes were closed off as emergency personnel, including divers, began recovery operations in an attempt to save the young boy who had just disappeared below the incoming tide.

Back at the carport Mina was sitting with Janet Stern, clutching her shoulders. Jake, still being held by the distraught Kathy, could not take his eyes off of Tommy's mother who just stared vacantly beyond the crowd of grievers and the curious. Jake was unfamiliar with shock and only knew what he was told by his mom that it was a state of denial or unbelieving. Naturally, Janet Stern did not want to hear that her youngest son had drowned, who would? They had not found Tommy at this point so perhaps he had not drowned. Maybe Johnny left too soon and Tommy somehow freed himself from the gripping mud and prevailing tide. Maybe he was hiding in the woods in shame, waiting for everything to settle down. His little muddy self would walk up at any minute laughing at everyone. NOT!

Thomas Sr. left work as soon as Christine phoned him. He and his Impala flew down the highway hoping that he would get there and find his son scared but breathing. Barbara, the second oldest of the Stern children had been at work all morning at the Dairy Queen. A friend brought her home and stopped in front of the driveway.

Barbara quickly jumped out of the car as she spotted her mother and ran through the crowd to get to her. Once beside her mom, she dropped to her knees and held her hand realizing something horrible had happened. She also realized that she wasn't going to get any sort of response from her, she looked at Christine and then over at Mrs. Willoughby who took one of her hands and gently lead her away from the crowd. A couple of moments later Barbara broke into uncontrollable sobbing as she embraced Mrs. Willoughby.

An image Jake will never forget as long as he lived is the black and white photo taken of Tommy's grief stricken dad, looking a lot like an older Tommy, leaning on the railings of the Church Creek Bridge while he watched divers scour the area for his son. For a split second there was hope in his eyes and then there was none as a photographer snapped this shot. The photo appeared on the front page of the Charleston Evening Post later that day, with the headline exclaiming young Tommy's tragic fate, matching Mina's earlier telepathic retort to the screaming siren almost word for word; Child drowns in Church Creek. How could she have known?

After nearly two hours, the rescue divers finally found what they were looking for, a young lifeless body. They attached hooks around Tommy's small muddy arms and hoisted him out of the sludge with a winch from one of the emergency trucks. Tommy Sr. watched in horror as the tragic scene unfolded, and his hopes and dreams for his young ball player vanished with water and mud dripping from young Tommy's lifeless, limp body.

Blue crabs had begun to feast on the young boy, and they reluctantly dropped from the muddy body as Tommy was dragged across the water like a worn out chicken neck and onto the banks of the disconsolate creek.

Kenny was there observing the entire event. He later shared his disturbing experience with everyone. He saw the photographer taking pictures. He saw a huge lump of mud with arms and legs resembling some scary creature pulled from the earth and towed across the water bed. If this was Tommy, Kenny assumed, he is definitely dead.

Tommy was caked in mud, with his face unrecognizable, like some sort of movie monster, a swamp thing of sorts. The mud had settled in and made home in his eyes, ears, nostrils and gaping mouth. There is no reason to believe he had survived after two hours of being deep beneath the mud and several feet under water. In an attempt to honor and respect the father of the victim, who was watching every move, and to follow proper protocol, the rescue team mocked a resuscitation effort and pretended to check Tommy's vitals for signs of life. When the obvious was evident they began to wipe away the mire from the lifeless boy's face. That's when Tommy Sr. let out a dreadful cry that had to have been heard several miles away to Tommy's carport where the neighborhood had gathered because everyone followed in with the same cry. This scream milled into Jake's inner ear, his brain, his memory and even his heart and soul and has echoed there for over forty years.

Jake Willoughby would never be the same. His childhood lost, replaced by the awkwardness of adolescence, and the dark corners of his imagination. This day can completely disappear forever into that secret account for all Jake could care. He wished it never happened. It was the worst day of his life. Why can it not just disappear from the memory as well, to funnel and spiral into the black crevasse of his abandoned splendor? Jake quietly prayed for this all to be a nightmare which he would wake up from, and run over to Tommy's house where he would be farting on his younger sisters and laughing about it as they ran in disgust.

Oh it is there now, in all its majesty, the ethereal beast that would try to consume young Jake Willoughby; the nightmare that would never end. The impetuous expedition of havoc receives the innocent and meek as the brave day wilts in the summer swelter.

Chapter 13

"A change came o'er the spirit of my dream."
~ **Lord Byron**

What causes nervous anxiety? What and where are the boundaries on which it lie and break surface and do harm? Is it controllable? Trauma and loss in any one's life certainly takes a toll on their mental state especially someone thirteen years of age. Jake was a perfect child, an energetic boy full of life and curiosity; a little spoiled at times but a fun loving, cheerful boy who enjoyed his family and friends, all of whom shared his enthusiasm.

Starting the moment Tommy died, and for the next several years of Jake Willoughby's life is a struggle to understand let alone survive. Jake never sat down with anyone, professional or otherwise, to discuss his problems. He never really had the time to think it all out or to analyze the situation. He wanted to sort out the events and their troubled consequences in his life to try, and find the justification of it all. He had to put them on the back burner and ignore them until the time was right or when he actually had the time.

Like dominoes, the thoughts about the events tumbled through the days which disappeared like sand in an hour glass. As Tennyson once said, "Time, a maniac scattering dust." Jake never did liked dust.

As he developed Jake noticed many changes in not only his personality but his overall looks and appearance. Each day the mirror brought into view another Jake Willoughby. The bushy haired lad was losing his baby fat as he grew taller with each passing day. He was becoming more mature looking by way of his facial features took on a more sculpted look and became more pronounced with arched brows and long thick lashes framed the deep mysterious and sullen eyes of night.

He started taking more interest in the way he looked and the way he dressed as well as in the way he talked and behaved around others, especially in public and around girls.

Jake had been a very shy kid growing up but now if he was comfortable around someone they would never thought him to be shy. As Jake matured he had a tendency to speak his mind no matter the consequence and not very diplomatic; something he eventually wizened up to.

Jake's mind was changing as well; it was growing with the rest of him. He was more curious, even more than before about life and everything about it; he wanted to enjoy it all. He felt that every moment had to be seized and savored before all is lost. He became more aware of himself and his surroundings including the people in his circle. Jake had always been impressionable. He curiously observed and studied everyone and everything around him, but an unknown dimension from within the dark corridors of his uncharted conception fought his gentle heart and trusting soul, at the confluence of body and time; his very actuality.

Recently Jake had experienced something but did not know what that made him a near nervous wreck about eighty percent of his conscious state. He was reeking in instability, insecurities and becoming more and more afraid of every approaching moment of each forthcoming long, uneasy day. Every heartbeat, every drawn breath and each bat of the eye dragged him further away from the normality of his joyful youth that he knew prior to the tragedy at Church Creek.

Other kids Jake's age are experiencing the best days of their lives. Every day he awoke with dread. He rarely smiled anymore. He became fidgety and hyper, constantly moving and always looking behind, ahead, around as if he expected danger. It was like a wanted, paranoid man running from the law but this is an innocent boy. Jake was as pure as the driven snow. He was honest, humble, gullible and naive. Why would anyone or anything want to do harm to his beautiful and sensitive youth?

All of his life Jake had longed for attention and approval. He enjoyed warm hugs from his mother and grandmother as he never knew that kind of closeness from his dad. Wavy was all man, masculine, indifferent and void of emotion, hence the unbreakable bond Jake shared with his older brother Ronnie, who in Jake's eyes was a grown man but found time to make Jake feel significant and equal.

Ronnie's affection for his little brother was genuine and he enjoyed spending time with him. Ronnie was always teaching Jake something, constantly praising him and awarding him with some kind of treat. When Ronnie needed a new wallet, watch, belt, or ball cap Kenny was offered first. If he refused then Jake became proud owner of the no longer wanted goods but he never knew the process before he took possession.

Ronnie had a knack for making Jake feel that he had earned the rewards in some fashion or another. Ronnie could sense when his little brother needed a shot in the arm and was always there; Ronnie on the spot. Jake looked up to his brother and admired him like no other. Perhaps Ronnie was much more mature than his years and saw something in Jake that no one else saw. Maybe he saw the changes in Jake that Jake himself could not explain.

Jake idolized his brother and wanted to be with him as often as possible. He wanted to be just like him, perfect. Everything seemed so right in Ronnie's cool calm and relaxed world. When Ronnie was near Jake wasn't the nervous wreck that he had recently become.

Wavy and Mina noticed this as well and convinced their older son to spend more time with Jake. He didn't really need convincing as much as he needed reminding. He was so preoccupied with Christine that he often forgot about Jake. Ronnie did genuinely enjoy time with his brother but he had hormones to conciliate to and he felt as if he may be falling in love. However, when he was with his little brother he gave him complete attention and Jake loved him for it. Jake would never forget the times that he spent with his brother which became some of his favorite memories.

Various times in his life Jake just wanted to go back to when the days were best. Time has a way of erasing the past. Jake started taking notes, keeping things in a diary of sorts and eventually writing a daily journal. Later in life Jake realized as he was sorting through some of his writings that he had forgotten some of the more horrific detail of his past. He often wonders how he survived; some of the things are best forgotten.

Chapter 14

"God knowest the secrets of the heart."
~ **Psalms XLIV**

Up until that tragic day in late June 1968, Jake Willoughby had the normal childhood. He was growing up in a lower middle class family. He had everything he needed, even if it was usually hand-me-downs, and pretty much got anything that he wanted. The Willoughby's never believed that they were poor, mainly, because they were healthy, happy and comfortable.
With humble Christian upbringings, Wavy and Mina were raised in the south when periods were hard-hitting for farmers. The values of their ancestors and old-fashioned virtues sustained them throughout their lives; they were survivors who inadvertently spoiled their children when afforded the opportunity with each generation passing.

The three boys had very loving, caring, and adoring parents, and they in return were very grateful and appreciative of them. Jake was ingenuous to the evil complexities of the world, and didn't know that anything or anyone bad or harmful existed. Before late June 1968, the entire world seemed like one big giant candy castle and the jubilant climb to the pinnacle was a sugary cavalcade of a trek.

Jake's home and his upbringing seemed perfect in his mind, and why wouldn't it? They had everything that they needed. There was always food, clothing, a respectable school, and a strong, hardworking father who provided the proper necessities for his family. His mother was a gentle soul that taught him right from wrong and *The Golden Rule* ~ do unto others as you would have them do unto you.

Mina taught all of her children to say their blessings before each meal, and to say the Lord's Prayer each night at bedtime. She taught them proper manners, which included saying yes sir and no sir, yes ma'am and no ma'am, open doors for women and elderly and to always be courteous to others. It's not that Wavy wasn't involved; it's just that

Mina had much more interaction and time with her children, while her husband worked to pay the bills.

Only two things stood out to Jake as not perfect in his world. An envious and obnoxious older brother, Kenny, and the time a couple of years earlier when he nearly lost his left leg in a leaf fire.

These two things alone could be pretty harrowing for any youngster, but not nearly as traumatic as losing your best friend so tragically and young, after looking him square in the eyes an hour before his death, and uttering the words *"I wish you were dead."* Before that fateful day Jake knew nothing of death. He was content other than when he found himself the target of Kenny's harassment. Jake loved the outdoors if weather permitted. If not, he found himself inside the house playing with Lincoln Logs, toy soldiers, drawing, reading, watching television or licking the spoon with fresh batter of cake or cookie mix that his mother would give him.

Jake had many favorite television shows, but his all-time favorite at this juncture in his life was *The Adventures of Superman*. To Jake this was the only Superman, the real Superman, the forever Superman. Jake loved everything about him; he had Superman comics, coloring books and when it became available, Jake received a Superman outfit for Christmas of 1964. As a youngster, every weekday afternoon at 4 o'clock Jake would view his hero on the gray, static laced image produced from the large, bulky television that sat on top of the wobbly homemade table.

In January of 1965, Uncle Hal was in the backyard burning piles of dried leaves early one clear, crisp morning. Young Jake was following Uncle Hal around, as he usually did, reminding the older gentleman of a faithful puppy. This time Jake was wearing his new Superman suit when a sudden gust of wind whirled across the blaze and a spark from one of the crackling leaves flickered into the air and landed on Jake's left leg, igniting the highly flammable material which immediately flamed up. Jake was unaware that he was on fire until he sensed something he had never smelled before, and will never ever forget; burning flesh, his own burning flesh. Jake first looked down at his right leg and saw nothing but then he looked down at his left leg. Smoke was rising from his ankle and he watched in horror as the vicious flames consumed his leg from the knee down.

Jake immediately screamed, jumped and frantically ran around in circles. Uncle Hal alarmed at what had happen, dropped the rake and swiftly ran to the hysterical youngster. At that same moment Mina hurried into the backyard with a broom in hand. She told Jake to lie on the ground and she tried to swat out the fire and brush off the blazing material. The flames darted out of the broom itself as it kindled, as Mina hastily dropped the fiery stick of sweltering straw. Without hesitation Uncle Hal grabbed the nearby garden hose, adjusted the nozzle, and simultaneously sprayed the broom, then gently fanned the cool water over Jake's smoldering leg. The two wrestled to keep Jake on the ground, and put the fire out completely with Mina's apron.

Next door at the Sterns' house, Christine heard the commotion and grabbed her mom. They brought their car over and hurriedly drove Jake and Mina to the emergency room at the Memorial Hospital in downtown Charleston. This hospital would be a place that Jake would visit often in his lifetime, for one misfortune after the other.

Inside the old Memorial Hospital, young doctors and nurses tended to Jake's severely burnt leg. Jake will never forget them pulling away the ruined flesh from his body with scissors and large tweezers. He will also won't forget the revolting smell that clung to his brain all of these years. He received third degree burns from ankle to just below the knee on the backside of his left leg. The awful scar is still there as a reminder that only Superman is fire proof. Jake swears he was not trying to see if the suit would burn or not, it was just a big coincidence.

After a week of daily visits to Dr. Grayson on James Island to get fresh new dressings of bandages, the young trooper was on his way to recovery. Jake was always the independent one. He would never consider bothering or interrupting anyone, especially his dear mother because she was non-stop busy around the house. During his early days of recovery he would literally crawl to the bathroom to handle his business rather than to inconvenience his mother. After the daily doctor visits ended, Mina would strenuously lift Jake with his assistance up onto the chest high deep freezer in the kitchen to tend to the dressing.

Jake and his mom were always very close. Willamina, meaning the determined protector, DuPont Willoughby was forty-six years old when she gave birth to her fifth and last child. There was a four year difference between Jake and Kenny. Mina and her baby boy Jake always shared a taut bond. To Jake there was absolutely nothing more soothing in the entire world than his mother's serine voice and gentle touch.

Ronnie revered his new adorable baby brother, but Kenny didn't care too much for his replacement. Kenny wanted to flush the brat down the toilet. He wanted to see the baby boy twirling, swirling and waving as he finally disappeared, "bye-bye baby boy, wave bye-bye," but he knew that the big headed boy would probably clog up the toilet so he left that idea alone. Kenny would work on getting him in other ways.

Kenny was unrelenting in his tantalizing of young Jake. He constantly called him names, laughed at him, and took away his food and toys from him. Kenny, prompted by so-called friend, even went as far as dangling his younger brother by the ankles over the Brownswood Road Bridge, terrifying Jake as he envisioned dropping the 20 feet into the mucky black water below.

Once Kenny and his entourage tied a nine year old Jake to a large tree out in the middle of the thick, dense woods beside the neighborhood, and left poor the terrified kid there for two solid hours crying his eyes out, screaming for help and nearly dying from pure trepidation before they returned giggling and laughing to untie the petrified child. Kenny had almost forgotten his little brother being in the woods until Mina asked him where Jake was. "Oops!" Of course he didn't dare tell his mother that he tied his brother to a tree in the middle of the woods for any source of wildlife to feast upon and then forgot about him.

Kenny was physically much larger than Jake and often times dragged his brother by the ears. Jake swears today that is the reason one ear is larger than the other. He got a kick out of picking on the kid and just could not help himself. Poor Kenny, he too had bigger problems lurking around the corner.

As the boys grew older Kenny gradually started accepting Jake, knowing that he was here to stay and that there was nothing he could do about it. He eventually warmed up to his little brother and accepted the hard fact that he was no longer Mina's favorite. As Kenny matured he treated Jake better, except when he was trying to impress his peers. Kenny soon realized his role as a big brother and role model, in fact, he became a little envious of how Jake looked up to Ronnie. Kenny knew he could not emulate Ronnie so he accepted he was just different.

Often Kenny would take Jake on walks to neighbor's houses to visit some of his friends but not the same ones that influenced the incident in the woods or the bridge dangling. Kenny wouldn't dare let them see him being nice to his little brother, so that is what made Jake think that Kenny actually hated him. Occasionally, Kenny and Jake would walk down Maybank Highway to *My Friend's Store,* and sit beneath the large sign and drink Cokes, eat penny candy and wave at cars as they passed by. This ultimately made Kenny start to enjoy the company of his kid brother, so they would do this more and more. They were getting along, until Kenny decided it was time to show off in front of his friends. Eventually he eased off on the picking, which surprised Jake and he even started liking Kenny, especially while Ronnie was away.

Kenny boogied to a different beat than his brothers. His outlook on life, his thoughts, actions, and behavior, and everything else about him was unique. A word not yet known by Jake that would best describe Kenny was unconventional, not in an odd or eccentric way but just in a non-conforming way. Years later there were other words not yet known to Jake that would describe his beautiful brother.

Chapter 15

"He that goeth down to the grave shall come up no more."
~ **Job VII**

June 27, 1968, the beautiful and fiery sun opened the account of a brand new day for everyone but Tommy. Thomas Nathaniel Stern, Jr. was laid to rest under the shade of an old live oak tree, on a hillside facing the historical Charleston harbor in Holy Cross Cemetery on James Island. In this final resting place, all are together in the darkness of the earth; the meek and mild and the mean and mighty; all now one dust resting with the worms never to leave.

The funeral and burial was attended by the entire Stern family and close friends and most neighbors. Strangely absent were Tommy's two closest friends, the pickle players. Jake Willoughby and Johnny Moore were not there.

Ronnie represented the Willoughby family as he stood by grief stricken Christine's side and carefully held her lovely arm. A mid-morning funeral mass then a noon time burial. Lunch followed for the tear and sweat soaked mourners.

Most of them were not hungry because they were still in a state of denial especially Tommy's mom, Janet, who was still in shock. Kathy, Julie and Barbara wept the entire service. They were close to their brother and loved him very much. This isn't something that happens to kids this age. It all seems so cruel and unfair. No matter how hard they try, they will never understand.

Mina believed that it would better for young Jake not to attend the funeral of his very best friend, with whom he had been quarreling just an hour before Tommy's awful demise. Jake himself, was sitting in his yard under the large weeping willow that he had always loved as if to hide from the world, but he was also trying to escape the insufferable humidity. He sat on the cool grass listening to the nearby squawk of a hungry crow. Even if his mom would have let him go, he did not want to or feel like he was able to attend Tommy's funeral. The entire episode was surreal. It was difficult to grasp the reality of the complete finality of his longtime pal actually being gone forever.

Over and over again Jake heard his own voice; *I wish you were dead.*

Over and over again he saw the look of disbelief in Tommy's green eyes. Jake had not been well for two days with these haunting sounds, and visions pulsating around in his head. He had not eaten nor slept except, only when his body gave out from sheer exhaustion.

This time three days ago, he and his best friend were playing ball, laughing, and living it up. Now only he lived, but why? Was he himself responsible for what happened to Tommy? Did he really wish this upon his best friend? Did he really make this happen? Jake was depressed beyond words; he was more ill than he had ever been in his entire life. Did all this really happen or was it imaginary? *Please be imaginary, PLEASE!*

Jake's last words to his best friend would reverberate through his mind for the rest of his life; it would also be his secret for decades to come. Jake was very mindful never ever to utter these words to anyone again, and definitely never let anyone know what he said to his best friend. Only one other person heard Jake curse his pal.

Jake suddenly remembered that there was a witness.

What if I do have this amazing power? What if word got out about this power? All of the Sterns would hate me forever and maybe throw me in jail. Everyone in the world would be afraid of me and hate me.

"Oh God," Jake bellowed aloud, "I am so sorry. Please Lord; please give me relief from this horror. Please forgive me, please!" For the next several months he would utter this mantra over and over again when he was certain that he was alone otherwise, he would mumble it to himself.,

The late afternoon summer shower patted down on the fresh shoveled dirt on the newest arrival in the quiet stone garden of tombs. A glistening, black raven sat above the grave of the latest resident on the lowest branch of the old live oak; its dead eyes glaring as its shiny black head twitched from side to side.

From directly above, a thunderous bolt of lightning shot through the cloudy, gray sky and struck the huge tree near Tommy's grave. It bounced back into the heavens after exploding the bark from the tree, just inches beneath the raven and slightly above the recently heaped dirt. The raven did not flinch; the only movement it made was the eerie, yellow eyes twitching from side to side.

A white mist of smolder slowly rises into the gloom filled sky, intermingling through the pounding rain, thus becoming a massive minatory cloud sitting over the murky graveyard. Lights flickered in shadowy buildings across the fog heavy harbor. The perfectly manicured lawn shimmered with droplets of rain, and the moss hung low and profound from the dampness.

Infinite circles of water from the middle of the stone fountain, centrally located in the land of the dead, made their way to the edge. The water flowed around the circumference to begin life anew with each drop of rain, as it became a novel wave within the boundless rings of ripples in the ivy draped fountain. So on, and so on, the alpha, and the omega, the first and the last, the beginning and the end.

Be careful for what you wish for.

Chapter 16

"To dread no eye, and to suspect no tongue,
is the greatest prerogative of innocence."
~ **Samuel Johnson**

One weekend a month the Willoughby family travelled over many rivers and through the woods into the farmland of the Pee Dee to get to Grandma's house. This is Jake's new favorite place in the world; this was a much needed break from the miserable shroud that draped his once precious and happy island. Like someone once said, a grandmother never runs out of hugs and cookies.

It was a two hour drive up Highway 17 north to Georgetown, then a lot of rural and desolate back roads northwest to Nichols, South Carolina. They were on the same roads that Wavy and his Sad Sacks had journeyed many years before.

The rustic, country landscape reminded Jake of the large books from first grade when learning to read and write with the pretty teacher holding the book with both hands with the pictures facing the wide-eyed classroom. The bucolic backdrop was sketched with large farm houses, reflective and inviting ponds, and sun sleek horses, hungry cattle, wondering chickens, and panting dogs.

The teacher would say, "Classroom, can you spell D-O-G? Classroom, can you spell cat C-A-T?"

Jake enthusiastically viewed ivy swathed water wells and large, vast farmlands full of produce. Strewn amongst the living and thriving was the opposite end of the spectrum with overgrown and neglected farms, abandoned and dilapidated homes and vine covered remains of tobacco barns. These were shaded by huge pecan trees, grandiose live oak trees and old rusty tractors with beards of weeds growing all around like a frowzy old man fearing to touch the razor.

Every few miles or so there would be a nice larger home and modern barn with new tractors beneath shelter. Jake observed and wondered throughout the miles of southern heartland and noticed in great detail every inch of Horry County right down to the purposely placed wagon wheels and exhausted , broken down wheel barrels reminding the weary driver of a by-gone piece of history. The good old days as Jake had heard them referred to as on many occasion.

Jake stuck his big curious head out of the rolled down window and let the fifty mile per hour wind blow into his eyes and mouth and through his thick dark hair. He looked into the side rearview mirror and was fascinated how his cheeks rippled from the breeze.

Even with the occasional overwhelming stench of decaying road kill Jake was far away from the salty creeks and putrid pluff mud. He could not wait to get to Grandma's where a garden of love grows in her warm heart. He knew she would have her famous brown cake to devour as she always made this favorite cake of cocoa specifically for their visit. Jake was also hoping that she would have her delicious country beef stew. Grandma's beef stew recipe was passed on to Mina whose beef stew became famous; time has a way of changing history.

Grandma's yard was acres and acres of beautiful sprawling farmland that included a thick green forest and several fishing ponds for which Jake could run, play and fish all day. There were always a few old dogs in which to share play time and one of the old dogs, Bullet, a black lab was especially fond of Jake and the feeling was mutual.

Jacob Todd Willoughby Sr. grew up on this vast land of play time as Jake thought of it. "Wavy" Willoughby was a tall fair-skinned kid covered in freckles who really loved to hunt and fish. He was smart student, especially in math as numbers came quick and easy to him. Young Wavy loved to play the guitar, and was fond of bluegrass and country music, specifically Bill Monroe, Roy Acuff, Ernest Tubb, and The Carter Family. Wavy learned all their songs as quickly as he heard them; he had a natural gift for music. Southern Gospel, bluegrass and country music were all that was available on the rural airwaves back then.

Wavy's father, John Oliver, was a prominent cotton and tobacco farmer at the turn of the century. "J.O." was an older gentleman when his son Jacob was born. Wavy had several siblings but spread out in age much like his own children with the majority of them being much older, grown and gone by the time the curly haired one came along. However, Wavy did have a younger brother by nearly two years. Olin Winston Willoughby nicknamed OWW, referred to by the word not the initials by Wavy and his friends.

When Olin's name was bellowed out it gave their parents obvious concern, OWW! These two boys did everything together. Where ever you saw Wavy his little brother OWW was always standing in the shadow of his big brother. That was definitely the good old days in the minds of those two growing up in the late twenties and early thirties in rural South Carolina. Much of the two brother's activities became folklore for the younger generations. One incident left a scar on Wavy's left ankle to prove the tale.

Ten year old Wavy was walking through the deep woods after picking huckleberries for the night's dessert as he passed the small overgrown centuries old family cemetery deep in the woods far off the beaten path. Normally he never thought twice about it but as he peered over he saw a frail old woman with long white hair sitting upon a very ancient tombstone. She looked at Wavy with deep-set black eyes, the blackest eyes he had ever seen, surrounded by gaunt, white flesh. The woman had no expression and her ghostly face was framed by a long sheer veil. She slowly lifted her right hand which was draped in long white veil of cotton and pointed a knobby pale finger with a claw like nail attached to it at the terrified lad.

A motionless Wavy was about to let out a scream but found no sound as her long crooked finger slowly motioned for him to come to her while she sat on a large faded tombstone. Wavy dropped the basket of berries, and ran as fast as he ever had in his entire life. He looked back only once and that was when the large diamondback rattlesnake struck and pierced its long fangs into his ankle. Wavy screamed, not OWW but HELP, and his brother came back running to him.

Earlier, Olin had gone ahead of Wavy, who insisted on getting every last berry in the woods. Olin did not notice the woman in the cemetery nor the rattler. Perhaps the wraith was trying to warn Wavy about the snake. Wavy survived, but stayed away from that path every day since. He often wondered who the ghost lady was, and who's tomb did she protect, or was it her own, but he would be too embarrassed by the consequential ridicule to ever inquire. Any future berries that needed to be picked in that neck of the woods, were picked somewhere else.

Jake and his new canine companion Bullet sat under the shade of a large pecan tree on the east side of Grandma's house near the pond. Jake dosed off for a few seconds, and he began dreaming about the old woman on the tombstone with empty, black eyes and solemn stare as she was motioning to him with that long crooked finger.

He was abruptly awakened by the terrifying, shrieking sound of some far off creature, and a wailing Bullet, who was responding to the eerie howling from the woods. Jake was more than ready to get back to the house with Bullet, as he had heard plenty of stories about ghost, hyenas, and other creatures, nearby at Gator Swamp.

Kenny sat in front of the twenty-seven inch solid state color television with Grandma. Kenny's attention was diverted from the screen while she brushed her long graying hair that fell nearly to her waist. He had never seen her hair down from the infamous bun, and was shocked at the length of it before she skillfully restored it to the top her head.

They both intently watched as Festus rambled on about the hill folk way of doing things while he trotted towards the Long Branch Saloon with Marshall Dillon to wet his whiskers with a cold drought beer. Mina was in the kitchen putting the away the dishes, something she never seemed to escape.

Wavy and Ronnie were down the street at Wavy's older brother, Melvin's general store and gas station, shooting pool. Father and son drank a beer together. Though neither uttered a word about it, they knew in their heart of hearts that this could very well be the last time for such an occasion; possibly the first and last beer together.

Wavy, with a tremble in his lips and a tear in his eye, looked at his son with pride. In between sips of beer and carefully aimed shots at colored and numbered balls, they snacked on one of Ronnie's favorites, boiled peanuts, something Uncle Melvin always seemed had on hand. Hank Snow was singing his best from an old radio sitting on a dusty shelf next to the green oil can.

The C5A's were roaring across the ocean… a world in chaos, are there really answers in the wind?

Chapter 17

"Beautiful is the bloom of youth, but it does not last."
~ **Theocritus**

For Jake Willoughby, the summer of 1968, which had started out so promising and turned into the season from hell, was finally winding down. A bittersweet occasion; Ronnie has just a few days left to console Christine before he ships out. The Stern family has changed, and rightfully so. They had lost their only son and brother; they are quiet and reserved. Janet Stern does not appear to be recovering from the shock of losing her youngest son; she has turned to alcohol for help.

A dark shadow has cast over the small neighborhood and everyone seems different than they once were. With the drowning death of one of its youngest, and happiest residents, and the impending departure of one of its, nicest, best looking, and most athletic residents, as he prepares for war; the community is depressed.

Jake and his friends all lost interest in baseball, especially the game of pickle. In fact, ever since the drowning, most everyone seems to have disappeared. A lot of the kids had to spend the last couple of weeks travelling with their families, and visiting their own grandmothers, or camping trips at Rocks Pond before school started back.

A dismal Jake has turned to his new best buddy, Bullet, for support. Bullet, brought home from Grandma's to help Jake in his grieving process, is a three year old black lab with the glossiest of coats, and the most joyful demeanor. Bullet is thrilled about his new buddy as well, even though he misses his tag-a-longs, and the great openness of his former home. Bullet stays right on Jake's heels everywhere he goes. He follows Jake on bicycle rides, lawn mowing, and trips to Staley's store on running on the side of the busy Maybank Highway. Jake thoroughly enjoys the lovable dog's company; he has never before had a dog of his own. In fact, the entire Willoughby family had never had a pet before, and they had taken a shine to Bullet. Was it enough for Jake?

Even though Jake seemed well enough on the outside, he hurt badly within. He had just lost his best friend, maybe from his own doing, and was about to lose his older brother, at least only temporarily, he hoped. Someone so young should not feel this way. Just days ago he was swimming at Green Hole and picking plums. He was walking down King Street with his hero and felt like king of the world. Now, with no one to talk to, he found himself confiding in his new canine buddy, who lapped up every word while they sat together under one of Jake's favorite trees.

Uncle Hal sat nearby in a webbed lawn chair reading the newspaper, or an encyclopedia. He sipping on his sister's refreshing, sweet tea while soaking in the summer sun and resting his tired, old war-worn body and trying to erase the horrors of combat, even just for a little while.

The world outside of Jake's seemed to proceed as usual. Jake did not at all like what has transpired in the last several weeks, none of this seemed fair, none of it seemed incited. Where did those awful words to his friend come from? Jake was muddled, he was disheartened and very tired. He longed for the endless days of summer, playing catch Ronnie and Tommy. He and Tommy would always find a thousand things to do, and it was the very best of times.

Jake did not know death until now. He did not know the true meaning of the word, nor did he know the permanence of it until now. Now, he thought about it more and more and he was extremely frightened by it. He did not want to die and he did not want anyone he knew to die, especially his family, and he certainly did not want to be responsible for it. What a miserable end of summer for young Jake. Each new morning as he washes away the sleepy, as Mina calls it, from his eyes, he sees a different Jake in the mirror. His dark eyes, like two unexplored caverns, leading to the tortured soul within that caves in on his existence.

I am Jake, I'm alive, I am here, and I don't want to leave! I just want to be free and happy again.

Jake gently patted Bullets black head and softly repeated the same line from early morning.

"I am Jake, I'm alive, I am here, and I don't want to leave. I just want to be free and happy again."

He peered from under the willow vines over at Uncle Hal who was savoring a cold sweet tea with an unusual look of delight on his tanned, experience lined face. Jake wondered if his uncle had heard him speaking aloud. He probably assumed he was talking to the loyal dog, maybe he thinks that his nephew is crazy.

Jake suddenly stared at his uncle and thought about the man and his past, something he never really considered prior. Uncle Hal, who was now reading his Bible, with a smoking pipe dangling from the corner of his mouth, looked so comfortable. Jake had imagined that his uncle had seen a lot of death with his four years in Europe during World War II. He dared not approach the man, who had very little to say. Jake loved his Uncle Hal dearly; he just didn't know much about him. What he did know, he learned from his mother, or from self-observance. He knew that his Uncle was a neat, organized, and intelligent man that loved to read and take long walks into the woods, observing nature. Jake was impressed that his uncle knew the name of every bird, plant, tree, flower, insect, or snake, as well as their Latin names and meanings.

Jake enjoyed being around his uncle, he was able to learn a lot of big words and pick up the habit of newspaper reading , something he started a couple of years down the road, from the sagacious old man. He was always well groomed, and nicely dressed. He walked like he was still the soldier he was twenty-five years earlier, straight posture, head and chin high. They would often take morning strolls through the woods where Uncle Hal would point out the different trees, birds, and shrubs.

The sweet smell of fresh, baked, buttermilk biscuits from his wonderful mother's homey kitchen caught Jake's attention and his uncle's as well.

"Get 'em while they're hot," he heard Kenny announce through the kitchen window.

That sounded great to Uncle Hal. He removed his reading glasses, carefully and meticulously folded and placed them in their leather case, and then slowly slid them into his right, front shirt pocket. He tapped the mouth of the pipe bowl in his palm, and removed a cotton handkerchief from his right, back pocket from his starched khakis. He wiped his palm and his pipe, cautiously tucking the stem of the smoking instrument behind the pocket protector full of pens and pencils of all colors in his left, front shirt pocket. He shook the handkerchief free of any debris while carefully, and perfectly, folding it with each corner matching the other, and slid it back into its proper place. He lifted his Bible, dictionary, and notebook, all neatly stacked like the perfect student would have done. He then grabbed the remains of the southern, smooth, sweet tea and the small, sacrificial ice cubes chinking in the quart size Mason jar. He turned towards the enticing aroma from those fresh, hot, buttered biscuits, and followed its enticement, and to refill his glass with real southern comfort; sweet tea.

A ravenous Jake is right behind the tall man with large, damp patches of perspiration on the underarms of his short sleeved khaki shirt. Anxious and panting, Bullet is in Jake's shadow. The young man is smiling for the first time since his best friend perished. With each step they all followed the clinking ice cubes.

The pale distance of time transcends beyond the revolutions of the earth and leaves trails of iridescent dust in the vast universe, dazzling generously and floating within regal galaxies throughout infinity.

Chapter 18

"Blue, darkly, deeply, beautifully blue."
~ **Robert Southey**

The early morning mist hit Jake's red cheeks as he pedaled his old hand me down bike as hard as he possibly could down the shady dirt road with Bullet right by his side, stride for stride. Visions had been gnawing at Jake ever since that fateful day, and finally, curiosity got the better of him as he headed out early before breakfast so as not to be noticed, to take a look at the last place his best friend Tommy had ever seen.

Many weeks had passed since the horrible tragedy that rocked the neighborhood and Jake's very soul.

Even though he had been to the fateful spot many times, usually with Tommy, and even a time or two with Johnnie, but never without the supervision of Ronnie, Christine or Buddy Barfield, he felt that he had to take another look, even if it meant disobeying his concerned parents. Why did he have the compulsive desire to see the scene of his best friend's death? He did not understand what possessed this urge; he only knew that he had to look and see to see the last things that Tommy ever saw, the visions that he took with him to where ever he went. He felt that it may help in some way to see, feel and connect with his friend's final moments for which he felt responsible. He had absolutely no general idea what he was looking for, or what he would see or feel, but he felt that just being there, that maybe something would materialize in some form or another.

Would this ease the pain? He didn't know if it would or not, but he had to try. Something that he could not explain possessed him to go. Jake assumed, if he arrived early, he would get there before any random crabbers. But most of all, he did not want be disturbed during his vigil. Jake had no idea whether or not the tide was high or low; it didn't matter, because he was going to go, regardless.

81

Jake reached the eminent path of departure and finality. This was Tommy's last sights, sounds, and smells. Being here somehow comforted him. The bright, morning sun burned the condensation from the deep, blue gleaming water and lit up the clear, wide-open sky.

As the dirt slope steepened, Jake jumped off his bike so that the speed and momentum would not take him straight into the mud of fate. He slowly walked his bike down the embankment with caution, and with his mind now going wild, and his eyes darting everywhere, he was wondering where it actually happened. He looked for solid ground; he trusted only the small point at the base of the slope would suffice. Jake sat his bike down and nervously looked all around. The morbid eeriness of it all would have freaked out most of his remaining friends, and definitely Kenny.

A strange feeling overcame him, and he felt as if Tommy was standing with him. After all, they had stood together many times on this very spot, but unfortunately, Jake had not been with Tommy on his final trip.

Possibly, if he had been with him, things may have turned out differently~ if only Tommy had not stolen his baseball. He wondered how Johnny was dealing with all of this. He speculated as to what the two of them had talked about before the incident. He pondered what exactly lead to the drowning. He knows Johnny's version, but was that the truth? It's hard to believe a character like Johnny, especially about something this severe. Jake was uncertain, so maybe he was looking for clues. Could something have transpired to cause a murder? No way, a kid wouldn't kill another kid!

The dark miasma of the sonorous underbelly, where bridge meets land, was cold and unnerving. Here he was, alone at the point of doom. He could not help but recreate the alleged events in his mind, imagining what Tommy did, or where he stepped or what he saw. Obviously, Johnny's foul face was one of the last things that Tommy ever envisioned- what a dreadful last site, *no wonder he's pissed*. Out of nowhere, billowy, white clouds were forming various shapes, high above Jake's head. The low tide reflecting the glorious morning sky was a glistening solar prism, lying between the tall amber strands of marsh grass, which resembled outstretched arms, desperately reaching to touch a rock idol on stage... or Tommy's outstretched arms, desperately reaching for something to clutch on to.

The bank on which Jake stood, was encased by the maiden morning mud which was shimmering in all its greasy, brown-gray glory. The fiddler crabs were scurrying in all directions while the hungry shore birds were attempting to feast on them. This was a splendid sight first thing in the morning and would make a grand photograph or painting. To Jake it had become a very bleak place, not appealing at all, and not like it had been when all was right in Jakedom. In fact, it was now the saddest place on earth he believed.

Standing tall, beside the unforgiving marsh, Jake took it all in - the view, the smell, everything. All of this was making him lightheaded and nauseated. Even years later, it's a sight that still lingers in the depths of his mind like a forgotten tattoo on someone's arm or back, only thought about when looking in the mirror, then it reminds you of your foolish past.

Every time Jake looks in the mirror, he sees that tattoo; dragged out from the eerie, dreary corridors like Tommy dragged from the wicked pits of the mire. The scene, like those fateful words, is etched in his suppression chambers, and in his unhappy heart, never, ever to fade.

An occasional car would pass over, causing the bridge above to rumble and shudder. Doodlebugs had made their prominent dunes all over the silky sand around the large pillars holding up the bridge. Mud daubers had their clay homes strewn throughout the concrete bottom of the connector. The shadowy corners of the bridge were still chilly from the moonlit night before.

The unmistakable stench of the pluff mud resonated all around the small distressing space that gave witness to Jake's death wish. Jake could hear the thumping of his own heart as it bounced off of the concrete pillars, and swears that he could hear the screaming ricochets of Tommy's very last breath.

Bullet had enough smarts to keep his distance, this was all new terrain for him and he didn't like it. The intelligent canine sensed something unfriendly.

The marsh critters greeted the day with excitement in search of food. The tall strands of Spartina grass met the pluff mud as far as Jake could see. The winding creek went on for miles, into kingdom come. If Jake had the vision of his one of his hero's, Superman, he could see HIS baseball as it made its way through drifting waters.

All tattered and gray now, the ball washed from the mud when the tide ripped through and rolled on its revolving journey when it descended twice a day. This ball has been on quite a voyage, with no end in sight. For something that he desired so desperately, Jake didn't get to enjoy the new ball for very long and ironically, it brought him much grief; it ended his love for baseball.

As Jake stood on the salty banks of the deadly marsh, he did not think of the ball at all. He looked out at the river where he had been many times in a boat with his dad and brothers. It had always been a pleasant place with great memories. Jake's dark wondrous eyes panned the immediate area. He picked a spot and decided that this was it - *the spot*, the spot where Tommy last stood. He inched closer to the softening mud, staring down at it, and he reached his long right leg out and put a foot on it. To his horror his foot found no bottom as it swiftly sank to his knee and he dared not put in his left foot. The more he tried to wriggle lose, the deeper he sank. OH NO!! Had he met the same fate as Tommy?

Jake's heart dropped to the bottom of his stomach like a ton of bricks. He felt as if he would throw up. Tears quickly filled his eyes. Terror blanketed him. His head darted around looking for help; anything, anybody. There was nothing or no one; all was quiet, except for Bullet. Jake wondered if Bullet could pull off a Lassie, and go get help. Did he have time? Was Bullet smart enough?

"Oh My God" Jake shouted. But, no sound came from his parched mouth. His wide eyes expressed complete and total panic.

Jake didn't have to say a word, Bullet sensed the danger that his master was in. The clever lab barked, ardently and deafeningly for help.

"Stay still, Bubba," roared a very familiar and extremely welcomed voice from behind Jake; just in the nick of time, just like in *The Adventures of Superman,* his hero appeared.

Ronnie had witnessed Jake's early and hasty departure from home, and decided that he better follow him. With no bike or car Ronnie had to walk toward the creek and it was nearly too late as the ferocious tide was surely greeting its unwelcomed visitor, Jake.

Ronnie pulled on his brother's outstretched arm, careful not to get in the same predicament. After what seemed like several minutes, he was able to wrap his mighty arms under Jake's armpits and pull his little brother from the powerful death grip of the hungry sludge.

Jake's muddy leg and foot re-appeared with no shoe, but that was the least of his worries. Jake embraced his brother as tight as he could and shook like the bridge above, as he bawled harder than he ever had before.

Bullet was excitedly running around the two brothers, and then when he had enough, he ran up the embankment, impatiently waiting for the two to follow. Jake finally got it out of his system; he never physically visited that dreadful spot again, neither did Bullet or Ronnie.

The mammoth cargo planes thundered overhead causing the steel span of the old bridge to shake giving added drama to the moment. Jake did not want to ever let go of his brother.

Chapter 19

"Youth is easily deceived because it is quick to hope."
~ **Aristotle**

Jake often wondered how what was supposed to be a summer of wholesome fun and delight could take such a drastic turn to horrifying gloom and doom. Ronnie's thirty day furlough was up, and it was the most dreadful day ever for the Willoughby household. In fact, the two days leading up to this day have been melancholy for the entire family. Very little was said due to the emotions resting on the crest of each spoken word. The family lacked an appetite because of the knots in their stomachs and Christine was just as despondent as the others.

Earlier that morning, Jake tried to muster up the courage to speak to his brother without bawling like a baby. When he approached Ronnie's bedroom door he saw the sad Marine packing his duffle bag while tears stained the items that he placed inside. That moment was too much for Jake to handle.

A very downhearted Jake hurriedly ran into the bathroom where he stared at himself in the mirror hoping to conceal any emotion, and the dam gave way as the tears came pouring. He tried his best to stop the crying but it emanated powerfully and didn't want to stop. This was without a doubt the saddest day of his life.

Now Ronnie had to be brave and hide all his emotions in front of his mom and family. He had to hold back those tears and realized it was the most challenging thing he had ever done. He took a deep breath, turned, and gave a somber glance at his beloved home for perhaps the last time as he climbed into the backseat with Jake and a teary-eyed Christine.

Kenny sat up front with Mina and Wavy as they headed to the Charleston International Airport in North Charleston. It was a good thirty minute ride, but it felt much shorter for everyone present. Ronnie did not want the trip to end. He kept thinking how he could get out of it; jump out at the next stop light and run for Canada? Nah, he was not a quitter and too much of a man for those little slant-eyed communist Gooks.

At the airport, the hugs were shared and tears were widespread. Saying goodbye and I love you flowed like the incoming tide at Church Creek. Mina constantly told Ronnie to be safe, write often, and say his prayers. They all stood side by side and waved as if Ronnie could see them doing so, while the giant jet roared across the lonely blue sky and disappeared into the thick white clouds swallowed by a magic dragon.

Ronnie had to spend the next thirty days in special training in San Diego, and then a couple of weeks in Hawaii before finally soaring across the immense ocean to the jungle of death.

Back home Jake has a few more weeks before going back to school. If the next two months were anything like the first he would just as soon stay inside and hide. There was plenty to watch on the bouncy television screen, he would turn the large dial between the three available stations. What used to be his favorites, he no longer showed an interest in such as *I Dream of Jeannie, Lost in Space, Gilligan's Island, Gomer Pyle,* and *The Beverly Hillbillies.* Even the beautiful girls and their smiling belly buttons were of no interest to Jake.

The only show that brought good memories was *Gunsmoke.* Speaking of *Gunsmoke*, Grandma loved *Gunsmoke*. Maybe another trip to Grandma's was just what he needed, but in the meantime nothing made him feel better, Tommy was gone and Ronnie was gone. Not Ronnie!

Jake would sometimes sneak into the backseat of the golden Chevy and pray aloud. "Please God, bring him safely back home." Often times he cried himself to sleep worrying about his brother and he hoped that Kenny never noticed. Finally, some good news that made Jake think that maybe he could feel a little better, a full weekend at Grandma's. Just the anticipation alone eased some of his despair.

The Fourth of July at Grandma's house included plenty of southern fare, lots of love, and most of all far, far away from Church Creek.

Poor Ronnie, he always loved going to Grandma's as much as Jake did, but instead he is in San Diego training to go to the worst possible place on earth. *My God, how he must be feeling.* Jake didn't want to think about it. He didn't want to think about anything really. He just wanted to run around Grandma's place with Bullet and Kenny, if he wasn't picking on him, and eat, eat, eat.

"Grandma's are moms with lots of frosting."~ Author unknown

As always, Grandma had her famous brown cake, never duplicated beef stew, the absolute best homemade buttermilk biscuits anyone had ever tasted and sweet tea that no one has ever come close to making.

Grandma always kept a little of her social security money set aside for the grandkids that she had folded up in her hanky and nestled deep inside her apron pocket. She always wore a flowery apron with pockets because it seemed that she was always cooking and cleaning. Just before they left to go back home she would pull the carefully folded embroidered lace handkerchief from the apron pocket and give Jake two or three dollars. Jake was sure Kenny and Ronnie received money as well, but he never witnessed her give it to them, and they were never around when she offered him his.

Jake thought for sure that Norman Rockwell had his grandmother in mind when he painted his *Freedom from Want*, the depiction in the photo remarkably resembled Grandma and her home, including the apron she wore. Even the spread on the table during late November with the elated eyes and yearning mouths were all the same.

Cigar smoking, greasy overall wearing Uncle Melvin rode down the long, sandy, cedar tree lined driveway in his cream colored 1963 Ford Falcon Ranchero, with three large white German shepherds in the open bed of the small truck. The huge dogs appeared to be guarding the two huge coolers full of ice, beer, sodas, and a couple of mason jars filled with Uncle Melvin's homemade scuppernong wine.

Bullet and the shepherds went crazy with delight when they saw each other. Yelping, barking, sniffing, pawing on one another with large drool dripping tongues fervently wagging in sync with their long tails.

They then chased each other enthusiastically around the house several times, eventually coming to a rest on the thick green grass in the shade one of the large pecan trees near the pond. Jake couldn't help but smile as the panting dogs laid in the shade patiently awaiting his arrival.

Everyone was there, except for Ronnie. Uncle Melvin and his wife, Aunt Eula Mae, Wavy and Mina, and Melvin and Wavy's younger brother Olin and his wife Aunt Betty Lou, and Uncle Hal. Along with Jake, Kenny, and their cousins, Sheila and Rhonda, who were Uncle Olin and Aunt Betty Lou's daughters.

Wavy, and his older brother, Melvin, set up large tables made from plywood resting on sawhorses, and covered them with several old cotton tablecloths. Inside, Aunt Eula Ma and Aunt Betty Lou, helped Mina and Grandma prepare the food and take it outside. Uncle Hal was setting up targets on the side yard near the pond for rifle shooting. All the men claimed to be the better shot. Well, we will soon find out who indeed is the better shot.

Kenny was in front of the television in the living room. Grandma's television was bigger and better than the one at home. It was a color set, although most of the shows were televised in black and white, and even more amazing was the remote control. This seemed to be the biggest thrill in Kenny's life at the moment.

The talking robot was warning Will Robison that there was danger!! Jake thought, as he walked past the living room, that there were a couple of cute girls on this show too, as he headed to wash up before eating.

The women folk, as Wavy called them, prepared from scratch the potato salad, baked beans and cole slaw. Uncle Melvin cut the watermelon into quarters, as Uncle Olin had turned a fifty gallon steel drum into a BBQ cooker and grilled up the very best hamburgers, hot dogs and ribs, which were favorites of everyone sitting at the large picnic tables. This group gathered together on the average once every couple of years, but this year would be a special treat.

Hopefully, according to all the talk that morning, they would get together again in November for Thanksgiving.

As usual the food was superb and extremely filling. Everyone was as "full as a tick", Jake overheard some of the adults say. That image nearly caused Jake to lose his lunch for a second, as he visualized a large, gray, blood filled tick that Mina pulled from Bullet just the other day.

The women pulled the leftover food from the table as the dogs chomped away at the scraps. Kenny helped cousins, Sheila and Rhonda, take down the table clothes and put away most of the chairs. The men grabbed their rifles for the rifle competition. Jake would not get to see any fireworks this year, as this was as close as it was going to get, but he still was dizzy with excitement anticipating watching his dad hit bulls-eye every time.

Uncle Hal and Uncle Melvin nailed soda caps to fence post forty and fifty feet away. Everyone gathered around the shooters as they took turns blasting at the caps. As predicted at the end of the competition only one shooter had hit the nail every time. Jake's father, Wavy Willoughby, was the shooting champion. Jake was proud of his father's mastery of his rifle. He marveled at his confidence and precision when he brought the rifle to his right shoulder, closed his left eye, took a steady aim and fired. It was astonishing to watch the soda caps fly away looking like metal washers when they landed.

Jake ran to the post and collected the remains of the caps to keep as souvenirs and trophies to show his buddies at school. The bullet holes could not be more perfect, dead center. Jake was in awe of his dad's shooting ability and his biceps, which resembled cantaloupes. Wavy's muscles were larger than Jake had ever seen, except the back of his comic books that showed an eighty pound weakling getting bullied. Then the weakling becomes Jack Lalanne in the caption next to the live sea monkey advertisement, but that's another story.

As the buttery sun melted into the horizon and radiated an assortment of oil colors, it co-mingled and effused with the inbound clouds with the pending darkness making its glorious appearance.

All of the men stayed outside and indulged in Uncle Melvin's homemade scuppernong wine, which must have been mighty good Jake thought, because they were into the third Mason jar by the time the last blink of sunlight was replaced by the half-moon floating over the distant tree line.

Jake and his cousins, Rhonda and Sheila, sat in oak rockers on the large front porch watching the lightning bugs dance in the night, while the women were inside putting away the leftovers and cleaning the dishes. Kenny, as usual, was in front of the television but now he was alone as he watched *Mod Squad*.

The men were as happy as Jake had ever seen them, and couldn't understand what they were hootin' and hollerin' about. He heard an occasional burst of belly laughter that made even the kids on the porch giggle. They didn't even know what they were giggling about, but it felt good to just laugh because it had been a while for Jake to enjoy himself.

Jake thoroughly enjoying the day and evening with the family, the food, the dogs and the laughter all made him relaxed, yet he was anxious about Ronnie, who would have loved all of this as well.

The stars above were the only fireworks for miles and the nearest city seemed like a million miles away. Jake didn't even know where the nearest city was, all he saw was shadowy trees, fields, frenzied lightning bugs and empty Mason jars.

This is one of those days Jake wishes he could withdraw from his secret account and visit over and over again. The memory bank doesn't suffice and time travelling would ideal to actually be there, to enjoy it all as he did when it took place the first time. To be able hear the sound of crickets in the air, the merriment of loving, happy men and the carefree cackle of women in the kitchen would be a great joy, along with the loyal dog's yelping at the croaking bullfrogs near the ponds edge, and the occasional giggling from the innocent kids in oak rockers creaking on the large, wooden porch. It would be wonderful to smell the southern, country, summer air again.

Meanwhile, far away from the gleeful rural upstate against a black canvass, there was a performance of the colorful array of fireworks bursting high above the atrocious mire of mud and shimmering waters between the briny banks of the barrier islands. Radiant yellow eyes, like that of a stalking panther, glowed from a thick wall of trees deep beyond the tall marsh grass.

Chapter 20

"War is as much a punishment to the punisher as to the sufferer."
~ **Thomas Jefferson**

Vietnam, formally the Socialist Republic of Vietnam, is the Eastern most country on the Indo China Peninsula in Southeast Asia. With an estimated 91.5 million inhabitants as of 2012, it is the 13th most populace country and the eighth most populace Asian country. The name Vietnam translates as South Viet and was officially adopted in 1945. The country is bordered by China to the North, Laos to the Northwest, and Cambodia to the Southwest, and the South China Sea to the East.

The Vietnamese became independent from Imperial China in 938 AD following the Battle of Bach Dang River. Successive Vietnamese royal dynasties flourished as the nation expanded geographically and politically into Southeast Asia until the Indochina Peninsula was colonized by the French in the mid-19th century. The First Indochina War eventually led to the expulsion of the French in 1954 leaving Vietnam divided politically into two states - North and South Vietnam. Conflict between the two sides intensified with heavy foreign intervention during the Vietnam War which ended with a North Vietnamese victory in 1975.

Vietnam is a long stretch of diversified landscape with climate changes between North and South. There are mountainous regions, jungles, deltas and beaches. There are small farms throughout the country side with many rice paddies along the number of rivers. It is beautiful country with many offerings which is why so many fought and died for it. The rolling green hills sprinkled with trees stretch for miles topped with mighty palms swaying in the monsoon winds. Tigers and snakes fill the jungles as well as many species of birds, plant life and other animals.

The late summer temperatures were much like South Carolina, very hot and humid. However, towards the end of the month the heat let off just ever so slightly as the heavy rains came and pounded the ground and gave some much relief to the entire territory.

Ronnie was a little more used to the scorching conditions than some of his clammy and complaining comrades which gave him an edge of resilience and perseverance along with his enduring athleticism.

United States Marine Corps Reconnaissance Division, Third Battalion based at Quang- Tri was Ronnie's new home. Arriving in early August fresh from special training in Camp Pendleton, California the eighteen year old Private First Class appeared to be a fighting machine on the outside but was a frightened child on the inside and no amount of screaming, spitting, brainwashing, and ass-kicking could change that. Dressed in heavy olive green jungle fatigues and getting used to his new environment still didn't keep him from missing family and home. Ronnie ached for home, he longed for his mother and his family and he desired the soft popcorn buttered lips of Christine.

Ronnie received many letters from family and Christine, and these hand written words from home kept him rejuvenated with hope and smiles. He read about the Fourth of July celebration at Grandma's house and how his dad won the shooting contest and he suddenly he became curious as to whether or not he, a trained marksman, could out shoot country born and bred, Wavy Willoughby, the best shot in all of Horry County. He wished that he could have stayed home at least one more week for that, of course, he never wanted to leave home and couldn't wait to get back.

After a month of sweltering heat at 100 plus degrees, Ronnie endured yet even more training; combat fighting, guerilla warfare, jungle aptitude, search and destroy mentality with the *if it moves shoot to kill mantra.* Feeling prepared and ready to deploy their new skills, Ronnie's platoon was soon sent on daily missions; enemy patrols, with Sergeant Conner at the helm, reporting every moment of their mission to Lt. Decker. The platoon set out on gunships into the jungle where heavy infiltration had been reported the day before.

The first mission was the worst. As the Bell UH1-E Huey landed in a high grassy area surrounded by jungle young Ronnie's heart skipped several beats and landed in the dark depths of his belly. He knew he was going to be sick, fortunately, he wasn't the first to jump out of the chopper; he knew that if he was, he would fall flat on his face from sheer fear.

His heart was now racing and pounding in his ears and drowning out the great gunship. This is it. This is what they had prepared for and they were now part of history. They were fighting in Vietnam and it was all over the news.

Ronnie's fellow Marines were all screaming at one another and he could not hear himself think. What they were saying was drowned out by the loud chopper, but he saw the intensity in their eyes and felt their spittle on his cheeks. He could see their moving mouths wide open and their eyes bulging with excitement as they were preparing to drop four feet to the ground and blast their weapons at whatever moved, hoping not to be fired upon in the process.

The young men knew that each mission could be death for them as each prior patrol always reported at least two or three killed in action, KIA, or wounded in action, WIA. Ronnie would prefer WIA if any fire came his way. Actually he would prefer none of this nonsense; why was he even here?

Why wasn't he home with his family where he belonged? This wasn't his war, his problem or his fault. Every day many young men his age were dying over this unassuming piece of land. Black body bags filled with boys in bloody boots were loaded and shipped home daily; he wants to go home alive. There was absolutely nothing he could do about it, except survive! And survive he would!

Ooh rah!!!

His heart was now deep below in the belly of the beast and he hoped he wouldn't crap in his pants as he jumped from the chopper. He was able to land in the high grass with his finger on the trigger and his eyes searching for gooks that he was primed to kill. In full pack with helmets atop and rifles ready, the brave, young Americans advanced towards the ominous and obscure jungle that loomed ahead.

Chapter 21

"There's a long trail a-winding into the land of my dreams."
~ **Stoddard King**

Wilhelmina DuPont Willoughby was a lovely woman. She was tall
with olive skin, long jet black hair and deep-black penetrating eyes.
She was generous by nature with a very caring soul which showed as
she constantly was giving and helping. She was sharp and quick with
wit and her bright eyes and radiant smile would light up the entire
county.

Although her parents have now passed she still has a large family with
a husband, daughter and four sons along with two sisters and six
brothers all which she loved dearly.

Mina DuPont grew up poor. She was the seventh child of meager dirt
farmers who lived just fifteen minutes southwest of Conway, South
Carolina with is thirty minutes west of Myrtle Beach, South Carolina.
She was born in 1915 in an oak and elm shaded small clapboard house
surrounded by widespread farmland. Her parents were older than most
folks having babies at that time and were God fearing, humble people
who did the best they could with what they had.

They were a proud hardworking couple that loved family, neighbors
and God. They had very little money but seemed extremely happy and
grateful. They raised and grew their own food; cows, pigs, chickens,
eggs, milk, vegetables and fruit including assorted berries, figs and
pecans. They had a horse for transportation and a mule for plowing.
They spent many painful hours and long days building their house and
plowing their fields to make a comfortable home for their children.

They made their own butter and soap and had a smoke house filled
with bountiful meat. Mina's mother sewed their own clothes and the
older children did the chores and helped on the farm until the
depression set in. After high school the boys all went to work for the

railroad so they could send money home to maintain the farm and keep the younger kids fed, clothed and in school.

Harold, Jake's Uncle Hal and Wilhelmina were closest in age and often mistaken for twins as they bare so much resemblance and were together all the time. They were always playing and singing on their long walks to school. Yes, it was the proverbial long walk down a dirt road through rain, sleet, and snow to school. Sometimes behind the barn near the woods Hal would pretend to be a preacher and Mina in the choir as they sang so pleasantly "Church in the Wildwood". These were warmhearted memories for Mina.

Occasionally they were able to join their father on his weekly Saturday visit to the general store in Conway; the big city to them. He would load them all up in the wagon pulled by their mule and travel on the lumpy dirt road to purchase much needed supplies with the money that the older boys had sent home. This was the time when the only thing making the news was The Great Depression, FDR and bank robber John Dillinger; these stories were quite often splashed across the headlines of The State newspaper that sat in the front display window as they walked into Burrough's Pharmacy for medication, usually liniment and maybe one stick of candy.

Mina would browse through the latest issues of the *Saturday Evening Post, Life* and *Look* magazines. The young country girl enjoyed reading about and looking at the pictures of the golden era of Hollywood. She adored Clark Gable and *Gone with the Wind.* Sometimes she would fantasize about living the life of a movie star; she definitely had the look and enjoyed poising for the camera.

As a child, Mina was somewhat spoiled being the first girl born in twenty years. Her father, Frank Monroe DuPont or Uncle Frank as he was known by the locals, had forgotten what it was like to have a baby girl around the house and farm. As she got older she was often seen feeding the chickens in the yard even though she wasn't much taller than they were at the time and pulling a pail of water from the stone well out in the front yard. Weary travelers would often stop by for cool, fresh well water and a glance at the lovely Mina.

On Sundays, relatives would travel long distances after church from other counties to have lunch with the DuPont's. Sarah Drew DuPont, Mina's mother, was renowned for her extraordinary cooking skills; she always made plenty never knowing who may drop by as they did not have a telephone in those days.

Mina was constantly assisting her assiduous mother with all the many chores around the house and farm. She learned to cook, sew and how to act like a lady; well-mannered and polite, just as she would teach her own children someday.

One summer day Mina was near the barn to finish some chores when she noticed that the old bull had managed to leave through the open gate that her father apparently forgot to shut. Uncle Frank had become a little forgetful being in his late sixties at the time. The large bull was quickly approaching with his head lowered and horns aimed at the slouching unaware old man when Mina noticed the aggressive bull and watched in fear at what was taking place. Without hesitation she grabbed the nearby pitchfork and ran straight towards the bull which then turned his attention to her and must have recognized the pitchfork and the fire in her eyes. The bull quickly huffed, puffed, snorted and lumbered his way back into the corral like a spoiled child who didn't get his way.

Another such incident happened years later when an old wood rat was inching towards one of her many nieces who happened to be playing in the front yard. Mina, who was standing on the front porch grabbed the hatchet from the woodpile near the front door and threw it with grace and skill and took off the head of the unsuspecting rodent. No one messed with Mina; no bull, no rat, nor man.

As Mina grew so did the attention of all the men folk in town. They would stop in their tracks when Mina was near. Some would stare, some would whistle and some would flirt but they were all careful because they knew her brothers and father and they did not want to tangle with any of them. Her father and brothers were all tall, strong, and intolerant of any disrespect towards their women folk. The majority of onlookers were always true southern gentlemen and town locals.

After high school graduation and no money for college, Mina found herself bored with the farm life and small town living; natural for a girl of 17. One of the Saturday trips to Conway, standing on the corner in front of Burrough's Drugstore, she did a double take when she noticed a tall blonde man she had not seen before; not in a while anyway.

John Paul Jones lived on the other side of the bays just a few miles away. He was now a grown, good-looking man who was a couple of years older than Mina. He had graduated from Conway High School a little earlier than she and had recently graduated from a military college in Charleston and was now a commissioned officer in the United States Arm and was home between assignments. Mina had never paid any attention to John before but today he stood out with dark gray fedora slanted over one eye. He looked very distinguished, which the young country girl admired and when he shot those steel blue eyes her way she was literally swept off of her feet. They soon were married and Mina headed to Syracuse, New York where John was stationed.

Wilhelmina DuPont Jones had two beautiful children; a girl, Sarah Diane and a boy, JP, Jr. with her husband John Paul. Mina was forced to raise her children alone as John found himself in Europe on a classified mission. War was brewing in Europe and with John gone for such a long time Mina and John eventually divorced.

Mina missed her parents and home, even after years of wanting to leave. Mina was growing unhappy and decided she belonged back in Homewood, the area where she had grown up so she loaded up her two children and headed home. After returning she knew she had made the right choice. Her parents were glad to have their daughter and grandchildren with them and they couldn't be happier.

With two children to raise she was blessed to have the support of her very generous and loving parents. The house was again full and lively for the first time in a while. Mina's siblings had either left to go away for work, to start their own families or were stationed somewhere far off with the military.

Mina was the perfect definition for motherhood. She always did the very best she possibly could for her children as they always came first. Mina sacrificed so her children would be comfortable; she ate little so as not to let her children be hungry and she worked hard but seemed very content in her little world.

The pilot of the bi-plane delivering the U.S. mail would fly low as he approached the Myrtle Beach Airport on his weekly deliveries. On one of his trips while preparing to land he spotted the tall lovely brunette out near the barn hanging a wash of clothes on the line. Mina, noticing the plane for the very first time, waved enthusiastically at the aircraft and the pilot in turn dipped his wing to say hello.

Several years later upon her return to the farm the pilot continued his routine of flying low to spot the beautiful and friendly woman and of course dip the wing. They never met one another but were always courteous to each other. Mina had fond memories of the plane throughout her long life when reflecting on her past and the changes that came about. Seeing an airplane for the very first time was a pretty big deal back in the day, much like when Jake saw the groups of Galaxies flying overhead for the first time, spine-chilling.

Chapter 22

"The bravest are the tenderest, - The loving are the daring."
~ Bayard Taylor

Summer vacation is winding down; soon Jake will start high school.
He knew that he better make the best of what was left of it. He decided
that that he was going to sleep late, watch a lot television and play
with Bullet well into the twilight when his mom would call him in to
wash up for supper. Unlike the last several years, he was not going to
play or think of baseball, and he was not going to think of Tommy or
Vietnam.

After a hearty breakfast, Jake finally reached the outdoors, and there
was not that usual cheerful greeting from Bullet. *"Oh goodness,"* Jake
thought, where is he? The more Jake called for his dog the more
uneasy he became. This was not the norm for the happy lab that was
always right there to greet Jake first thing every morning with big, wet
tongue lapping away at the boy's face.

Jake searched everywhere and loudly bellowed "Bullet, here boy,
come on boy, Bullet, come here Bullet!" No Bullet. Kenny broke away
from Mina's skirt and the scratchy television as soon as he heard all
the noise; he too had become very attached to the black lab. The two
hopeful brothers hopped on their bikes and rode around the
neighborhood calling for their dog. They rode out onto the highway
looking and calling.

They feared the worst and it could be seen in each other's eyes. They
knew they better not stray too far from home so they turned around
and headed back, hoping to be greeted by the big lovable buffoon.

It was lunchtime, and still no Bullet. Jake was extremely anxious and
not very hungry; neither was Kenny and now Mina was worried.
During summer vacation she had been driving Wavy to work so she
could have access to the car in case of an emergency, much like when
Jake's leg was on fire when she had hoped and prayed that a neighbor

was handy and willing. The three jumped into the gold Biscayne and started riding around searching for their beloved pet.

While on Main Road Mina decided to head down towards the railroad depot that once housed the post office and still handled deliveries from train. Not that Bullet would be five miles from home but there may be mail from Vietnam. This was across the street from the tomato sheds which were all quiet now as peak season for the red fruit had passed.

As they slowly approached the side of the railroad track, much to the dismay of the Biscayne riders, appeared a black object. Mina pulled over to the side of the road just in front of the black, flaccid dog. Kenny and Jake jumped from the vehicle before it had completely stopped with Mina soon following them. It was indeed Bullet. How did he get this far away? This was not like him to stray this far from home. It appeared that he was hit by a slow moving train or maybe a car but he was indeed dead. Jake thought how much more of this could he take? His heart was broken, he had a sick stomach, his head was spinning and his limbs trembled as the madness within was about to make its inglorious appearance.

Jake was beside himself. This deplorable sight of his beautiful dog and new best friend unnerved him. He looked at his mom for relief and for answers. Mina pulled her youngest son into her bosom and he looked at his brother for some sort of comfort while his eyes welled up with tears. Kenny rubbed his brother's head and patted his shoulder actually showing compassion for the down trodden little twit. Jake felt that the air around him was polluted and filled with revolting germs that would attach and rot and destroy whatever it wrapped around. He felt the thickness of the germs glaze over the palms of his hands; he frantically blew at them until he felt satisfied that they were free from the evil and wicked pollutants.

Can anyone help, PLEASE?!

From the thick forest beyond the tracks glowing yellow eyes watched as the sad and broken Jake collapsed to his knees in front of his dead pal. Mina also knelt beside her youngest son and put an arm around his neck.

In the distance the fierce rage of an incoming train whistle bounced between the trees and alarmed the countless birds who immediately took to the stunning blue openness. The three grievers stood up, and walked to the car while they waited for the passing train. They then removed an old wool blanket from the Chevy's trunk that Wavy always kept on hand and slowly walked over to their lifeless pet.

Mr. Pickett, a friend and owner of the nearby general store just happened by on his way back to the store after making a local delivery. His old Ford pickup truck slowed down and parked just in front of the fallen dog. He helped them load the animal into the bed of his truck and he offered to bury it on his property.

Bye Bullet, thanks for the love when I needed it most. Sorry you left so soon.

Unseen, a cool swirl of white mist rose above the nearby tree-line and hovered like a cloud between the roasting sun and the black forest as though it was waiting for instructions.

Chapter 23

"That way madness lies."
~ **William Shakespeare**

Obsessive–compulsive disorder, OCD, is an anxiety disorder characterized by intrusive thoughts that produce uneasiness, apprehension, fear, or worry, by repetitive behaviors aimed at reducing the associated anxiety, or by a combination of such obsessions and compulsions.

Symptoms of the disorder include excessive washing or cleaning; repeated checking; extreme hoarding; preoccupation with sexual, violent or religious thoughts; aversion to particular numbers; and nervous rituals, such as opening and closing a door a certain number of times before entering or leaving a room. These symptoms can be alienating, time-consuming, and often cause severe emotional and financial distress.

The acts of those who have OCD may appear paranoid and potentially psychotic. However, OCD sufferers generally recognize their obsessions and compulsions as irrational and may become further distressed by this realization.

Obsessive–compulsive disorder affects children and adolescents as well as adults. Roughly one third to one half of adults with OCD reports a childhood onset of the disorder suggesting the continuum of anxiety disorders across the life span. The phrase obsessive–compulsive has become part of the English lexicon, and is often used in an informal or caricatured manner to describe someone who is excessively meticulous, perfectionist, absorbed, or otherwise fixated. Although these signs are present in OCD, a person who exhibits them does not necessarily have OCD, and may instead have obsessive-compulsive personality disorder, OCPD, an autism spectrum disorder, or no clinical condition.

Despite the irrational behavior, OCD is sometimes associated with above-average intelligence. Its sufferers commonly share personality traits such as high attention to detail, avoidance of risk, careful planning, exaggerated sense of responsibility and a tendency to take time in making decisions. Multiple psychological and biological factors may be involved in causing obsessive–compulsive syndromes. Standardized rating scales such as Yale-Brown Obsessive Compulsive Scale can be used to assess the severity of OCD symptoms.

In 1968, OCD had not yet made public awareness, though it was being studied by doctors and researchers. Jake simply believed he was losing his mind at the tender age of thirteen and a half. Over forty-five years later Jake has not divulged his deepest, darkest secrets to anyone. It now seems like a distant long-ago nightmare to Jake, but it nearly destroyed him during his teen years.

Jake wanted to step back in time, even for five minutes, to try and understand what was happening to him, but was skeptical because he feared that he would never return to present reality. All Jake knew was, that things weren't right in his world and he was extremely fearful. He desperately wanted to be normal and unscathed. He wanted to be free from the nervous habits, as his mother described it, and other time consuming rituals that he so seriously tried to control to no avail, and hide from everyone.

On the outside, Jake looked like the typical kid. Nicely dressed and decently groomed, other than a little dust on the freckled cheeks and his uncombed, windblown hair. Jake was tall for his age and had a handsome face, highlighted with an infectious smile and large, sparkling, brown eyes; traits he inherited from his mother, which she often reminded him of.

However, on the inside, Jake felt that he was completely unraveling. He felt his mind and spirit was spiraling out of control at such an enormous pace that he thought eventually he would crash, burn and evaporate into the wind. He would be gone forever as a microscopic fragment of dust riding the summer breeze across the island whispering through the mighty oaks and dancing through the billowy white clouds over the farmlands, majestic rivers, mountains, ocean and ultimately vanishing into the infinite universe.

Jake first discovered that something was not quite right in Jakedom soon after Tommy passed away. That tragedy was immediately followed by Tommy's replacement, Bullet, being killed. Bullet was given to Jake to cheer him up and get his mind off of Tommy. Of course, his greatest heartache was Ronnie heading far away to Vietnam and facing the possibility of being killed too.

School is now just around the corner and Jake is not sure how to handle all of this. How can he continue to hide all of these ridiculous and repetitive and time consuming practices that he has recently developed?

Jake had first perceived something odd on what started out as a pretty terrific day. Uncle Hal had befriended the owner of Pineland Riding Stables on Brownswood Road which was about three miles from the Willoughby household. Mr. Brown, as he was known, had a love for horses and had a few on hand.

The old man turned his hobby into a business by offering riding lessons and horseback rides through the many trails that he had developed. He also offered boarding for the horses of the owners who went on vacation, or just weren't up to the commitment any longer. Uncle Hal came to know Mr. Brown over a period of time at Staley's corner store.

Uncle Hal loved the outdoors; nature, trees, dirt roads, woods, and long walks. He also loved to read and was often spotted underneath one of the many shade trees in the Willoughby yard sitting in a lawn chair reading a book, the newspaper or one of the family's encyclopedias. He spent many years in the United States Marine Corps and fought in Europe during World War II. When Hal came home he had no visible scars but had developed a penchant for alcohol, which became a daily habit to help him escape the horrors of war.

It soon elevated to the point where he would go into drunken binges and stay inebriated for days, sometimes weeks at a time, causing him to lose good jobs and his driver's license. That explained why he had no car and why he lived with his sister Mina. She was the only one who seemed to understand him and truly love and care for him. Mina understood that alcoholism was a disease and that someone should not be frowned upon or rejected when they most needed support, especially a family member.

Hal's other siblings looked down on the man. The only one in the family who had spent most of his adult life in the military and half that time in combat during the worst of times; he felt very fortunate to be alive. No one could ever imagine the horrors that he had witnessed and took part in. Because of his drinking he was disowned by his siblings other than Mina. They couldn't relate to his problem nor did they seem to want to relate ~ cast the first stone. In later years Jake and Mina were always quick to defend their Uncle Hal when others would criticize the poor man long after his death and unable to defend himself.

Jake never understood how ignorant some of his cousins could be, especially the ones that considered themselves highly educated and devout Christians, yet they were quick to pass judgement on anyone who drank anything stronger than coffee.

"Love one another and be kind to each other," Mina would say. "Do unto others as you would have them do unto you"

Like everyone else, Uncle Hal had grown attached to Bullet. He was as sad as Jake after the dog was killed. He decided to ask Kenny and Jake to go with him on one of his walks down the dirt road to the stables so the boys could see and maybe even ride the horses and feed the chickens. Maybe the diversion would help all of them in their grief and the boys could play with the many dogs that wondered around in the shade of the tall pines and the shadows of the stables.

The one thing Uncle Hal did not mention to the boys because he wanted it to be a surprise, was the huge peacock that made home at the stables. The boys had never seen a peacock, other than the one on television advertising for one of the three networks.

When they passed over the small rickety bridge Kenny snickered at his little brother. Jake was reminded of the terrible time when Kenny dangled him by the ankles and threatened to drop him into the cold, black, water full of deadly moccasins. Jake shivered with the frightening thought. Kenny became frightened too when he wondered if his brother might tell on him to Uncle Hal. Jake never did; not to Uncle Hal or anyone else.

As Uncle Hal and the boys passed through the main entrance there was a tall gate decorated with galloping wild stallions made of wrought iron hanging high above the ground. A white wooden fence on either side of the dirt roadway and tall, shady pines lined intermittingly down the trail gave it a cool almost cave like prelude to the large rows of stables and barns.

Beautiful red-brown horses gazed in the pastures and a couple of palominos stood near the fence. This caught Jake's attention right away as he had seen this horse only one other time. This was Little Joe's horse on the television show *Bonanza*.

The palominos were black and white in color, similar to a cow. The horses seemed gigantic to Jake and Kenny, who at first were intimidated, having only seen horses on television until now. Uncle Hal was raised around horses so he was quite comfortable and wreaked of confidence which he hoped would make the boys feel more at ease.

Mr. Brown met the trio at one of the stables where he had a pitchfork full of hay that he had lifted from the bed of his '65 Chevy pickup and tossed it into one of the stalls.

Mr. Brown was a tall, darkly-tanned man in his mid-sixties with a leathery looking face and gray bushy hair protruding from a sweat and dirt stained cowboy hat sitting on the top of his large head. There was always an unlit cigar in the left corner of his mouth which had left a permanent brown stain just below his lower lip. His short sleeves were rolled up to reveal huge biceps, the product of years of feeding horses. His large muscular arms were adorned with medium size tattoos that had faded into obscurity. The one on the right forearm acknowledged his chosen branch of military and the one on his left bicep inked the name of a pretty freckle faced lass from his long ago past.

Mr. Brown walked with a slight limp that he sustained during the war. He talked with a long and slow, southern drawl but laughed with a booming, hearty laugh that made everyone present laugh with him. Jake wondered how the cigar did not fall from his mouth and why it was not lit or smoking. After careful observation, he noticed the sogginess of the chewed end was stuck to the old man's bottom lip like it was glued in place. Jake enjoyed the smell of cigars and pipe tobacco but detested the smell of cigarettes which seemed to be just about everywhere.

The always joyful and garrulous Mr. Brown was expecting the company and was excited to see the young lads. He took everyone on a walking tour of his pride and joy. In the background Jake kept hearing an unusual sound like some sort of large bird or chicken; it kept squawking and got louder and louder. Finally, on the third row in a corridor between stables, stood the most magnificent bird that Jake and Kenny had ever seen. The male peacock stood about three feet tall and had a lustrous blue-green plumage and a large crown atop his curious head. He turned his attention towards the group of admirers and began screeching louder and faster.

The beautiful bird lifted its train to show off its colorful feathers they were long and a lighter green than the rest and each had a lavish circle at the top or end, depending on your sense of direction. The boys stopped in their tracks and waited to see what the huge bird and men were going to do. After realizing that it was harmless Jake and Kenny walked around the creature in awe. Sensing his splendid grandeur, the bird began strutting his stuff.

By late morning, the August sun began taking its toll on the visiting trio who were sweaty, thirsty and hungry. The late summer heat also took its toll on the horse poop that seemed to start piling up all over the place. In fact, it was all Jake could breathe. When he looked around he saw dog poop, chicken poop, horse poop, and peacock poop - everywhere a poop-poop. The vile air was getting the best of visitors, but it was affecting Jake somewhat differently. Recognizing the disgust by young Jake, Mr. Brown led Uncle Hal and the boys to his office which was air-conditioned and smelled much better than the outdoors.

Mr. Brown proudly opened the vending machine with his huge ring of keys and allowed everyone to pick and choose the snack and soda of their choice. This thrilled the two boys beyond belief. Kenny grabbed a lemon-lime soda and a bag of peanuts and Jake seized a cola and his favorite, a pack of nabs. A very grateful Uncle Hal snatched an orange soda and a moon pie; no doubt taking a trip back to his youth when a treats were rare.

Inside the cool, clean office the walls were decorated in a variety of photos of horses and some with young men in military uniforms under large palm trees. Instead of looking at the pictures, Jake felt a sudden desire to look at the bottom of each shoe to make sure that he had not stepped into the very bountiful poop that scattered the area. Perhaps he was urged by the stink that hijacked his nostrils. He looked not once, but three times at each shoe bottom before he was satisfied that there was no poop on his soles. Jake believed this was odd and embarrassing and hoped that no one had noticed.

After his first big swig of the cold beverage Jake felt compelled to look again at the bottom of his shoes, after lifting each foot three times to assure he had no poop to worry about, he nearly cried. He looked at up at each person in the room to see if they detected his sole searching. He wanted more than anything to run and hide, but where?

The boys were directed to the bathroom where they could wash their hands before handling their snacks. Kenny washed like he always had, but Jake washed like he never had before. Over and over and over again, three separate and complete washes. Jake nearly used up the entire bar of soap which he had to wash as well before he started on his hands. After each wash he looked at the towel in preparation to dry his hands but was not satisfied that his hands were clean. Something grabbed his hands and turned him to the sink, again and again like he had no control. Three times seemed to be the charm for whoever or whatever wanted Jake's hands washed; the same number for looking at the bottom of his shoes.

Jake was frightened nearly to death. Was Tommy doing this to him? Maybe the old ghost lady that his dad had seen when he was a child? Jake was petrified. He did not know what to do. He thought he was a good kid until those fateful words to Tommy on that doomed afternoon just a few weeks ago.

He was sorry. He was sorrier than he ever had been in his life. He would take it back if he could, and he would never say it to anyone again, ever.

Suddenly, he nearly jumped out of his skin when he looked into the mirror; he had forgotten that Kenny was in the room with him. He was more afraid that it was Tommy or the ghost lady than he was his brother but he didn't want Kenny to suspect any of this craziness. He hoped Kenny hadn't witnessed this strange unexplained ritual, but of course he had. Kenny was standing right there behind him the entire time.

For the first time in his life Jake saw an unrecognizable look in the eyes that had always picked on him and seemed to hate him. It was a look of compassion and caring; a look of sympathy. Then Kenny did something he had never done before. He reached over and pulled his anxious little brother into his chest and tightly hugged him and said, "I'm here for you, Bubba." They then left the restroom and the two boys never spoke of this incident to anyone or each other again. It was their little secret. Jake loved his brother and forgave him for all that he had done to him.

Maybe there was some good to this strange thing that was happening to him. Jake was hopeful that it wouldn't happen again after they leave the stables. Perhaps these stables were built on some ancient Indian burial ground. Something strange definitely has happened in the last several minutes. Jake did not know what but knew that he wanted out. He no longer wanted his nabs. He wanted to get home quickly, because he wanted his mama.

Chapter 24

"The wind passeth over it, and it is gone;
and the place thereof shall see it no more."
~ Psalms CIII

Jake and Kenny now had a weekend job at the Pineland Riding Stables even though Jake wasn't quite sure that he wanted to go back to poop paradise. He would have to think about it, especially after the episode in the bathroom. Uncle Hal, Kenny and Jake walked the long dirt road on the edge near the trees so that they could have a little shade. Jake pulled up the rear stepping into the tracks of the older two in front of him. Kenny did the same with Uncle Hal. Three people, one set of tracks. This this humored Jake as kept peering backwards to make sure the tracks were perfect. Uncle Hal pulled out his light blue Bugle Boy can and lit up one of the cigarettes that he had rolled earlier in the morning.

Jake never understood this smoking habit that was enjoyed by most of the adults that he knew, and figured it was a way of life; just like brushing your teeth. The white plume of smoke drifted off into the wide array of greenery that bordered the road. Jake watched it as it faded into the forest. He couldn't help but think of Ronnie, who began smoking when he joined the Marines and was headed off to some thick, dangerous jungle...sad. Then he thought of Tommy and how he would have loved the stables and horses and the chance to work there. Jake could just see and hear the overly animated Tommy enthusiastically telling everyone at home about the peacock, in that excited high pitched voice of his...sad.

As the group entered the neighborhood and the hot paved road they could hear in the distance that familiar melodious sound of the ice cream truck. Kenny and Jake looked at each other with exhilaration and then sadness, because they both knew neither of them had money. Then, a glimmer of hope as they both had the same thought at the same instance; perhaps Uncle Hal would have some money. The two boys looked up at their uncle at the same time. How could he refuse not one but two sad puppy dog faces? He could enjoy a cold grape popsicle himself.

The boys were ecstatic as the carnival sounding chiming became louder and louder. They could smell the burnt fuel as it funneled its way from the exhaust pipe while standing in line ordering their favorites.

Jake got an orange pushup, Kenny, a nutty buddy and Uncle Hal got a grape popsicle, along with the enjoyment of seeing his two nephews being so content. The three walked home, quickly eating their frozen treats before the August sun melted them away and before Mina found out about all the junk that they had eaten. She had prepared a healthy lunch, which they had to pretend they had room for when they got home with their exciting adventures of the day to share. What a day!

After a couple of hours and a hot soapy shower Jake plopped down in the middle of the living room floor with his legs crossed to watch *The Adventures of Superman*; the black and white scratchy Superman in syndication.

Chapter 25

"The passing ships slip away as night brings me home;
will we ever meet again, dear friend?"
~ Jake Willoughby

This was the most anticipated summer of Jake's life, the one he looked forward to more than any other. It was the one that seemed like it took forever to arrive, then with the horrible turn of events seemed as though it would never end; finally it did.

The last weekend wasn't the fun he had hoped it would be because Jake and Kenny found themselves in the busy chaotic stores with Mina. They were not looking at toys, but trying on clothes and shoes; getting notebooks, pencils and lunchboxes, etc. Jake was going to miss his old Superman lunchbox, but freshmen in high school do not tote around cartoon colored lunchboxes. In fact, after day one, the lunch box was traded in for cafeteria food.

The boys also got fresh haircuts from Uncle Ted, who always enjoyed seeing his nephews. The Willoughby boys were always well groomed, well dressed and well-mannered, which Mina was very proud of. However, this coming year would prove to be an arduous test for the proud mom. This year marked the end of innocence for both Jake and Kenny.

On the first day of every new school year Jake always found himself a quite nervous. He was too nervous to watch the *Disney's Wonderful World of Color* the previous evening and his stomach bothered him too much to enjoy breakfast. The prospect of meeting a new teacher and new classmates as well as leaving his mom and Uncle Hal with the safe surroundings of home nearly worried Jake to death.

Ughh! He felt as though he was going to throw up and he really hated that feeling. This day would not be good. He knew eventually that it would get better, or he hoped so anyway. He knew most likely that he would like his teacher and he would meet some really nice, new friends. He really needed new friends right now but just the unknowing of it all and the fierce anxiety of the day brought on by the anticipation was terribly frightening and made it difficult to get out of the door.

"A case of butterflies in the stomach" Mina said.

Jake did not know what that expression meant. He knew he had not eaten any butterflies. He knew he was a nervous wreck, so that must be what it meant.

"Do I really have to do this, I feel sick?"

Months of doing pretty much anything he wanted to suddenly turn into doing everything that he didn't want to do.

"You have to go to school," Mina said firmly. "Look at Kenny, he's excited about going."

Kenny looked just as sick as Jake did. Kenny was a rising junior, his third year of high school. This is Jake's first; whatever happened to Dick and Jane? Oh they were going to be there too, just several years older and differently dressed.

"You excited Kenny?" Jake asked his older brother.

"You are kidding right? This is the worst day ever."

Mina decided to use her ace, "Ronnie expects you to do well in school and be a good boy, ahem, good young man."

That was all that was needed. Jake followed a very slowly moving Kenny to the corner of the yard where all the neighborhood kids waited for the bus, including the entire Stern family minus one. The older kids seemed happy with their long hair and patch covered denim. The younger kids not so much. A few parents stood by patiently with their children as the big, yellow bus came screeching to a halt. *Well, this is it,* Jake thought. *I need to make Ronnie proud, along with Mom and Dad.*

Mrs. Walker, Jake's new teacher was a tall, slim woman who kept her blonde hair on top of her head in some sort of bun, much different from Grandma's. Her pleasant face was adorned with black horned-rimmed glasses. She seemed nice enough, though not nearly as sweet as his previous teacher, Ms. Dorn, who Jake really liked a lot.

Mrs. Walker introduced herself with a generous voice, then slowly scrawled her name in chalk on the large, green chalk board. As she turned to her right, Jake could not help but notice the size of her breast since they protruded like torpedoes. Jake believed they were very large for a teacher. They looked like honeydew melons that were about to burst right out of the solid white cotton blouse. This reminded him of his favorite commercial with actress Jane Russell wearing a cross your heart bra.

Jake was now very much enjoying himself; he couldn't take his eyes off of his new teacher. One button was all there was between heaven and arithmetic. One tiny piece of thread on the button held on for dear life. Jake intently watched the button's Olympic feat against all odds, hoping that it would be defeated and the duel torpedoes would spring into the classroom. Unfortunately, Jake's wishes for the button and the thread to break weren't coming to fruition anytime soon and it was down to business.

Mrs. Walker went down the list that she was holding and called out each name. She made each child stand up as they heard their name called out and then she made them sit in a certain order of which she alone decided. Alphabetically the names were called and based on last year Jake knew exactly when he would be called and where he would be sitting. He was usually in the far back, which he preferred. Hating to stand up and speak in front of everyone, he knew he was about to called on and was mere seconds from losing yesterday's eggs, grits, and orange pushup.

The class was not the same as last year as there was one major exception. There was a new girl, which Jake did not yet know but wanted to badly. Normally, Willoughby was the last name called which suited Jake just fine. It gave him the opportunity to learn the names of anyone new and watch everyone else make fools of themselves. Taking mental notes and paying strict attention, he quickly learned what to do and what not to do. He became prepared and actually appeared to be quite smart, but he wasn't prepared to share his summer. Sitting at the back of the class kept him separated from his friends, which was probably a good thing for all involved.

"Jake Willoughby!" Mrs. Walker said, in a booming and discernable tone.

Jake nearly crapped in his chinos because he had not heard the new girls name yet and assumed that he had a few more seconds on the clock. He nervously stood and stuttered his name while scratching the side of his hip with one hand and inadvertently doodling onto his scalp with a number two pencil with his other hand causing the entire class to break out in laughter. Jake wanted to die inside. He couldn't stand being laughed at especially in front of the new, pretty girl too. He wanted to blow away the cooties and check the bottoms of his feet. His cheeks were now tomato red and Mrs. Walker told him to have a seat sensing that he was too nervous to tell everyone about his summer.

"Lisa Wilson," Mrs. Walker said, in a flat voice, disrupting Jake's pity party.

What the new girl, the pretty girl? Are you serious, she is sitting behind me? She saw me make a fool of myself, so I guess she laughed at me too? This day is turning out as expected. Since she is close by that may be an advantage.

Lisa Wilson was the prettiest girl Jake had ever seen. She had black curly hair just below the ears with big, round crystal blue eyes, full lips, big white sparkling teeth and a spatter of freckles across her nose and cheeks just like Jake. In Jake's mind she was perfect. Her skin was smooth, soft and tan from the summer vacation. The hormonal teen stole a glance every chance he could especially when she first walked past him to have her seat. He liked the way her behind jiggled in the tight little plaid woven skirt.

Jake would discreetly peer over his shoulder and sneak a peek. He completely froze when faced with her beauty and just wanted to stare at her. He was not expecting her to come alive and he certainly didn't expect her eyes to meet his. He was caught completely off guard not knowing what to say and if he did, he wasn't sure that he could say anything even if he tried.

He bashfully grinned, and then quickly looked away when he realized that she was actually looking into his eyes. *"Oh my goodness,* Jake thought; this frightened the living daylights out of the poor kid. *Hide me* he said to himself quietly, with lips moving.

I should have spoken, why didn't I speak to her? Hello, I'm the Moran that drew a hole into the top of his head just now; pleased to meet you.

Much to his surprise, this day took a pleasant left turn out of nowhere; gigantic teacher boobs and the most beautiful girl sitting right behind him. Everything was shaping up to be much better than anticipated.

Who was she, where did she come from he kept questioning himself. *Okay kiddo. Sit straight, look ahead at the big boobed teacher because she is staring at you and Lisa is staring at you too.*

Jake was a nervous wreck. He just knew Mrs. Walker was going to change her mind and ask him about his summer vacation. He had not rehearsed the answer to that question and he could not tell anyone even though most of his classmates knew about his summer. Lisa did not know and he could not let her know about all this crazy crap that had happened to him.

That his brother the Marine is off to Vietnam and that he very possibly killed his best friend; and somehow he was most likely responsible for his dogs death too. Wow! Did anything good happen over the summer? The trips to Grandma's house, the short time with Bullet, drive-in movies, downtown visits, riding horses at the stables in Poopville.

He didn't know what to say if he was called to do so. He silently prayed that he wasn't going to be called on because he thought that he may throw up, wet his pants and cry like a baby all at the same time; one big, fat urine soaked bundle for the world to see and smell.

Stay away pretty girl; I'm a bad, smelly boy!

Mrs. Walker was not looking at Jake after all but at the new, pretty girl. Jake was sure that the buxom teacher took it on herself to make the introductions to spare Lisa, who was already a nervous wreck. He then took another glance behind him and Lisa appeared very calm and confident. Jake liked that. He wasn't sure why or what about it he liked but he knew he liked it a lot. He was positive that he didn't dispel that kind of confidence but wished very much so that he did.

Mrs. Walker continued, "Class, we have a new student that will be part of our educational family."

How corny, Jake thought. *Okay button, pop, POP-NOW*!!!

"Blah, blah Pennsylvania, blah, blah John's Island, blah, blah brother, blah, blah welcome her", rambled the owner of super thread. Everyone in the classroom clapped, even Jake.

Wow, no one ever clapped for me, he speculated.

Jake noticed that his pals Billy Burns, Barry Grimes and Rusty McDaniel were all were staring at his new sweetheart; uh oh, this is not happening. He had to make a move and he had to make it quick, but how?

"Class, in front of you is a notebook; open it to page one," ordered Mrs. Walker. The button was still hanging tough, literally by a thread but hanging on. Jake waited patiently hoping that a big sneeze would pop it loose.

"Blah, blah, blah, blah, blah…" No doubt that Mrs. Walker moonlighted as the teacher for Charlie Brown and the Peanut's gang.

The muffled Mrs. Walker went on interminably; the class had to write her name, their name, what books you read and what you did on vacation. Finally, that beautiful bell on the wall shook the room and everyone in it; time to head to the first real class. Jake was accustomed to being in the same room with the same teacher all day and he assumed this would be difficult to adjust to.

Oh man, where is that piece of paper with the class schedules on it? I can't find it; I'll just follow my pals. The pals were as confused as Jake. I'll follow Lisa!!!

Jake was so glad that he came to school today without much fuss. The time has arrived for that magic moment to take place and to do something impressive, he thought. How about drop your notebook, text book, pencil? One or the other would suffice, but Mr. coordinated dropped all three, unintentionally drawing a roar of laughter from the classroom. Jake wondered if this was this a good laugh or a bad laugh? Even Lisa was chuckling ever so slightly. *Do they think I'm clumsy? Does Lisa think that I'm funny or just a big dumb klutz?*

Jake very nervously gathered up his materials and nearly fell over backwards when the beautiful, the one and only, blah, blah, Lisa Wilson, blah, blah Pennsylvania, blah, blah, handed his pencil to him.

"Huh?" Jake asked,

"Your pencil," Lisa said.

"What about it?" Jake asked.

"Wouldn't you like it back?" Lisa asked, in the sweetest voice Jake had ever heard.

"Oh, yes, thank you very much," mumbled the visibly shaken youngster.

"You need to sharpen it because the point broke off," the silky soft lips from one of God's very own angels said.

"Um, okay. Do you, um, I'm not sure where to go, do um you?" stuttered God's gift to articulation; and so it began - high school.

After what seemed like hours of fog another bell finally rang; lunch, the best part of the day. The grounds were sandy and very shady from the large protective limbs of the aged trees and as everywhere on the island large live oaks dotted the landscape with long gray strands of Spanish moss hanging nearly to the ground. This was a sight that Jake would love his entire life.

St. John's School was a glorious place. It was built in the early forties and once served grades one through twelve. It was the most modern and largest school on John's Island. Up until then students gathered in small frame houses. It was also home of The Mighty Islanders championship football team.

"Jake!" Kenny called out to his younger brother.

Kenny promised his parents and himself that he would look after Jake at school. Kenny yelled, out again over the noise of the multitude of spirited kids.

Kenny, with a *Lost in Space* lunch box in tow, grabbed his kid brother and they walked to a large crowded picnic table on the edge of the grounds. There, they squeezed in the middle of jovial group of guys all dressed identical. They sat down, and with limited elbow room, began to consume their bologna and cheese sandwiches. With mayo and mustard dripping from the corner of his mouth, Kenny ate like he had not eaten in days. Jake slowly nibbled on his sandwich. Kenny exchanged several niceties with the other ravenous students while Jake scoured the grounds for Lisa, constantly darting his head from one direction to the next. No Lisa.

In the center of the grounds was a huge merry-go-round that everyone was jumping on and off of. Nearby was a set of monkey bars, Jake's favorite on any other day. Kenny prodded Jake to race to the monkey bars to prove who could out do his little brother. Jake wasn't too interested in racing.

Jake knew that he could outrun his brother besides; he was preoccupied with looking for the angel from blah blah Pennsylvania. Billy and Rusty found Jake and they all headed to the merry-go-round and still no sight of the angel, where could she possibly be? She was for real right? Jake started to wonder if she was indeed a real angel, with all the stuff that has been happening lately he could sure use one.

The bell rang to resume classes and Jake was disappointed that lunch was over and that he never saw Lisa, but he was excited that he would see her in class. The noisy bunch entered the classroom and took their seats. Jake anxiously awaited the arrival of the Miss one and only… she never appeared. Jake frequently twisted and turned his head until he felt that it would fly off, the equivalent of the spinning contraption in the middle of the school grounds. With his dirty knees shaking uncontrollably beneath the wooden desk, he tried to comfort himself with thoughts that Lisa was in the bathroom or the office. *Maybe she was lost. That was it, she was lost and he should have been there for her. That's what he should have done, why didn't he?*

He started retracing the events… After he sharpened his pencil, he turned around and she was gone. He never saw her in any of his other classes. He hurriedly ran and ignored all of his friends to get to the school grounds to look for her, and that's when Kenny called for him. Now, the beautiful girl is lost and frightened and Prince Charming dropped the ball, or did he?

Lisa never returned to class, and after asking several questions Jake learned that there never was a Lisa, or for that matter, there weren't any new students. How could this be? Jake was more confused than ever. How could he possibly see this person in such detail and feel such emotion only to have her not exist? Bologna is bad enough the first time around. Jake did not want to taste it after it had plunged to the bottom of his belly and somehow made its way back to the inside of his mouth.

He sat slumped at his desk with no one behind him. Troy Varner sat in front of him, Michelle Underwood to the left, the off white wall with a map of the United States to his right. At the front of class with bright lights overhead Mrs. Walker sat at her desk sorting through some papers with super button still intact. Just behind her on the wall were two large green chalkboards with the alphabet written in cursive and print hanging over them.

Jake slowly lifted his right leg and foot to peer at the sole of his shoe to make sure that it was poop free. Abraham Lincoln and George Washington stared right at him as if he were the only person in the room. Like they knew everything about Jake, they knew he was waiting for that button to pop loose and this made him even more anxious. As a younger kid, Jake learned his left from his right because of the scar on his left leg. He carefully and slowly looked at his left foot, no poop. With both feet poop free and planted on the floor Jake felt compelled to do this same ritual twice more while nervously looking around to see if he was spotted by anyone other than George and Abe. When the coast was clear he looked at each elbow three time each, first the right, then the left and back to the right again. Then he had to blow the cooties from his palms, three times on the right hand and three times on the left hand and back to the right hand three more times. If he were interrupted he would have to start the entire ritual all over again ~ so button, you've waited this long, DO NOT POP NOW!

Jake knew that his knees were dirty because he could clearly see them. He could not easily see the bottoms of his feet or his elbows and it's a good thing that he was not worried about his butt because he probably would not be able to pull that one off without being spotted.

What was that Mrs. Walker? Oh, I was just making sure that I didn't sit down in a pile of crap while I was at lunch.

Why am I doing this? Jake asked himself, with a troubled expression in his big brown eyes and a disconsolate heart. Lisa would help, if only she existed.

Chapter 26

*"Pillars of flame in spiral volume rise,
Like fiery snakes, and lick the infernal skies."*
~ Joseph Trapp

At the very moment Jake was envisioning his angel Lisa, his older brother Ronnie sat looking up at the full bright moon that was illuminating his small encampment in the thick brush. He was thousands of miles from home, somewhere northwest of the Da Nang Air Base in Vietnam. Ronnie, like Jake, always loved the full moon, and to think that everyone that has ever lived has looked up and wondered at this same moon is very humbling. Of course he was not thinking of the time difference, but tonight Ronnie was imagining that his beloved family and girlfriend stared upon the same moon at the same second and he could see the yellow glow reflecting in Christine's large, dreamy eyes.

Ronnie's attention shifted as he heard a noise in the brush. Maybe this bright moon was not such a good thing while on patrol in the jungle. Despite hiding beneath large trees and heavy shrub, they were still in the spotlight while looking for the enemy. Ronnie slowly raises his M-16 rifle with finger on trigger ready to blow away any Viet Cong that may be intruding. Ronnie is a member of one of four Reconnaissance forces sent ahead to explore and search for any signs of the enemy. *Humping,* as the Marines called it, is as close to hell on earth as they could imagine.

Marine Recon was sent out by their platoon leaders usually in groups of four or nine to scout out the surrounding areas for enemy activity. Most Marines preferred the nine groups as they would have two point men and the remaining men could try and catch some shut eye. The most unsettling nights would be during the four day hump with a small group of four.

The days were not much better, in heavy, full pack; steadily walking in the excruciating sunlight except to urinate or check something out, the four young Marines would warily walk through the impenetrable green and sinister jungle searching for the enemy. By nightfall the group was exhausted and hungry but dared not sleep because this was when most likely the Viet Cong would attack. The tired and weary Marines finished off their one can of rations and drank slowly, the nasty, warm water from their canteens.

Mina had been sending care packages to Ronnie that consisted of some of his favorite foods, which usually didn't last very long after he received it. However, he made sure that the Kool-Aid would last by sharing very limited amounts. The Kool-Aid was an essential item because it helped kill the vile taste of the local water, which contained only Lord knows what. Ronnie wouldn't even think about it because it was too disgusting but had no choice but to drink it since their supplies were so inadequate.

Jake loved shopping with his mom and helping put together these packages which usually contain travel and heat friendly items such as Vienna sausage, Slim Jims, dill pickles, chewing gum and many other goodies, as well as the favorite of most Marines, Kool-Aid. Mina would also throw in some soap, deodorant, razor blades, toothbrush and toothpaste.

Jake would excitedly help her wrap these large boxes in grocery bags turned inside out. They would hurriedly drive to the John's Island Post Office on Maybank Highway to send them straight to Vietnam. Jake could just see his brother opening the packages with that big boyish grin of his all over his face just like at Christmas.

Then Ronnie heard the disturbing noise again, but this time it was a little louder. All four Marines were now prepared for the inevitable of what lurked in the darkness beyond. Ronnie quickly prayed to himself as he strained his eyes to see what evil lies. In that same instant the loud roar and thrust of an adult female tiger ripped through the foliage and leaped towards the men as they fell backward, away from the attacking monster of a feline, whose paws and claws were the size of the combat helmets.

The yellow eyes had the violent and fearsome stare that the worst of nightmares could not produce. This tiger was hungry and meant to kill, so did the barrage of M-16's that unloaded into the belly of the beast. The tiger went down in mid-flight. The four Marines fell backwards onto the ground, scared out of their wits and very fortunate not to be torn to shreds at this moment. One of the Marines unloaded his weapon and cursed the tiger with every foul word that he could think of and another Marine soiled himself. A shaken Ronnie and the steady Doc quickly attended them knowing that the gunfire and screams would bring out the enemy.

"Lock and Load!"

That was the most terrifying instant in young Ronnie's life and he had experienced many since crossing the ocean.

"A cigarette would be nice," some fool whispered.

They all nodded in unison, but knew that was out of the question. Being home in my bed would be even nicer Ronnie told himself, looking up at the moon one last time as he tightly gripped his rifle.

The four fretful soldiers formed a tight circle with rifles pointed outwards. The dead tiger had one last nervous movement in his rear leg that surely sent the remaining urine down the legs of the jungle fatigues and into their boots. The man on the moon wore that crap eating grin of his. Why couldn't he have warned them? Ronnie had never seen a tiger before and this dead one is the only one that he would ever want to see again.

Back on John's Island, in the privacy of his bedroom, Jake was looking at the bottom of his left foot for the third time in three seconds. He then looked at his elbows and began blowing his palms. His anxiety was taking control. In the background, from another room, the small transistor radio gave everything it had to Crispian St. Peters pleading with all to follow him; he'll show you where it's at.

Chapter 27

"And thou O sun, thou seeist all things,
hearist all things in thy daily round."
~ Homer

The letters from Vietnam became less and less frequent which made the family's hearts heavy. Mina continued to send the care packages and Jake continued to help her with them. Ronnie's letters arrived more often before he arrived in Vietnam. Even during his last stop in Hawaii he even found time to write Jake and remind him to be a good boy, obey Mom and do well in school. He had time for separate letters to Mina, Kenny and Christine. In Quang Tri, Ronnie's first base in Viet Nam he had less time to himself as they had to train for what lies in the jungle. Then the dreaded patrols began which put him out of touch for four full days. At home everyone was nearly as nervous as he was in the jungle.

Jake was a complete nervous wreck, to the point of often vomiting. The odd rituals continued at an unsettling pace. He found himself constantly straightening things; everything had to be upright, level, with even distance and to be perfectly centered. Everything that he had control of had to be absolutely perfect, never tilted left or right. His penmanship had to be flawless with textbook formation, such as the letter A had to look like an A not a U, same with the letter O, the lines all had to connect. The t's had to be crossed with equal distance on either side and the i's had to be dotted with the dot perfectly centered over the body of the letter.

If he messed up something, he could not write over it because that appeared too shambolic, he would have to start all over with a new sheet of paper, no matter how many words or numbers had to be rewritten, or length of time involved. If it wasn't legible to him, it would not work. Everything had to be in straight lines and in order, according to his creed. Paper, envelopes, books, magazines, all neatly stacked in a perfect square, never compromising. Corners of pages could not be bent or wrinkled. Absolutely everything had a place and that's where it should be, in place. Otherwise, it would make him extremely uneasy. He couldn't stand stains on anything; clothing, paper, floors, etc. Everything had to be in pristine condition according to Jake's doctrine. He obviously didn't look at himself in the mirror very often, with the unkempt hair and dusty cheeks. If he did look in the mirror, he was usually too busy wiping away the dust or Windexing away the smudges to notice himself.

The daily grind and boredom of school with no Lisa continued for Jake. The days shortened and a chill entered the air, which caused the leaves to change from green to scarlet, tan and orange, then finally detach from their home, drifting freely through the autumn breeze and coming to rest on the cool ground. For whatever reason, as Jake grew older he always he found that he preferred fall and winter over spring and summer. He would close his eyes and transport back to those simpler days when the air was cold and he could feel and hear the crumple of leaves beneath his feet.

Jake had always loved rolling around on the ground and covering himself in leaves. Many times as an adult he would find himself wanting to do just that, and he would look around to see if anyone would notice and then he would dive into a mountain of leaves that he labored over for the past hour, but it was well worth the extra effort. Once in a while, every grown man deserves a leaf bath.

Jake also loved the cool touch of rain dancing on his face. Often times he would close his eyes and lift his face to the sky to allow the water to wash away the grime, sweat and cooties of the day. Jake and Uncle Hal on many occasions would sit in the carport or on the front porch and watch the rain bubble up in small puddles as it dispensed from the rooftop. No sounds, other than the cool rain dancing on the puddles, both men alone in their thoughts. Rain is a tender and nostalgic sound for Jake. With generous rainfalls later, it always sooths his soul, relaxes his heart and guides him into a peaceful sleep, just like rain on the tin roof of his dad's shed in the backyard, when days were innocent and life was simple with abundant hope just beyond the horizon at the rainbows end.

Jake clearly remembers sitting under that tin roof with his Uncle Hal, they would watch tree frogs skip across puddles to the dry ground while the serenity of the rain drops would relax their minds, sometimes it seemed like hours just sitting there enjoying the gift of rain. Though Jake never dozed off, he did come close to it. Years later, during Jake's visits home, he would steal a moment for himself while it was raining, to sit beneath the tin shelter and close his eyes to ruminate, while no one knew where he ran off to. The tiny green frogs would burp and bounce from the golden leaves to the moistened bark and hurdle their way to the watery puddles below.

On countless rainy days in his future, Jake would sit alone to look and listen to the melancholy raindrops. The teardrops would well up and trickle down his cheeks as he recalled those days of old with much fondness. He would always think that Uncle Hal had done the same thing when the two of them would sit together. The bobwhite would bring a smile to Uncle Hal's face as he evoked his youth. Then, when day gave way to night, you could hear the Whip-poor-will singing in the nearby woods. Jake now likes to think that the call of the Whip-poor-will is dear Uncle Hal saying hello.

Twilight in the fall meant beautiful sights, sounds and recollections for Jake. Maybe the cooler air gave him a serenity that soothes his spirit and relaxes his mind, body and soul. During his youth, twilight also meant that it was time to come inside and finish up any homework, to wash up and eat supper with the family, then maybe squeeze in a little TV time before bed. During the weekends, Friday and Saturday nights, Jake usually watched television until he fell asleep on the couch while Kenny was wide eyed enjoying some B grade horror movie in the comfort of *his* recliner.

Wavy Willoughby rarely watched television. He did not have one growing up because they weren't invented yet. He spent most his time outdoors; farming, hunting, and fishing, that's what you did to survive. Wavy's only entertainment while growing up came on weekends when he would play guitar with his buddies and listen to all his favorites on the radio.

Later on in life Wavy enjoyed sitting with the family and watching *The Red Skelton Show* on Tuesday nights. Jake had never seen his dad laugh very often but ole Red always brought a chuckle to his father's stone face, as would *Hee-Haw,* the next year when it premiered. This made Jake feel good to see his dad smile. The smiles were hard to come by with a child in harm's way.

Wavy was always up at the crack of dawn as he was accustomed to and went to bed after the local and national newscast. He enjoyed a good night's sleep so as to be to be energized for a full day's work. No one knew what went on in Wavy's mind because he was a very quiet and reserved man when it came to his thoughts and emotions. He kept most of his feelings to himself.

Who really knew what Ronnie was going through in that terrible place? The closest clues came in the form of the nightly news, which was extremely distressing to say the least. Common now in Jake's world is the deep down wretched sensation in the bottom of his stomach just waiting to leap out and destroy the day. Despair stained his life.

Jake continued with the anxious routines of looking at the soles of his shoes and stretching to peer at his elbows, along with the compulsive urge of blowing his palms. He could not restrain from the need to constantly check these things out. Along the way he picked up some new habits as well. Jake became more and more nervous. He found himself repeating thoughts and sentences in his head. He started talking to himself aloud, but not loud enough to be overheard. He started making up friends and characters to play with because his friends were dwindling down. The imaginary friends were there at his beckoning call. Lisa Wilson came back on occasion, but only in Jake's mind, which is the only place she had ever been.

Jake started observing the way he walked, careful to avoid cracks, corners, and any kind of object that may lie in his path. His steps had to be precise and in sync; otherwise he would back up and walk more cautiously. Everything within his vision had to be unsoiled and in perfect order and with absolutely no clutter. Jake could feel the filth and evil, which he called *cooties,* circulating in the air. He could feel the malicious smut touch the palms of his hands and he had to immediately start his lengthy routine of blowing his palms with a deliberate and hard breath to free them from the atrocity that had attached. He would blow three times for each palm to remove any foreign matter. If a sink was available he would wash with soap and hot water over and over again until he felt comfortable; a certain number of times on each hand, sometimes mumbling incantations as if warding off evil spirits. If he physically walked in a circle, he would have to reverse his actions to keep from being "locked" into the inconceivable state of ruin. He was compelled to do these things, otherwise something horrible was going to happen to someone he loved or even to himself.

Jake knew that all this was not normal because he had not been this way until this past summer and he has not seen anyone else doing these dreadful things. He was terribly afraid of what was happening, but he was even more afraid to tell anyone in fear of the consequences. Jake's insides were eating away and his mind was swirling in a nervous muddle of a cyclone of sorts. Too much uninvited desolation going on his life and he wasn't sure how to handle it.

"What can I do?!" Jake would scream aloud to no one in particular.

Maybe Lisa is right here with me in a ghostly way. I did see her after all, so she has to be somewhere; in your mind dear boy, in your mind. Daydream believer?

Jake hoped that perhaps Lisa would guide him back to where he belonged; in the land of normality with family, friends, ice cream trucks, Whip-poor-wills, baseball, brown cake and loyal dogs. Jake started asking about visiting Grandma because that always seemed to help. Everything is perfect at Grandma's ~ *just don't go into the woods.*

Chapter 28

"No sky be heavy if the heart is light."
~ **Charles Churchill**

Lying in bed each night Jake found it impossible to sleep. It was only after many months that he discovered a way drift into slumberville. He would close his eyes and float in his own little space ship, far, far away. No worries at all, just the glitter of stars as he coasted by completely alone. This was his serenity; ALL HIS ~ not to be taken away like HIS baseball. This was almost as gratifying as going to Grandma's, but it wasn't the same.

The family visit to Grandma's that October reintroduced Kenny and Jake to their half-brother, James Delano Willoughby, whom everyone called Jimmy. Wavy's first marriage gave him the one child who had lived with his mother in Virginia. Jimmy was a tall, well built, good looking, loquacious and charming young man with that signature wavy red hair and freckles of his father yet had the opposite temperament of Wavy. Jimmy's temper was short and as red hot as his hair and everywhere he went he seemed to leave havoc in his wake.

Jimmy seemed to be a bright and funny lad with a loving spirit. He enjoyed playing practical jokes on people. He meant no real harm; he was just a prankster at heart. Though a fun loving athlete he tended to go a little too far and his short fuse would usually get the best of him. Jimmy never learned the art of rationalization and patience. Jimmy would hit first ask questions later which lead to many altercations, fisticuffs and trouble.

Wavy never got to spend much time with Jimmy, due to each of the boy's parents living far apart and starting families with new spouses. Jimmy never cared for his stepfather, and really didn't know his real father well, so he had a boulder on his shoulder. Wavy did get to spend a little time reintroducing himself to his oldest son when Jimmy, his mom and stepdad moved back to South Carolina from Virginia after several years.

With Jenny's appeal to Wavy for some advice and support the two of them persuaded Jimmy to join the Navy after high school in hopes of calming him down and cooling him off with some strict discipline. As it turns out the Navy couldn't handle the son of Wavy either. Not wanting a bad influence on his other kids and with very little patience with rebellious behavior, Wavy asked his mother if Jimmy could stay with her for a while hoping that the rural countryside would dampen the fire.

Brown cake, beef stew, hot buttered biscuits, sweet tea, butter beans, fresh corn on the cob. Even though Mina had learned to replicate her mother-in-law's cooking it just wasn't the same as being there at the table with the sweet old lady. Grandma always enjoyed the monthly visit. Jake could sense that she was sad and hopeful about Ronnie and a little skeptical about Jimmy whom she didn't really know. Grandma decided that this was an opportunity to get to know her grandson and maybe it would be good for all involved. With herself getting up in age it was difficult to tend to the daily chores, even with Melvin's help who himself was getting harder to get around.

Kenny and Jake never really knew their half-brother because he grew up living with his mother. Jimmy never had the fatherly guidance that may have been just what he needed. The two youngest Willoughby boys were excited to see their older brother and willing to accept him into their lives and get along just like one big happy family. Jimmy wanted to know his younger brothers as well because ultimately his goal is to leave the farm and be close to the city where there would be ample bars, booze, billiard, and broads.

Jimmy eventually started spending more time at Uncle Melvin's store fine tuning his billiard skills, and his appetite for the cold amber ale. He pretty much ignored his grandmother after a short while which did not sit well with Wavy or Uncle Melvin whose beer inventory was rapidly being depleted by one thirsty young fellow. Wishing he had known in the beginning about Jimmy's affection for beer, Uncle Melvin gave Jimmy a job hoping to kick his drinking habit and maybe teach the boy some responsibility. Jimmy also started helping his grandmother more with the chores.

Jimmy's job at the store was to attend to the customers, who were mostly a handful of locals and old timers, at the gas pump. Jimmy was to fill their tanks, clean windshields, and check the oil and tire pressure. He also had the task of bringing them anything that they may want from inside the store, taking their money, giving them the proper change, and sending them on their way with a big smile. He would wave them goodbye through the rearview mirror proudly adorning his four barrel coin changer on his belt, tire gauge in shirt pocket, and oil rag hanging from his pants. Uncle Melvin anticipated that staying busy with a work schedule and responsibilities would keep his nephew out of the beer supply and out of trouble.

This particular weekend was slightly cool and breezy which Jake enjoyed and he stayed outside playing with Grandma's mutts and Uncle Melvin's white shepherds. While running on the farm with the dogs Jake was preoccupied and actually felt happy and carefree for the first time in a while. He had no desire to check his feet or elbows and he truly felt good... everything is better at Grandma's.

There was just something very special about this place to young Jake and he could not put his finger on it. It was peaceful and quiet with no creeks, mud or bullies. It was full of love, respect and support, and everyone seemed so happy, content and considerate. Grandma and Uncle Melvin were always positive and pleasant. As he grew older, Jake would always have the best memories of this wonderful place. Jake loved the hustle and bustle of city life but found as he aged that his heart belonged to the great outdoors with nature, mountains, rivers, and large trees; the great wide open.

As they rode in the car in vicinity of Nichols, Jake noticed that with every passing vehicle came a wave of the hand by both parties whether they knew the other driver or not. However, in this small farming community in the sixties most everyone did know each other; it was a similar and smaller version of John's Island at the time. Wavy missed his childhood growing up on the farm. He often took early morning strolls across the landscape and woods taking his sons along, and telling them stories from his youth. Jake was always excited to hear his dad talk about the good old days.

Jake would run hard and fast down the long sandy cedar lined driveway of his grandmother's home with the rambunctious dogs on his heels. When they reached the front porch Jake would stop and wave at the gossipy folk giving the oak rockers their daily workout.

The panting dogs seem to say hello as well. Then it was off to run around the large farm for a while, and then the dogs and Jake would plop in the thick grass near a sweetgum tree.

Relaxed, Jake would just sit stare and at the reflection of the heavenly sky on the tranquil water; a time and place that he would visit often as an adult. All he had to do was close his eyes and a gentle wind would whisper across his dreamland and he would drift off to Grandma's and his heart would dance in the sunshine of his long lost youth.

Chapter 29

"Oh Hell is deep an' Hell is wide.
An' Hell ain't got any bottom or side."
~ **American Negro song**

The East side of the Indochina Peninsula was still tremendously hot in October though the temperatures had dropped a few degrees since summer. Heavy rains would come often and stay for days which would bring slight relief except when on a four day hump. The soggy ground made for an even more tortuous experience but this day however was high and dry. Ronnie and his best new buddy, Corporal Ben Stedman, and seven others were straining to listen through the loud noise of the Bell UH1-E Huey for their orders.

"Lock and Load!"

Two at a time the Marines dropped into the high grass and crawled the fifty yards to the jungle where they did a head count and with every trained skill and preparation they headed into the unknown.

Webster's definition of the unknown: *not known or not well-known;* also: *having an unknown value.* Ronald Willoughby's definition of the unknown - *scared as hell*!

The clanging of guns, equipment, and the grunting and groaning became common as did the stench of blood and body waste. But the dread of being heard by killers was always forefront in Ronnie's mind. He was constantly aware of any little sound that he made for fear the VC would hear them and gun them down.

Into the tropical mist, and beyond the shadows of the evergreen forest the tense but ready Marines approached with eminent caution. Like entering a cave dark and cold, the sun could not break the sheltering leaves of the palms and the lofty Hopea Odorata trees, also known as Black Star. Surrounded by mangroves, brushwood, eucalyptus, conifers, and large, woody vines resembling the native pythons and boas, the young men became more and more anxious. They could not see anything other than the claustrophobic wilderness that seemed to be closing in on them.

It was very dim and obscure, and the only light that they received was erratically riddled through the distended verdures every ten or fifteen feet like a drunk man holding a flash light while having epileptic seizures as he tried to walk a tightrope. The occasional shriek of laughing monkeys swinging through the trees, and the rustling brush by a wild boar nearly shattered what was remaining of the Marines already tried nerves.

They knew this forest contained many killers. Some with assault rifles, others with large fangs, venomous fangs, and some with sharp claws. Over the last several weeks in the jungles the Marines have spotted a tiger, three bears, a crocodile, pythons, boa's, water buffalo, jackals, skunks and wild oxen, and they knew that there was much more hiding in wait. *A friggin wild, killer zoo,* Ronnie thought.

They have also seen Viet Cong armed with AK 47's and Simonov SK's not to mention grenades and rocket launchers. They have seen pujil's, which are sharp pointed bamboo rigged as booby traps, and they have seen the results of these weapons and the horror in the eyes of those afflicted. This group of nine tired Marines have witnessed and tasted the terror of war many times in the last couple of months but still nothing prepares you for a journey into the unknown.

The platoon leader would tell them just before each trip to "Keep your eyes and ears open, and your finger on the trigger…and watch your buddy's back!"

John Wayne and Gomer Pyle did not prepare Ronnie for this. The training and coaching did not prepare a young innocent soldier for how to handle what was on the horizon of hell. No one knows what is unfathomable in the soul which is the profound scars from war except those who survive, and they do not want to talk about it. The wretchedness of a true living hell is not a place you want to revisit.

Oh God, please get me out of this place. Please let me see my mom and family again. Please Lord. Please Jesus. I am begging you. Ronnie prayed to himself as he stepped on a dry branch that brought eight machine gun barrels in his direction.

After a deep sigh of relief and the forehead wipe with the back of the hand, the soldiers continued on.

After three days in the jungle the small group of soldiers finally saw the sunshine as it rose over the top of a small mountain burning away the cloudy mist that hovered around the ridges and cliffs. This sunrise is a far cry from the luminous outbreaks of spectacular and stunning shades over the many creeks and rivers of Charleston, South Carolina, and the surrounding Sea Islands.

Before the Marines, Ronnie would often ride to Folly Beach and enjoy a hot cup of coffee on the pier as the sun rose into the azure southern sky and wonder what was on the other side of this great mass of ocean. As a child he would stare into the horizon and fascinate about the pirates who sailed and terrorized in these very same waters. He would enjoy the reflection of the full moon on a clear spring night, and would throw a line hooked with sand shark pieces into the surf hoping to surprise Mom and Dad with a large catch. He would let the low country sun polish his pimple blemished cheeks, and he had the luxury of the magical sound of the crashing waves as they rolled into the helpless sand dunes. He would relish watching the sea oats dance in the summer breeze entertaining the bronze, giggling girls in their scanty bikinis.

Not this morning however. This morning brought a monster mountain scattered with eerie palms, menacing boulders, and Black Stars with black hope; the feeling in the abyss of the belly. The young warriors were exhausted, mentally and physically, and they wanted no part of this hill or what was on the other side. The hill was dubbed "Mother's Ridge" by the Recon forces that have already visited. Either because they longed for their mothers or because it was a mother you know what but most likely it was a combination of both. This is apparently one of the many locations where the enemy is reinforcing its supply and volume for the region.

That bottomless, empty feeling of desolation overcame Ronnie as he watched the sun take its place over the tree scattered formation in the vista. The morning sun usually brightens Ronnie's spirits especially after not seeing it for three days but today it just accentuated the doom ahead.

The group of Marines did a quick and silent head count. They tried their best to rejuvenate knowing very well that they needed every ounce of energy that they could muster. Eyes bright and heart full they marched on with their rifles ready and backs humped from the heavy load. They cautiously waded through the high grass and the winding creek that bordered the hill like a moat surrounding a castle.

The knee high muck only weighted down the already burdened soldiers as they trudged through the muddy rocks onto dry land with one large Hopea Odorata greeting them at the base of the mount bordered with many huge boulders. It's now or never, Ronnie thought, as he looked at his buddy, Ben who looked like he had just seen Wavy's ghost lady in the woods as they tried their very best to march onward. Half way up the dreary hill side crouching behind a large boulder, Ronnie peered over his shoulder and looked back at the small river glistening in the daylight and the green shadowy forest where he had just spent three horrific days.

From the distance it actually appeared to be stunning, reminiscent of his hometown of John's Island; the place he longed to be right now. Even the forest seemed pleasing compared to this mountain where they stood visible to any enemy target sight. The Radioman who was close behind the leader and the point man kept slipping on rocks as the leader radioed in their location numbers. Ronnie just knew that any second the entire group would collapse like dominoes into the waiting creek below. Humiliation from the rest of the platoon back at the base would be all punishment he hoped for at this point and that would be really, really nice if that's all that came out of this four day hump of misery and torment.

"What did you do in the war, Daddy?"

"Well, let's see son. My platoon and I were on the side of 'Mother's Ridge' with the enemy just on the other side. and when we encroached the peak, the fat Radioman suddenly slipped on a rock. He went tumbling into the lieutenant and they both came rolling into the rest of us like bowling balls knocking all the pins down into to the river below. Well, the enemy heard all the commotion and stood at the mountain top pointing and snickering at all of us as we dumped the water and fish from our helmets. After a long laugh they turned and walked away."

"Ha, ha Dad, that's funny."

"Yes it is son, yes it."

Taking a quick breather under the shade of the last tall palm tree, the tight bunched group looked at the top of the hill that now was only a few feet away. Who was going first? Did an ambush await them? The young Marines would string out and have to crawl the rest of the way and arrive together with two men in rear. The fat Radioman again struggled but giving him credit, he has been one helluva trooper. Final instructions on the radio, one last look at the rear, and at each other then up into the heavens with one final prayer on their parched lips. The grubby fatigues and mud caked boots held their own too.

Ronnie shot a quick glance at Ben with "Born to kill" scrawled on his helmet and his cigarettes tucked inside the band which he hadn't smoked in several hours, maybe days. With his baby face, Ben looked like he was born to do just about anything other than kill. Ronnie took a deep breath as did the others, and with the thumbs up they were off to the races.

"Kiss me Christine," he mumbled, remembering their very first kiss on prom night.

Rocks, weeds and brush blocked a clear view of the other side of the hill. Quiet…all is quiet on the eastern front. All the men were listening intensely for any kind of sound, and hungry, fat Radioman's gurgling belly was the only sound. Ronnie used his forearm to wiped the sweat and grime from his brow and his long eyelashes, and blew dust from his horned-rimmed glasses. He peered down at his dirty Timex; 8:38 am. He wondered what time it was on John's Island. He knew his mama was praying and worrying, and of course cooking; that's the three things she did best.

I've got to get back home. PLEASE LORD, LET ME GET BACK HOME… this is unbelievable. I've never been more afraid in my life!

For some odd reason Ronnie could hear Porter Wagoner singing "Green, Green Grass of Home". He fought hard to hold back the tears. He took a deep breath with lips quivering and eyelids fluttering he looked up into the heavens and smiled.

Chapter 30

"The nearer the dawn the darker the night."
~ HW Longfellow

With the end of daylight savings time and season's change, the days are much shorter now than they were during the summer. By the time you had a snack and finished your finished homework it was pitch black outside. That was Jake's only complaint about fall and winter. Jake missed playing around outside with his pals. He was stuck in the house to only be able to watch the television news, have supper, take a shower and go to bed but not before Red Skelton said goodnight.

After that he was shortly joined by Wavy and Uncle Hal. Mina was in the kitchen washing the last of the dishes as she peeped out of the window into the dark night. She could see her brother's shadow in the dim lantern light as he prepared for sleep in the converted bedroom/workshop in the back of the house.

The small moth covered light on the front porch faintly illuminated Kenny as he sat gingerly rocking while looking up, and wondering at the vivid stars millions of miles away. Several yards away the pale light from Christine's bedroom appeared forsaken, shimmering through the darkness of the large swaying weeping willow. The rest of the Stern house was as dark as their hearts have been since late June.

A quiet evening with bright stars, occasionally from out of the woods a bobwhite whistled his name into the big open night sky which was kind of late in the year to hear from Mr. White. Not far behind, a screech owl retorted the quail.

Jake lay in the darkness of his room with his eyes wide open as he adapted to his surroundings. He could see the small, empty stand where his new baseball once proudly sat. The only thing on it now was a faint powder of dust.

Tommy, where are you? Lisa, where are you? Ronnie, where are you? God Bless you all.

Jake bolted upright with an anomalous feeling in his tender young heart. He was so tired of being sad. He pulled back the curtain and looked out of the window into black night. He saw the one lonely light in Christine's window and Jake imagined that she was writing a long letter to his brother filling him in on all of the events since she last time wrote two days prior. Jake knew that she too was sad; her entire family was sad. He wondered if everyone besides Christine were asleep so soon or just lying there like him, miserable. He laid back down into his soft comfortable bed.

Above his head his Apollo spacecraft hung by fishing line from the ceiling next to the Gemini and the Mercury ships. He imagined, How cool would it be to be sitting in one of these space craft flying through the universe cruising past stars and looking down on mother earth far below?

Jake laid his head on the forgiving down pillow which was Ronnie's pillow as he pulled his quilt up over his head. He covered all but a small opening to breathe and see through. Then he pretended to be in the Mercury space ship all alone; *The Adventures of Space Boy.* No elbow or sole searching here.

Just inches away on the other side of Jake's window pane, a pale figure lurks in the hedges. It leans forward and peers into the dark room and whispers, "Hang in there Buddy, this is just the beginning," Tommy said.

Just a few feet from Tommy, in the distant moon shadows beyond a large azalea, Kenny stops rocking and turns towards the whisper with eyes wide open. The old willow ballets in the evening breeze with the vibrant moon above giving luster to the countless stars which twinkle and glitter, they seem so close yet they are so far away.

Chapter 31

"Hereafter comes not yet."
~ **John Heywood**

The luminous October sun was beaming on the mountain top with both sides equally bright and vexing. The Marines have no idea what the sun sees and no idea what awaits them on the opposite side of the ledge. This could be their very last seconds on this beautiful earth; why in the world has it come to this? Innocent young men who love God, family, and country are sent into hell to die in vain, simply because they cannot afford college nor have the smarts to receive a scholarship. These unfortunate youngsters die so that the rich and condescending can continue to have the good life. Of course there are the few, the proud, the Marines who want to be there, but are their fight and sacrifice appreciated or respected?

Seven helmets, fourteen alert eyes simultaneously popped up over the edge of hell and the side of the hill. Like Marty Feldman getting two fingers in the rear and coughing, the fourteen fretful eyes randomly danced around the entire hillside and saw no sign of life. A single, tall Black Star stood halfway down the center of the elevation surrounded by long brushwood that could easily hide the enemy. On the opposite side, a few small eucalyptus trees and several large boulders scattered over the terrain that the Marines could not see from their point of view; this made a perfect opportunity for an ambush by the Viet Cong.

With the two Marines keeping watchful eyes in the rear and the thumbs up from the platoon leader, the front seven slowly encroached with rifles prepared as they began to crawl towards the edge of the ridge. Fat, stomach gurgling and sweat soaked Radioman sluggishly made it too. The uneasy soldiers keenly listened for any sound and cautiously watched for any movement. Their Marty eyes still scanning the hillside of Mother's Ridge as they now were on an opened flat plateau just above the bordering boulders and brushwood and this was not good.

146

They sat like fish in a fishbowl. They had no way to see what was beyond the boulders and brush; they didn't want to toss grenades in case no one was there. That would waste ammo and surely set them up as targets on the hill top where they could easily be hit by enemy bullets, grenades or rocket launchers. The PL puts his left hand up and his weary squad halts. He then whispers to F.S.G.S.S., (fat, stomach gurgling, sweat soaked) Radioman who was pouring perspiration by the bucket that they have no cover going down. Just who in the hell set up this idiotic patrol anyway, Ronnie asks himself. He is thoroughly loathing this situation; he could die. For what and why?

Begrudgingly he has to do as he is told. On their bellies with hand and finger signals they decide to spread out slowly. Six feet between each of them and the two pulling up the rear spread out as well with rifles pointing at where they had just left. The point man on left leads out as the point man on right follows with a slow scuttle followed by the other five in alternate succession. This continued for what seemed like an eternity with their hearts skipping numerous beats thru each dusty movement until they reached the shade of the Black Star. The two flankers stayed back behind small boulders to cover the rear and the gap between them and the front seven.

Ben looked at Ronnie, who hesitantly looked back and they both appeared to have aged ten years in the last half hour. They were all filthy and drenched from the humidity and fear. Their eyes sullen from the four day hump but the adrenaline was pumping. There was no time to be somnolent because these were either kill or be killed seconds.

The nine young Marines looked at each other in amazement as they were all still alive and they could not help themselves from smiling. The rolling tears broke the smudges of dust and dirt and formed odd irregular lines resembling a fragmented spider web down their cheeks which gave them all an evil façade. This must have frightened the crow that sat atop the large Hopea Odorata above them because he made a ghastly squawk that nearly caused the Marines heart failure. This would surely alert the enemy, damn bird! From the emanated stench, there was no doubt that Radioman had a soggy bottom.

Ronnie's black eyes followed the silky sheen of the large blue-black wings as they flapped across the sapphire sky and disappeared into the bright lemon sun. Now all they could hear was their own heartbeats, what a beautiful sound that was.

The dirty and terrified yet determined group of young Marines nervously slinked downward through the brushwood, past the welcoming eucalyptus with its unusual and fresh scent. The death hunters reach the very first of several boulders which of course happened to be the smallest one around. Should they continue the crawl or should they quickly dart towards the larger boulders? They silently moved their lips among themselves to resolve the next horrific move.

It was decided that the point men would each crawl to the nearest and largest boulders in their directions, and then they would motion for the rest. The point men followed the same routine until lastly they reached the bordering rocks and bushes. The two Marines were pulling up the rear and searching to see if they would need to shoot.

Again, there were seven helmets and fourteen eyes slowly rising above the rock that separated men from boys, life from death and heaven from hell. The ridge was flat and dusty with huge boulders connecting it to the rest of the mountain and the tops of several tall trees just at eye level due to the large drop off just beyond the boulders. They had all had finally arrived.

They all breathed a sigh of relief with gleaming reprieve in their eyes. After catching their breaths the Marines started shuffling to the flat rock not realizing that between the boulders and the drop off was enough room to hide several crouching and armed Viet Cong. Ronnie planted both feet on the rock and fretfully looked around. He felt somewhat relieved and a little safer. So far so good, he thought. All they had to do was walk to the edge and peer over and down the huge cliff which had to be thirty feet ahead on the other side of the big rocks. When all nine Marines were safely on the ridge the PL radioed in the details as the Radioman continued to sweat and his fatigues were now completely drenched and muddy.

Ronnie wanted to wipe the sweat from his glasses when he suddenly saw a peripheral shadow beyond a boulder and several flickers. The lightning fast bursts were the difference between life and death and before they could react the Marines were gunned down by several Viet Cong who jumped up over the boulders with rifles blazing. The VC were awaiting and watching from the ridge and when they realized that the incoming Marines were not backing down they planted themselves between the line of boulders and the cliff; a perfect ambush.

Upon seeing the flash Ronnie immediately fired in that direction, as did a couple of his comrades. They had no time to vocalize the imminent danger, just shoot. Three of the VC went screaming over the cliff immediately after being hit with American bullets. The PL was on the radio and could do nothing but catch several Russian bullets in his face and chest before he fell to the ground and a blood spattered Radioman squeezed off a couple of rounds before he went down in a heap. Ben, slightly in front of Ronnie took the brunt force of the hail of bullets that came towards Ronnie who was squeezing off several rounds as he turned to run for cover. Ronnie, with his large backpack full of equipment and supplies felt a stinging, burning pressure in the middle of his back and the same thing in his right ankle as he fell hard to the dusty rock.

All nine Marines had been shot; their motionless bodies lay on the flat ridge bleeding out. The five remaining of the twelve VC approached the dead Marines with their smoking Suminov SK's aimed at the bodies in case they needed to finish them off. Ronnie could hear them speaking in their native tongue but did not know what they were saying. He knew by the sound what was happening and he knew that the least little movement or groan would end his beautiful life and he was not going to die here on Mother's Ridge; maybe in his mother's arms at another place and time but not today, not here.

Months of preparedness and a life time of being the runt made Ronnie stronger, tougher and more determined than the average nineteen year old. The VC poked bayonets into the fallen Marines to make sure that they were dead, and then they robbed from the bleeding bodies wallets and watches and whatever else they had the desire to steal. The longest and hardest moments of the teenager from John's Island, South Carolina's life were unfolding as his dead comrades and friends were being stabbed and robbed. Could he survive this? He had to, he had no choice. He was not going to die today. He wasn't going to let his family down, and he wasn't going to break Christine's heart. He had a full life yet to live and these slant eyed bastards weren't going to take that away from him.

A wounded Ronnie was alert and breathing very slowly so it would not be noticed by the enemy. Should he start blasting or pretend to be dead? Where was he laying in proximity to the enemy and how were they spread out? Without proper answers he decided to remain still and no matter what pain he suffered he would endure what they offered and he would survive; green eyes and lips of cherry await thy return.

The enemy's harsh shrill voices were getting louder. If only he knew what they were saying. Their footsteps and scuffle of their boots were more pronounced as was the dust right at his helmet when it came; the cold steel, stained with the blood of his friends, blade pinched into his right rib cage. It then stopped and retreated; not what he was expecting, THANK GOD! Ronnie was frozen in those few seconds as he dared not breathe or squint. He had to have no movement at all and pretend to be dead because it's now or never with no second chances so it has to work ~ NOW!

Ronnie was hoping it was over because he didn't know how much longer he could hold his breath. He prayed to survive as they grabbed his right arm and removed his still ticking Timex at exactly 9:53 am. The gunship carrying the U.S. Army Air Corps roared onto the scene as the VC ran without firing to the safety of the rocks but did not make it as the Air Corps snipers made careful aim and took down the enemy one by one before they could hide. The merciful chopper hovered over the dreadful sight of the fallen U.S. Soldiers.

Ronnie could hear the beautiful sounds of his rescue. He believed his lungs were about to explode as he finally breathed for the first time in what seemed like hours. He even managed to crack a smile as the tears ran down his beautiful dirty cheeks. He opened his eyes and realized he did it! Above him, beautiful blue sky and the harsh scent of gun powder filled his nostrils.

He desperately waved an arm so the Air Corps could see that he was alive and needed immediate help. Ronnie wondered if his friends had survived like he had. He hoarsely called out Ben's name with no response. He then called out the other eight names with no response. At last the Air Corps jumped to the plateau and upon inspection it appeared that Ronnie was the only survivor. Therefore the only one needing immediate attention. Three of the soldiers spoke as they lifted him onto the gurney.

"You okay, Buddy? We're going to get you out of here, you're going home Marine!" Those were the most glorious words Ronnie had ever heard.

Ronnie was carried out by the U.S. Army Air Corps who were the brunt of many Marine jokes but they were now his heroes. As they all reached the bottom of the hill they were physically but not mentally away from Mother's Ridge. What a mother of a ridge that was and forever will be!

Ronnie tightly closed his eyes in complete awe that he has survived; he prayed and thanked God for these men and his survival. He hasn't even thought about his pain or the extent of his injuries. All he knows is he is alive and the other eight members of his platoon are not. He can smell life…how sweet it is!

Chapter 32

"If it were not for hope, the heart would break."
~ **Greek Proverb**

Willamina DuPont Jones was a very strong-minded and resolute woman. After returning home in 1941 with her two children she was determined more than ever to make sure that she did the very best she could at raising them. With her mother watching her children she was able to find odd jobs within the community and in town. She was very busy working and teaching her children how to grow into courteous, respectful and hardworking adults with strong morals. She taught them to say their prayers morning and night and to always be thankful and gracious.

The growing DuPont family was a very humble and very well thought of and respected throughout Conway and surrounding bay areas. Family values was always a strong virtue and daily supper together was a ritual that would never stop; during which they would always share the news of the day, the local gossip, many laughs, and hearty, down home and delicious meals.

The family were meager farmers and the little money that Willamina brought in went into the fruit jar for savings. She learned to get by with what they had but managed to make ends meet but they were never able to be splurge on anything too expensive.

JP, Jr. or just JP loved living on the farm where he managed to get into just about everything. He was a good looking lad who was growing like a weed and had the gift for gab right from the beginning. He would often stand on the front porch and mimic several of his boisterous and outspoken uncles or even his granddad who also had a loud voice that would carry throughout the nearby fields. JP was a fun loving lad and a welcomed addition to the farm. Even the wide assortment of farm animals loved him since he kept them fed, watered and always offered a gentle rub and soft words.

JP's little sister Diane would often tag along where ever her big brother roamed off to but was always under the careful watch of her mom and grandparents. However, one day they were able to slip behind the barn undetected and six year old JP managed to pocket his grandpa's pipe, tobacco and matches. Needless to say, within minutes the two tikes were as sick as two old dogs and as green as the long-needle pines that surround the farm. After a firm paddling on the rear, JP decided that he would never smoke a pipe or steal again.

JP waited anxiously at the end of the day for his mother to return home from work in town and bring home the grape jelly which she had promised him earlier that morning. JP loved the jelly on his grandmother's biscuits and his mouth needed a change of taste after the pipe episode. He looked out the window every five minutes until finally he saw his beautiful mom with arms full of brown grocery sacks.

He quickly darted out of the front door and down the few concrete steps already tasting the sweet jelly in his mouth. As he grabs to hug her one sack was knocked from her tired arms and the glass jar of grape jelly crashed and splattered onto the concrete walkway. It would be another month before jelly again was afforded and a lifetime of a memory for hungry little JP. As an adult JP loved to tell that story, especially when he was hungry.

The end of World War II brought much needed respite into the DuPont family. Mina's brothers came home along with the neighbors, except one. Audie Chestnut, one of Mina's many admirers died when his plane was shot down by and exploded somewhere over France. That was disheartening for everyone in the area, particularly Mina's mother, Sara. She was thrilled beyond words and grateful to God that three of her sons were safely home. She was ever so happy to prepare their favorite meals over and over again. However, the young men wanted to get out on their own, start a family, and make a living. Bob joined the railroad through connections from his older brother Bill. Ted joined a war buddy down in Charleston and opened up his very own barbershop on John Street. Hal stayed in the military.

The feeling of elation from the war's end was soon interrupted by late autumn with dismal news for the DuPont's. Sara became very ill and weak until finally her doctor admitted her to McLeod Infirmary in Florence. Mina stayed by her mother's side attending to her every need while JP and Diane stayed with their Aunt Lucy and Uncle John and their many children whom lived across the highway. Mina had always been very close to her mom and could not stand thoughts of the looming loss.

One cold December afternoon, Sara asked her daughter for some oysters of all things. Mina searched high and low until she found them but by the time she got back to her mother's room she had passed. Mina was sick with grief and guilt for not being with her at the exact moment. For a lengthy period Mina believed that perhaps her mom would have lived had she not been gone so long. Guilt can destroy if you allow it to but as time passed she came to the conclusion that it was God's will.

Although she loved her dad, Mina could no longer stay at home; she felt a desire for a change. Her brother Ted from in Charleston was the only one of her siblings that could or was willing to accommodate her. With her brother John living across the street from her dad she felt that he would be okay even though he would have to adapt to living in an unusually empty house. The old man kept himself busy outside tending to everyday tasks. Mina loaded up her things and little JP and Diane, cranked up the large Buick and headed south to the low country down forest lined highway.

Charleston, South Carolina was rich in history and loaded with opportunity. The stately peninsula dotted with longstanding beautiful antebellum, Greek revival homes, historical buildings and churches and surrounded by water and beaches. Tall palm trees and mighty oaks, azaleas with barrier islands seemed like paradise to the farm girl. *The Holy City,* as it is referred to have many tall church steeples dotting the sky line seemed to be calling young Mina as she nervously drove over the narrow Cooper River Bridge.

This bridge raised high in the sky and then dropped like a roller coaster which scared Diane but not fearless little JP. He wanted to ride over it again. The kids were excited as they looked out of the large windows on either side of the black 1938 Buick and stared below at the water, ships and small islands that separated Mt. Pleasant from Charleston.

This was Mina and the kid's first trip to the historical city by the sea. The city had so much to offer compared to Conway. JP had heard stories about ghost, pirates, swashbucklers and the Civil War. The little fellow couldn't wait to see Fort Sumter, the Battery, the Old Slave Market, historical churches with hidden grave yards and of course the sandy beaches. He was ecstatic; he wasn't missing his grandpa or the farm animals, not yet anyway. Diane was happy too, especially about the beaches and living with her cousins, Frankie, Christopher and Emily.

Mina was fervent about her new beginnings but felt a little overwhelmed with all that faced her. She was not a quitter and would not be discouraged. She would tackle it all with positive boldness, one step at a time. She put her trust in her God and had complete confidence that everything would be just fine. The spirited woman was determined that she and her children would make it.

Mina missed her parents, her siblings, nieces and nephews. She even missed the rural country side and the farm life but having had a small taste of the world outside of Conway she yearned for more. She loved her hometown but had grown bored with the country life and wanted her kids in the city. She knew with time that they would all adjust.

"No need to look back," she would remind herself, "We've got a lot to do kids" talking over Hank Williams singing "Your Cheatin' Heart" from the small car speaker.

Ted, his wife Lenora and children Frank, Christopher, and Emily all lovingly welcomed Mina and her children. They lived in a mid-sized craftsman style home with a large front porch just a block from Hampton Park. It was also near the Citadel, the military college of

South Carolina. Eventually, Hampton Park became Mina and the kid's favorite place to visit. They would stroll along the huge, timbered park to visit its zoo and picnic at one of the many tables or even on the soft green grass. They often would feed the squirrels fresh roasted peanuts that they purchased from the small store near the parking lot. Mina particularly loved the magnificent oaks and the array of colorful azaleas and the quaint pedestrian bridge over the duck pond.

Hampton Park was peaceful and quiet yet near the center of Charleston. Consisting of 60 acres the park in the peninsula was named after Confederate General and former Governor of the state, Wade Hampton. It was once a plantation owned by John Gibbs known at that time known as The Grove. It became a Race Club, The South Carolina Jockey Club in 1835 where the socialites would gather and enjoy live music from the band stand and watch the horse races and drink and eat. During the Civil War it was used as a Union prison where more than 200 prisoners died and were buried. Their graves later moved and the Gibb's heirs donated it to the Library Society who turned it into a park. Many years later a zoo was added.

The nearby neighborhood was quiet and shady with hundreds of old trees with blocks of white framed homes lined with sidewalks. Mina and the kids were fascinated with their new home. The backyard was huge and grassy and fenced in with large shade trees bordering the entire yard. This was the perfect place for all the kids to play.

"This is a good place," JP shouted.

"Yes it is," Mina said, "Always remember we are guest here. This is your gracious uncle's home and we must respect it and take care of it as if it is our own. You must obey Uncle Ted and Aunt Rosie and be nice to your cousins, understand?"

The kids looked their mother square in the eye, earnestly and sincerely, "Yes, Mama," they both replied simultaneously. "Can we go to the zoo now?" JP asked almost immediately.

Mina laughed, "Maybe tomorrow, right now, we've got to get unpacked and situated and I know you kids have to be hungry."

Chapter 33

"Man's common curse to mankind - folly and ignorance."
~ **William Shakespeare**

While Mina and her two children were settling into her new home and environment, just over a hundred miles away a young Wavy was picking his old Gibson acoustic guitar he nicknamed Nellie, after a high school sweetheart. Wavy's love for music matched with his skills and talent got him hooked up with other musicians during high school. Wavy along with banjo picker Spivey Ford and mandolin player Guy Hamilton formed a country- bluegrass band they called *The Sad Sacks*. The youngsters were actually a pretty good band for three untrained country boys. They learned to play several of the more popular bluegrass and country-western songs as well as a few gospel tunes. The hubristic threesome performed at most of the school functions, holiday festivals, social events, picnics, weddings, carnivals and anywhere else they were allowed to.

As word spread they were paid to play their music at a few of the local taverns and honkey-tonks as they soon became known. Like wild fire the news travelled and soon Wavy and his *Sad Sacks* were playing their music at the nearby small towns of Green Sea, Floyd, Aynor, Tabor City, Mullins, Conway, Wilmington and Myrtle Beach. The good looking and talented trio rapidly were getting more and more prevalent with each performance and were quickly discovered by the females all around the area. A swarm of girls would flock to see and hear *The Sad Sacks* perform.

Wavy was drifting further away from the farm and his chores but he was making pretty good money and always gave a portion of it to his parents. Wavy's exceptional finger picking and train whistle became very popular. This matched with his long red side burns, crooked grin, and trademark cocked to one side fedora which was becoming legendary in the Pee Dee Region. The fledgling band of hillbillies, as they were labeled by some locals started getting more bookings than they could keep up with. They were travelling as far as Murrells Inlet, Florence, Dillon and Lake City. Their price per performance increased but without proper management the boys blew the cash as fast as they got it and never branched out as far and wide as they could have.

They should have made their way to Nashville where their talents possibly would have made them big stars. Instead, the new found money went to their heads and was thrown away furiously and frivolously before the group ever made it out of the state. The boys started buying old cars and turning them into hot rods. They were drinking heavily and carousing with multiple women at a time. They were crashing cars, destroying motel rooms, getting thrown out of ocean front restaurants all along the South Carolina coastline. This behavior gave them a reputation they did not need and was frowned upon at the time. Eventually their performances were weakening and their appearances were less.

After performing at The Tear Drop- Inn in Little River, the only place that they hadn't been thrown out of yet, the drunken musicians piled into mandolin player Guy Hamilton's black '44 Pontiac. The wild and loud hellions were headed to Myrtle Beach to quite literally tear up the town. On a rural back road as he took a big swig of the brown stuff, Guy lost control of the speeding Pontiac. The doomed vehicle left the road, went airborne and struck several large pine trees before flipping over and resting on its top in a small creek fifty yards into the woods.

In the wee morning hours of darkness Wavy awoke lying on the damp earth with a horrible headache and covered in dry blood. The reveler had been thrown free from the wreckage and was excruciatingly sore, bruised, and scratched and very fortunate to be alive. His head, wounded and cloudy tried to make sense of what had happened. Once the fog in his banged up head had cleared and his blurry eyes regained focus he carefully pulled himself up by clinging onto the tree that he was thrown into. Once standing, he sluggishly limped over to the upside down car to see if he could help his friends and band mates. It was no use; Guy and Spivey were dead, either from the crash or from drowning in the creek. Wavy could not believe what had happened; he could not believe that his best friends were dead. He knew that if he didn't quickly get help that he would probably join them.

An unusual cold front rushed through the thick woods and the wind eerily whistled through the branches. The sun was still sleeping and curious critters were inspecting the scene of unfamiliar events. Wavy soon noticed a familiar piece of paper floating on a huge oak leaf near the wreckage. He noticed how much pain he was in as he reached down to pick it up. Scribbled in big loopy girl writing was written the name Jenny Hill and an unacquainted telephone number. Jenny was the black haired beauty that tended bar at The Tear Drop-Inn.

Jenny had been flirting with the tall lean Wavy every time he came to do a show but Wavy was always so focused on his music that he didn't pay her much attention except tonight after she sent him a cold one after he sang his favorite, "Wildwood Flower". Wavy cocked his fedora in her direction, raised the cold beer, winked and took a gulp. After a few cold ones Wavy finally mustered up the courage to talk to the big breasted beauty and escaped with her telephone number.

Wavy was still buzzing and suffered a bad bump on the head which caused much dizziness and pain; it also dampened his thought process. He knew it was dark and that he was in the middle of nowhere covered with blood. He was sore, wet, dirty, cold and afraid. He couldn't find the road and knew he couldn't get his friends out of the car.

The trunk had popped open and the top of his hard guitar case was resting in the cold water. He struggled in great agony but wrestled his prize possession from the heap of torn up metal. He limped off into the woods with Nellie strung over his shoulder and a little guidance from the gracious blue moon in the sky, all the while being spied upon from the shadows of an old birch tree.

Jenny Hill was anxious to hear from Wavy Willoughby but doubted that she ever would so she was startled when her telephone rang at four o'clock in the morning. This call woke her up from a deep sleep and Wavy was the last thing on her mind; she thought perhaps it was an emergency in the family.

"Jenny? This is ah Wavy, uh Wavy Willoughby, with *The Sad Sacks*," said a very strained and shaky voice from the other end of the telephone.

Jenny was exceedingly excited, yet cautious due to the sound of Wavy's voice but figured him to be awfully drunk.

"Wavy Willoughby," she said, with a long southern drawl and sexy rasp.

"I figured I would never hear from you again handsome."

Wavy, lightheaded and in severe pain said, "You don't know how close that came to being true."

Wavy was staggering inside a telephone booth at a small gas station that the band had passed earlier. They wanted to stop for cigarettes, beer and gas but it was late and the place was closed. Wavy had no idea where he was headed when he left the wreckage but heard a couple of cars pass by in the distance and followed the sound until he saw a street light. It was all he could do to stay conscious but knew he had to get to the road or at least near it so he could follow it without being noticed and that's when he spotted the dim and familiar sign of the filling station.

Wavy was sitting in the dark beneath a huge elm tree waiting patiently when he passed out. Jenny finally pulled into the gravelly lot of the filling station. She did not see him at first so she looked all around the area while slowly encroaching the small building. She was starting to get agitated but was startled when she noticed a figure passed out against the tall tree. She saw the famous guitar case with studded sequins spelling *Wavy* shining in her headlights leaning up against the tree. A knee was propped up against the case and on the top of the knee was the familiar gray fedora although was now torn and tattered. The frightened brunette carefully pulled alongside Wavy then hastily parked her green 1941 Ford pickup. She jumped out of the pickup to lovingly tend to her future husband.

Jenny drove Wavy to the sheriff's department in Conway so he could give them the details of the accident. During the ride he filled her in the best he could while nodding in and out of consciousness. Jenny then took Wavy to the Conway Hospital to have his wounds tended to. The sheriff questioned Wavy again later that afternoon and told him not to leave town until the investigation of the crash was completed. The distraught and heavily medicated Wavy obliged.

The Times and Democrat reported the next day the car crash that claimed the lives of two-thirds of *The Sad Sacks* based on reports from the sheriff's department. Guy Hamilton and Spivey Ford were found in the creek mid-morning after the fatal crash. The lead singer and guitar player for The Sad Sacks, Wavy Willoughby was recuperating in the Conway Hospital from injuries he sustained from the tragic crash. At Wavy's request, Jenny notified his parents who along with his brothers checked on him in the hospital later that day. After leaving the hospital, Wavy continued his recuperating process in the arms of the young and gorgeous Jenny Hill in the loft of her parent's large barn in Little River.

Sone after his recuperation, Wavy and his young new bride, and of course Nellie arrived at his parent's home. Nine months later James Delano Willoughby came into the world and three months after that on the one year anniversary of the car crash Wavy Willoughby and his new family moved to Charleston, SC. There they moved in with his brother Olin until he could find them a place of their own. Wavy went to work at the Naval Shipyard with his brother Olin.

After two more years the young couple realized they were incompatible and just too different from one another. Since neither was willing to compromise they divorced and Jenny and Jimmy moved back to Little River to live with her parents. Wavy sold their home in Hanahan and moved to downtown Charleston and rented a carriage house off of Lomboll Street, three blocks north of Colonial Lake until he could find something else. Unbeknownst to Wavy Willoughby, one lovely Mina DuPont Jones worked at Mellis' Pharmacy on Broad Street one block from the lake.

Chapter 34

"The gaudy, blabby, and remorseful day
is crept into the bosom of the sea."
~ **William Shakespeare**

J.P. Jones, Jr. worked for the railroad in Champagne, Illinois and would spend his vacations in Charleston, South Carolina to visit his mother, sister and half-brothers. With twenty years between them J.P. and Jake were not very close but J.P. took a shine to his little brother and enjoyed doing things for him and with him. J.P. had no children so this was an opportunity to sharpen his fatherly skills.

On one of his visits at the Army/Navy Surplus Store on King Street, J.P. found olive green military fatigues for his little brother who proudly walked around the yard like the little soldier he pretended to be. This was a few years before Ronnie became a Marine. When Ronnie left for Nam he left behind training boots and a USMC cap that Jake would wear when playing soldier. Both were a few sizes too big and the shirt and pants were a few sizes too small, but he would wear them anyway. He would run through the yard with a stick for a rifle and an old cap gun for his .45 pretending to be shooting down Gooks that hid behind every hedge bush, tree and corner of the yard.

Classmates Steve and Chuck Garner along with Billy Burns from down the road took notice of his soldier outfit and immediately wanted in on the war games. The kids were busy shooting each other similar to the game of tag which they also often played with Kathy and Julie. After growing bored with the confinement of the yard they took their war to the woods across the street where there was a huge variety of dense bushes, vines, and trees to hide behind. Finally, the neighborhood started showing some signs of life again. The kids were running around laughing and yelling with dogs and cats following them. It was good to be a kid again and with the days shortened so too was the fun.

Jake, dirty as usual, entered the house at the same time the telephone was ringing. Right away Jake knew that something was wrong by the look on his mom's face and the tone of her voice as she spoke on the phone. Jake froze as did Kenny who had overheard some of the conversation from the other room and ran to see what was wrong. Mina was urged by the person on the other end of the phone to say the word "Roger" at the end of each sentence or word when she was ready for the other person to speak. This was military talk for received or copy. The caller was not Ronnie and this was not good. Jake's battered and bruised heart has been through the wringer lately and just took another nose-dive deep into his belly.

Mina never ever showed fright or fear to her kids. Both boys were about to be ill with the certain news they were about to hear and they each had a hand on their mothers shoulders. Tears came to Mina's eyes for the first time that Jake or Kenny was aware of and it frightened them both.

However, things started looking up when she said, "He is okay then. He is alive and on a hospital ship. Can I speak with him? Roger."

The boys burst into tears of joy as they stood, stared and listened to every word that their mom "Rogered."

"Hey son. Lord has mercy. My dear sweet boy are you alright? Oh, Roger."

Everyone could hear a distant and scratchy voice on the other end of the phone.

"You did? When? Where? How bad? Oh my God! Oh, Roger!"

Wavy and Uncle Hal quickly joined the two boys who all now circled Mina resembling a football huddle. They all listened intently.

"You are, when?" Oh, um Roger. Thank God Roger!"

There was a sigh of relief from everyone present.

"I love you too, oh, thank God, Roger!"

163

After many tears and *Rogers*, Mina was able to catch her breath and tell the boys that their brother is alive. She went on to tell them that he had been shot twice; once in the back and once in the ankle but he was recovering nicely from his wounds on a hospital ship. He would be headed to San Francisco and then he will fly home for good. "God has mercy!

Chapter 35

One Saturday afternoon Wavy walked into Mellis' Pharmacy for a Coke and pack of smokes when he caught the eye of the tall and lovely Mina. After that moment, the romance began. They each grabbed a vanilla ice cream cone and walked the two blocks past the old two story homes. They both loved the porches also known as piazzas and verandas on the sides of the homes instead of the front. This was to allow cross ventilation from the sea breeze to break the hot and humid summer afternoons on Colonial Lake.

Colonial Lake is a tidal pond and a neighborhood park in the heart of the peninsula of Charleston. It is popular for strolls with kids and dogs as well as walkers, joggers, and in many cases lovers. It is encircled with a wide cement sidewalk which is encircled with oak trees, palm trees, and oleanders all growing from healthy green grass. The park is also sprinkled with park benches and is simply a beautiful place facing the Charleston harbor and replicated sunsets.

Wavy and Mina found a bench under the largest live oak tree at the lake off of Broad Street. They sat and giggled their way through the ice cream and the scarlet sunset and this is where they spent the next dozen Saturday afternoons.

On the twelfth Saturday after meeting Mina, Wavy had a big surprise in store; he knew in his heart of hearts that this was the woman that he wanted to spend the rest of his life with. He saved every dime that he could from his paycheck to make this moment perfect. Wavy had never been much of a romantic but with the help of some friendly female neighbors eagerly waiting with loads of advice and ideas. He packed a picnic basket with cheese, crackers, grapes, strawberries, pears and a blanket. With Nellie slung over his shoulder Wavy set out on the most anticipated day of his life.

The majestic chime of all of Charleston's historic church bells rang in unison adorning the southern city in spiritual charm and grace which added romance and drama to Wavy's already anxious day. Mina worked the early shift at the pharmacy this particular Saturday and her boss Mr. Mellis told her that she could leave early so that she could spend most of the day with the man of her dreams, one Jacob "Wavy" Willoughby.

The tall, red-headed Wavy arrived early, parked behind the pharmacy and grabbed Nellie from the backseat. He reached into the trunk for his sweet grass basket full of goodies and walked straight into the front door wearing the biggest smile anyone in the building had ever seen. The olive skinned Mina met his smile with a huge one of her own. With a tortoise shell beret holding back her long black hair she looked absolutely divine in her white linen dress accenting her curves and long legs. Her black eyes mirrored Wavy's excitement.

Mr. Mellis waved the young couple away with his own toothy smile and with Old Charlestonian dialect told them to have a very wonderful day and not to do anything that he wouldn't do. His son Larry handed the beaming couple each a cold Coke and Mina traded him her soiled apron.

"Please Mr. Wavy, before you go can you do the train whistle, please," Larry pleaded.

Wavy was happy to oblige. He did his best Roy Acuff train whistle, sounding just like the real thing, roaring right through the middle of the pharmacy startling patrons within and passerby's on the sidewalk. Young Larry's eyes lit up as if he were hearing it for the first time and not the dozen times that Wavy honored his wish. Larry's dad was just as enthused as the youth each time "The Walbash Cannonball" whistled on Broad Street in Charleston, South Carolina.

Everyone was laughing and smiling on this perfect Saturday morning. Wavy and Mina walked hand in hand on the shady sidewalk towards the lake. Wavy's heart was about to jump right out of his chest and his nerves were nearly shot by the time they crossed the tree lined street to the beautiful lake. While they ran across the street, Mina teasingly asked Wavy for the third time, what was in the basket and for the third time he told her it was a surprise.

Neighborhood skateboarder, Henry "Hank" Stovall, was going around the lake on his bashed up but trusty board when he caught a glimpse of the smiling couple as he bee-lined towards them. Wavy spread a blanket on the soft grass for the lovely Mina as she crossed her long legs, and sat down with Wavy holding one arm for support.

Hank has long had a crush on Diane and was always out for brownie points with Mina and Wavy. But the twelve year old just didn't get it that Diane was too old for him and is just being polite when speaking to him which he misinterpreted as sincere interest.

"Good morning Miss Mina and Mr. Wavy," the young towhead boy yelled a good thirty yards away, as he quickly approached.

"Good morning Hank. How are you on this lovely day?" Mina sparkled with enthusiasm.

"I'm fine. No falls yet today but I was scraped up pretty good yesterday though," the boy with the blonde flattop responded, with a long southern drawl. "You wanna see my knees?"

"No thanks. I'm sure that your mother doctored them up just fine and they must be healing quickly for you to be out here at it again today."

"Yes ma'am."

"Mr. Wavy are you gonna play your guitar?"

"Yes Hank. I thought I would serenade Miss Mina while we are having a cozy and private picnic." Wavy said, while he winked at the boy.

Young Hank was suddenly blushing and quickly took the hint then he was off with a big gap-toothed smile across his face.

"Ya'll have a pleasant afternoon. I'll see ya later and don't forget to tell Diane I said hey." Hank hollered over the noise of skateboard against concrete as he glided away.

Mina said, "Such a sweet boy and so polite."

Skeptical and wise Wavy tolled back, "Almost too polite if you ask me."

Hank looked back in caution and then hopped off the board, flipped it in the air and confidently grabbed it with one hand. He then reached into the back pocket of his denim jeans with the other hand and withdrew a crumpled half pack of filter less Chesterfield's with the other as he jaunted onto the grass and dashed behind a large oak. He produced some stick matches from a smashed box from his front pocket then hawked his bubblegum into the lake as he drew onto the cigarette as he fired it up and savoring the smoke inside his mouth as if it were the best thing in the entire world. He inhaled the smoke into his young lungs then closed his eyes and dreamed of Diane sharing the cigarette with him.

"That gal is gorgeous and one day, one day..." He said, pointing his cigarette at the non- respondent tree. Granddaddy long-legs appeared on the boy's wrist and he squealed and jumped back like a frightened little girl trying to knock the spider from his arm. Ashes dropped from his secret cigarette which landed between his fingers burning his tender skin. Hank shrieked more loudly and tossed the cigarette into the lake then jumped on his board and sailed down the sidewalk towards Rutledge Avenue.

Proud and nervous Wavy sat across from who he believed was the most beautiful and charming woman in the world. He could not stop grinning even while digging through the basket and pulling out his idea of a romantic picnic. All the while Mina is looking at Wavy with wild eyed amazement and anticipation. Wavy plucked a red seedless grape from its stem and tried to gracefully mimic his sweetheart. He could not quite pull it off as juice from the fruit squirted onto Mina's cheek and she giggled with delight. Wavy was embarrassed and certain that he had just blown the afternoon, or his entire life for that matter. Mina, still smiling, asked Wavy if he had a hanky.

Dumbfounded, Wavy thought she asked him if he had a hankering.

"A hankering for what?" he asked, while nearly choking on the grape peel.

Mina chuckled, "No, no, a hanky, a handkerchief for the grape juice, silly."

Feeling even more idiotic than before and feeling his hopes and dreams sinking away with each second Wavy stuttered "Oh, oh yes of course, a hanky, I knew that."

"Sure you did," as the ruby red lips puckered in response.

Wavy reached into his back pocket and produced a white, cotton handkerchief and nervously reached over to gently wipe Mina's rosy cheek. She closed her eyes and ever so slightly puckered her lips for the tense gentleman to take them unto his own lips. With much relief Wavy soon obliged and he finally breathed again. They sat beneath the oak and smiled at each other for a very long time.

Wavy finally reached for Nellie and started strumming. He cleared his throat and began singing the song "You Are My Sunshine."

Even the seagulls stopped snacking and quacking to enjoy the serenade.

Mina's heart was thumping away and tears came to her black eyes.

"That was so beautiful honey."

Again Wavy cleared his throat. "Why thank you."

"Just a little something hmm, I um, hmm thought I would do for you. My throat won't seem to clear, sorry."

Mina just gleamed at the nervous fellow sitting in front of her. She thought he is such a wonderful, darling gentleman.

Again, they are back at it with the staring and long silence. Finally, Wavy reached into the sweet grass basket. He dug around for a few seconds and came up with a small black felt covered box. Mina gasped. Wavy held the box in the palm of his left hand, opened it with his right hand and picked up a shiny, golden ring with a beautiful small diamond proudly gleaming on top. Mina eyed the jewel with tears of joy in her beautiful black eyes. She eventually looked into Wavy's eyes when he began to speak.

"Mina, make me the happiest man in the world, please dear. Would you marry me?"

Mina was shocked, yet exhilarated and exploded "Yes, yes I will marry you Wavy Willoughby!"

At the same moment in the near distance the sounds of the skateboard and Hank whistling "You Are My Sunshine," bounced across the silvery lake.

A small elderly man with a well-trimmed white beard, gold wire rimmed glasses, black suit and red bow tie smiled and gingerly clapped for the young couple as he leisurely walked by.

"Congratulations, you're a lovely couple. You both sing well too," he said.

In accord they both said, "thank you."

A seagull squawked and flew from the shade of a nearby oleander to a large palm and impatiently waited for the couple to toss more bread. The melodic bells continued to fill the peninsula with their beautiful song of hope and happiness. Life is good.

Chapter 36

"The job called for an accountant but a dancer got it."
~ Caron De Beaumarchais

Knowing that Ronnie was safe and leaving the hell of war and military service behind him for good brought a great relief to the Willoughby family, especially young Jake. He believed having his hero Ronnie soon home again would cure his current ailment. Ronnie left Vietnam but Vietnam never left Ronnie.

The past eight months have been extremely hard on Jake and it all started with the news of Ronnie joining the Marines and pretty much everything went downhill from there. What happened in the past eight months will linger in the shadows always and rear its ugly head at random times throughout the rest of Jake's life.

The fall of 1968 saw an increase in Jake's nervous habits as his mother referred them to herself in a soft whisper while she noticed him one day constantly checking the soles of his shoes. Mina just figured that her youngest son was a bit hyper and may be bored but she never thought that perhaps nerves played a role in his actions. For the past eight months Jake became more and more nervous as the subsequent events played out in his life.

Jake started living with the horrible feeling that something bad was always just around the corner or an eye blink away. He felt that the only way to prevent these horrible things from happening was to do certain routines and rituals to prevent them. Somehow, these habitual practices eased his anxiety. He was compelled to persistently perform these rites in order to protect his family, friends, and himself from some horrific and dreadful circumstance or event.

Jake's anxious rituals were physical and mental to the point that they snatched control of the teen. They eased his worry and made him feel more secure about everything but they were evaporating his time and thoughts. Jake was even more alarmed when he realized that he often repeated statements aloud to himself when he was alone.

Jake found that numbers played a significant role and he had absolutely no control of this behavior. If the phrase that he uttered to himself didn't sound satisfying or strong enough the first time he would repeat it with emphasis. He felt that the more he said it the better the odds of being heard by whomever or whatever, and fix the situation. This also frightened him and made him even more nervous. Jake would avoid walking over or through or near corners of walls, sections of sidewalks and floor tiles to prevent horrendous and tragic things from taking place. Not only were the anxious routines and repetitions of phrases controlling him.

Jake hoped that he was just overly superstitious and soon it all would just fade away but all of a sudden Jake became extremely orderly and neat. Things had to be in perfect order and dimension like stacks of paper, magazines, and books all had to be lined up and facing flush with his eyes. Absolutely nothing could be upside down; ever. They could not be even a centimeter out of place. All corners had to touch and lineup. Pictures on walls had to be straight and his shoes would have to be in perfectly straight rows when he took them off. The toes would have to be evenly in line and pointing straight ahead. Nothing could be out of order in any way shape or form, especially numbers.

Somehow Jake deleted the number four from existence. Four was Jake's number of devastation for some reason. The number four in Jake's mind was absolutely taboo and he did not know why. He could not explain it; he just did not like the number four. He was afraid of it and he couldn't even stand to look at it even though it was totally unavoidable at times. If he ever had to say the number he would blow the cootie dust from his palms then wipe his hands on the tops of his thighs.

Sometimes he could feel the cootie dust still there and he would have to discreetly blow again at his palms, always looking to see if anyone noticed. He usually had to do this three or five times, but never, ever four times. Anything and everything in his world had to be as close to unspoiled as humanly possible. Dust, dirt and crumbs were not expectable in Jake's biosphere, inside his home. The great outdoors was a different story as there wasn't much he could do to change what went on outside of his house except to avoid cracks and corners, and definitely not step in any poop.

Most of Jake's nervous practices went undetected as far as he could tell anyway and he went through great lengths to hide his habits. As far as he knew no one had any idea that inside he was a complete nervous wreck. With all this chaos swimming around in his brain and the uncontrolled time consuming actions holding him hostage he felt nauseated and very afraid for the majority of his waking hours.

Jake found himself drawing and reading a lot more to take his mind away from this monster. Jake loved history so he enjoyed learning about George Washington, Abe Lincoln, Teddy Roosevelt, the Wild West and General Patton. Even reading had its bumps in the road as he found himself repeating certain lines and words over and over again but never four times.

Jake has made up his mind. He's a kid and he's going to be content. He's going to enjoy youthful things and be cheery. He was going to try his hardest to be happy and who knows what tomorrow will bring?

…Good intentions.

"Please God bring Ronnie home!" Jake would cry out to himself. He knew if Ronnie were home that everything would be okay again. He would not be so nervous and upset. He knew if his brother was safe then he too would be safe.

Chapter 37

"Along the cool sequestered vale of life,
they kept the noiseless tenor of their way."
~ **Thomas Gray - Elegy written in a country churchyard**

The past summer had shaded Jake from the blazing rays of the sun with the under belly of leaves in cool, bright emerald. The change of season has brought a chill into the low country's brackish air. Those same leaves once so heavenly and welcomed gave their rule in the summer sun. They secured Ronnie during his visit home as well as cooled Jake, Kenny, and Bullet as they played beneath the tall trees. They sheltered that eminent baseball before it became an idol tortured. They shaded Johnny and Tommy on their ill-fated trip with the pilfered treasure to the mystic creek of shadows and whispers.

Like Tommy and Bullet, the leaves served their purpose then left the boughs of home to softly sail beneath the clouds in the autumn breeze. The ornate golden, scarlet, purple and copper facades of yesterday's beauty and grace float freely and effortlessly across the days departing sunset of dazzling hues and southern charm until gently landing on the dark, rich, low country soil. The shadows in the twilight of the evening brought coolness across the marsh and the flicker of starlight onto the perpetual rolling waters under the moss-filtered moonlight framing the tall steeple of St. John's Episcopal Church on the sandy Angel Oak Road.

Centuries before the proud Cusabo, Algonquian language meaning 'good water', Indians made their home village on the river banks. They minded their own business and lived their lives just yards away from the pluff mud that sucked away the life of young Tommy Stern.

The *good water* turned evil after the demise of the proud Cusabo and now their vindictive spirits haunt the marshlands and creeks. The church steeple stands guard over the oak covered cemetery with its ancient tombs draped with the long veils of Spanish moss shading the names of early American settlers. Some of these settlers built the church and its ministry but some were part of seizing the land that was once the territory to its native son, the Cusabo Indians.

Some graves belonged to hungry farmers trying to make a life on the land that they inherited and they knew nothing of the natives except maybe a few folklore legends.

The haunting sound of the watchful old screech owl penetrates the darkness lingering across the final resting place of forgotten souls and settles in and wraps itself in the conspiracy of silence of the graceful church and ethereal grave yard. One small black mass of clouds drifts in front of the cluster of iridescent stars resting in the bright path of the full Harvest moon. The eerie mist settles over the Willoughby house and drops a gentle, cool rain onto the dark, quiet domain. The beautiful melodic raindrops dance around the shelter of slumber, inducing dreams of wonderful days to come.

For Uncle Hal, the peaceful drops on the tin roof of the side shelter of Wavy's workshop where he regularly sat when the rains came reminded him of careless and innocent days of his lost past. He closed his old eyes and all was right again in this wicked world.

The innocent and dead slept. The weary wanted. The angry and evil crept as the rain poured.

Chapter 38

"My youth shall wear and waste, but it shall never rust."
~ **William Congreve**

Great things are about to happen, Jake believed as he stretched his head to inspect his elbows to make sure that that they were free of anything but clean skin. Ronnie is on the mend and heading home. Halloween is just around the corner then it will be Jake's birthday with breaks from school to follow. Thanksgiving and Christmas were all approaching quickly... "Fun, fun, fun, 'till your daddy takes the T-Bird away..."

Saturday morning, ah yes. A full day was ahead. Jake watches Uncle Hal pat his cheeks with Old Spice aftershave and tells Jake to hold out his palms where he sprinkles a little of the fresh smelling liquid from the unique cream colored bottle. Jake, following the earlier que from Uncle Hal, pats his own cheeks and sniffs away at the distinctive and lingering scent. Uncle Hal grins with pride and affection. Jake has decided to give the stables another chance since giving up on it after his first visit. Perhaps the perfume will hide the stench of poop.

Kenny had been working there two days a week after school and on Saturdays making himself a little Christmas money. The three Old Spice men enjoyed a beautiful, crisp fall morning stroll down the dirt roads to the stables after a big breakfast Mina had prepared for them. Jake had already forgotten the negatives of the stables - the reek and filth along with the birth and discovery of his nervous habits.

Jake was thinking of that glorious peacock and the beautiful horses and the chance to ride one and pretend to be Roy Rogers or Gene Autry. Kenny had been feeding and grooming the horses and shoveling their waste to put out to pasture. Today he was finally going to get to ride one along with his little brother with the guidance of Uncle Hal and Mr. Brown.

The enthusiastic comrades walked down the long sandy, entrance to the stables which reminded Jake of Grandma's driveway except this was bordered with white wooden fence with intermittent tall pines instead of tall green cedar trees. The horses grazed in the pastures shadowed with the roaring C5A-Galaxies flying overhead in sets of three, destination to you know where. Jake had noticed that the amount of cargo planes seemed to have increased over the last several weeks but that didn't concern Jake because, thank God, his brother was no longer involved with that dreadful place. Jake's brother survived and that's all that really mattered to him as far as Vietnam was concerned. Ronnie would be home soon and all would be well in Jakedom.

Uncle Hal gave wild eyed Jake a boost onto a black and white pony; "I'm little Joe Cartwright," he said, with a wide grin exposing his large front teeth and stretching the little patch of freckles across his red cheeks. Uncle Hal gently led the pony with the worn lead rope attached to the bridle through the pine straw covered paths and trails that wound around the stables. Jake was thrilled and at first a little skeptical but knew that Uncle Hal had control of things.

Jake quickly became comfortable, in fact; he wanted to go a little faster so he could catch up with Kenny who was riding Flame, a beautiful, large thoroughbred with a white patch the length of his face. Kenny too wanted to go faster but Mr. Brown was careful not to let go of the rope and he could not run so the boys had to settle for just sitting atop the pony and horse and moving at the older gentlemen's pace. The trails were clean and offered smells from the many different trees and brush throughout the great wilderness. Jake noticed a couple of odd odors drifting into his nostrils and wrinkled up his nose in distaste.

"Skunk," Mr. Brown said.

Jake and Kenny both were taken back as they had never smelled or seen a skunk before and didn't want to start now. A few feet away everyone wrinkled their noses again as they drifted through another vulgar odor. "Lima beans," a grinning Kenny said. Everyone broke out laughing.

The boys were home in time to wash off the skunk and lima beans and to gobble down grilled ham and cheese sandwiches and tomato soup prepared by their mother. With full bellies they watched Kenny's favorite Saturday shows, *The Monkee's* and *The Archie's*. Jake didn't care too much for these shows. He only liked Veronica and the blonde girl but he knew that his brother was enjoying them even at his age. Somethings you just never outgrow.

Jake still had an entire Saturday afternoon to play with Billy, Stevie and Chucky, and hopefully hangout with Kathy and Julie too.

Since late June Johnny Moore, the ball thief and coward has kept to himself. No one has seen him except at school and even then he is quiet, withdrawn and avoids eye contact. He is a year or two older than Jake so he never sees him at school anyway. Once in a while Jake will see Johnny's dad drive by on the way home from work but other than that you wouldn't know they exist. Too bad they ever did, Jake thought.

Three sets of three cargo planes fly over again, "Wow, where they are going," asked Stevie.

"Vietnam," Jake said flatly.

"Oh," Stevie said, obviously embarrassed knowing that Ronnie was over there.

Jake just shrugged it off. The boys headed out into the nearby woods which they considered their forest to build a fort. They followed the path made by Mina's cat, Fluffy. Jake was familiar with the path since it was the same one that Kenny and friends lead Jake to his long afternoon of trauma in the woods. To the boys it seemed as though they went very far away but they were only a couple of football fields away from Mina's motherly ears. Jake wondered why no one heard him screaming for help on the day that he was tied to a tree and left for some wild animal to rip and shred for supper. Anyway, that was then and this is now - Saturdays are good!

They dragged with them the necessary tools in Kenny's book bag, which was a little payback, Jake thought. The boys were having a blast. They had to make several enthusiastic trips back and forth to carry the needed wood scraps that Wavy had lying around his workshop

The entire time that they were in the woods Jake had the uneasy feeling that they were being watched. Every time he turned to investigate there was nothing there. However, one time he could have sworn he saw a shadow and even heard a rustling in the thick brush. He brought this to the attention of his voracious buddies and they all cautiously approached the area that the sound came from. After seeing nothing they figured it was just a cat or possum.

The boys did notice an unusually cool feeling in that particular spot and assumed it was from all the density and shade harboring the previous night's lower temperature.

Finally, the fort was finished. They inspected their handy work and stood back in admiration. They congratulated each other on a job well done but were too tired and hungry to play in it so they all headed back to their respected homes. There they had a snack and watched a little television but later that afternoon returned to their fort to play soldier or whatever for an hour or so before it got too dark to see. Lastly, they would head back home to wash up, enjoy supper and stay in for the evening. They would anticipate a full day in the forest the next day where they would pack a bagged lunch and bring a canned soda or two so that they would not be interrupted. Boys will be boys.

Chapter 39

*"The museum is seldom a cheerful place- often induces
the feeling that nothing could ever have been young."*
~ **Walter Pater**

Mrs. Walker was patiently teaching more than twenty-five students, excluding Lisa, long division and proper grammar. She was also teaching them good manners, which were welcomed by Mina Willoughby. Jake had always listened intently and took schooling and learning seriously. He especially liked American History and was very passionate about. His grades were always in the top of the class but lately he's been a little noisier than normal and slanting more towards the unruly clowns in the class and not applying himself as he used to.

Stevie, Billy, Chucky and Rusty were the talkative ones. They were the class clowns and very disruptive. Jake had always been shy and quiet, especially in class but as he got older he was easily egged on by his buddies. This bothered Mrs. Walker because she knows that it's because of the disorderly kids and she hates to see a good pupil mottled by peers.

Mrs. Walker had one on one talks with Jake about his unfounded behavior and it worked for a short period but eventually the attention craved teen wondered back over to the rowdy side. This prompted a telephone call to the Willoughby household from a concerned teacher. Mina sat her youngest down and explained the importance of paying attention and doing well in class. She prayed that she got through to her adolescent son.

Jake loved field trips. The class would load up on one of the big yellow school buses and leave the building for the day. Last year they visited Hampton Park which always was and will be one of Jake's favorite places as it's under the radar in current Charleston standards. Today, they unload from the big yellow bus on the corner of Rutledge and Calhoun at the first museum in America. The Charleston Museum was established in 1773 when South Carolina was yet a British colony.

It was a beautiful, old building with tall white columns in the front standing on a large plantation porch. Jake halfway expected to see the Colonel all dressed in white kicked back in a rocker eating chicken and sipping tea. Several large, mature oaks, crepe myrtles, palmetto's and azaleas scattered around the entire block that hosted the museum and dozens of hungry pigeons.

Jake had been on the grounds before when his mother would come to town on Saturday mornings to buy plants and flowers that had been carefully grown and cared for by many local older ladies that gathered around the sidewalks leading to the museum. They would park their vehicles in front and around the vast grassy front entrance to the museum where they would sell the beautiful results of their efforts from their yards and small gardens. Jake would stare at the building and wondered what was inside. Mina promised that one day they would take him inside. That one day finally arrived but it was Mrs. Walker and not his mom taking him in.

After a chaotic period a straight line was formed. The students entered as they were remind by Mrs. Walker to be quiet. The front foyer was large, eerie and depressing with an old musty smell to it; very old and malodorous. Jake was actually frightened somewhat. It resembled an old haunted castle that Jake had seen illustrations for in one of his many books. Jake's eyes were darting everywhere; he was waiting for instruction on where to start.

"Ooh, ah, look up," Mrs. Walker said, pointing at the ceiling.

Jake's big brown eyes shot upward and all he saw was Mrs. Walker's big cotton covered breast. Man, he really wanted to see those things without clothing. He then followed the direction of the finger to the ceiling and there hanging in mid-air was the scariest looking thing he had ever seen. It was the fossilized skeleton of a prehistoric whale. It was huge, hideous, and exceptionally creepy. All the kids just stared in amazement.

Mrs. Walker ushered the studious group into the main area and Jake was awestruck because he had never seen such things. Mrs. Walker read the descriptions of each display and items therein to the curious and enthusiastic kids. Then Jake saw the second scariest thing he had ever seen in his young life, a real mummy. It lay out in an old coffin and was displayed in what appeared to be a glass case. The cloth wrapping was deteriorating and brownish orange in color. Jake could see where the eyes had once been in this old Egyptian corpse.

Jake got the willies and really needed to clean off now. He felt filthy and had to blow the bad from those sweaty palms. Jake learned with time how to conceal his habit in public. He would slowly and inconspicuously blow his palms in a very nonchalant manner. He did the same thing but looked at his feet and elbows. This took a lot more effort to make discreet than he would like but he eventually satisfied his compulsive urges, poor kid. Here at the museum he was fortunate to be able to hide behind a large column to do his thing.

Then in another large vile reeking room attached to the ceiling was the only fossil in the world of the largest flying bird ever. Jake and his buddies were pretending to be chased by the giant creature running and ducking from its giant claws. Mrs. Walker had to call down the playful teens.

Meanwhile, Mina was at home preparing supper for her men as *The Dick Van Dyke* show continuously fluttered up and down on the black and white screen and Wavy was busy at work. Kenny was at school learning about mummies and pyramids in Ancient Egypt while Uncle Hal, sporting a cardigan sweater was reading the daily newspaper while sitting beneath the tall sycamore tree as the bark peeled away and fell to the ground along with the large leaves that had shaded him a just a few short weeks ago. And far, far away wishing that he could be present, Ronnie was resting in a wheelchair smoking cigarettes and reading a Playboy magazine on a hospital ship headed to San Francisco.

No one knew of the nuisance and torment that young Jake was suffering; no one but Tommy that is and Jake was unaware of this. Jake's mind was spinning like a top and he felt that it would never stop until it just gave out or exploded. This was no way for a kid to feel.

Jake was frightened. He knew that he could always approach his mom about anything but he was scared and embarrassed about his situation. He was constantly on the verge of collapse with tears pouring from his eyes at any given second unless he was preoccupied…His clownish buddies helped a lot.

Jake also found that drawing helped somewhat and he became quite good with sketching. He liked to draw people, trees, birds, barns, mountains, and landscapes. Wavy sketched a lot and often showed his youngest son how to draw cars, fish and *Dick Tracy*. Jake developed and interest and showed natural talent. He then started drawing more than normal to keep from going completely insane. He would lose himself in the shadows of the charcoal and create some good drawings for a thirteen year old. He would sketch Lincoln and Washington while looking at their cartoon colored portraits on the wall. His drawings would look more realistic in the color gray. One of his favorites was of the crucifixion. He had meticulous detail with dirt, blood and cuts all over the body of Christ.

When Jake couldn't draw or be with his buddies he felt that he was about to lose his mind so he would walk inside his closet, shut the door, and get on his knees and pray. Sometimes when it was available he would go the backseat of the Biscayne when no one was around and he would pray there just like he used to do when Ronnie was in Vietnam; it worked then so why can't it work now.

Chapter 40

"Innocence is ashamed of nothing."
~ **JJ Rouseau**

With the American space program at its peak it's only natural that a teenage boy would be fascinated with spaceships, rockets, spacemen and going to the moon. When the vertical hold was working and even when it wasn't, Jake watched every Gemini and Apollo lift off on television. America was heading to the moon and Jake wanted to watch every moment of it. The moon, Jake thought, so far away and so mysterious yet there it was every night staring you right in the face. Jake thought of all the great and famous people that looked up and wondered at the very same moon that he stares at each night.

Over time the space program took the place of Jake's love for toy soldiers and eventually baseball which now put a very sour taste in his mouth after this past summer. Just the mention of baseball or the sight of it on television nearly made him sick. Thanks to Mina's inveterate persuasion with Wavy, young Jake had accumulated various model rockets, toy rockets, pictures of rockets, some hanging from his ceiling, some on shelves, some on dressers and tables.

Jake started building his own spaceships with large paper towel boxes his dad would bring home from work. Jake just loved the idea of being alone in the black abyss of the universe. He felt serine and content; he felt in control. He would pretend to be an astronaut and would soar through the galaxies and past planets and stars in search of exciting new worlds. Alone in space everything seemed perfect. There was no one to bother him, tell him what to do or argue with. Everything was clean and in order just the way he wanted it. This was just pure contentment for Jake until his belly growled.

"Mom, I'm hungry," Jake yelled, from the large box.

Stevie and Chucky Garner, the twins down the street and Jake's classmates, war buddies, and fellow explorers of the woods were members of Eden Rocket Club. As a member you received a cool membership card and a catalogue offering many rockets to purchase. The little spaceships ranged in size and price and were all launched from a pad usually in the Garners backyard since they had less trees that could possibly intercept and snag a free falling rocket ship as it came back to earth with the assistance of a parachute.

The least expensive rocket turned out to be the most popular in the neighborhood. It was made of balsam wood and packed with filler and explosives. It was nothing more than a small amount of gunpowder which made it no more dangerous than a firecracker when in responsible hands and supervision. Still though, the excitement of belonging to the club, having your own membership card, and picking out and ordering your own rocket was a great feeling.

Then following the mailman around the neighborhood every day in anticipation was exhilarating for Jake and his friends. Just like the days when they would order something from a cereal box or comic book. They would tell each other, "you know back when we were kids." After the long wait of five to seven days the boys would receive their rockets. They would put them together launch them on Saturdays. The spaceships would blast off into the sky for about thirty to forty feet and float back to the ground with their little parachute about twenty or thirty yards out. The ships were good for one launch, and then you had to buy more launching powder etc.

They never had the extra money to enjoy more than one launch a month but three guys meant three rockets so they had three exciting launches. It was a long month and a lot of chores before the next mail delivery that may even be an upgrade to a better rocket but that meant more money and more chores. So, where to get the money was the question. They would look for grass to cut even though fall had settled and no lawns needed mowing.

Jake became so desperate to purchase a rocket that he went back to work at the stables again even though this was the place he was sure that caused all his nervous fixations to come into play. After a vigorous afternoon of tossing hay from the pickup truck into horse stalls and checking his feet and elbows every couple of minutes Jake was exhausted but he had two dollars.

The three determined boys would ride their bicycles up and down Maybank Highway and Brownswood Road looking in drainage ditches for thrown out soda bottles to cash in for deposit money. This was before there was a litter law and respect for the environment. The ditches were full of soda bottles and everything else that someone wished to discard by way of their car window. The three managed to collect quite a few bottles and would redeem them at Platt's Grocery Store on Maybank Highway for five cents a bottle.

They got enough money for one rocket upgrade and a three way ownership that seemed like a great thing when browsing the catalogue but turned into a nightmare once the rocket arrived because they failed in their excitement to discuss where the rocket would sleep at night. After a week of sleeping at each of the homes of the three boys the rocket found its permanent home somewhere deep in the woods which lead to many explorations in search of the tiny spaceship but no sight of the spaceship itself.

The boys finally settled on the less expensive gliders that you can purchase at Morrison's Department Store on James Island. Soon, gliders became all the rage and there were many balsam planes flying all over the neighborhood. This turned out to be more fun much more often. It was also quicker and easier to use than the Eden Rocket Club and parents liked the gliders more because they were more safe and affordable. However, the boys missed harassing the mailman. So the boys often would order junk from cereal boxes or comic books like the good old days just to have some mail arrive in their names and to keep the mailman busy.

One Saturday Jake received a letter in an airmail envelope which usually meant Ronnie. Jake anxiously tore open the envelope that had been mailed all the way from Hawaii; it was indeed from Ronnie. It was just a few lines to let his little brother know that he was thinking of him and that he was okay. He was recuperating on a hospital ship and would be home soon. He also told Jake to make good grades and be a good boy or he would not bring him anything back.

This made Jake's day. He was already a good boy making good grades and he would see his beloved Ronnie soon. Maybe he would be there in time for his birthday or at least by the holidays. Things were getting better and he hoped that soon all this crazy stuff in his head which made him do crazy things would be gone.

Chapter 41

"Many demons are in woods, in waters, in wilderness, and in dark pooly places ready to hurt and prejudice people; some are also in the thick black clouds, which cause hail, lightning and thunder, and poison the air, the pastures and the grounds."
~ **Martin Luther**

Jake loved his trusty old bicycle and has been on it as much as possible. It is an old, rusty hand-me-down which was the cause of much joy for both Ronnie and Kenny and it takes Jake everywhere that he wants to go. Jake spends most of his time pedaling around the block over and over again. He enjoys riding with no hands especially quickly around the corners although many times he has fallen and scraped his knees. This doesn't seem to bother him because he always got right back up and did it again.

After becoming bored with the circle he ventured into the newer section of the neighborhood looking at the houses, the yards, the cars, and any people that may be out and about. He was also looking to see if he recognized anyone from school, especially a freckle faced brunette named Lisa. Jake had rode on the main roads before but with other people and was always told by Mina to be careful, look both ways and to be on the right side of the road.

The traffic on the rural roads back then was scarce and no one other than Mina believed it as dangerous. She would always tell her kids as well as their friends to be careful. Jake decided he was going alone on Brownswood Road and rest on the shoulder at the old wooden bridge. He carefully leaned on the railing and gazed below at the dark murky waters that quickly flowed under the shadows of the bridge and flanking trees rolling beyond into the thick dark forest that encircled his neighborhood.

Jake thought of his brother Kenny and his brother's friends dangling him by the ankles and threatening to drop him in. That would not have been a good thing because he probably would have drowned. Drowned like Tommy did but he didn't think that anyone had wished it on him like he did Tommy. Jake started the entire elbow, sole searching and cootie blowing ritual as well as the repetitive mantra after thinking about Tommy. He felt that by thinking these horrible thoughts that whatever evil swallowed up Tommy may do the same to him and these bazaar rituals would actually keep away the evil. He wondered that somehow this brook may be connected to Church Creek just a couple of miles away.

The water sounded refreshing as it passed over the larger protruding rocks and an old algae covered log from a fallen tree. Just at the end of the log on the grassy bank sat a coiled, fat water moccasin. A startled Jake did a second take then anxiously hopped on old rusty and pedaled north. It was difficult to steer his bike with one hand while blowing away the cooties on the other. He nearly lost control and crashed into the railing that would surely have sent him flying right on top of the awaiting reptile.

Heading north meant going towards the horse stables. Jake decided that would be a good place to go to earn a couple of dollars and get his mind off of the gloom and doom even though he forgot about it being a poop village. Jake truly loved dirt roads except when a speeding car would pass by leaving a cloud of dust in his face which followed by bogging down in the thick sand on the edge of the road. The woods between the bridge and the stables were thick with tall pines, oaks, poplar, hickory and many other varieties of trees and brush.

Jake passed a small barely visible trail; in fact he had never noticed it before. He figured that it must lead to the rear of the stables since it so close. Jake turned his bike around and stopped in front of the overgrown entrance. It was covered in pine straw and leaves but definitely had been a road or trail at some point in time. Curiosity got the better of him and his adventurous spirit was hungry so he pedaled forward and entered the dark path.

The path was bordered on both sides with old crooked post that was tangled with barbed wire and leafy vines. Jake now thought that this pathway maybe lead to someone's home or a moonshiners still but he hoped it would take him to the horse trails that he had been on before. Jake rode cautiously down the winding trail. He didn't see the huge spider web as he blasted right through it and he swiftly stopped. He dropped the bike and franticly started wiping off the sticky web hoping that he had no encounters with spiders.

Suddenly, a booming out of nowhere piercing scream shot though Jake's eardrums scaring him nearly to death. The garish and horrific scream came from a creepy old man who jumped from behind a huge tree. This man had wide, yellow eyes and a malicious, malevolent face and he ran towards Jake with both arms outstretched with his gnarly black fingers with long filthy nails clawing out at Jake. The old man reached down and grabbed a long, thick tree branch then ran after Jake trying to club him with it. Jake was already frightened from the spider web and now he nearly pissed his pants and probably would have if he hadn't froze solid for a split second waiting for his heart to beat again.

The rebarbative screaming and yelling continued.

The toothless, screaming devil was nearly on him when Jake knew he was going to die a horrible death if he didn't move quickly. He jumped on his bike and tried to pedal but the bike wasn't moving because he was two inches deep in mud. Oh no, not mud he questioned. The pernicious old man had blocked the road and Jake though maybe he was leading him to a whole village of toothless devils with yellow eyes all screaming and running after the small boy on the old rusty bike. Jake quickly hopped off of the bike and desperately pushed it to dry ground all the while thinking he was about to die.

"Don't fail me now," Jake said to his bike as he jumped back on and pedaled as hard as he could to escape the terrifying old man. No sooner than he escaped the muck the bike started sliding on fallen pine straw. It alternated sides with each push of his strong legs as Jake's knees were scraping the ground every time the bike tilted. He was afraid to look back he knew the devil would bite off his face.

Jake gazed back over his shoulder and the evil man was staring right through his young soul with the meanest eyes Jake had ever seen. The monster was still screaming that loud ghastly sound. Jake had never been more afraid in his life. "Please Lord, get me out of here. I will never ride alone in the woods again; oh I want my mama. MAMA!"

Jake prayed and cried as he continued pedaling hard and fast then the worst thing that could possibly happen happened. The rain came down in buckets or cats and dogs as he heard Uncle Hal say on many occasions. Where was Uncle Hal anyway? The ground became soggy, his tires again were stuck in the mud and he could not move.

The approaching toothless devil was grimacing pure evil; his yellow, fiery eyes were even livelier as he thrilled in Jake's mishap. He started walking fast towards Jake with his stick waving in the air. Jake fell off the bike into the mud with the heavy rain pounding in his eyes. Jake started crying and yelling for help as the old scary monster was closer. Jake finally managed to stand up and grab his bike. He pushed it as he ran deep into the woods away from the bogeyman that Kenny had always warned him of. Jake now knew that the bogeyman was real and he has seen him face to face.

The rain fell harder as it began to sting as it hit Jake's body and face. Jake could barely see where he was going as it got darker and the woods got thicker. The yellow eyes behind were like headlights as they got closer and closer. Jake ran into a large, fallen pine tree that blocked the muddy trail. The impact knocked him backwards which was the last place he wanted to go. While he was frantically pushing himself up out of the mud only to sink further he looked straight into the black eyes of the pale ghost lady who slithering behind the shrubbery.

"Oh crap!"

Jake clumsily turned over onto all fours and pushed with all of his might until he was stabilized on his feet. He was not quite upright but he was close enough. The hard rain kept pounding into his eyes nearly blinding him but he tried to keep his head bowed for protection and reached his arms out to guide his way.

Jake struggled with fingers, toes and everything in between to get over the colossal log which was nearly to his chin. He looked on either side of the fallen log and it stretched into the darkness where he did not want to go as he felt the devil's noxious breath on his now muddy neck.

"Oh Crap, what do I do?!"

He didn't want to engage in a fight because he knew he would be eaten alive so he leaned his bike against the tree, put his right foot on the seat to give him a better advantage and climbed and clawed to get to the top. Decomposed bark crumbled loose and Jake dropped back and fell on his bike which cracked a rib or two. Jake howled and screamed loudly, as he fell into the mud.

Jake started kicking his feet and legs to get out but the mud was now above his chest and rising. He sank deeper and faster with each movement. He looked up above into the tall dark trees with the silvery rain drubbing his eyes and there on one of the large branches sat his dead best friend Tommy smiling at him with a mendacious grin.

"Jake, are you okay, Jake? Jake, you were having a nightmare," Mina said to her youngest son as she was awaking him from a deep sleep.

Mina had heard him screaming and immediately ran to his room where he was tossing and turning and screaming for help.

A clammy Jake opened his eyes to find his sympathetic mother sitting on the edge of his bed with her gentle hands on his shoulder. He grabbed her and hugged her tightly and knew she would protect him from the bogeyman. Jake knew that his mama would always protect him no matter what. That is the one thing he always knew he could count on his entire life.

Chapter 42

"I wanna go home."
~ **Ronnie Willoughby**

Recuperating on a hospital ship floating in the Pacific Ocean while lost in a drug induced dream about the young farm girl wearing pigtails and dressed in a blue and white plaid dress who is also lost in a dream as she clicks her ruby heels together and repeated the axiom three times in hope and desperation.

There's no place like home; Dorothy Gale's ageless statement rang true to everyone, especially Ronnie Willoughby.

There were only three major television networks in the day and choices were slim but once a year during the spring *The Wizard of Oz* would come to visit. This year it blew into town on Mina's birthday so it was a good day all the way round. It was Ronnie, Kenny and Jake's favorite movie and the anticipation was almost as exciting as Santa Claus. Jake was frightened by the wicked witch and the flying monkeys yet he couldn't resist the thrill, much like that of a rollercoaster ride. He enjoyed being scared for a few seconds as long as it was only a few seconds. He knew the ending of both the movie and the coaster ride; he could endure anything that long with a positive ending in sight.

As Ronnie awoke he stared at the ceiling and he looked across the ward at the other wounded soldiers, all of whom were wrapped in bandages on different parts of their bodies. Most were healing quickly and heading home. Ronnie solemnly stared at the sleeping warriors. Some were snoring and some were twisting and turning to get comfortable. It was their first shot at real sleep in a long time due to the morphine and pure exhaustion from combat and their fight against death. Ronnie recognized no one as they were from different branches of the military but with one common goal; rid the world from communist rule but mostly to protect one another while in combat.

Ronnie was tired of lying on his back and was over the constant nausea from sea sickness. He was sick of the crappy food, the constant barrage of foul language, the smell of alcohol and iodine and he didn't like all of the agonizing screams echoing throughout the ship. He was thirsty, which was a constant and couldn't wait to drink good old John's Island water. "Cool, Clear Water", he could hear his Uncle Hal singing the Sons of the Pioneers western song.

Ronnie craved a cigarette, he craved his family and John's Island and his mom's cooking. He craved Wavy's finger picking bluegrass melodies, the noise of Kenny picking on Jake and craved Christine with her soft warm body and gentle touches along with her childish giggle. He wanted to be home. He never wanted to leave home again and he would never, ever wear olive green again. "I wanna go home," he hoarsely uttered to no one there. The young wounded soldier was near tears but he wouldn't dare let these wounded soldiers see blubbering from the only survivor from the Mother's Ridge ambush.

In his attempts to sleep, Ronnie had reoccurring visions of blood and eight dead comrades with their bodies tattered and shredded from war. The screams from his buddy, Ben in his final seconds all haunts him even in his conscious state. He tried desperately to block it all out and make it go away and to pretend it never happened. Ronnie would close his eyes and think of making love to Christine out beyond the pear orchard where everything was peaceful, easy, and blissful. He could hear Wavy strumming his guitar and singing about an intoxicated rat and he would drift away for a short while only to awaken to the same horrible stench and maddening surroundings the next morning while being poked and prodded by doctors and nurses.

"There's no place like home, there's no place like home, there's no place like home."

Chapter 43

"O'er the nights brim, day boils at last."
~ Robert Browning

"Nothing can stop me now…cause I'm The Duke of Earl." Jake heard Gene Chandler exclaiming from Kenny's room on the portable Admiral record player. Jake was watching *Gomer Pyle USMC*, as Gomer and his girlfriend are unable to make a decision on what to do for the evening. Jake laughed to himself then said aloud "Step aside Gomer, let big Daddy take the wheel, ha-ha. I'll show what to do with Lou Ann."

Wavy had already turned in for the night and Mina was finishing up the dishes. Ronnie was on the mend in the San Francisco Bay and Uncle Hal was lightly rocking on the front porch enjoying the singing frogs, crickets and the garrulous bobwhite. Jake was so pleased that he was home in his safe living room and everything was good.

The day had been a decent one after he realized that everything that had happened in the woods was only a terrible nightmare. He couldn't help but think about it all day because it was so intense, distressing and realistic. Jake knew one thing for sure; he would not dare travel down one of those side roads ever again. Jake looked over at his beautiful, soothing mother who was watching the television and munching on popcorn. Down the hallway he heard Kenny singing "At the Hop" and over at the large picture window he could see Uncle Hal's shadow moving back and forth under the dim porch light. He felt safe, real safe as he lay on the couch. He put his head on the big fluffy pillow and drifted off to sleep… good night sweet Prince. Good night Gomer, good night Lou Ann.

Bad night for sleep young fellow as the nightmares continue…

Jake loved fishing; he found himself sitting on the bank of an unfamiliar pond beneath a large red maple tree with a cane pole in hand and the line in the water which reminded him of Tom Sawyer.

The bright afternoon sun mirrored itself on the crystal pond as Jake pulled the bill of his straw hat down over his heavy lidded eyes. He dropped the pole from his hands into his lap after dozing off and after what seemed like hours something heavy tugged at his line nearly pulling the pole out of his lap. Startled, he looked up and was surprised to see the moon instead of the sun lighting the pond. He quickly grabbed the pole and pulled vigorously as his feet were sliding in the damp soil out from under him.

Where is everybody? He pondered, realizing that he was alone. "Where am I?" He added aloud, looking around at the strange surroundings.

Jake could hear hundreds of crickets and bull frogs harmonizing in the cattails on the edge of the pond as if cheering him on or perhaps they were cheering for whatever had hooked old Sawyer on the grassy bank. The moon was full, never brighter as it illuminated and orchestrated a night at the opera with the correspond stars. Jake's heart beat faster; he didn't believe he could hold on to the pole much longer. This had to be the granddaddy of 'em all and he wasn't gonna let it get away. He heedfully continued to pull on his line trying not to break it.

Heavy footsteps impinged just behind him and as he turned what he saw made him drop his jaw and his pole. A nearly complete emaciated and decomposed Tommy ran at him with pure hate and evil in his eyes, just like the old man with the large stick but this time it was his best friend with whom he felt responsible for his death. Jake tried to scream but no sound came from his parched mouth. Tommy got closer with outreached arms.

Jake had no choice but jump into the moonlit pond and swim under the water as long as his young lungs would allow. He desperately felt the need to breathe as he attempted to push himself upward but something had grabbed his left leg and it was pulling him back. He fought as hard as he could but whatever had a hold of him was winning. Was it Tommy or was it whatever had taken his bait?

Oh my God! Is this it? He thought while his lungs were filling up and near explosion. *Please forgive me God*…Jake knew he was a goner and his last thoughts were of his family, especially his mom.

At that same second the sodden branch that had tangled on his pants leg snapped into and Jake bolted to the surface at the same second he was taking his last breath. His drenched head burst up out of the dark water as he gasped for air. Tommy sat on the bank beneath the maple tree where the leaves were scarlet in the alluring path of the moon. His pale contrast overwhelmed his frightened friend.

"How does it feel?" Tommy said, with a sneer; "Except you got a second chance, look at me…Thanks, Buddy!"

Jake's eyes widened in extreme fright as he felt his body fluids doing what they had been threatening to do for some time. The same thing he wanted to do, get the hell out of Dodge. Again, something grabbed him tightly but this time it was his right arm. As he shifted around to see, Kenny was standing over him looking very fretful and concerned.

"Jake, wake up, wake up Jake," Kenny said, shaking his brother to come to.

"You stole my baseball you stupid jerk!"

Kenny realizing that Jake was still asleep continued to shake his brothers shoulder until he awoke.

"Oh heck, Jake you just crapped yourself!"

"Kenny, is that really you?" Jake looked at his brother in total surprise and yet relieved, literally.

"Yes it's me. You okay? I think you had another nightmare. You go to the bathroom and clean up; I'll change your sheets."

Jake gladly obeyed his brother's command.

"I'm sorry," Jake said feebly, looking back at his sympathetic brother.

"It's okay. I'm sorry about the nightmares." Kenny was heartfelt in his concern for his little dumb brother. "Maybe you can tell me about them tomorrow if you feel like it."

Jake would never forget the compassion that he saw in his brother's eyes. Kenny quietly removed, replaced and washed the soiled sheets so his little brother could have a good night's sleep.

Chapter 44

*"Forgotten mornings when he walked with his mother through the
parables of sunlight and the legends of the green chapels."*
~ Dylan Thomas

Kenneth Terrance Willoughby was an apple cheeked, happy and
lovable child. He was always a mama's boy, hence the resentment
towards newcomer baby Jake. Kenny always had a twinkle in his eye
and a deep from the belly loud and hearty laugh that pulled in and
made you laugh with him. He was an endearing child to everyone that
knew him as he grew from an adorable fat baby to a tall, husky,
affable teen.

Kenny was always close to Mina who was the love of his life, his
precious mama. Kenny stayed close to Mina even as a teen. He would
be in the kitchen as she cooked, sat beside her at the dinner table and
would be with her in the den when winding down watching television.
He would always go shopping or running errands with his mother and
was never far from her side.

Kenny was very different from his brothers. He had dissimilar interest
and preferred to hang with the girls most of the time and showed very
little attention to sports or masculine activities except when his dad
dragged him along for fishing or crabbing. No one really seemed that
concerned about it, occasionally at school he endured some hounding
but that came to an abrupt halt when Ronnie stepped in. Ronnie was
typically close by until he graduated leaving Kenny to fend for himself
and their youngest brother.

As Kenny grew older, the less he wanted to be outside, the less he
enjoyed the outdoors. It seemed that the television took control of his
spare time which disappointed his father. Kenny also loved music and
commonly had a transistor radio jammed in his ear while his eyes were
on the television set. Jake wasn't the only Willoughby boy that was
changing but no one would ever have imagined Kenny's future.

As he matured, Kenny wanted to spend even more time with his mom and his sister Diane. His sister had spent considerable time with young Kenny from the moment he was born and she always felt very motherly towards him. Truly, it possibly primed her for motherhood and it was definitely a big help to her mother besides she loved the little boy like her own.

Diane would always say there was just something special about Kenny that no one could define. Maybe it was his big happy eyes, adorable cheeks, delightful behavior and infectious laughter. Even after Diane was married and had children of her own she would have her chubby little brother over at her house as much as possible. He was much like an older brother to her children and babysat them on many occasions. They became very fond of their uncle and likewise.

Chapter 45

"Happiness is not a destination. It is a method of life."
~ **Burton Hillis**

Bryce was twenty-three when he first set his eyes on the lovely Diane who was just sixteen and still in school. He was the only son of Dr. Wilbur Adams and Florence Hutchins Adams. Dr. Adams was the only family medical doctor on John's Island during the thirties, forties and early fifties until he succumbed to heart failure in the very same home which served as his office.

Bryce was a tall, thin man with light brown hair whom Mina often said resembled Leslie Howard who played Ashley Wilkes from *Gone with the Wind.* Being an only child; a spoiled youngster therefore very set in his ways and used to getting everything he wanted including a beautiful teenager knew immediately that the young, flirty brunette would someday be his bride. The two started dating and married two days after she graduated high school against the will of both sets of parents.

Diane and her new husband honeymooned in Jamaica and 10 months later they were the proud parents of Paul Hutchins Adams. Hutch as he was called was Mina's first grandchild and two years after that came Mina's first granddaughter, Sara Drew Adams. Then one year after Sara was born Mina had her final child, Jacob Jr. who was already an uncle the second he entered the world; already Jake was dissimilar.

Diane lived off Angel Oak Road on several acres in a large 1920's clapboard farm house surrounded by live oaks and azaleas. It was bordered at the south end by Bohicket Creek also known as Church Creek because of St. John's Episcopal Church on the corner and magnificent southern crimson sunsets. "One of the prettiest places on the island," Diane often boasted of her home which actually was a very true statement. It had a large dock leading out to the river and Bryce had a couple of boats.

Quite often Bryce would take Wavy and his boys fishing and oyster gathering around many of the Sea Islands and even into the open ocean where they would land many prized catches of grouper, sheep head, sea bass, red snapper and countless dolphin.

Wavy also enjoyed the fishing which he grew up doing but had not had that luxury in the last several years so when the opportunity presented itself he jumped on it. On several occasions Wavy would take Ronnie, Kenny and Jake around the islands in the Jon boat and they would load up on the red drum or whatever that would take the hook. To Wavy, these were quiet, relaxing and the best of times. He preferred boating in the early mornings knowing when the fish were hungry.

Of course it was always a struggle to get the boys up that promptly and sometimes he just went alone. Wavy had always been an early riser, having grown up on a farm. He liked to jump on things right away to get it over with noting there was no sense in wasting the day away. Like the fish, Wavy and his sons were hungry too and would eat fried smoked sausage sandwiches on the boat that Mina would prepare for them. In proper season, they found time to cast many a net for enough shrimp to fill three deep freezers. Wavy thoroughly enjoyed these outings with his sons and just enjoyed nature in general as he favored the outdoors.

Jake and his brothers would frequently suck from the shell the salty bivalve mollusk known as oysters that Wavy would pluck fresh from the muddy shorelines and toss into the boat. Jake was sure that he had swallowed pounds of the mud over the years. They had many close calls in the sludge as the tide would recede and the Jon boat would become stuck and a friendly local would always drift by and toss them a line and tow them away from the ravenous muck.

Lots of time they all were thoroughly astounded when they would watch the playful porpoises come right up to the boat. Wavy loved it as much as his sons did. Jake never forgot the time when Ronnie dove in and swam with two of the jocular mammals alarming everyone in the boat.

Diane Jones Adams was a social butterfly. She loved being around people and loved the attention that came with it. She regularly hosted parties and gathering for reason or not; to her life was a party and that was reason enough. She was proud of her home and had every right to be. She was also proud of her striking good looks that she enjoyed showing off as well. Diane, given that she was a born flirt really knew how to entertain. All the men from several neighboring sea islands enjoyed the gatherings even with kicks in the shins from their wives or significant others for giving too much attention the lovely and beautiful hostess.

Diane would have her family over as much as possible. They particularly enjoyed the cookouts which usually consisted of salad, baked potato with sour cream and a large medium- rare T-bone steak seared on an open fire. In season there would be many oyster roast and shrimp boils as well.

They also loved the views along the creek, sitting beneath moss draped branches of the many grand old oaks and of course the soul seizing sunsets. The sunsets at Church Creek were magnificent and glorious. They were frequently enjoyed from the back porch, patio and dock by the residents of the estate along with their family and friends. However, Jake's favorite thing about the property at the time was the huge coy pond near the house.

Many, many times in his early life Jake had passed over and under the Church Creek Bridge. It was a stunning spot; the Spartina grass, the creek mud, coastal birds, the tall trees swathed with long strands of Spanish moss hanging over the inviting river on the horizon with its zigzagging tributaries and inlets encircling the island. It was an artist or photographer's dream.

Many times he would sit on his sister's dock and just stare into the horizon wondering what might be at the other end. The overwhelming scent of the pluff mud was something they all had grown up with and appreciated. Jake was born into the world respectful of the eloquent pluff mud, the fetid redolence, the greasy, gray realm that bordered his island.

Little did Jake know that sitting on the dock and taking it all in that one day this exquisite place would become the passage of his most horrifying experience and that it would ruin many lives; it became his least desired place on earth.

Chapter 46

"The dreadful dead of dark midnight."
~ **William Shakespeare**

It's now Halloween; creepy, scary, and fun. The air is cold and the trees are bare. Nature compliments the occasion with its own touch of magic. At school, Mrs. Walker wore a black mask and gave the kids that did not dress up in costume the same sort of mask to wear over their eyes which reminded Jake of the Lone Ranger.

She had the students each take turns reading aloud ghost stories that she had selected. After the stories they drew pictures of scary things such as black cats, witches, ghost, and Frankenstein. Then after lunch they had a little party where she gave each student their very own bag of treats. They would drink a small paper cup full of fruit punch and eat their candy and toss paper airplanes across the classroom. Jake thought he was back in grammar school.

Jake loved legally breaking the rules because there were no consequences or discipline. The rambunctious boys had to be asked to quiet down on a few occasions but overall it was a great day of school; fun for a change. As he turned to look at Mrs. Walker's buttons Jake's heart skipped a beat for a split second when he believed he saw Lisa Wilson behind one of the costume mask.

After a double take he realized it was Donna Hill, another pretty brunette. The kids lined up and took their turns behind the blindfolds and dunked their faces into the large metal tub of water that held several red apples. They each bobbed until they each had one in their mouths. Jake's newfound phobia would not allow him to participate.

"Uh, I don't like apples." He lied.

The bus ride home was noisier than usual due to the sugar rush and the extra flow of adrenaline brought on by the party and the excitement of dressing up and Trick or treating later on.

Jake and Kenny hopped off the bus in front of their house along with the four remaining Stern kids, the Garner twins, Billy Burns and the soundless, sullen Johnny Moore who always sat alone in the rear of the bus.

Quietly everyone turn their heads to watch the remote teen drift in the direction of his house with his head drooped as far as it possibly could leaving everyone to wonder how he even knew where he was headed.

Several months had passed since the drowning of Tommy Stern and his siblings seem to be pretty much back to normal at least on the outside. They didn't appear to hold any kind of grudge towards Johnny concerning their brothers drowning but they kept their distance from him just the same. But Johnny, who was more responsible for what happened to Tommy than Jake, seemed to be getting worst by the day. He rarely spoke and his looks were haggard and insipid; unfortunately he didn't need to wear a costume because he was already frightening the heck out of people without one.

Johnny would not be Trick or Treating; he did nothing anymore but go to school and return home. Jake had assumed that he was the only one being tormented by the past summer's tragedy but when he looked in the mirror he seemed to look ordinary and healthy, unlike poor Johnny who was downright startling. Jake's mask of horror was wrapped around his poor little brain and squeezing it like a vice.

Later that evening Kenny was over at the Stern's house helping the sisters get into costume. At home, Jake was being outfitted by Mina and his visiting sister Diane who brought over her kids Hutch and Sara to make the rounds in the neighborhood since their neighbors were few and far between.

Everyone was wearing a thin plastic mask with exaggerated faces attached to the head with a thin elastic string. Some wore old white sheets and some adorned old clothes that were way too large. Others had on really cheap outfits made out of some flammable material like the Superman suit.

In a large freakish group Frankenstein, Dracula, and Zorro along with the Lone Ranger, Barbie, a princess, a cowboy, a wolf man, a genie, a sad clown and a funky pirate went from house to house knocking on doors, ringing doorbells and yelling those famous words in perfect harmony.

"TRICK OR TREAT!"

The brown paper grocery bags were filling quickly with all sorts of candy and a couple of apples. The after dark activity kept the kids, especially the boys from feeling the cold air except when an occasional breeze would jet by and then the group would hover together to feel the warmth of each other's bodies.

Diane lead the group of kids with the oldest being Kenny and Barbara Stern. Jake always had a mild crush on Barbara because of her pretty face and curvy figure. Now she had the highly developed body that he couldn't stop staring at and even more so tonight as she seemed to have grown giant breast in a matter of hours.

Barbara was dressed as Barbara Eden's genie. With the chilly night air she had her mother's shawl wrapped around her shoulders and occasionally it would slip down and Jake would get a quick glimpse of her stimulated breasts protruding through her halter top and get a quick glance at her smooth flat belly. It was happening.

Jake had been noticing several sets of female breasts lately; Mrs. Walker's and Anna Mae's super huge booby traps at Staley's Store but they did nothing for him like Barbara's just did. He'll never look at boobs the same again as they were sticking out for everyone to admire. Until now he had never noticed that she even had breasts, in fact, he doesn't remember ever paying any attention to her at all. Jake never knew just how big Barbara's were until now, even bigger than that day in the bikini at Green Hole. *Wow,* he thought, *Halloween brought out the breasts in all the females. Too bad it's just once a year.*

Now he just HAD to see some more boobs. Barbara was fifteen and the prettiest girl Jake had ever seen and of course she always ignored Jake. He looked over at her younger sisters Kathy and Julie and they were very pretty but they had no breasts. None that he could see anyway ~ oh wait, Kathy's boobs seemed to grow bigger as he gaped at them, the chilly air helped with that.

Kenny the clown stayed close to Barbara but he never noticed that every time that she bent over or took a step, Jake anticipated fallout. He was in dreamland and enjoying himself for a change. He felt a little jealous that Kenny was hanging with and bumping against the enormous boobies. *Zorro may have to prod forward~ where's my sword?*

Barbara often would lean over to inspect her bag of goodies and Jake made sure that his Zorro mask lined up properly so he could assess the situation. *Would the flash light be too obvious?*

Jake just recently learned that he truly liked boobs. He had never paid them much attention until the lovely Mrs. Walker showed up in his classroom. The nerve of some people, causing young boys to become anxious and all, you know? Now between all of his anxious irrational rituals he developed a new fixation, he had become a lover of boobs. Boob gazer! The Sears circular advertising women's underwear was his new favorite read. The curvy, near nude women seemed to avert his attention somewhat from all the craziness. Jake liked them; he surely liked them a lot. Jake was quite excited, he felt that he better eat some candy.

Another quick look at Barbara's practically bare chest… yes, yes, yes, the night was getting colder and the boobs were getting bigger… all around him…ah, to be stampeded and smothered in a barrage of giant boobs. Suddenly Jake realized that he really loved Halloween.

"TRICK OR TREAT!"

The group came upon Johnny Moore's house; it was completely dark and deathly quiet. The pitch black yard and the eerie house appeared black and empty. It resembled a haunted house that Jake had been hearing about in some of the stories that Mrs. Walker had them read today in class.

Out of nowhere Kenny, with his arms outstretched in zombie form, blurted out in a ghoulish voice, "They're coming to get you Barbara," from *Night of the Living Dead.*

Barbara screamed, "Stop it," as she irritably pushed Kenny away. This girl needs some cuddling Jake thought.

Kenny couldn't stop laughing.

"You're mean," Julie screamed, in defense of her sister.

The Stern children were quick to walk past the Moore house as Diane called for them to slow down while she jogged towards them in the cold October air. The willows whistled as the cold breeze sailed through their long relaxed branches while the sounds of delighted kids on the other side of the block echoed when they examined their bag of treats.

Inside the shadows of his cold bedroom, Johnny Moore peeped through the blinds of his window as he heard the commotion outside. The deep set, sad eyes watched the motley crew as it watched his house. Johnny missed Halloween as last year he lived in a much larger neighborhood and wished he had never moved. Johnny blamed his parent for this as he was new in the neighborhood when he befriended Tommy and stole Jake's baseball. Now he knows that he can never be friends with anyone because no one likes him and everyone at school whispers about him as he walks towards them or past them.

Johnny was blamed for the death of the very popular and likable Tommy Stern. Johnny has had several very bad months since and had quit eating and quit talking to his parents. He barely made it to school each day and he quit bathing. Everyone had noticed a foul odor about him. He spent most of his time staring out of his bedroom window at his could have been friends and could have been fun.

Johnny never was much of a good kid. He was always breaking the rules and stealing and lying. He never obeyed his parents; he was a spoiled, lonely child. He knew he did wrong but just didn't care. As the group passed his house and went to the next one.

Johnny got closer to his bedroom window careful not to be seen as he watched them walk away. He was startled when he saw shadows on the walkway lurching towards the front door which was one lone trickster. Johnny, still peering through the curtains, wondered who was who behind the mask.

Chapter 47

Fridays were always a good day at school. Mrs. Walker was always in a good mood and her Friday blouses seemed to be more revealing than normal. Two fun days in a row and they go by so quickly but still excited all the students. The morning bus loaded up with happy kids anxiously discussing their Trick or Treating with one another. When the bus pulled up in front of Johnny's house all kids eyes stared out of the large school bus windows at the ambulance parked in the driveway.

Whenever you see an ambulance you know something bad has happened. The medics slammed the rear doors shut and got inside with no rush at all. When everyone realized that Johnny wasn't boarding the bus, the whispers began as the bus slowly passed the yard. The bright red ambulance backed out of Johnny's driveway into the street and slowly went in the opposite direction of the school bus.

The kids ran to the rear of the bus and gazed out of the windows and watched the ambulance, hoping to catch a sign of someone. There was no one anywhere. Not in the ambulance windows and no one was in the yard. This was the opposite of the chaos in the Stern's yard, back in June. The house and the yard all appeared to be eerily quiet with no sign of life at all.

"What in the world has happened?" Everyone on the bus asked at exactly the same time.

The noise and clatter got louder. Abruptly, the good mood changed and that sickening feeling entered Jake's belly again. That uncontrollable nervousness and depression along with his sweaty palms felt soiled and contaminated like they were covered in a contagious disease. In his mind they were filthy and he desperately needed to blow away the evil before something dreadful happened to him or his family and he didn't care who saw him do it.

This alleviated the immediate urgency but not totally resolved because what he really wanted to do was to scour them with hot soapy water. He wanted to look at the bottoms of his shoes to make sure that they were clean even though he knew that they were pretty spotless. They're clean, everything is okay Jake told himself as he utter that sentence to himself three times before he felt that maybe, just maybe they were clean and that it could wait until he got off the bus and could run behind a tree and checked like he often has in the past.

Jake started to feel as though he was losing his breath and he quickly needed fresh air. Maybe the complete routine would help; he quickly looked to see if anyone actually maybe looking at him instead of the ambulance as it turned on to the main highway towards town. He quickly looked at each elbow the very best that he could, of course he could never see the entire elbow but just the effort of seeing the majority of it eased his tormented mind somewhat.

Jake gazed at each elbow three times intermittingly and could no longer wait, then the same with the bottoms of his feet, then he blew each palm three times. Finally he was breathing better. Everyone on the bus was too busy gossiping about Johnny's horror to notice Jake's horror, everyone that is except Kenny who left his seat next to Barbara and made Stevie move so he could sit next to his busy little brother.

Kenny gave Jake a big apple cheeked beam with dazzling large lashes framing his big brown eyes. He put his right arm around his shoulder and told Jake "Everything will be alright. After school we'll walk to Staley's and get a Coke and a moon pie, then we'll walk over to the stables and ride."

Jake huge eyes were filled with tears and he knew that he needed help. He knew that something was dreadfully wrong with him. For a split second he wanted grab his brother and cry and confess but there were way too many witnesses and he couldn't possibly take that chance; it was awkward enough as is. The show of support from Kenny at that moment meant more to Jake than anything. He later regretted that he never got the opportunity to tell his brother that.

At that precise moment, Johnny Moore was riding to the morgue at Memorial Hospital in the very same ambulance that carried the body of young Tommy Stern, earlier in the summer. Two young boys from the same neighborhood are now dead, only a few months apart. What was going on? This was beginning to become really creepy, and Jake just hoped that he wasn't next.

The next day, they all found out what allegedly happened to Johnny. The story goes; sometime around midnight on Halloween night Johnny had decided he had enough of the guilt. He knew that everyone blamed him for what happened to Tommy almost as much as he blamed himself. Johnny had picked on everyone as soon as he moved in the neighborhood but really gave Tommy a hard time trying to influence him to become mean like him. He could feel and see everyone's hatred of him. Tommy was well liked; he was not and never was.

So, after sitting in his dark room and listening to kids outside having a wonderful time Trick or Treating and just enjoying each other and life as a child, he decided this world was not for him. He stripped himself of his clothes, climbed into the tub with his Case pocket knife given to him by his grandfather this past Christmas and the same one that he used to carve his initials into Angel Oak. He planned to carve again, only this time deeply into both wrists and he writhed in pain until he bled out and then he passed into another world, a world full of lost tormented souls.

"I wish you were dead."

…Had some spirit overheard Jake and took vengeance against the ball thieves? Why would any spirit side with me, Jake wondered?

Out of the three that were playing pickle, which is defined as a predicament, with Jake's new ball that day; Jake was the only one left. He felt that the nervous habits and routines were eventually going to cause him to lose his mind. He became frightened; think of something pleasant ~ quickly!

213

A vision from earlier in the evening popped into his head at that very second; big boobs made it easier…tit for tat. Jake almost smiled. He decided to just fantasize about all of the mammary glands he had seen in the past evening. Maybe this would take his mind off of all of the awfulness.

Chapter 48

"Our birthdays are feathers in the broad wing of time."
~ **Jean Paul Richter**

To celebrate his birthday they were all there; Jake's best of the best. Stevie, Chucky, Billy, Kathy, Julie, Barbara, Kenny and nephew Hutch and niece Sara both of whom happened to be older than Jake. A platter of small turkey sandwiches, a large white birthday cake and vanilla ice cream was ready to devourer. The group gathered around the cake as Mina lit the candles and lead them into the birthday song. Jake, with a sheepish smile made a wish and blew out the candles. Jake wished that the anxious habits would quickly go away and that Ronnie would hurry home.

They ate plenty, drank Kool-Aid, played pin the tail on the donkey and opened presents. Jake received what looked to be and smelled a lot like a brand new burgundy V-neck sweater. He had never owned a new sweater before; one that no one had worn out or out grew. This excited him very much since he had wanted one for some time. He also couldn't believe that he received a new pair of cowboy boots. No one had better steal them; you know what happened to the last guys?

Wow, what is going on? His old boots became supper for the Church Creek mud when Ronnie pulled him out of its hungry mouth. From his friends he got a couple of reading books, some comic books, candy and a yo-yo. Jake was hoping for a new bike but was reminded that if he was good that Santa Claus may bring him one. For years now Jake had been hearing rumors amongst his friends and classmates that Santa did not exist. Jake just could not imagine that because he loved old Santa almost as much as he loved Grandma's brown cake.

The kids played and enjoyed themselves despite what had happened last the last few months with Tommy and Johnny. This is Jake's first birthday that he can remember celebrating without his best friend. Tommy's sisters were all present and they seemed fine.

No one knew Johnny that well and they all blamed him for what happened to Tommy and as Jake heard others say, "What goes around comes around."

Jake was grateful for his gifts and for his friends and he verbalized his sentiments to them. He was also thankful for family, even Kenny; under his breath he mumbled these thanks to the good Lord. The excitement and noise thrilled Mina. She loved children and loved pleasing her own making them happy and having everything that they needed and if possible everything that they wanted. She didn't even notice that she was tired, a good tired. She had been up all night roasting a turkey, Jake's favorite, even though Grandma would roast one in just a few days for Thanksgiving.

Jake loved turkey sandwiches and so did the other kids and since that's what they wanted, that's what they got. Besides, it was a good, healthy birthday meal that would feed the entire family for days. Mina stayed up late tending to the turkey and got up early to bake the cake.

Mina was approaching 60 years of age but her young son and his friends energized her and kept her youthful, that's the way she felt anyway. She thoroughly loved doing these sorts of things for her kids and was extremely pleased that Jake came along otherwise there would be no more babies or young ones to tend to. It wasn't easy at her age but she did it all with a smile, never once complaining.

It's a mother's instinct to worry about her children and she did her share of that. Ronnie in Vietnam was causing her the most stress, Kenny and Jake constantly getting scratched and bruised and going through band aides and bottles of mercurochrome was a daily ritual. Speaking of rituals, she couldn't help but notice some of Jake's nervous habits and bothersome quirks when she would peak out of the windows to make sure that he was okay.

She prayed that this was something that he would quickly outgrow like one of his older brother's sweaters. Mina believes that it all began right after Tommy's drowning and that Jake missed his buddy and had too much free time on his hands and his edginess got the best of him.

Who thought of taking a child to a phycologist in those days? Mina's only familiarity with therapist was by watching one of her soap operas. She and her family worked issues out the old fashioned way ~ own their own through faith and prayer.

Chapter 49

"The world loves a spice of wickedness."
~ **Henry Wadsworth Longfellow**

Jake was excited because he knew it was going to be a long and fun filled weekend at Grandma's. He knew that there would be lots of great food, playing all kinds of games with his cousins, running around with the dogs, and learning to shoot pool at Uncle Melvin's store. He believed that this was the great break that he needed; maybe this would cure all of his woes.

Maybe he should just move to Grandma's he thought, while he was trying to fall asleep the night before the anticipated trip. He wondered why his dad even left there. What a great place. Why would anyone want to leave this magnificent open paradise to move to Charleston of all places? Jake never appreciated *his* beautiful and historical hometown until after he left it some forty years later.

Wednesday night before Thanksgiving, the men managed to get into the homemade scuppernong wine while they shot pool. Jake was the only kid there because Kenny was watching television with the women, including cousins Rhonda and Sheila. The older men lost patience with the rookie after a couple of hours and started playing for money. Jake sat on an old frayed barstool and watched the men get drunk and start stumbling and mumbling. *This is better than television* he thought.

After a while he caught a glimpse of the grotesque stuffed bobcat that sat on a shelf over the back counter in attack mode staring at all who entered and usually frightened any newcomers. He wondered what Uncle Melvin must have felt like when confronted with the large cat and how lucky he was to see it before it attacked. He wondered how he would react in the same circumstance. The ticking of the Pabst Blue Ribbon clock next to the dead cat made Jake nervous and antsy; so did the late hour. The loud, drunken men didn't help matters either. He discreetly checked the soles of each shoe three times each. On the final lap he noticed gum on the bottom of his left shoe. He had almost taken for granted that they would be clean and was quickly switching to the elbow check when he had to do a double take to make sure. He nearly freaked out when he thought it could be dog crap, but under further investigation he knew it was gum. *What idiot would spit out their nasty gum for someone to step in?* He spent the next several minutes in the filthy bathroom. Thank goodness that there paper towels available, nice, thick, brown heavy duties at that. He placed a couple on the floor to rest his shoeless foot on while he scrubbed the bottom of his sneaker with several more that were doused in the yellowish soap, he prayed it was soap, that barely squirted from the mucky, moldy dispenser. When all was said and done, the soap past the sniff test, he washed his hands, soaped, and rinsed three times each. He was again compelled to look at each sole three times each. While he was in there he could see his elbows in the foggy mirror, right, left, right, left, right, left.

"Make sure you flush that toilet at least twice." Uncle Melvin growled.

Jake was mortified. *Why at least twice? Had he been spied upon? Was the door cracked open?* He nervously appeared in the mirror, a frightened child. He felt lightheaded and afraid.

"Why?" He finally yelped.

"You been in there a while, that toilet will back up if you don't flush her twice." drawled his kind uncle.

"I was only washing my hands."

Everyone chuckled.

Jake carefully turned the faucet handle with a paper towel and dampened it and then used it to turn the knob to liberate himself from the stifling stench of the urine wrenched den of filth. He entered the smoky dark room with a huge worried grin on his face.

"You okay son?" Wavy inquired.

"Yasser."

Jake was wondering what was going on at Grandma's with Mama and Kenny. The darkness had settled in for the night and it was pitch black outside. Jake remembered all the stories about the "haints" and other scary creatures just beyond the woods in Gator Swamp behind Uncle Melvin's Store. Jake did not care; he wanted to get to Grandma's house. He was really panicky for some reason and would feel better with his mother. He did not know the telephone number to his grandmother's and he dared not ask the pool players. Jake did not want them making fun of him, not that they would but he didn't want to take that chance. He has learned that people say the darndest things when they're drinking that scuppernong wine. He gently sneaked out of the back door of the store that faced the side of Uncle Melvin's large white frame house which seemed very dark because Aunt Eula Mae was at Grandma's with everyone else.

Jake wondered slowly and carefully to the side of the store as not to disturb the partiers or the many dogs. He ducked under the window displaying an illuminated Pabst Blue Ribbon sign all the while looking towards the forest at the edge of the store and thinking of his nightmares with the terrifying old man running after him in the woods and the one with Tommy at the pond. He thought of the old ghost lady his dad had seen many years ago in those same woods. He got chills and became very scared. He wondered if there may be some connection with the ghost lady and him, who had the ghost lady been and why was she roaming the woods? Maybe there was more about his dear old dad than he was aware of.

Jake knew that he better bolt, but at that exact split second an owl must have seen Jake and let out a loud screech just over the roof of the store which in turn startled the dogs, and bolt he did. Jake never ran so hard in his life.

Can I make it?

What Jake assumed was hyenas, started barking loudly and chasing him. They were nearly on his heels and Jake never looked back. He just kept running as hard as he ever had.

It was a pitch black night, except for the one dim street light at the front of the entrance to the store. Jake used his instincts and prayed that he didn't fall in a ditch. Three hundred yards, but it seemed more like three hundred miles to Grandma's drive and then another two hundred yards to the front porch.

Can I make it?

At that instant, the bright quarter moon lit the way to Grandma's driveway entrance. Thank God, because he did not want to run into the woods. As he approached the drive, he quickly turned right and could see the dim lights on at the front of the house.

The tall cedar trees on either side of the sandy drive also frightened Jake because they were so tall, shadowy, and intimidating in the dark, like fortress walls.

He felt barricaded and breathless. He had to get to the house as fast as he could. He could see it, he was almost there. Please Lord, just a little further and a little faster. The dogs barked louder, as they snapped at his heels. It sounded like a dozen hyenas and hopefully he would not become supper for the scavenger dogs. He didn't want to be torn to threads as the vicious dogs ripped at his flesh and yanked out his heart. This was not the way Jake wanted to go. Maybe it was the way that Tommy, or whatever *it* was that had been haunting him, wanted him to go.

"Faster Jake, faster, HELP, HELP!" Jake screamed at the top of his lungs.

The screaming enticed the dogs even more.

Kenny came running onto the front porch followed by several women, as all the flood lights lit up the entire front yard. Jake jumped completely over the hedge row in front of the large porch and completely bypassed the seven large cement steps that lead to the top of the porch and right into the arms of his loving mother, whom he embraced securely, while trying to catch his breath.

The hyenas turned out to be three of Uncle Melvin's white shepherds, who were doing just like they had been doing for the last few days, following Jake around. As the frightened boy ran faster, so too did the dogs, having fun at Jake's expense, while he ran for his life. Everyone, especially Jake, was relieved when the dogs stopped at the bottom step as trained to do. They looked at each other like they were wondering what all the commotion was about this late at night.

The next morning, Wavy awoke before everyone as usual. He showered and dressed, and then he woke up Jake and Kenny, he couldn't find Jimmy. They all put on their jackets and went for a morning walk through the woods behind Grandma's house to look at the ruins of his grandfather's old home that had been destroyed in a fire many years before. This is something Wavy did on every trip home although he was careful to avoid the nearby area with the cemetery and the ghost lady, a place he had not visited since the snake bite.

Wavy and his sons enjoyed the crisp morning air, with scarfs around their necks and faces to brace against the wind chill as they got thicker into the woods. Jake just knew at any second something was going to jump out at them, and he was not let down. Jimmy shot out from behind a large pine tree and yelled, "BOO!" at the trio, startling everyone, including his dad.

Jimmy laughed at the petrified three. Kenny grabbing Wavy's left arm and Jake grabbing his right had to be a sight because Jimmy could not stop laughing and he was actually bent over nearly touching his toes. Wavy was not amused nor were Kenny and Jake who ran towards Jimmy as if they were going to kick his freckled-faced butt. Jimmy teasingly ran around in circles and then... BOOM, dead center against Jimmy's freckled forehead slammed an old hickory hoe handle as he stepped on its upward blade. Jimmy, dumbfounded, was knocked back several feet and nearly fell to the ground as he fought to keep his balance, reminding Jake of a goofy Jerry Lewis. He was more shocked than hurt, but a little dizzy, as he slowly sat on the ground to wait out the wooziness.

Kenny and Jake had the last laugh, as they all started picking blueberries. A frail Jimmy lifted himself off of the ground with a growing knot in the middle of his forehead. He knew he got what he deserved, and shrugged off their laughter and helped pick berries. What they all didn't know is that they were just mere inches from the chilly cloud of mist and haunting eyes lurking beyond the blueberry patch. Suddenly came a howling screech from deep in the forest, behind the old, long forgotten tombs of the century ago farmers. They all looked at each other with penetrating fear. Jimmy had been out here earlier all alone, or so he thought. Now he feels as though something had been watching him, maybe sizing him up for breakfast.

"Let's get the heck out here." Kenny whispered.

Confident and brave Wavy who no doubt heard this a thousand times growing up in these woods shrugged it off. "Not until we get all these berries."

"Well let's hurry then," Jimmy chimed in.

Jake looked up at his brave dad for safety and confidence and then plucked away at the juicy fruit.

They couldn't sense it nor see it; however, it did size them up.

They could smell wood burning in the fireplace and knew that everyone was up and a huge breakfast was to be had, they headed back, with their handkerchiefs full of huckleberries so that Grandma could make her fabulous muffins to compliment the grits, eggs and country ham. All washed down with Eight O'clock coffee. Jake looked at his Timex, 7:38, close enough. He giggled to himself.

Chapter 50

"In the sun that is young once only, time let me
play and be golden in the mercy of his means."
~ Dylan Thomas

And so Rockwell's painting come to life; Thanksgiving, 1968, just outside of Nichols, South Carolina, a late fall chill touches the surrounding forest of Grandma's house as smoke from the old stone chimney breezes through the cedar, pine, holly, poplar and pecan trees. The family is gathered inside at two large tables, one of which was brought from outside. Mina was thrilled that she did not have to roast another turkey; Grandma roasted this one and baked a large ham as well.

Everyone missed Ronnie as usual, but took comfort knowing that he was alive and well, recuperating and heading home soon. Just down the road, Uncle Melvin's wife, Aunt Eula Mae, baked and slaved over her own stove and brought the festive results over to Grandma's. Mina made the oyster stuffing, Uncle Olin's wife, Aunt Betty Lou, made the butter beans and okra. All the women enthusiastically pitched in to assist Grandma with the pecan pie, pumpkin pie, red velvet cake and of course, Grandma's famous brown cake.

The large family gathered around two cloth covered picnic tables and gave thanks to the Good Lord. They passed plate and platter and ate and ate until they were miserable.

"I'm full as a tick," Uncle Melvin said, while rubbing his bulging belly, drawing laughter from the hearty group.

Kenny would clear his throat or nudge at Jake when he noticed his little brother looking at the bottoms of his feet as a friendly reminder not to. Jake was startled that his brother had noticed and was deeply afraid of those consequences. This charming gathering made quite a picturesque and delightful country setting. The quaint and jolly laughter of all his loved ones, the smiles and genuine joy filling the air, one would think that Jake was a very happy boy. Jake seemed to no longer have the capability or propensity to be truly happy, this horror would shadow him most of his life. Deep inside his soul was always a feeling of dissatisfaction, anxiety, apprehension, and restlessness.

Ronnie couldn't get home soon enough. Jake was getting worse and he knew it. He would blow away the cuties from his palms almost every time he touched something or when he heard unpleasant words or news. He had more reoccurring, unpleasant thoughts and he felt that such thoughts were causing terrible things to happen to him and his family and friends. He couldn't stop the thoughts as they would just jumped into his head and the only way to make them go away was to go through the motions of awkward and consuming rituals.

Jake took comfort in touching the family bible every time that he passed by it sitting on the large table in the living room although he always had to make sure it was flush with the lines of the table, otherwise there would be something horrible lurking in the future. Just the quick touch gave him an inner peace. He could feel it flow from his fingertips into his arms and filling his body, he felt cleansed and protected.

Jake would look at pictures of Christ and the crucifix on the wall and feel rapid relief. He felt best looking into the eyes of Jesus Christ in the painting because right now Jesus was the only person he felt could help him because Ronnie was still floating on the Pacific Ocean on a huge ship having the time of his life or so Jake assumed.

"Please help me Lord," he would say three times, blow into his palms, look at the bottom of his shoes and check his elbows. "Everything is going to be alright." Three times he would repeat always careful not to be spotted by anyone.

Several times a day Jake would look at print of Jesus on the wall, touch the bible, avoid corners and cracks, wash his hands, dry them and repeat that process two more times, and make sure that everything around him was straight not crooked. He would walk into the kitchen where his mom spent most of her time, to take a look at her and smile and say "I love you." If none of that would feel exactly right or made him feel at ease, he would repeat it all until it did feel right, and if the fourth time was right, he had to do it again to avoid the number four.

Jake was spiraling out of control; something had a hold of him and it was exhausting to say the least. Jake was frantic in his thoughts. Was he cursed because of what he had said to Tommy? Jake believed that was his only explanation; Tommy's ghost seized control of his mind and very soul and would not let go, until he perished.

This is an awful way to live. Jake cried to himself after he would hide in the backseat of the Biscayne and stare up at the heavens. He would pray for Ronnie's return, pray for peace and happiness, pray that this horrendous curse would go away and that Tommy, or whomever, or whatever, would forgive him and leave him alone.

On many of occasions, a desperate Jake would ask aloud "What can I do?" while staring at the back windshield of the gold Chevy with tears streaming down his freckled cheeks.

…"Pass the pumpkin pie," Kenny yelled at Jake as he gulped down a swallow of the very best sweet tea known to mankind and interrupting Jake's daydream.

Later in the evening Wavy grabbed old Nellie, his beloved Gibson acoustic guitar, and picked and sang about lost love, tears, beers, lying, crying, dying and one very intoxicated rat.

The next morning the group enjoyed another hardy breakfast then the boys packed their gear and loaded the Biscayne and everyone said their goodbyes. Separately, Jake and Kenny received Grandma's secret gift of cash and both paid her back with huge hugs.

The long drive home was always a huge letdown for Jake and Kenny even with their stash of cash from Grandma's old hanky. Their woebegone expressions could be seen by Wavy in the rearview mirror so he would start singing one of his joyful favorites such she'll *be coming around the mountain.*

The next big event was Christmas; they were saving every dime and looking at every sales ad in the paper, along with the old faithful Sears and Roebuck catalog. Jake especially enjoyed the lingerie section; somehow he just had to get him one of those Playboy magazines. Jake kept his cash in his new, black, Marine Corps wallet, given to him by Ronnie at the beginning of the summer. Jake loved the smell of new leather and kept sniffing at it.

Even with the cold November air outside, Kenny rolled down his window for fresh air because the heat blowing from the front was stifling. Kenny pointed at a young man walking on the side of the road in curious wonder because he wasn't wearing a jacket or sweater and seemed to be in the middle of nowhere. Jake leaned out of the window for a peek, and out of the window went the new wallet full of cash.

"My wallet!" He screamed.

Wavy slowed down the Biscayne and pulled over to the side of the road. The young man was walking towards the wallet, Wavy slipped into reverse and backed up to the wallet and jumped out and grabbed it. The young man stared at the older man and vice-versa, reminding Jake of Matt Dillon and some poor idiot in a gun fight. Wavy had the odd feeling that he had seen those eyes before. He got back into his car and handed the wallet to his youngest son. Jake had the best parents and he knew it. He loved them both so much.

He looked over at Kenny, he even loved him too. Jake sniffed his wallet; he was so thrilled to have it back, he just knew that it was a goner but thanks to his brave dad, he had it back.

"Put that wallet in your pocket," Mina shouted, as the golden Chevy cruised down a quiet Highway 17 South towards Charleston.

"Yes ma'am," Jake said.

"Right now young man," Mina said.

"I am, I am!" Jake said.

Jake was thinking to himself as he peered out the window at trees and clouds that this was not one the better visits to Grandma's which is rare because the trips are usually very pleasing and relaxing. He wondered if anybody or anything was behind that.

After making sure that the door was locked, elbows, soles, and palms were clean Jake snuggled up into the corner of the large backseat opposite his brother and drifted off to sleep.

Chapter 51

"The world in solemn stillness lay to hear the angels sing."
~ E.H. Sears

Almost six months after he left home for his journey as a soldier and a patriot, Ronnie returns as a decorated Vietnam Veteran with two purple hearts; a true hero.

Jake, Kenny, Mina and Uncle Hal searched the Charleston International Airport terminal looking for their beloved son, brother, nephew, and American Hero. Soldiers returning from Vietnam were greeted by war protesters who actually cussed, spit and yelled at the very men in uniform who fought for their freedom. Their freedom to be selfish assholes, Ronnie realized. Ronnie's welcome home was not quite as dramatic as displayed on the evening news with only a couple of Vietnam Vets landing in Charleston that early afternoon.

Mina had kept the two boys out of school so they could give their brother a warm and loving family welcome while Wavy had to work and Christine could not get out of school due to an exam. The animated foursome ran all over the large area together with the excitement of kids on Christmas morning. There were lots of people in all sorts of clothing but no Marine Corps uniforms. No one thought about making a large sign with Ronnie's name on it and holding it up. They were running out of breath and becoming uneasy.

Mina started calling out her son's name, "Ronnie!"

Kenny followed suit, "Ronnie!"

Then Uncle Hal and Jake joined the "Ronnie!" quartet.

Curious people were looking at the group with empathy as their eyes exhibited all their anxiety and angst. One professional looking businessman figured out what was going on and he tapped Uncle Hal on the shoulder and pointed to the next room. They all ran to the adjoin area and stood beside one another and looked all over the smaller room.

Still no Ronnie until Uncle Hal noticed the young man in a Marine uniform standing in the rear corner of the room by himself with his back turned towards the entrance of the room as if he were ashamed and hiding.

All four walked over to the front staring intently and hesitantly because from the rear and side this person did not resemble their Ronnie. Standing in the front now it still did not resemble Ronnie but he recognized all of them and his deep-set eyes lit up with exhilaration as he looked at each one of them and ran into the arms of his mother for the lengthiest hug Jake had ever seen. Jake wanted his turn too.

Jake believed that Ronnie looked much older. His hair was very short and he was much thinner. His eyes looked exhausted and he was sporting a new mustache which is something Jake had never seen on his brother before. Finally, Jake got his turn and his big brother attempted to lift him in the air and said "Oh my, you've gotten big, Bubba," and opted to hug him instead so not to embarrass him or hurt himself. Ronnie broke his first smile as he stared at his little brother then ran his hands through his thick black hair which made Jake smile too.

Uncle Hal grabbed Ronnie's duffel bag, which surely brought back memories for him. Ronnie handed over his carry-on bag to Kenny, after he gave him a big hug. Jake was wondering what was in those bags. Was there anything in there for him? Were there guns, grenades, bayonets, oh man?!

The ride home down Main Road on John's Island was the most exciting trip down that long rural road that Ronnie had ever taken. A thrilled Mina drove as her beautiful son took it all in… *HOME AT LAST*. He had missed the towering moss draped oaks, the familiar cars and faces, the small stores, and gas stations. He couldn't believe that he was actually excited to see his old high school again. He had survived pure hell and was finally home. He had dreamed of this day over and over again for nearly six months and now it had come true.

Ronnie was overjoyed and probably the happiest that he had ever been in his entire life. Quietly, he thanked the good Lord for his safe return and vowed never to leave home again. As they passed the railroad tracks he went from being joyful to sad in a quick instant when everyone pointed at the railroad track and told him about Bullet.

He looked at Jake and said, "We'll get us a new dog, Bubba." While he placed his woolen, olive green dress cap on his little brothers head.

Jake smiled from ear to lopsided ear. He knew now that everything would be alright because his hero was home.

Once home on John's Island, Ronnie opened the door to his bedroom and fell spread eagle in the middle of his bed in full uniform and that's where he stayed for nearly two full days. "We're home Toto, we're home ~ home sweet home."

Chapter 52

"The devil's behind the glass (mirror)."
~ **H.G. Bohn**

The first Saturday afternoon after Ronnie's return had the kids in the woods picking pears from Staley's orchard just behind the Stern's house with the Staley's approval of course. Jake, Kenny, Stevie, Chucky, Kathy, and Julie were filling up brown grocery bags with the green delights. As they got near the end of one of the rows they heard and awful noise coming from the bordering woods. They didn't know if to approach it or run from it. The noise got louder; it sounded like a woman screaming in severe pain and agony.

"Oh crap!" Kenny yelled.

"That's Christine." Kathy shouted, quickly running into the woods, followed by Kenny, Jake and Julie.

The unusual noise was definitely coming from Christine and Ronnie. Jake was totally muddled.

"What the heck are they doing?" He asked Kenny. "Why is he hurting her?"

Kenny didn't know much more than Jake about what was happening but knew that this must be sex which he knew very little about and Christine, despite her screams looked as if she were totally enjoying it. Ronnie looked like he was envisioning the Gooks who wiped out his entire squad and instead of a machine gun he was blasting away with his manhood. He was definitely passionate; he was putting everything he had into his rapid thrust.

"I don't think he's hurting her, I mean intentionally. I think that's um, I think that they're um."

Kenny scratched his head trying to figure out what to say and how to say it and thought that he better not say anymore in front of Julie.

"We'll discuss it later. Let's all get back home now."

Kenny led young Julie away from the suggestive scene that was taking place on the blanket but didn't realize that Kathy had stopped Jake. The prissy Kathy knew much more about what was happening than she should have and swiftly grabbed Jake's dirty hand gave and him a very unusual smile. She then reached over and kissed him on the lips in broad daylight in a wide open field for the entire world to witness. Jake nearly freaked out; he just knew that Tommy's ghost had something to do with all this craziness. Instead of allowing her to kiss him he stepped back and immediately looked at the bottom of each shoe three times and didn't care who saw it. He blew away at his palms, he looked at his elbows, again three times each, and he was desperate for help.

Jake nearly screamed out to his brothers when Kathy kissed him again but he settled down somewhat. Then came something that he was sure wasn't supposed to happen; Kathy's tongue entered his mouth and this was the weirdest thing Jake had ever known. Her tongue swirled around his own tongue and then it ran itself over his teeth as if it had a life of its own and explored his entire mouth like some exotic creature. Jake did not know what to do; he just stood there with his arms dangling at his sides and let this pretty girl clean out the inside of his mouth with her tongue while her sister was getting pounded on by his hero brother. These were some of the strangest and most baffling moments Jake had experienced and they were getting more bewildering by the second.

"Put your tongue in my mouth." Kathy whispered when she pulled her mouth away from Jake's and stared at him intently.

"Why?" Jake asked nervously.

"Just do it; you'll like it. Do what I'm doing," she said confidently, and glared at Jake like she could not understand his resistance. "Don't you like my tongue in your mouth?" she whispered in her best Ginger Grant. Jake thought about Ginger and thought how good it did feel with her tongue roaming around his own. No longer reluctant and finally beginning to relax he did as he was told, and was actually starting to get into it when he realized that he had a large protuberance in his jeans.

Jake remembered that during one of their games of hide and seek Kathy had kissed him on the lips before, but not with her tongue in his mouth. Kathy must have realized Jake's surrender and felt his eagerness against her tummy as she reached for it and started caressing his denim. Jake sensed a gratification that he had never known before and he felt a desire he had not known. It was then came the second shrillest scream Jake had ever heard in his life. He and Kathy both jumped and nearly lost their breath. So much for Jake's excitement which disappeared like a frightened bird.

Christine sounded like she was in pure agony, and apparently Kathy wanted the same punishment, because she again grabbed Jake's groin.

"Do that to me." She said, while trying to unzip Jake's pants.

Jakes eyes tripled in size. "Do what?" He asked, literally ignorant to the demand.

"Sock it to me!" Kathy said, like a crazed, possessed woman. "Let's make it like they're doing."

It? Make what? What is she talking about? He wondered to himself.

"Right here in the wide open?" He asked, pretending to know what she was talking about.

Jake felt as though he had stepped into the twilight zone and his entire world had changed yet again since he stepped out of the front door of his safe and secure home.

"Um here?"

No one had to answer that question because another more imperative question was asked. "What are you two doing?" Kenny asked, spoiling the mood of the hot and bothered duo. Jake was actually thankful, sort of.

The two quickly stopped and turned as they assumed that Kenny and Julie had walked back home. When Kenny realized they were not all walking together, he and Julie turned around and walked back to get the other two so they wouldn't get busted by Ronnie and Christine. Besides, it would give those two the opportunity to finish doing their thing. He then saw that Jake and Kathy had started up their own thing. Kenny quickly walked in front of Julie so she wouldn't see anything even though she just saw her other sister naked with Jake and Kenny's naked brother.

"Uh, nothing, we uh, we were just um, we were coming, sorry, and we had to talk about something."

"Kathy, take Julie home. I have to talk to Jake a minute."

"Wow, wonder where she learned all that?" Kenny asked his little brother. "I guess she has been sneaking around and spying on Christine."

Jake shrugged his shoulders, "I don't know."

"The kissing felt really good though. Would it be okay to kiss her and what about the tongue? That seems gross but it felt really cool."

Kenny tried his best to describe his knowledge, but he wasn't sure that it made much sense.

"Anyway, I think that's all that Ronnie and Christine were doing, just making out in a far more advanced stage, I think, I guess, it's called sex. But remember, that's something you do after you're married."

"Well why are they doing it then?"

"I don't know."

"It must be painful?" Jake asked, oblivious to the situation.

"It sounded like it didn't it? Makes you wonder why they do it. But, you don't need to be finding out; you're too young for that. I'm not sure if you even need to be kissing at your age."

"Dang," Jake said, visibly disappointed. "What about you, have you kissed a girl yet?"

"Of course."

They caught up to the rest of the group and Jake turned back to see if Princess Crazy Tongue was following. Sure enough she was walking like Jake had never seen before other than in the movies. She had a confident little strut to her and a devilish grin to accompany it. She reminded Jake of the predator cats he had seen on *Mutual of Omaha's Wild Kingdom* just before they lunged at their target for the kill, the kill? He gulped. Jake was downright frightened and this was a good time to run home for lunch. In his haste he had dropped his bag of pears and he grabbed Kenny's bag so that Mina wouldn't be disappointed and he darted towards the house.

Inside the comfort of his bedroom Jake went over the events of the past 30 minutes in his very troubled head. First, had he been absent from school when all this information was given out? Is this something he should know and was behind on? Why had he missed this information? Or, is Kathy really crazy? If not in school then where did she learn this stuff? Why, when she saw her sister in torment did she react this way? And what the heck did the Marines teach Ronnie anyway?

According to Kenny you should be married before having sex. It is the proper thing to do anyway. However, as he visualized Christine's nakedness and her large boobs again in his mind he started becoming stimulated; he kind of liked it. He remembered the kiss a while ago and how great it felt. He remembered the times in the closet while playing hide and seek and once the initial shock wore off that he liked that too. Now he was regretting the fact that he didn't get to stick his tongue in her mouth during those times. He just didn't know what to do.

Kissing Kathy became his main emphasis. Next time he'll do it; he'll stick his tongue in her mouth. Now he knew why she had that devilish grin. She knew that she would be the center of his attention from now on. Not the elbows, the soles of his shoes, or dirty palms. Nothing but her tongue and fingers and the sizzling little secrets inside her faded tight jeans would now be what Jake was most anxious about. How did a girl her age know these things? How did she learn to manipulate a boy at this early stage in her life? He figured that she learned all this from spying on his hero brother and her sister. Jake now possessed that same devilish grin that was pasted on Kathy's pretty face.

"Can't wait to play hide and seek." He said aloud. "Ha, ha, ha."

He didn't know why but he continued stroking and the new adrenaline was overwhelming like when Kathy had stuck her tongue in his mouth. The feeling was incredible; the best he had ever felt in his life. He was out of breath, excited and confused all at once. His dark eyes were glazed over and out of focus.

"Oh, oh, oh, oh man, this feels great!" He couldn't believe what was happening and how good it felt, hoping that no one would walk in on him.

The sensation was awesome. Jake thought of nothing else for the next hour except that incredible feeling that overcame him, and of making out with Kathy.

I've got to clean and wash clothes without anyone knowing about this. Is this normal? Dang that felt good. I know I shouldn't but I really wanna do that with Kathy. I bet it would feel even better inside of her. I guess that's what makes 'em scream like they do, heck, I wanted to scream. He thought to himself.

"Dang that felt great, what a rush. I'll sock it to you all right!" Jake just stared at the ceiling. "Kathy, you want it, you're going to get it - *SOCK IT TO ME BABY!*"

Chapter 53

*"The first age of man is when he thinks of all the
wicked things he is going to do; the age of innocence."*
~ **Author Unknown**

After a quick early afternoon shower, which was very rare for Jake, he put on a change of clean clothes, splashed on some of Uncle Hal's Old Spice all over his face, brushed his teeth and swiped Ronnie's brush across his head then he felt nearly brand new. Some tongue would do the trick, so off to Kathy's house he went. Apparently the girls were all in the woods picking pears according to their half sober mother.

Jake went row after row of pear trees and saw no one. Then he heard a cackle of laughter from afar made by several girls. He walked towards the sound and stopped in his tracks when he saw Barbara, Kathy, and Julie peeping into the woods and holding their mouths with their hands to try and keep from laughing but it didn't work. He now understood, based on the location and the red faces he assumed it was his older brother again pounding away at their older sister; two things Ronnie couldn't get enough of when he returned home from Vietnam, ice cold water and Christine.

Jake now knew what they were doing in the woods during Ronnie's summer break and his dumbass was actually picking red ripe plums. He also understood how Kathy and obviously the other girls learned such things by spying on their sister and his brother. Jake pondered. Why haven't we been taught these things? Instead we've been sneaking around to see someone else doing it. Are we too young? Is this bad? They seem to enjoy it and now I know I liked what I felt, wow! Jake realized also that he had no desire to do his crazy routines.

"Man, this could be better than an apple a day."

Earlier in the summer Jake didn't know any of these things. He was picking plums, pears, playing pickle, building forts and model rockets and this was enough to be content but he had no clue. Now, however, Jake's blood was boiling and he wanted more. He wanted more of what Kathy could give and do for him. He cannot forget how good it felt when Kathy last kissed him and what she said, how she said it, the way she looked when she said it, and how good it all felt.

She cured me of my nervousness ~ that pretty little gal may have created a monster.

While the red faced girls enjoyed the show at the edge of the pear orchard where the woods stood tall and dense, Jake was not quite sure what to do; make his presence known or just walk away? The more he thought about what his brother was doing and the fact that all these girls were watching it unfold made him want some action too. He knew that Barbara's giant boobs were just 30 yards away. He knew that Kathy's crazy tongue and happy fingers were just 30 yards away; if his brother could do it, why couldn't he? Before he could make a decision he was spotted by none other than old Crazy Tongue herself. She transformed right before his very eyes and in a split second she went from giggling little girl to confident vixen. Oh, Jake thought, that first instant always made him very nervous as she walked his way with the swagger of a supermodel.

"Oh crap." Jake mumbled to himself.

How does this girl know all of this crap? He was befuddled. I've never seen her this way in all these years. Did she learn all of this by watching her sister? What was Jake to do?

Jake was tempted to run like hell and then remembered just what he came for, poor kid, he was shivering in his sneakers as he waited for the inevitable. He became anxious and sad thinking that maybe he wasn't cured after all. He connected the dots, nervousness equals habits and very much wanted to look at his soles, his elbows, and blow the cooties out of his palms. He knew that may freak out his predator who was six feet away at this point but had she not seen his routine in the woods just the other day? And that's when she really attacked him. Boy, he couldn't do it fast enough, soles, elbows, and palms… blow, blow, blow, baby, faster, faster, here she comes. Jake nearly crapped himself as Kenny ran up behind him with a copycat of Jimmy and screamed, "BOO" in his big ears.

Jake quickly turned around and started pounding his fist into his brother's chest. Kenny, who could not stop laughing, very successfully blocked the last few thrown blows and started running around in circles as Jake's eyes filled with tears.

"I wish …" Jake nearly said those same horrible words. He caught himself in the nick of time when remembering the fate of the poor soul that he last yelled out these words to. There was no sincerity or thought to it. He just screamed it from impulsive anger.

Jake stopped as he dropped his hands to his side, turned his head to look at unexpectedly extraordinarily attractive Kathy. She just stood there with her head cocked to one side and her hands on her hips wondering what these two fools were up to. Kenny knew that Jake was about to be Kathy's supper. He walked past the two when he saw the more interesting happenings 30 yards away.

Christine wrapped in a GI blanket and nothing else was yelling at her sisters and chasing after them while Ronnie was frantically trying to buckle up his kaki chino's that would one day be Jake's. The young lovers and their love nest were busted and they knew they would have to find a more secretive spot but damn it was fun while it lasted. Ronnie was pulling his blue polo shirt over his head with a very pissed look on his face as everyone ran away from the pear orchard as fast as they could, even Kenny, who up until that point, thought everything was so hilarious.

Standing on the Stern's carport, thinking that they were safe, the group split up as Kenny and Barbara went into the house leaving Jake, Crazy Tongue and little blonde, curly haired Julie standing and looking at each other. Jake wondered what young Julie thought of events on the blanket. Jake and Kathy's eyes met and the rest of the world didn't matter, it was just the two of them looking into each other's souls, or more likely through each other's clothes. They just stared into each other's eyes for several seconds; brown and emerald emulsion of dreams and they would not disconnect. They knew what they wanted but what about Shirley Temple here? Shirley, being smarter than people gave her credit for saw what was unfolding and took off into the house as Ronnie and Christine, finally dressed, walked from the side of the house. They did not see Jake staring at them earlier as he was several yards away so they were not sure what he knew, but they knew the look that that the youngsters were giving each other and it was not appropriate at their ages, so they must have seen more than they had assumed they saw.

"What did you two see out there?" Ronnie asked angrily.

"Nothing at all," Jake said.

Kathy just shook her long brown wavy hair with a certain gesture that made Jake feel that he was still going to put his tongue in her mouth despite all that had just happened, but where? Kathy knew they could go to the best place possible, the scene of the crime where no one would be returning. Ronnie and Christine walked into the house then Kathy, smiling, grabbed Jake's hand and off they went. Jake felt a certain exhilaration he had never experienced. He had no urges to look or blow or mumble and this was good. He only had an urge to kiss this girl and discover whatever was hidden in those tight faded jeans. Finally, a cure at last he thought.

The two did not speak a word as they walked back into the woods past the rows of pear trees to the far end into the thick brush that separated the lovers nest from the rest of the world. There lay a blanket, a small transistor radio and a half eaten pear.

"Are they coming back?" Jake nervously asked.

"Are you kidding?" Kathy said, with the confidence of a grown woman as she sat on the blanket and turned on the small AM radio. "They did what they set out to do, trust me."

Trust ~ The Monkee's were singing about how much they believed and Jake himself was starting to believe.

Jake just stood there looking down at this beautiful girl and her gorgeous brown hair as it hung just above her pouty lips. Kathy opened her world and pulled back her colored cotton dress that revealed that she was open and ready for whatever. What Jake saw changed his life forever; he had never seen it before, but overheard Ronnie and his buddies talk about *IT*, so this must be *IT*.

All the guys at school talked about *IT*, how they wanted some, needed some, got some. He wasn't sure how, but he was going to give *IT* a try, because all the guys were wanting it and he was a guy, so he should want it as well, besides, that is what Kathy wanted. Jake went to his knees in front of the devil's throne.

Kathy grabbed his hands and pulled Jake into her hot frame.

"Kiss me," she said.

"Uh, okay," Jake said sheepishly, even though this was exactly what he had been waiting for.

Jake inquisitively looked into her eyes as if he were expecting instructions.

"With your tongue," Kathy whispered.

"Uh, oh, um, okay." Jake put his tongue in her mouth.

"Mm, hmm," Kathy moaned.

He too loved the sensation of the "French kiss", as he heard Kenny and others call it.

He was going to make the kissing last as long as possible. He nervously looked around the woods as "Come on baby light my fire" was belted out by The Doors from the little plastic box. He saw a fire in her eyes, a want that fueled the pyre, her lips puckered to receive his own lips and at last they met. Kathy sucked on his tongue just had he had been anticipating for days. Jake tackled her tongue with his and this slobberfest went on for several minutes. Jake became more excited than he had in his life; he was becoming rock hard and steaming hot.

"What do you want to do?" She whispered.

Jake honestly didn't know of anything else to do other than to continue kissing. He did not know what was next and was hoping that she would guide him along. Kathy, looking like a zombie with glazed eyes and slack jaw aggressively grabbed Jake's wrist and made him massage her breast.

"That's it Jake, yes, keep doing that." She said, as her breathing labored.

Jake could not believe his luck; he finally had a handful of boob, make that two hands, two boobs.

Kathy finally had enough of this tongue wrestling. "Do it!"

"Do what?" He asked, obviously very nervous.

Jake had never been in this situation before; he was scared nearly to death for a lot of different reasons. Mostly he was embarrassed. He just knew that he had missed that day of school and he felt like the biggest idiot in the world. Amid the moping and groping, moaning and groaning … Master sprang to life. When in doubt, whip it out.

"WOW!" they both squawked.

"Oh crap Jake!" Kathy said, as she bolted backward several inches.

Her hands lead Jake down the bold road of no return…manhood.

"Try to set the night on FIRE!" Morrison screamed.

The hot, dreamy essence of a desire binged afternoon. They both shrieked as they looked into each other's reflective and dazed eyes; the emulsion of dreams complete.

That's when *IT* began for them both.

Kathy didn't wait very long to spread the word amongst her girlfriends who all anxiously wanted to make it with him. Poor Jake, still not completely sure of everything except that he just experienced the most paramount feeling he had ever known, and that he had no yearning to do all the nervous routines when his world was being rocked by a beautiful girl. All Jake knows is, he missed a very important day of school and that Kathy absolutely loves Master, *from I Dream of Jeannie*, and that Master loves Kathy and her magic carpet ride.

Chapter 54

*"The moon is hid; the night is still,
Christmas bells echo in the mist."*
~ **Alfred Tennyson**

Kenny and Jake loved Christmas; who didn't? The excitement of it all was always exhilarating and much anticipated by the two boys.

The decorations, the music, the television shows and movies, the commercials, the food, the scents, the tree, the wreaths, the village beneath the tree with the carolers wrapped in scarves singing their little hearts out.

They loved the shopping, the wishing, the hoping, the atmosphere, churches, bells, the ornaments, the tinsel, pictures with Santa, animated shows on television, the visitors, the gifts, all the sights, sounds, smells, flavor, and all the noise of hustle and bustle.

The spirit of the season soaring through the cold December air made it the best time of the year. Jake knew too that it was the favorite time of the year for everyone in the household just by the constant smiling and laughing. Everyone was so happy; the peculiar and disheartened summer was behind them.

The fresh aromatic scent of the Frazier fir seemed to rejuvenate their souls and refresh the attitudes with hope of a better year.

Ronnie was out of Vietnam and the Marines, although it was not yet official. He was safe and most importantly, home where he belonged. Home with the eggnog, apple cider, hot spiced tea, pecans, old fashioned hard candy, oranges, tangerines, cakes, pies, puddings, mixed nuts, chocolate, all being devoured by the truckloads it seemed.

The bare, limber branches of the willow softly swayed in the December air as the last of the red and yellow leaves from the neighboring trees frolicked in the air as they quietly drifted to the cold and firm John's Island soil. The jaybirds, cardinals and squirrels scrambled for food and Wavy was good with the woodwork and made sure that his handcrafted feeders were full at all times with the help of Uncle Hal.

The white smoke from burning oak puffed into billowy swirls from the brick chimney and floated off into the woods. Inside, the huge fire roared with excitement and warmed everyone as they sat admiringly in front of it.

Some watching the fire, others, warm and toasty watched the *Andy Williams' Christmas Special* with Bing Crosby as guest while Mina sipped on warm tea, Kenny drank eggnog, and everyone seemed cozy and content.

What a special feeling Jake thought, what was once the norm now seemed like a rare privilege to him and his family.

Jake lay beneath the tree near the fake snow starring at the little village with the villagers and carolers. He pretended to be in this place which appeared to be London, England based on the shop windows, store fronts, churches and old homes.

The snow coming down hard as the horses carried town's people to Christmas Eve services. Jake found himself right there with the carolers enjoying every minute of it with his huge scarf and paperboy cap pulled tightly on his head and donning large rubber boots.

This is what life is all about; the love of family, the safe and warm home, this is true happiness Jake believed, enjoying the copious repose of his surroundings.

Jake was wondering what kind of Christmas gifts he would buy for the girls, not giving any regard to his family. He would use his chore money from dad and combine it with the five dollar bill Ronnie left on Jake's dresser from his first paycheck from after coming home as a salesman at the Mary Janes' shoe store on King Street.

"I want it to be this way all of the time." Jake wishing it would never end.

"I'm dreaming of a White Christmas…" crooned Bing in the background. Kenny jumped up and said, "Jake, let's go into the kitchen." While the adults continued to watch television Kenny and Jake sat at the kitchen table and wrote letters to Santa.

Kenny kept trying his best to keep the dream alive and encourage his little brother to do the same; the innocence of childhood, untarnished and unequaled.

Jake began to compose his letter to Santa trying to keep it short and to the point but he did not take into count that he should be limited with his wants as his family finances were meager. He didn't quite realize that his parents were responsible for purchasing his wishes.

Dear Santa,

I hope you are fine. I am well. I've been a very good boy, I've listened to my parents, I've done my chores, I make good grades in school and I say my prayers every morning and night, sometimes more… This is all I want you to bring me if you wouldn't mind:

A new bicycle, some cool Hot Wheels with a race track, and new cowboy boots, lunar module, etch a sketch, a Spiro-graph, some good books to read and some new clothes because everyone laughs at me, plus a new jacket for Kenny cause his is all torn up with the pockets hanging down. Everything doesn't have to be new but it would be nice.

Please give Mom, Dad, Ronnie, Kenny, and Uncle Hal, Grandma and Barbara what they want too.

Thanks again Santa.

Yours truly,

Jacob "Jake" Willoughby

"You don't want much do you?" Kenny's sarcasm hurt Jake's feelings.

"I guess it is a lot huh?"

"You've been good but not that good," Kenny laughed.

"I included you too."

"I'm just kidding. I guess the more you ask for the more you'll get. I may ask for more too."

"What do you want?"

"Some peace of mind," and upon first hearing that desire, Jake thought it to be odd, but totally related very quickly.

On a cold Saturday morning downtown Charleston on King Street was busier than usual with all the shoppers crowding the sidewalks. Jake, Kenny and Mina fought their way through the crowds. The green garland with huge, silver, gold, and red bells hung from the street lamps. Jake and Kenny both loved the hustle and bustle of the crowds.

As they headed towards the marked off areas for the Christmas parade, Jake window shopped as Mina called it. He loved the store front windows and decorations; it reminded him of the jolly village beneath the large tree. Woolworth's on King Street was one of Jake's favorite places because they had great décor, merchandise and food too. Western Auto was several blocks away and offered no food, besides; Jake didn't want to go into that place ever again.

The happy three found a spot at the counter and ordered their favorites. Jake and Kenny had submarine sandwiches and Mina had tomato soup. Yuletide songs serenaded from a ceiling speaker, festive patrons drowned out the words but Jake enjoyed the melodies as he gulped down his sandwich and a Coke. He was anxious they would be late for the parade and not get a good place to stand to get the free candy that was thrown to the onlookers by none other than Santa himself.

"Let's go." he kept saying.

"Calm down." Kenny yelled.

"We have plenty of time." Mina reminded them.

Jake peered down at his worn out soles, peeped at the elbows and blew his palms, and mumbled some Jakeish gibberish which always alleviated the madness for a spell. He wanted to get the lunacy out of the way so he could enjoy the parade and make those manic dashes for candy.

High school marching bands, local celebrities mostly newscasters and a very Happy Indian Princess which Jake and Kenny were on her television show the year before, and then finally, there he was, the big red jolly ole St. Nick himself.

Oh wow! Santa is throwing candy right to me Jake thought, but was shoved out of the way by some bully. Kenny tripped the bully and got all of his candy and gave half of it to Jake. The bully got up as if he was going to take a swing at Kenny but Mina grabbed his shoulder and told him to go find his mother and leave her boys alone or he would be in deep trouble. The shaken bully scurried off.

The parade ended and they trudged through the crowd to the gold Biscayne parked on Beaufain Street admiring the decorations, seeping in the smells of nearby restaurants and chewing away on their free bubble gum. Both boys were cold and snuggled tight against the warmth of their beautiful mama who wrapped her arms around her two youngest children's shoulders to protect them from the cold breeze. No matter the size of their children, mothers will always be mothers.

On the way home they stopped by Morrison's Department store on James Island and got some more icicles and tinsel for their tree. Mina grabbed a couple of boxes of chocolate covered cherries to give out as gifts as the boys ran to the toy section. Jake nearly froze dead when he saw *his* baseball sitting on the shelf. It was new and in the box and it quickly made him become sick. The submarine sandwich was resurfacing in a real big hurry. RALPH ripped all over the shiny floor, the coloring books and sprayed all over the plastic housing that kept GI Joe safe from Jake's weapon of mass destruction. Kenny jumped back in total surprise as he saw chunks of mayo covered tomato splatter into the cuffs of his/Ronnie's old hand-me-down chinos which were now Jake's.

"What the heck?" Kenny was startled by the explosion from his little brother's mouth. "Are you Okay?"

Jake slowly nodded his head sideways.

While Kenny gawked at the damage he knew they had better run.

A pale faced Jake nodded his big head in a negative motion.

"Let's go, quick!" Kenny grabbed Jake's jacket and practically dragged him from the scene of the crime.

They stopped an aisle away from Mina and Kenny took Jake's scarf and wiped off his pants and Jake's jacket and mouth in that order and tossed the scarf behind tall rolls of wrapping paper.

"There, no harm, no foul, let's go, Bubba."

Jake, dazed and confused, was lead to the fresh, chilly December air that waited outside of the hot stuffy building. The boys stood beside the Biscayne waiting for Mina who soon appeared smiling with relief that they were alright but a little concerned that they dashed out without her knowledge.

She had no clue as to what just transpired inside the stuffy store. She had spent several anxious minutes combing the aisles looking for them. She assumed that they were outside or hoped so anyway and quickly went to the checkout with her few items.

She didn't notice Jake's ashen face and missing scarf because Kenny stood in front of his little brother to hide him. Looking down to hide his guilt he noticed a slimy chunk of tomato sitting in the cuffs of his khaki's; quickly he swung his upchuck catching leg behind the other one like a clumsy ballroom dancer, nearly tripping Jake in the process.

"What mischief have you two been up to?" The suspicious mother asked.

"Nothing, it was just so hot in there that we had to come get some fresh air," Kenny said.

"Hmm," Mina's nostrils winced to a familiar and unfortunate odor.

"Just get me home." Jake mumbled behind Kenny's ear.

Jake's black eyes rolled into his head and the taste of acid overwhelmed the inside of his mouth. His entire face shuddered from the uninvited tang.

Where was Crazy Tongue when you needed her? Aw, thinking of Kathy suddenly made Jake felt a little better. A game of hide and go seek would definitely cure this ailment. She would have to be pretty darned desperate to stick her tongue in that mouth right now… you just don't know boy.

Chapter 55

"Don't pluck a green apple; when it is ripe it will fall itself."
~ **Russian Proverb**

Christmas break from school started with a half a day of school which concluded with a party. Jake was thankful when it was all over because of all the girls with their red cheeks ablaze had been pointing, staring and giggling at him when he would walk past after Kathy shared her secret in their eager ears. Jake felt ashamed because he assumed the girls were talking about his habitual routines. Maybe Kathy had told them that he didn't know how to kiss and that all the other boys were better or that he didn't know about *IT*. Jake was in a big hurry to get home.

After a mid-day snack prepared by Mina, Jake answered the knock at the door. It was Teresa Hamlet, the sixteen year old pretty little blonde from the other side of the neighborhood. Jake had always thought that she was cute but since she was a little older he never knew her well.

"It's a nice day don't you think?" The flirtatious girl asked Jake. "You wanna pick some pears?"

So the word spread quickly and it must have been good. Jake thought, *If I eat another pear, I'm gonna be real sick.* Then he caught on. *Oh, what to do?* He studied the girl standing in front of him; the dazzling sparkle in her big blue eyes, the shoulder length blonde hair, and the alluring smile sucked Jake right in.

"Sure!"

Jake was enjoying his new found discovery and notoriety. "Man, this is going to be friggin great!"

The two walked right pass Crazy Tongue's house and into the nearby woods. Crazy Tongue just happened to walk past the picture window when she spotted the pair. She did not at all like what she was seeing. They were both smiling and laughing. Kathy bolted to the door, down the few steps out of the house and into the woods. She watched as Teresa grabbed Jake's hand and the two strolled behind the third row of pear trees, what? *That's our spot* Kathy said to herself. She ran down the dirt trail to the third row and stopped and watched for a bit. Her blood was boiling, she was in a rage, and she was out of breath and wanted to kick some blonde, blue-eyed butt!

"Hey!"

Kathy startled, turned in shock to find her older sister Barbara behind her.

"What's wrong, why did you run out here in such a big hurry?"

Kathy now was as nervous as she was angry and did not know what to say. She knew she had to stop what was about to happen in the woods but needed to get rid of her sister first.

"I thought I saw Fluffy run back here like she was being chased.

"FLUFFY, FLUFFY!" she called.

She knew the noise would startle the two sneakers and hopefully stall or abort their intentions.

"Fluffy!"

She continued to call louder as she patrolled to the end of the row followed by her curious sister.

"There is no sign of her so let's go." Barbara said. "Cats are fine in the woods, she'll be back."

Jake heard Barbara's sweet voice and thought of her like he had never before.

"Oh my gosh, what are they doing here?" Teresa whispered..

"Uh, I don't know, sounds like they're looking for my mom's cat." Jake said, in an aw shucks sort of way.

"Let's hide behind that big tree over there," Teresa pointed.

"Uh, maybe we should just leave," Jake said.

"What?" Teresa almost shouted, but caught herself and whispered rather loudly, "No way, Jose!"

She grabbed Jake's sweaty palms and they tiptoed through the horse weed and around the mound of dog manure to the large oak and crouched behind it and hid behind the moss.

"What's this? Oh, Ronnie and Christine never came back for their blanket and radio," Barbara laughed.

"I guess we better leave it," Kathy said, in a hurry.

"Yeah you're right, come on lets go." Barbara said.

Kathy's bright emerald eyes scanned the area before leaving and then she noticed the shadow behind the tree.

She grinned and studied. "Oh my God there's a wild boar!" she shouted. "Run Barbara run!"

Barbara did run but so did Jake and Teresa. Kathy just stood there smiling that self-assured smile of hers as the two would-be naughty doers ran right smack into her.

"How are the pears kids?" Kathy asked, in a sarcastic tone.

They both looked up into the oak tree.

"Uh, plenty of pears," Jake said, pointing at the Spanish moss.

"Ha, I see," Kathy said suspiciously. "Teresa, do you know that wild boars love pretty little blondes. I think you should get on home before you become supper," she added with a little feistiness.

Barbara stopped and turned around in disbelief at the two who came running from behind the oak.

"What are you two doing back here?" she shouted.

"Uh, picking pears," Jake, Teresa and Kathy said in unison.

Jake just stared at Kathy's green eyes and pink lips and his heart did a summer salt. He loved the way she stood, the way she talked, her cool confidence, everything about her. He felt a certain jubilance and pride; he had never, ever felt this way before. Previously he had only thought of her as just one of the guys but now she was someone very special. Jake saw nothing but Kathy and he almost forgot that Teresa was even there.

When he thought of her he had no desire to look at the bottoms of his shoes, elbows, or blow cooties, or mumble phrases to himself. Kathy's hubristic expression made Jake's heart flip, pound, and flutter. He was aglow and all three girls knew it. Jake now only had eyes for Kathy and she knew it, so did Teresa. Barbara studied what was happening as she too had heard about Jake; my how big news travels. She was a little more than interested herself despite her sister and the fact that Jake was a dumb kid.

"So Jake, let's see it," Barbara said.

Kathy lost her composure and stepped back with mouth agape. Teresa's eyes bugged out and turned her attention to Jake's jeans.

Jake, doing his best Gomer Pyle, said "See what?" in a slow southern drawl.

Barbara was now more strident than ever. "See the pears; let's see the pears that you guys picked." With unyielding posture she pointed at their empty hands.

Teresa finally spoke, "Ah, we were just getting started."

Kathy was proud of her quickness and said, "Oh, good, so we'll all pick some pears so where's your basket or bags?"

Waiting for and not receiving a response; "It's winter time dummies. I don't see any pears, do you Barbara?" Kathy challenged.

Barbara now knew where her sister stood so she would just have to wait until another time which would be better anyway. She knew eventually she would have "lover boy" to herself. She has noticed on many occasions how Jake has gawked at her large breast. She would give Jake something that her little sister couldn't. Barbara was a hormonal and curvaceous sixteen year old, extremely desirable.

Jake slowly eased back and separated himself from the girls and approached the nearest pear tree. He looked up and saw no pears but attempted to climb it anyway to try and avoid the disconcerting awkwardness and trepidation as he was hid from everyone.

The three girls followed suit and Barbara winked at Jake as she walked by and whispered in his ear, "Meet me here this same time tomorrow."

"Uh, okay," he whispered back.

Jake nearly looked up the crafty girl and then caught himself. Crap, this is getting better and better, Kathy who? He started pondering that whatever it was that Kathy had conveyed to everyone must have been really good. He felt immensely better about himself and everything in general, so much for hiding. He decided to stand tall in the middle of it all. Nothing can stop the Duke of girls he sang to himself laughing.

Chapter 56

"Most dangerous is that temptation that
doth goad us on to sin in loving virtue."
~ William Shakespeare

That was probably the longest twenty-four hours of Jake's life. Not wanting to be spotted by Crazy Tongue, Jake rode his old bike to the end of the neighborhood and entered the pear grove from the street entrance. He was back tracking but knew it would be well worth it. Would Barbara do the same he wondered; surely she was smart enough to know to hide from Kathy.

He hid his bike in the bushes at the beginning of the third row of mature pear trees with their heavy branches hanging to the ground. The winter air rushed through his black hair and chilled his ears now turning tomato red. He saw no sign of big boobs Barbara and he kept hoping she soon would be there. He walked to the end of the row feeling dejected and turned every few seconds to see if she was behind him.

"Dang it," he muttered, kicking at an old fallen branch.

"Well, I'll just go find Kathy or Teresa since I'm all cleaned up."

Just as he was about to turn around he heard that familiar, raspy voice of Barbara.

"Hey, over here," she summoned.

Jake was hoping that whoever that was didn't over hear his rumbling and would look in the direction of Kathy's and his and secret love nest which was another hand-me-down from older brother Ronnie. Slowly he approached the bushes and peered over to the other side and to see Kathy resting on her elbows lying on top of the battered blanket. There Jake saw the most beautiful face and largest cleavage he had ever seen - "POING"! Just like the Grinch's new found heart, growing three times larger and busting through the frame.

The little radio was stating something to a young girl. "Don't you just love Gary Puckett?" Barbara asked.

"Yes, I really do, I really do."

Jake was climbing through the brush not knowing who the heck Gary Puckett was. All he knew was the world's most beautiful boobs and the attached girl love him. Jake was now sweating as he took a step closer to loveliest things he had ever seen.

Barbara was the prettiest of all the Stern girls although all of them were beautiful but Barbara was stunning. She had the figure to compliment the face and the sexy, raspy voice. Jake wanted to pinch himself because he wondered if all of this could be true. Was she just messing with him or was this some trap? He had been admiring this girl for years but knowing she was so much older he never believed this was possible. *Way to go Master,* he thought. I'm gonna have the prettiest girl in school he said to himself ~ Oh man, dreams do come true.

The two looked into each other's eyes and closed them as they slowly moved closer to each other. Jake could feel her firm breast on his chest and then their lips lastly met. Jake could not believe that this was happening. He could not be any happier and felt he was the luckiest guy in the world. This was every guys dream and here he was tongue wrestling the most beautiful girl in the world. Barbara was a virgin and truly relishing the circumstances.

Jake was in awe of the entire situation. They were both breathless and swallowing each other's saliva as Barbara started licking Jake's ears and then his neck. Jake was getting chills all over his body and started caressing her large breasts. Master had never been so excited. Barbara pulled off Jake's sweatshirt and pulled up his under shirt and started kissing his chest, and then she looked up at him and whispered the greatest words Jake had ever heard in his whole life.

"Do the same to me," she whispered in Jake's ear.

Jake had never been more eager to oblige any request ever. Do this right; don't mess up because he wanted more of this every day. He also did not want a bad reputation with the other girls. The December air had made her already huge breast firmer than Jake could have ever imagined and he loved every second of it.

Normally, the two of them should be freezing but they were on fire. The two blazing adolescents engaging in coitus lost themselves in each other for several smoldering hours. Jake was a wild man while he let loose with such energy he never knew he had. His buddies were playing with spaceships and toy guns while he just rocked the most beautiful girl in the world!

"Oh man, this is so awesome." Barbara said, as she tried to catch her breath.

Jake had never been this blissful and euphoric. He could not stop smiling while catching his breath and admiring Barbara. Their two bare bodies were stuck together like glue from each other's perspiration. Jake inhaled Barbara's sweet aromatic fragrance as he nestled his nose into her exquisite forgiving hair. This was no dream. This was the real deal and Jake could not believe his good fortune as he glared into Barbara's eyes.

The azure sky and flaming sun observed as the two explored each other. Jake, becoming quite the explorer in the last day remembered doing the same thing to Barbara's little sister, Kathy just hours earlier. Jake wanted them both and what the heck, maybe Teresa too. Dusk was approaching and the two finally dressed. They were surprised that no one was out in the woods looking for them, especially Kathy but he was too into it to even worry about that. Just a few days ago this lovely girl would not have given him the time of day. He cannot believe he just nailed that.

Barbara was now captivated by this "little boy" as she used to call him and now he was all hers; she liked to think so anyway but how to explain it to her girlfriends who also think of Jake as a kid. She knew too that her sister was crazy about him but not for very long.

In less than twenty-four hours, Jake was close with two of Tommy's sisters in a way he never, ever thought about, or even knew about. Now he could not get enough. This was better than anything he knew of, even brown cake. No elbows, soles, or palms, just pure ecstasy! He just had to keep it up - Teresa, you're next baby!

Forty-three hours after the greatest pleasure in his life Jake met blonde and gorgeous Teresa on the same blanket. Teresa was a complete knockout; a Barbie doll come to life. She was taller and thinner than Barbara but about the same age with perky breast bursting to get out of her sweater blouse. Jake, always obliging, removed the sweater and freed her perkiness which was indebted to the young man. He thought *this whole making out thing just gets better and better with each girl.* Who is next he wondered. Take care of business at hand then worry about who is next - Unleash the beast!

Just several hours earlier Barbara snuck Jake through her window and into her closet late at night. Christine was at the Patio Drive-In with Ronnie. The bedroom was all hers but she did not want to take a chance so she led Jake into the small dark closet where she could have him. While trying to suppress her natural desire to scream and without thinking she grabbed the nearest thing for support which turned out to be her clothes hanging on a light rod that was to either side of the walls in the closet space. As she came closer to cresting the clothes came falling and so did she. Startled and recoiled Jake just stood there as she went to the floor and she landed safely on a pile of dirty clothes.

In the bedroom just inches away Kathy was dreaming. "Oh Master," she whispered in a deep slumber.

Barbara wanted Jake all for herself and all of the time. Jake wasn't ready to be tied to just one girl. He hadn't even considered that an option because there were too many for the picking; just like plums and pears when in season. This was the coolest thing ever!

Barbara, though not wanting to, skipped a day from seeing Jake because she had to go Christmas shopping with her mother and Christine. All she could think about was someone she never gave two thoughts about a couple of days earlier; the young dirty faced neighbor that was her little brother's best friend. Now she would wake up each morning and think of Jake; she was fixated with the kid. She had already forgotten about Teresa although Jake had not and he was knocking on her door the very second the Stern women left their driveway.

During the ride into town Barbara was going over in her mind different schemes on how she would hook up with Jake and sneak around Kathy. She was not aware that Kathy and Jake had been intimate. She suspected that they may have made out but did not think that they knew enough to go all the way; little did she know. She was unaware of her little sister spying on Christine and Ronnie. The little sneak had watched and learned and then she used her knowledge on poor unsuspecting Jake who just happened to be in the right place at the wrong time.

This little vixen got Jake hooked on salacious desires way too early in his life. Though Jake would contradict that sentiment as he was enjoying the heck out of it while he could. Besides, he wasn't doing the nervous habits as often; he traded one for another. It seemed like a good one to him at the time, at least until he got caught.

After she got home, Barbara quickly went to the Willoughby house supposedly to borrow some sugar.

After Mina gave her a cup of sugar Barbara asked casually "Where are the boys?"

"Kenny's at the stables with Uncle Hal, Ronnie's at work, and Jake is riding his bike with Chucky and Stevie".

"Okay, thanks for the sugar, I'll tell Mom you said hello."

Chapter 57

"The way to fight a woman is with your hat, grab it and run."
~ **John Barrymore**

Before Barbara went meandering around on her bike, which she rarely rode, she thought that she would walk through woods to check the love nest behind the pear orchard. She really didn't know why she would go there except that it seems to be the hot spot lately and something compelled her to do so. She just knew that some sort of action would be taking place there like her own amatory act just a day earlier.

Taking the long way to the spot like Jake did, Barbara's heart nearly stopped when she heard Teresa's squeals coming from behind the bushes. What other girl besides Christine and Kathy knew of this place she thought. She then remembered Teresa being here with Jake just the other day. No, no he wouldn't, would he?

Sure enough her man was pounding Teresa like a maniac. Barbara was in shock and tears. She could not speak; if it was going to be anyone else she thought it would be Kathy, not the beautiful blonde from the other end of the neighborhood. Kathy had indeed created a beast; Jake was relentless for his age especially considering just a couple of days ago he was clueless to it all.

Jake was on a mission and he did not exactly know what the objective was except to stay as busy as he could because it kept him from thinking of the compulsions that lead to his ridiculous habits and detrimental rituals; copulating became intrinsic and irrespective for the distressed adolescent and besides all of that it really felt good.

Barbara just stood there and watched as the two enjoyed each other. She was waiting to hear the same words Jake had whispered to her but they never came and for that she felt some relief no matter how small. She expected to be spotted but the busy bodies never looked up, they kept their eyes only at each other.

She gingerly stepped back out of the scene careful not to make any noise. She did not want a confrontation not knowing the outcome. She knew she had some work to do; she sadly walked home contemplating her next move.

As she turned the corner to leave the orchard another hurdle to jump, little sister Kathy, who Lord knows why was headed to the hot spot herself. Poor Jake better wise up and find another place and soon. Barbara's eyes lit up as she realized this was the answer to her problems; it just fell right into her lap. Kathy had been suspicious of the two because of the way they had been looking at each other and she was jealous of her sister because she wanted Jake all to herself. She also recognized what Teresa was up to.

"What are you doing back here," Kathy asked her older sister.

"I was just going for a walk when I heard all this noise back there at Christine and Ronnie's love nest. I assumed it was them and took a peek, but guess who was going at it? You'll never, ever believe it."

Kathy was fearful of the answer, but asked anyway "Who?"

"Jake and that cute blonde from down the road," Barbara said, with a twinkle in her lustrous emerald eyes.

"Teresa?" Kathy was beside herself; her green eyes were now bulging from her pretty little face. "What are they doing?"

Barbara was feeling sorry for her sister and feeling victorious at the same time. She looked indifferent when she told Kathy that the two were rocking each other's brains out just now.

Barbara was tremendously upset by what Jake was doing, but she knew that he would be all hers if everything went according to plan. Kathy took off to the love nest as fast as she could run. Barbara, holding back a huge smile waited a few seconds and then slowly followed behind her contentious younger sister. She could not miss this for the world; she just hoped that Kathy wouldn't hurt Jake. Teresa she could care less about.

C5A's roared overhead as the two girls ran toward the end of the row of low hanging pear trees. Barbara intentionally measured her step as she wanted to watch not interfere. Kathy busted through the brush like Deacon Jones after a quarterback. There was no vestige of Barbara's claim. All she found was the well-used blanket. She was consumed with anger and would have shredded them both to pieces had they been there. Breathing heavy and confused she was wondering if Barbara had lied. That would be fine with her because that would mean Jake did nothing wrong.

Kathy heard footsteps behind her and quickly turned. She did not expect to be followed so she was startled when Barbara was standing in front of her.

"Where are they?" Barbara asked sardonically, stretching her head to see around her little sister's shoulders.

"Were you messing with me?" Kathy asked, catching her breath.

"No, I swear they were making it right here just a few minutes ago."

Kathy was ready to punch somebody. "

Are you sure it was them?" She asked impatiently.

"Of course, who else is that stupid?"

"Did you do stare at them? Why were you here, really?" Kathy demanded of her older sister.

Their instincts made them both look at the large oak tree because they both have hidden there with the same guy in the same situation. At least ol' Jake had been keeping it in the family, up until now that is. Kathy practically lunged at the tree in a fierce rage resembling a hungry leopard. This alarmed Barbara because she could just as well be the target of this aggression and she wasn't quite sure she could take Kathy on in this state of fury.

No one was behind the oak. The two girls, both unaware of each other's curiosity were searching the area very keenly with their gorgeous and fretful eyes. No sound, no Jake, no Teresa, nothing. The girls walked the small clearing and beyond, still nothing. Barbara knew what she had seen and wondered how could they possibly vanish in mid-air?

Kathy was convinced that Barbara was messing with her so that she could have Jake all her own. Kathy then jabbed her fist square in the right eye of her older sister. Shocked and dazed, Barbara fell backward onto her firm round bottom and bounced straight up again. She grabbed her right eye in disbelief. She had one arm in front of her face to block any more blows.

"What the hell was that for?" Barbara screamed at her little sister. "I didn't do anything. Your stupid little boyfriend was making it with another girl. Don't take that crap out on me. Get a grip you little bitch!"

Barbara was also wondering if Kathy may have spied on the two of them, which could to be the reason for this hostility.

Kathy jumped into her older sister with fist flying. Barbara was pissed that her plan had backfired, and she now was ready for battle. She blocked every punch that Kathy threw. She managed to hold her sister's raging arms and flip her soundly onto her back, and then she placed her knees on Kathy arms stabilizing her until she eventually gave up the fight. The difference in age and size saved Barbara from a terrible ass whoopin'. Kathy's eyes were red and full of tears. Barbara's right eye was bloodshot and quickly swelling.

Covering her own ass, Barbara leashed out "Look girl, don't flip out on me. I know what I saw. Jake and Teresa were frigging' getting it on here just a few minutes ago. They were right here making it."

Spittle flew from Barbara's lips onto her sister's face as she tried vigorously to explain to Kathy what she saw. Kathy kept moving her head from side to side in order to keep the spit and grass out of her nose and mouth so she could breathe.

"They must have heard us and peeled out. Instead of fighting each other we should have searched the other rows. I know they have to be hiding behind one of these trees. It's too late now, they're probably home. Why do you like that kid so much anyway? Look at what you did to my eye you dumb little girl. I ought to blacken both of your eyes right now!"

Kathy was exhausted; she cried hard and nearly lost her breath. Barbara realizing there was no fight left in her sister got up off of her and brushed the dead grass off of her back, nearly feeling regretful for her dumb kid sister.

"You wanna go look for them or you wanna just go on home now?" Barbara asked softly.

Kathy, looking at the ground and still trying to catch her breath, mumbled "Home."

Chapter 58

"No fools are so troublesome as those who have some wit."
~ **Francois de La Rochefoucauld**

Jake and Teresa had heard the two sisters talking in the distance and quickly covered and ran in the opposite direction trying to avoid them and took the really long way out. Jake had not looked at the soles of his shoes or his elbows or blown cooties from his palms in three days but he sure felt like doing it now.

If the girls had not wasted time fighting they would have caught the two zig-zagging between pear trees on their way out of the orchard, getting tangled and scratched by briars, and fighting through long vines, tripping over logs and jumping ditches. All of that in a matter of three short minutes.

It had been a long time since Jake had been this far out in the woods and Teresa never had so she had to trust Jake because he seemed to be in the woods most of his time for one reason or another. Jake recalled several months earlier when he and Uncle Hal were taking one of their strolls together in this vicinity coming upon a giant water moccasin on the edge of a brook too wide and too deep to cross. Uncle Hal picked up a fallen branch and chased away the deadly creature.

They walked the southern end opposite the snake and finally came upon a narrow enough stretch to cross without getting wet or snake bit. They ventured through the forest, Jake trusting his Uncle to keep him safe. They ended up walking all the way to Brownswood Road and came out of the woods directly in front of the stables and near the old trail that Jake had dreamed about being chased by the scary old man.

Jake knew from memory that they could leave the woods going this direction but wanted to be closer to the neighborhood and Teresa's house.

Jake decided to make a sharper turn south into the dense untraveled forest which made up of nearly every tree and foliage imaginable. Jake amused himself by thinking of the haunted forest in the *Wizard of Oz*.

"Hope there's no flying monkeys around."

"Huh?"

"Oh, nothing."

The lovely blonde, reflecting on what transpired earlier, was still in heaven and wanted more but knew another time was more suitable as they tried to escape the wrath of two scorned sisters. More confident than ever in his life, Jake trekked through the shadows of the tall mature trees and the thick, tangled brush. Teresa pleasantly followed her man. With no end in sight after hiking longer than he thought was required, Jake became a little apprehensive but did his best not to show any doubts to the lovely girl. If Teresa were not with him he would be very afraid. His insides said panic, his pride said, be cool. Jake quietly prayed, as he often did when faced with a dilemma.

"How much further?" asked the honey sweet voice of the second most beautiful girl in the world.

"Should be an opening any second now," Jake said, trying to hide his frustration.

For comfort Teresa grabbed Jake's arm as they walked through the endless woods and he very much liked this. He turned to her, smiled and kissed her lips. Teresa very much liked that. The brush and vines got denser the further they walked. This frightened Jake considerably, who stopped and looked around alarming Teresa for the first time who noticed that Jake looked somewhat uncertain. She grabbed his arm tighter and locked sweaty hands.

"Are we lost?" she asked timidly.

"For heaven's sake no, just a little further," The brave lad said.

"You have been saying that for a while now."

"Well we can always go back the way we came, there is definitely a way out."

She now knew they were lost and she also knew that it would be dark before long and her parents would be looking for her.

"Jake, I'm getting scared!"

Jake stopped in his tracks; he turned to face the pretty girl and gently kissed her lips and gave her a tight hug.

"Don't be afraid, we're almost out of here. I promise." He too was afraid but hid it well.

She kissed him back and smiled.

"Jako, over here," A very familiar and haunting voice said.

Jake was glad he had good control of his bowels because another opportunity to crap his pants came and went in that split second. Had he done that he would have lost Teresa forever and by the time she spread the word he would be right back to where he was a few days ago except worst. Everyone, including his buddies would make fun of him for crapping in his pants. Only one person ever called him Jako. Pale faced, Jake turned to the sound, and he saw nothing.

"Did you hear that?" He asked the beauty queen.

"No. Hear what?" She grabbed his arm tighter and he felt she would pull it from its socket.

Jake knew he heard a voice call him and he knew who it was. He thought this was a cruel joke and he was ready to bust someone up. They walked through the thick vines and briars towards the direction from where the voice came with Teresa following just behind him.

A row of tall, massive pines draped in bare wisteria and kudzu vines which bordered a white structure of some sort. He walked closer, pulling beauty queen along with him as he stepped over branches, logs, stumps and dried leaves.

Jake recognized it to be an old building hidden in the thick brush. It resembled several of the old buildings that dotted the John's Island landscape; a small white clapboard church built in the early 1920's and later converted into a school house. Jake had never known this building existed and he wondered if Uncle Hal, who spent several hours walking these woods, knew about it. If he didn't, he couldn't wait to show him.

Then Jake realized he had discovered another love nest only this one was even better because Teresa was the only one that knows about it. It could be their love shack but could they ever find it again and can they even find their way home now? He would have to leave a trail of broken branches or tied ribbon made from his trusty handkerchief leading from it.

The small framed building with collapsing porch was over grown with weeds, shrubs and vines just like the once upon a time yard. During the summer Jake would not even consider getting close to the ramshackle building due to snakes, lizards and other scary critters that made this old building home.

The two teens approached slowly and with caution and Jake wondered if those same critters may be inside now seeking warmth from the December chill.

"What is it?" Beauty queen asked..

Jake did not want to cause her any more unease than he had already.

"This is our new home away from home baby doll," said the proud and enthusiastic Jake while he hid his trepidation by what may be inside.

"I like it," Teresa said.

Hand in hand they stepped over vines and stumps to the nearest window which was filthy and cracked. Using Teresa for support with one hand, he used the other hand to shield any sun or reflection as he peered into the window. Jake wasn't aware if he controlled his bowels or not and he wasn't even aware if he lost consciousness after he saw

Tommy Stern, Johnny Moore and Lisa Wilson all inside the building sitting at an old wooden table facing an unrecognizable person in the shadows of a dark corner.

Jake's heart literally skipped several beats and he blacked out and fell to the ground which caused Teresa to scream bloody murder. She tried to see what may have knocked him down; she was more concerned about him than she was her own safety. She reached down to pull him up and her shrill scream must have brought him back into her world as his eyes searched for focus and found her sparkling blue eyes.

"Oh my God, Jake what happened? Are you okay?"

Jake sputtered as he tried to lift himself with her assistance but kept spinning until he crashed against the old building and fell to the ground once again. Teresa was scared, and screamed for help. She just knew something bad had happened to Jake and would probably happen to her as well.

"Oh crap, are you dead?!" She asked, grabbing his shoulders to turn him around.

Jake's forehead was bleeding immensely from the impact and this made Teresa scream again. This poor girl wouldn't be able to talk tomorrow with all the screaming she had done today. All she could think of now was that all this had happened because of that jealous little twit that wanted *her* man.

"I will kick their ass if we ever get out of this," she yelled at Jake.

Jake's head was wobbling back and forth as he tried to gain focus. He felt as if he had been hit in the forehead by Mickey Mantle and his Louisville slugger.

"Uh…um…ah… ow…uhh…ugh," then it came, the watery vomit.

This is happening too often and all for the same reason Jake thought. He's got to catch Tommy once and for all, this craziness has to stop.

"What happened?" the beauty queen screamed.

"I, I dunno, um. Will you look in the window?"

The frightened girl hesitated but then reluctantly did as she was asked. Wiping tears from her eyes she peered in just as Jake did at the same exact spot and saw only four long tables that were once used as school desk and several rickety old chairs.

"I see nothing but old tables and chairs," she said.

"You don't see anyone? Look again," asked Jake.

"See anyone like whom?" Teresa was beyond herself now and not about to take a second look.

"Who did you see?" she yelped, now very afraid. "Someone's in there? Oh crap, they must be hiding, who is it?"

Jake knew his answer would scare away this lovely girl that he wasn't ready to give up just yet.

"I dunno, I thought I saw someone in there but maybe it was my own shadow," Jake lied.

"Oh my God, let's get the heck out of here," she screamed.

Teresa grabbed Jake's hand and this time she led the way. He was worn out and weak looking but managed to crack a half smile as he watched Teresa's voluptuous behind bounce as she ran slightly ahead of him.

"Shake that thing," he smirked.

"You like it Jake?" she said shyly while looking over her shoulder and smiling.

Jake grinned and nodded his big bruised head up and down.

Within 15 minutes they exited the forest almost directly behind her house; three doors down to be exact. She had Jake sit on a webbed lawn chair on the patio while she ran into her house and gathered a glass of lemonade and a wet rag for Jake's head.

They both drank gulps of the cold beverage while she cleaned his head, then she reached over and kissed it.

"My brave man," she said, while softly patting away the blood from his messy forehead.

"Ha, thanks, thanks for fixing me up and getting us outta there."

"Anytime dear. So is that really our new spot? Who do you think you saw? Do you think it's safe? When do you wanna go back?" she asked, in rapid succession.

Awaiting a response, Teresa smiled at the tattered boy making him realize just how lucky he is to be with her. She sat in front of him staring into his eyes with both effulgent beauty and beam.

"Yes it is baby doll. That is, if no one is living in it. Maybe we'll check it out again tomorrow. Yeah tomorrow would be groovy."

Putting on a front and pretending to be the brave man she thinks he is but knowing after seeing what he saw or thought he saw, he is far from brave. He definitely did not want to go anywhere near that place again.

From atop a mammoth loblolly, a lone black raven peered down on the two young lovers.

Chapter 59

*"The majestic river floated on, out of the mist and
hum of that low land, into the frosty starlight."*
~ Matthew Arnold

The beginning of the trek starts from the Atlantic Ocean is the mouth
of the Edisto River. As the moon swops places with the sun and gives
luminous light to grace the glimmering stars, the shadows and
tenacious waves of ocean crash into the limpid banks and unyielding
oaks of the resilient island. The zealous river forms serpentine creeks
and winds its way through miles of marshland into earthy forest to
replenish the secret soul of the cool, quiet pool behind the wild fruit
grove.

Within a six mile stretch of Church Creek water flows just yards away
from the Angel Oak and borders Jake's sister, Diane's house and
freely drifts beneath the dock that the Willoughby's, including Jake,
had fished from for years.

The tides rise above the banks where Tommy perished and continue its
inexhaustible journey below the wooden bridge that Kenny dangled
Jake from. It flows onward in many twist and turns behind the old
dilapidated school house that was discovered by Jake and Teresa to the
huge farm pond in the dark forest that no one knew of and rests finally
behind the pear orchard.

Jake was unaware that this was the same body of water. He never
thought to connect it because of the distance and the direction in which
the creek turned. The green algae and fern covered banks of the stream
took on new life as the water surged its melodic journey through the
dense and dark John's Island forest aiding as a refuge to coastal birds,
abundant wildlife and many species of wild flowers and, the
unknown... amid the darkness lurks evil.

By the time the imperturbable water streamed over countless rocks and under numerous logs and rushed to the edge of the old school building it was rich in mineral and cold as ice. It would be a refreshing place to swim in the dead of summer if it were not for snakes and possibly gators. Neither Jake nor anyone else for that matter knew that this creek reached far into their own terrain and encircled the pear orchard and opened up into a large farm pond that sustained several crops and farms many years before.

The pond in the middle of the forest was full of fish despite the inhabitant of several slider turtles. If Wavy had known this he would have been there every afternoon with his trusty old cane pole and frosty Blue Ribbon with his three sons by his side.

The owner of the property became too old to maintain the farm and with no children to carry on the tradition the acreage became neglected. The property was overgrown and hidden for decades just like his huge home 300 yards up the hill which was shadowed by a giant live oak and smothered in Spanish moss. The unpaved road that leads to the uninhabited and neglected dwelling was also over grown with ivy and weeds. What was once a thriving plantation with many occupants and several farms now resembles a haunted forest.

No one dared venture deep into these woods not even hunters. The nearby cow pasture and horse farm was owned by a distant cousin to the desolate plantation owner who sold the land to a real estate developer and quickly it became the neighborhood in which the Willoughby's now reside.

With a new day breaking and Christmas just three nights away Jake greeted the morning with a slight headache and bruise on his forehead. So much has happened the last three days and he just lay in his bed taking it all in and planning the new day. Barbara had come by the night before after the episode in the orchard to just visit and wondered where Jake was. Mina believed this was peculiar because of their age difference and the fact that the pretty young lady never before gave two hoots for her youngest child. Mina told Barbara that Jake wasn't feeling well and turned in early.

Barbara thought this odd since the night before he was bouncing her butt in her closet; maybe the poor dear is just worn out she assumed. She is pretty sure that she saw Jake with Teresa but began to doubt it after finding no evidence or perpetrators when she and Kathy returned to the scene. How could she have imagined that? She is convinced that she saw them together but she would get him back even though her first plan had failed.

She left the Willoughby house then back tracked to Jake's bedroom window and slightly tapped on it. She could hear the theme from Hogan's Heroes from within the walls. Kenny curiously came to the window while looking over at Jake, and saw his brother put his forefinger to his lips for him to keep quiet.

"Barbara? What are you doing?"

Hearing this, Jake pretended to be asleep.

"Just wanted to see if you guys wanted to do something," she said.

You guys? Kenny thought this was odd. Why on earth would she want to do something with Jake?

"Nah, we're down for the night. Jake's already asleep and I'm watching television," Kenny whispered.

"You want some company?"

"Better not, Jake is asleep and doesn't feel so good. He bumped his head earlier today."

Jake grimaced, faking the excruciating pain.

Barbara was surprised and said, "Oh goodness how'd that happen? Is he okay?"

Kenny was still surprised at her interest thinking that Kathy was the only one with the hots for his little brother.

"I think the klutz ran into a tree but he's fine now. I'll see you tomorrow, okay," an irritated Kenny said, as he was a little tired of whispering to the window pane.

"Okay, I hope he feels better. Sweet dreams boys,"

Barbara skipped off hoping that Jake would hear her well wishes and raspy voice. Now she felt really confused and anxious. Ran into a tree? Hmm, what is going on? He and that blonde tramp were running from me. Well I hope she followed his dumbass into the tree and that she feels like crap too.

Whew, Jake thought. He didn't want to have to explain the bump on the head and better get started making up an excuse when older brother Kenny saved the day.

"What was that all about?" Kenny questioned.

"Not sure, maybe she had a message from Kathy," Jake lied. "But thanks for covering for me."

"You owe me sewer breath."

"Okay."

When Jake woke up the next morning he really did not feel that well but knew he would need to get up and eat breakfast. Once he was finally awake he remembered what he saw in that old school house. The previous afternoon's events were blurry to him with the bump on the head coupled with the lack of sleep and exertion for the last few days. He was drained and needed to recoup. Maybe some orange juice would help. But wait, did I really see Tommy, Johnny and a girl I made up? No way, I'm just exhausted. I need to take it easy, get some rest, and decide how to approach the Stern girls.

Jake smiled when he thought about his adventures with all of the lovely girls. Had he been a braggart like his buddies he would surely be a legend for having been intimate with three of the prettiest girls in the area and in a three day period at that. He knew that he couldn't tell his friends for two reasons; they wouldn't believe him and it would get back to all three girls and that small knot on his head would be nothing in comparison.

Many thoughts and ideas running through his head made him even more muddled, what to do, he asked himself.

"Jake, you feel like eating?" Mina asked.

"Yes Mom, I'll be right there." That answered that question.

As he sauntered into the kitchen Mina and Kenny gawked at Jake's head wound which was now purple and scabbed.

"I still can't believe you ran into a tree, you dummy," Kenny said teasingly.

"I didn't run into the tree. I tripped over something and fell into the tree."

"Clumsy."

Mina quickly tended to the bump and gave it a gentle kiss to make it all better, just like she has always done for each child when they encountered a bump, bruise or scratch.

The excuse was fathomable since Jake was constantly coming home with various wounds; "All part of growing up" Wavy would tell a fretful Mina.

Jake gobbled down his grits and eggs with fried bologna and toast. Then he gulped down a glass of milk and two small glasses of orange juice to chase down the two aspirin Mina gave him. After a shower and fresh clothes and a renewed outlook he headed out on his bike to see if any of his flock may be wandering around.

Kathy was sitting by the picture window looking for Jake and when seeing him she confronted him in the street.

"I've been looking for you mister. What happened to your head," she squawked.

"I tripped and fell. You wanna do something?"

"Sure, watcha got in mind?" she whispered looking around to make sure big sister didn't over hear.

"Grab your bike, let's find a new spot," Jake said.

Jake knew of a path behind Staley's store that led to the middle school which was now deserted for Christmas break. They circled around the school to make sure that it was vacant and then they rode up to the cinder block water pump house. They took their bikes inside and noticed there was no floor and no blanket, just cool, damp dirt. Jake kissed Kathy on her pouty lips then looked into her green eyes and said "I missed you."

Kathy kissed him back, and then asked, "So where were you the last couple of days?"

Prepared as of late, Jake said, "Just around, you know with the guys, the stables, the woods, you know, stuff like that. Plus I've been shopping with Mom and Kenny."

He was convinced it would die right there.

"Oh yeah, hmm, not according to any of your buddies or your mom." Barbara said, she saw you getting it on with Teresa in our spot too, you sorry pig, as if it weren't already bad enough.

Taking in air and swallowing hard, "What? She just said that to mess with you, I would never do that."

Kathy was not buying that.

"Heck, you were trying to get her the other day when I caught you. Unfortunately, I didn't catch you yesterday. I guess you outslicked me when you finally did it." She was noticeably holding back tears and her voice shaking. "You didn't even know about such things until I taught you, why can't you just be with me?"

Jake didn't know what to say except "No, no she was trying to get with me. I don't know why but it wasn't the other way around. Barbara is lying. Now hush the silly talk. You're right; you are the only one, I promise."

Jake lied, he didn't want to lie, he just didn't see any other way out of this.

Kathy knew he was lying but she had him now and she had to make him want only her. "Okay Master, come here and make me happy."

Chapter 60

"Oh sleep, O gentle sleep, nature's soft nurse."
~ **William Shakespeare**

Apollo 8 orbited the moon on the day before Christmas Eve and sent back for the world to see on television images of a lonely earth floating in the dark galaxy. Ironic setting in the serene soundless space yet on that blue and white planet was about to end the year that would forever change the world and Jake Willoughby; a year of seismic social and political change across the globe and burgeoning protest of civil rights and anti-Vietnam demonstrators and of course the tragedy of the war itself.

For Jake, this year seemed to be one let down and tragedy after another where there were a few bright spots and towards the end of the year something sweet and exciting happened when brand new doors opened for him in the form of the opposite sex. Not just their bodies but he started to appreciate their personalities, their moods, their ideas, and their fashion. Learning more about the girls gave Jake a whole new respect as he got to know them through and through.

Jake appreciated them as individuals and he found that he loved the sparkle in their eyes, the things they said, the way they said it, he loved the way they think, the smell of their soft hair, the dimples in their cheeks, their lips, the shape of their bodies, the curves, the smoothness of their skin. He also learned he that he loved barefoot girls and he really liked their pretty feet and toes. He discovered that he loved what the girls could do for him and how they did it. He found out several things about each girl that turned him on and excited him. In other words, he loves girls and just a few months ago he never gave them a second thought. The world is full of girls and this prospect thrilled Jake immensely.

These exciting and new changes confused Jake though and annoyed him in a way because he wasn't done with being a kid. He missed the fun times with his buddies and the innocent games with the girls. He missed the walks and lessons of nature from Uncle Hal. He missed crabbing and fishing with his dad and brothers. He missed baseball, and most of all he missed Tommy.

Jake knew that Tommy wasn't coming back, but what about the others and the things that he could do something about? The thing is it seems that the nervous habits are always taking control of him when he is not banging the girls.

Christmas Eve arrived. Jake, Kenny, the Stern sisters, Teresa, just about everyone, was so excited that Santa Claus was finally coming. All the music, the shows and festivities along with the hustle and bustle lead to this day. Jake started worrying whether Santa would bring him anything. He obeyed his parents and elders and did well in school. He knew that was all he was supposed to do as far as he was concerned.

Jake assumed that Santa would not know about what he said to Tommy, after all, Jake felt that that comment was well justified but he did not know that his friend would actually die. He was very sorry and would never, ever speak those words again.

Apollo 8 crew told the world that there is indeed a Santa Claus, which led the hopeful children of the world to believe that the astronauts had seen him while floating around the earth. They also read the book of Genesis and the world got to watch and listen thanks to the evening news, which brought such a feeling of hope, unity, and peace. But those wonderful and fleeting feelings never last long with restless and aggressive humans with attention deficit. The war in Vietnam raged on, protesters continued their march and something kept an eerie watch over Jake Willoughby.

Charlie Brown and friends sang as they gathered around the blockhead's newly transformed tree with the hand drawn snowflakes falling around them in the cold night.

Jake wished for snow. He loved snow because something about it made everything seem so pristine and serene; a spiritual feeling and healing.

Kenny sitting at the other end of the sofa eating his favorite dessert, peanut butter and jelly mixed together in a large beer mug.

Ronnie was off somewhere with Christine as usual as Jake grinned because he knew what big brother was getting into but he couldn't help but wonder where? Mina was in the kitchen with Wavy preparing Christmas dinner.

Teresa and Kathy were both at home wrapping the presents they had gotten Jake. Teresa had a sweater and Kathy had some British Sterling and a Ouija board for him. More Christmas shows came on and the boys were too excited to sleep but were warned that Santa would not visit until they went to sleep.

Jake speculated if the girls had gotten him anything and he was confident that the chocolate covered cherries that he had gotten for all of them would be good enough. After their third trip to the water pump house only Kathy had hinted that she had gotten him something. He wondered how he was going to exchange gifts with all of the girls. "Man, this is going to be a real pisser. How did I get myself into all of this?" he said, to the anxious face in the dresser mirror.

"Get to bed boys," Wavy barked from the kitchen.

They both had a twin bed that had once been bunk beds, because a third bed was Ronnie's, but now he had his own room after Uncle Hal and Wavy added onto the back of the workshop and converted it into Uncle Hal's bedroom. Kenny turned on his radio; appropriately enough Deep Purples' "Hush" was wrapping it up when they both heard Mina communicate to them,

"Hush boys."

They both giggled. After turning down the volume, Kenny searched the dial for Christmas music, and "The Little Drummer Boy" put them to sleep.

The astronauts aboard Apollo 8 were photographing the quiet earth as Christmas day unfolded; they were thousands of miles away drifting amongst the stars, the place where they had always stared at and dreamed of being someday. Now, they are actually there in space; a place that they never imagined they would be in real life. They quietly orbited the moon while the world looked up at the stars and wondered. On Christmas Day, the astronauts looking down at the earth so far away, made them lonely and melancholy. The earth looked so small and irrelevant, the universe so vast and infinite.

Outside in the cold distance…

Chapter 61

"At Christmas play, and make good cheer,
for Christmas comes but once a year."
~ Thomas Tusser

Jake awoke on Christmas morning at 6:33 am. He was more than excited and interested to see if anything had been brought to him after this unbelievable year. *What if he got nothing?* Oh my God, he couldn't bear to think of such tragedy at this moment. He needed Kenny to wake up and go into the living room first.

"Kenny, Kenny, wake up, wake up Kenny." Jake loudly whispered.

Kenny had always been a heavy sleeper and finally rolled over. He had forgotten the significant occasion of Christmas.

"What, what is it?" Kenny asked more alarmed than annoyed.

"It's Christmas!" Wild eyed Jake told his brother.

Rubbing his eyes, Kenny suddenly sprang to life and instantly jumped from flat on his back from the bed to floor standing straight up on both feet in one fluid movement so quickly that Jake was in awe of his brothers' athleticism.

"Let's go." Kenny said eagerly.

"Okay." Jake said, deliberately waiting for his brother to make the first move.

Jake suddenly had that knot in his belly, that anxious, uneasy feeling that he became so adapted to this past year and he became apprehensive about leaving the comfort of his bedroom. After opening the bedroom door and entering the cold hallway, Kenny turned and was surprised that his brother was still in the bedroom and told him "Come on, Jake."

Kenny knew that all the years before Jake was always the first one into the living room so this behavior was a little baffling but not enough so to keep him from charging into the room full of pretty paper and surprises brought by the one and only Santa Claus. Kenny was nearly seventeen and refused to not believe in the magic of Christmas despite all that he has been told. He was easily drawn into the festivities of innocence because of his little brother who also refused to give up on the magic of it all. Ronnie was snoring in the other room as was Uncle Hal in his room behind the workshop. Something they must have learned in the Marines.

"Oh my God, look Jake, Jake come on, look!"

After Jake checked his soles, his elbows and blew into his palms three times each he felt safe to walk down the hall although careful to walk dead center between the walls with perfect measurements between each shoulder. When turning the corner and entering a room he had to have at least a good six to eight inches between his shoulders and the corner of the wall just to feel free of any evil cooties. These rituals somehow relieved in his troubled mind.

A Norman Rockwell Christmas, a drugstore greeting card, and a department store calendar, all came to life right there in their living room. The cinnamon fresh aroma of hot sweet potato pie filling the house. The tall decorated tree centered the room of treasure where every color imaginable sparkled and glittered and met the boy's enthusiasm with an array of dazzling animated excitement. Garland with colorful bells, balls and bows draped the fireplace mantel which hung large, full stockings of green, red, and gold. A vast array of vintage greeting cards that had been mailed by family and friends with affection and grace also highlighted the mantel.

Beneath the twinkling and vibrant tree were dozens of assorted gifts in various shapes and sizes, wrapped in colorful festive paper. Beside the tree was Kenny's drum set, next to it was a brand new Western Flyer Bicycle that Jake had wished for. Between the bike and fireplace was a dizzying assortment of new and exciting goodies for them all. On the other side of the fire place hung a new suit that Ronnie had needed for job interviews, next to that was a long and curious gift for Wavy, wrapped in three different themes of paper and highlighted with a large red bow attached in the center.

Jake could not believe his eyes; Santa had come through for him. He received an Apollo spacecraft model and four shiny new Hot Wheels cars with a race track. Jake was overwhelmed with tears and disbelief. Jake ran to all the bedroom doors knocking, banging and shouting "Wake up, Merry Christmas, wake up everyone, wake up!"

Kenny received an Etch-A-Sketch, Spirograph, and a multi board game set that included checkers, chess and Chinese checkers. Ronnie received The Beatles *White Album*, The Rolling Stones *Beggars Banquet* and a new record player to spin them on. All three received sweaters, socks, and underwear.

After two full hours of ripping gifts open and strewing colorful paper everywhere with Christmas songs in the background, the first knock at the door came.

Beautiful Barbara with her long wavy dirty blonde hair with adorning red bow hanging over the shoulders of her picture-perfect figure displaying her new dress. Her fluttering long, dark lashes enhancing her lively emerald eyes and the captivating and radiant smile that greeted everyone one.

Jake was still stunned by her attractiveness and affection. He could hear Gary Puckett harmonizing with The Union Gap in his head and feel her warmth in his arms. She smile and gazed right into his black eyes. Jake's heart melted. He had been struck by the thunderbolt of love. He was suddenly ashamed of the box of chocolate covered cherries he was going to give her. "Merry Christmas everyone, Jake," she said, with her raspy voice as she stared at her handsome boyfriend while he was admiring his shiny new bike.

She had carried in a large bag of gifts for everyone from her family and handed it to Mina. At that instant the door barged opened and Kathy stormed in and if Jake were a Christmas candle he would surely have melted.

"Merry Christmas!" she belted.

Jake looked at the fireplace and believed if fat Santa could fit in it, so can he. He should be able to climb out of the top to one of the large trees, shimmy down, and run into the woods, never to return until he was a ripe old man, and everyone would have forgotten who he was.

"Hey Kenny, we got Twister, we all need play real soon." A very excited Kathy said.

"Oh great, I love that game." Kenny shouted back.

Jake was a complete nervous wreck with both of his girls standing right in front of him. He looked up at his dad and uncle as they entered the room from the kitchen both holding mugs of hot fresh brewed coffee. Jake was hoping that the two older men would divert the attention with some conversation or offers of hot chocolate and eggnog.

Jake's worries would all dissolve in three quick seconds when he stumbled backwards over his Hot Wheels box into Kenny, who fell against the tall package leaning on the wall which was a gift from Ronnie to his dad. The gift fell against a chair then exploded with a loud, deafening explosion that terrified everyone in the room, quickly followed up by the screams of horror from Mina and the girls as they saw blood splatter from the chest of the stunned and staggered Wavy, who sat just inches from where Jake stood. Jake beheld his dear wonderful dad in disbelief, not realizing that he was covered in scolding coffee and splotches of blood. He did realize at that very instant, that he may have killed his own father.

Who would load a shotgun and then gift wrap it?

"OH MY GOD!" Kenny screamed.

Wavy had been shot in the chest by his own gift. The gift that was proudly purchased by his son, Ronnie, who gave it to Kenny to wrap. Ronnie had purchased the shot gun from a friend and it did not have a box and would take an entire roll of wrapping paper to properly hide it. Kenny sat it in the corner of the bedroom until he and Mina got back from Morrison's Department store with more gift wrap paper. Unaware of it containing a shell, Kenny did as he was asked to do by his older brother.

The shell had been placed there late one evening by a curious and exhausted Jake who grabbed the shell from the nearby box thinking that it could be easily removed. The shell wasn't coming out as easy as it went in. Jake was afraid to mess with it any further and had planned on asking Kenny for assistance since he was too afraid to ask Ronnie. With all his frolicking and escapades Jake forgot about asking anyone and totally forgot about the gun until that very second when it blasted.

Jake watched in absolute fear as the dark, red blood drained from his happy-go-lucky father's chest, the point of impact. Wavy's eyes displayed total surprise, but to calm down his family he smiled and acted unruffled. Maybe he knew that it wasn't as serious as it appeared but Jake never knew what his dad was thinking. Complete chaos erupted but Ronnie took charge and ordered the girls to grab towels and sheets. Uncle Hal immediately ran to the telephone to call for an ambulance. Ronnie and Mina grabbed towels from the girls and applied them to the wound.

Kenny and the girls were in a state of panic. Jake just stood there in astonishment while his brother and mother tended to his father's blood soaked chest. Something Jake will never forget is how casual and relaxed his father appeared when he looked over at him and smiled.

"It's okay, I'll be alright," Wavy said, in a very stable and tranquil voice that had a very calming effect on the entire room.

Barbara was squeezing Jake's arm with both of her hands which went unnoticed by Kathy who was clutching Uncle Hal and Mina. Hal was standing between Kathy and his sister with his large comforting hands on both of their heads as blood trickled down into their hair. Kenny crying his eyes out was helping Ronnie and Christine with the towels. Christine was literally walking up the steps to the front door when the blast occurred and hurriedly ran inside.

The very same ambulance, Old Red, was in the front yard within five minutes. This time it would transport someone alive for a change. Wavy has always been a stout and easy going fellow; nothing seemed to rattle him. Not even a shotgun blast to the chest. His strength comforted his family in time of crisis. Thank goodness that Ronnie bought birdshot and not buckshot, otherwise Old Red may have had another casualty on board.

Jake was just inches from the flash as it discharged. If he had been one more step or inch away he would have been on the ambulance, the third child death in six months from the same neighborhood. Uncle Hal took two pellets in his left wrist but no one ever knew it and they were still there until the day he died.

The most anticipated day of the year besides Ronnie's coming home quickly turned into a disaster. Everyone followed the ambulance to the Medical University of South Carolina where Wavy was efficiently observed and taken into surgery. After nearly two hours one of the surgeons let the family know that Wavy was going to be just fine. This was the Willoughby family's Christmas miracle.

Needless to say, the entire family was relieved after that news but until that very second they were all extremely distraught, especially the three boys who each had a hand in this catastrophic incident. Kathy and Barbara were at the hospital as well as their older sister who was at Ronnie's side. The younger girls had witnessed this terrible event and after the ambulance took off they ran home to spread the news.

Jake was a complete nervous wreck but did an excellent job hiding it. On the inside he was a typhoon out of control. He mumbled to himself multiple prayers. He went into the "what if" scenarios over and over again. The elbow, sole, palm expedition went on unnoticed. His insides were eating away and the guilt was destroying him. This kid has gone through a really horrible year.

The rest of the family that was supposed to come to the house earlier and share in the cheerful festivities including dinner all showed up at the hospital before Wavy's surgery was complete. Mina, realizing that her husband would be fine used his inspiration to keep the rest of the family calm.

In the recovery room Mina was allowed to visit her husband as he slowly came to.

She smiled at him as he opened his eyes and said, "You're going to be just fine sweet man."

Wavy winked and smiled back, then said, "I know, now that you're here. Is everyone okay? Can I see everybody?"

Despite the doctor's request, all the kids came in and Wavy assured them that he was going to be up and at 'em in no time.

The three boys all apologized and Wavy waved them off, "Accidents happen no one's at fault. Save me some ham okay." he whispered.

After realizing that Wavy would recuperate and at his urgency they went home for a quick bite. They gathered Wavy's gifts other than the shotgun and prepared a plate of food and another one with desserts. They quickly went back to the hospital to celebrate Christmas with their dad and all breathed a sigh of relief that everything would be okay.

"You can't keep a good man down. Heck, we'll be picking and grinning for New Year's." Wavy reminded everyone.

After alternating two at a time visits for several hours the exhausted boys were ready to be home since they knew that their dad would be okay and that their mom would stay with him. Ronnie drove Christine, Uncle Hal, and his two younger brothers home and the Stern family followed.

Back on John's Island late that evening, the remaining family and the Stern girls quietly celebrated again exchanging gifts and eating and hung around and helped with the dishes, cleaning and the putting away of the food. Jake had forgotten about his new, never rode bike, and he had also forgotten about the carnal escapades with the girls. Jake wasn't aware that Teresa had been by earlier. One of the neighbors broke the news to her so she decided she would get with Jake the next day.

As darkness settled in so did fatigue. The entire family was exhausted and dozed off where they sat or laid. Ronnie and Christine were in Wavy's recliner and Kenny was on the floor beneath the tree while Jake lay on the other side of the tree against the wall as if to hide from everything and everyone. Kathy and Barbara were both on the floor as well but not too close to Jake to arouse any suspicion. Uncle Hal sat on the front porch slowly rocking and gazing up at the Christmas stars. Mina was at the hospital in a chair close to her beloved husband praying and Wavy was resting comfortably in his hospital bed.

Chapter 62

"See how the morning opes her golden gates."
~ **William Shakespeare**

As the novel cerulean dawn began, a relaxed, gray December mist rises above the southern point of the Stono River and the sleepy banks of the Church Creek, which was occupied with ravenous shorebirds. Dancing on the sparkling water were crystal glimmers of the prevailing waves shining like a great widespread blanket of diamonds. Behind the pear orchard, the omnipotent sun awoke from darkness and spread its daunting marvel on the indolent and inconspicuous pond and lifted it from the bosom of nocturnal solitude. The dewy droplets resting on the sagging leaves would soon dry as the unsympathetic frosty air seeped through the ambiguous forest surrounding the old abandoned school house hiding beneath the grandiose branches of ancient oaks and innumerable mature and shielding towers of trees.

Within the dilapidated ruins of ghostly shadows mimicked the faded echoes of the gospel congruence for development and evolvement of young minds. The brisk air breathed and whispered through the branches and creepers within the obscurities of the forest whose flock have witnessed what human eyes would doubt and never trust.

The floor weary youngsters awoke with aches and pains and soreness that they were unfamiliar with. Without hesitation and with the quickness of a lightning bolt, Barbara planted her lips on Jake's as he was coming to; this brought his first smile in over 24 hours.

Ronnie had taken advantage of the exhausted and passed out bunch and brought with him to his room his darling Christine, where she slept all night with her head on his shoulders.

Barbara had secretly wished for the same with Jake and her. Kathy too, was missing the intimacy between Master and herself.

After breakfast, they all took two cars and headed to see Wavy, who was awake and ready to go home even though he knew that the doctor's orders were for him to stay put for a couple more days. Mina continued to stay at the hospital and sent the others home; they would pick her up later that evening.

During the ride home Jake was silent, but to himself he thanked the good Lord for his father's recovery. He had never been more afraid in his life as he faced the prospects of losing his dad. He just got Ronnie back after months of constant worry, then this, on Christmas day of all days. Thank you Jesus! Thank you, thank you for saving my dad and brother, Jake mumbled.

Finally, Jake would get to ride his new bike and Kenny could bang on his drums. After a couple of hours of riding his bike with pals Chucky and Stevie, Jake was ready to ride a female. He couldn't seem to separate the Stern sisters, so he took the Western flyer to the other side of the neighborhood where the blonde, dimpled beauty queen resided. After feeding each other chocolate covered cherries in her backyard and making out behind the storage shed, they knew that they would probably get busted unless they went into the woods. Teresa wanted to have the privacy of their new spot anyway. Jake had forgotten about Barbara's brand on his neck and Teresa never noticed it until later.

"You feel like going to our new spot?" Teresa anxiously asked.

Jake laughed and did his best Curly Howard "Why sointainly!"

Giggling hand in hand they hurried deeper into the woods as someone extremely livid and very provoked watched them from behind a large cottonwood tree. Cardinals greeted the new visitors with cheerful song but it was really a cautioning plea for help.

The few remaining leaves of golden complexion released from their final desperate grasp caught ride with a passing breeze and methodically pirouetted to the earthly ground. Come hither if you dare into the mendacious facade of tranquility.

Chapter 63

"That's the darndest thing I ever saw, and I've been to the fair."
~ **Wavy Willoughby**

Wavy Willoughby wanted to spend more time with his wife and kids, quality time. This had been a perplexing year for all. Just recently he had noticed some peculiarities in his youngest son. He thought back to a month ago when the family went to the Coastal Carolina Fair on Dorchester Road. It was a cold mid-November afternoon. The wind was unusually brisk and cold and lent it's cool freshness to rejuvenate the spirit and tone.

The fair visits once a year every November for nearly a two week extravaganza of food, drink, fun, ride, exhibits and more. Mina and Wavy separately as kids growing up in the rural south enjoyed the fair as most kids did. Wavy especially enjoyed the agricultural exhibits and the huge barns filled with familiar livestock. Jake was not as fond of the animal barn as his dad, especially after twirling and swirling at high rates of speed... and you young man wanted to be an astronaut?

Jake suddenly had flash backs of the poop festival at the horse stables. Oh man, now it was pig, cow, chicken, goat, turkey, llama, even elephant poop everywhere. It saturated his senses and covered every molecule as it drowned his pretty pink lungs. It flooded from his ears, nose, and eye sockets and anywhere it could find an opening even his pores.

Jake felt as if he was sweating poop. He felt grotesque and macabre. *Oh God, help me!* He nervously looked around for one of his girls and of course there were none. He really had to look at his soles, his elbows, blow his palms and wash his hands. What to do?

Jake moved along from one of the smelly swine exhibits in an attempt to get everyone else in his entourage to start moving along. While they slowly crept across the saw dust strewn concrete Jake stopped.

He assumed the coast was clear as he raised his right foot and saw it was clean, then he raised his left foot saw it was clean too. After repeating this idiocy two more times he stretched his long neck to peer at both his right and left elbows, and as far he could tell they were both clean too, but he had to look two more times. Looking around quickly to see if he was being spied upon, he brought both of his hands together as if he were holding water in them, brought them within two inches of his lips and blew hard three times. They didn't feel clean so he ended up blowing into his cupped hand eighteen times before he was satisfied that he had blown away the evil, the impurities, the epidemic, whatever it was that would torture him and family if he didn't.

As Wavy walked into the prized bull exhibit, he saw out the corner of his eye, that Jake had stopped following and carefully angled himself as to see his son, and not be caught. Wavy slowly turned to see if Jake would try to catch up when he saw his youngest son looking at the bottoms of his shoes. Wavy chuckled because the stench was strong enough to make anyone wonder if they had stepped into a brown mound of bull poopy. He then saw Jake repeat the process twice more, and inspect his elbows and thought how odd, but remembered overhearing Mina mention Jake's nervous habits to Ronnie, Kenny or Hal, and how he would outgrow them. Then Jake began his palm blowing ritual and wouldn't stop. Wavy feeling empathy towards his son had enough and said,

"I've seen about all I need to see and the odor is starting to get to me. Let's all go out and get some fresh air and a Coke." He put his large hands on Jake's sad shoulder, and guided him out into the sunshine where they were greeted by a hodge-podge of aromas representing the wide array of abundant fair food.

With bellies rumbling they all headed to one of the nearby vendor trailers and ordered a little of everything. The sat at a proximate picnic table and indulged, as they people watched. And the fair thinks that they can charge for a freak show? Just sit in the parking lot and watch for free as the freaks amble to the entrance gate to pay to get in, Wavy thought with a smirk.

Chapter 64

"Beyond the twilight is evil."
~ **Friedrich Nietzsche**

The television news actually covered two things that weren't depressing; the wedding of Julie Nixon and David Eisenhower and the splash down of Apollo 8. If you could stay awake a couple extra hours you could enjoy any of the countless variety shows that offered something for everyone and lots of laughter. Lord knows laughter and good times were needed by all, especially the Willoughby family with young Jake at the forefront.

The week between Christmas and New Year's Day flew by; Wavy recovered nicely in the hospital and came home to his attentive wife and family. Jake and Kenny played with their new Christmas loot and Jake's headache disappeared despite Kenny and his drums. Ronnie worked away at the shoe store in between Christine snacks and no one ever did find their new love nest. Barbara continued to sneak Jake into her closet late at night. Jake and Teresa hooked up a couple more times and Kathy stared at the ceiling of the water pump house at least once in the past week. Jake felt that this lascivious craving was the only thing that kept him from going completely insane, so have at it.

Christmas vacation was nearly over and it would be most difficult to work the three girls in with such limited time so he did what he loved best and was getting quite good at it. He was also becoming quite the deceit. Teresa and Jake gave up on their new house since Jake seemed to defy gravity whenever he was around it. He knew he saw Tommy, Johnny, and Lisa inside that building so he was not about to go near it again. He still has yet to figure out who the heck Lisa is.

While "Mrs. Robinson" by Simon and Garfunkel and Joe Cockers' rendition of "With A Little Help From My Friends" seemed to be the only songs on the radio that week. Jake never would have believed it but he actually started to enjoy Kenny's barrage of noise on his drum set. Per Mina's request Kenny had to stop playing his drums once

Wavy came home from the hospital which was the day before New Year's Eve. Then eventually the drum set was moved to the workshop much to Uncle Hal's dismay.

Uncle Hall never let anyone know that in passing he would stare at the drums and a time or two he actually sat down in front of them and tapped away with the long wooden sticks. Doing nothing more than making a racket and embarrassing himself, he quickly gave up that little experiment.

Diane decided to have a quiet New Year's Eve party at home on the dock with just the immediate family. Mina was afraid that Wavy wasn't strong enough to attend so they stayed home and probably slept through the incoming New Year despite the noise of exploding fireworks. As darkness settled in, Kenny, Jake, Ronnie and Christine joined Jordan, Hutch, Bryce, and Diane on the dock for fireworks. The kids enjoyed finger food and sodas while Bryce and Diane enjoyed Chevas Regal and Moet Champagne with their steamed shrimp and bacon wrapped scallops.

With a cold breeze blowing from the creek into the dark night following the reflection of stars on the river to the heartrending spot, the silhouette of long drooping branches covered in moss hanging over the creek at low tide lent it an even more ghostly expression as the shadows intercepted the moonlight.

Jake thought he saw someone walking in the gray thick mud towards the bank. He came to the conclusion that it was the branches of moss. That had to be it right? His curiosity caused him to simply stand on the dock and stare at the spot where Tommy perished. He didn't know why he was obsessed with this or what he may have been looking for. When someone from behind grabbed his shoulder he nearly jumped out of his shoes and fell into the river. Kenny standing there in his favorite mint green cardigan sweater was bellowing out that famous laugh of his. Jake turned and looked at his exuberant brother and his first reaction was stopped by the belly laughter. He didn't know what to do or say as he took a deep breath, finally he muttered "wise ass." Kenny laughed even harder when he realized he wasn't in trouble.

Jake's three girlfriends were unaware of the party for which Jake was very thankful since he had a tough week being deviously creative, now he could exhale and breathe easier. Jake was pretty sure that he had been clever enough to keep either girl from knowing about the other one. He had allowed enough time for the dust to settle before he whipped Master out again. He was also sure that no one else knew of his escapades with any of the girls. Though he believed that Kenny was suspicious of him and Kathy, he figured that was okay since Kenny seemed to be on his side as of late. Jake even felt as though he missed spending time with his brother and maybe he should encourage a walk or bike ride to My Friend's Store for a Coke and ice cream sandwich now that Kenny had a job and extra cash. This way he could spend time with his brother and feel him out as to what he knows.

Jake was kind of excited to spend some more time with his brother. As Kenny became older, he seemed to be more elusive and mysterious, and starting to become more like dad, Jake thought. He didn't realize that Kenny was feeling the same way about him. Like Wavy, Kenny's few words were measured and clever, and his thoughts were complex and always outside of the box, totally unique. A quality Jake admired about both his dad and Kenny. Kenny's eyes always seemed to be far, far away and he didn't make eye contact with anyone anymore. However, he still loved funny television shows and he really loved music, occasionally, out of nowhere he would sing a tune from a favorite song or catchy jingle or give that famous belly laugh of his at something funny on television.

Kenny was always a happy child and constantly displayed it in those beautiful eyes of his. He did very well in school and loved world history the most. He was very interested in ancient Egypt, the pyramids, and mummies and such. Jake's love of girls made him curious about Kenny's lack interest in girls and never having a girlfriend. Kenny was good looking enough and was funny and thoughtful. Jake just figured that he was focused on school and his weekend job at the stables and had no time for a silly girl. Kenny was liked and respected by all and loved by his teachers who often sent complimentary notes on his report card back home to his parents, something Jake envied. Jake's notes from teachers usually informed his parents that he didn't apply himself and was too concerned with being the class clown and they would like a conference to discuss the situation; a drastic a change from Jake's first couple of years in school.

Chapter 65

"Variety is the soul of pleasure."
~ **Aphra Behne**

1969 was going to be a better year Jake promised himself. He made several resolutions that he whole heartedly intended to keep. His mother had taught him very early on that prayer was the answer for anything and everything. Jake wanted to be worthy; he wanted his mother, his father and God almighty to be proud of him. He truly was a good person and wanted whatever evil that followed him to be blown away just the way he blows away the cooties from his palms.

First, he would pray several times a day for wisdom, guidance, and peace of mind. Jake wants and needs to resolve the death of his best friend. Second, to once and for all bring an end to this uncontrollable nervousness and anxiety that makes him do these crazy things, the bad habits, such as making sure that his soles are clean, his elbows are clean and that there is no need to blow his palms. Needing not to say and do things more than once, and things do not always have to be perfectly clean, straight, even, and in chronological order. Jake feels that if he cannot stop these things, that he will go absolutely insane. He wants to relax, he wants more than anything, to have comfort and calm.

"Please God help me with this," He expressed to himself, not three times, but five times, because two of the times weren't perfectly enunciated, or something distracted his focus. Therefore, it wasn't right and wouldn't work. He then blew the cooties from his palms until they felt cleansed, three times on each palm, one or two times just wouldn't fulfil the need, it would not work.

Third, he felt that he was in love with all three girls, but he felt in his heart of hearts, and deep down in his gut, that what he was doing was wrong, and he needed help in making the right decision. In every aspect of his life Jake knew that his choices in the past year have not been so good, and he really wanted help with this. He wanted to do the right thing, just like he always had before the summer of '68.

Jake didn't realize at the time that girl number four just moved into the empty house five doors down, and would be in his homeroom class... and girl number five was waiting behind the large oak at the end of the playground. Poor Jake, something had a hold on him, and he didn't know what. All he knows is that his little world was spiraling out of control and he felt helpless.

Mary Smith moved into the neighborhood in mid- December and since it was so close to the holiday break had not attended school yet. She was a curvy red head with blue eyes and larger boobs than Barbara and she had noticed Jake right away seeing him on his bike mumbling to himself. After a few minutes of small talk she followed Jake to the fort in the woods that he had built with Chucky and Stevie. Jake could barely wait to get her top off so he scouted the area and made sure that no one had spotted them riding into the woods.

Once they reached the fort, they dropped their bikes and climbed the three steps into the little wooded fort, and before Jake could make the first move, Mary grabbed his face and thrust her tongue into his mouth. Jake immediately grabbed her large happy boobs and squeezed them like he expected them to honk, and he then pulled off her blue cotton sweater. Underneath her top he found the two largest mountains of love that he had ever seen in his life. They were bigger even than anything the department store ads had to offer in its underwear section. Jake didn't know that they could grow so big; he was smiling from ear to ear.

Mary was pretty happy herself, and she nearly started to hyperventilate. Jake was indeed The Master. He was just a kid, and he was banging like a rock star. Now, he has another girl to hide from the others, as if the stress from three girls wasn't enough. Oh well, at least he wasn't elbowing, sole searching and cootie blowing.

The thing about tree forts built by amateur teenagers is they are usually not very well constructed. Jake and Mary were not the only ones making noise and through their moans they failed to hear the nails and boards giving away to the extra weight and consistent pounding. As they laid there collecting their breaths the rickety floor collapsed and down went the two nearly nude teenagers in broad daylight. Fortunately they were in the middle of the woods where hopefully they weren't seen or heard by anyone. It was just a five foot drop to the ground but it was enough to scare the hell out of them both and give them a few scrapes and bruises along the way. It was a good thing they were separated otherwise he may have a flattened her or he may have actually bounced off those giant boobs and never stopped.

When they hit the ground Mary stopped screaming once they figured out what had happened and they could not stop laughing. Mary had a cute giggle that Jake really enjoyed but come to think of it he likes every girl's giggle.

"What a rush man," the wide eyed girl howled at Jake.

"Yeah it was; a real pisser about the floor though."

Chapter 66

"He who finds first love finds nothing."
~ English Proverb

Jake headed home on his bike after busting the bottom out of the tree fort, and was surprised to see Patty Singleton sitting in a lawn chair on his carport. Jake knew who she was but didn't know her well. He knew that she was very pretty and had thick, wavy, black hair that hung all the way to her butt. She had very large, round, firm breast and a perfect bottom that was high and firm. She had pronounced eyebrows that arched over long ovals that housed deep set black eyes with thick lashes. She spoke with a lisp and Jake stared at her luscious lips which were perfectly plump and pouty and painted in a soft pink.

Patty was one of Barbara's many friends. She was sixteen, same as Barbara, and had quite an appetite for boys. She had already had sex by the time she was thirteen, with an older boy and had been getting nailed often by Billy Burn's older brother Bobby. She had experience, and was about to rock Jake's world. He hadn't seen anything yet.

Barbara made the huge mistake of bragging to Patty about her relationship with Jake. Patty, being competitive and promiscuous, now wanted what her best friend had, even to the point of taking away her man. Patty now focused her desires on one Jake Willoughby. The poor kid can't catch a break.

In her hand was a transistor radio playing "Baby It's You" by the band called Smith. Not a word was said, she deliberately and slowly lifted one leg onto the plastic arm of the lawn chair, exposing her womanhood, and she teasingly blew Jake a sensuous kiss with her large inviting lips. Then she slowly ran her long tongue over the bottom lip, wetting it. *Dang it*, Jake thought, I'm running out of hiding places. The only place left was Wavy's workshop, which Wavy wouldn't be using anytime soon, and hopefully Uncle Hal was out and about. Still, neither spoke as Jake stared at her open thighs and she gave him that come and get it look. Jake carefully sat down his new

Western Flyer, still beholding Patty's temple of pleasure, and he walked over very confidently. A completely different Jake emerged from just a few short weeks ago; he took her hand and led her around back to the workshop. He found the hidden key, looked around, and gingerly opened the squeaky door, then nodded for her to enter.

After five minutes of tongue twister. Patty whispered, "Dang Jake, why have you been hiding from me?"

She stared at the cute boy in disbelief. "Far effing out, this is going to be frigging amazing!"

Then she looked up at a blushing Jake, whose eyes were now glazed over. They quickly ended up on the floor, a floor that would not give out, but there were no promises on the shelving.

The low volume of Tommy James singing from the small transistor was bouncing off of the wooden walls in the small room. "I Think We're Alone Now" hopefully was loud enough to drown out the amorous noise. No worries about cooties, elbows, or the soles of his shoes, though perhaps, he should have been worried about the cooties. Jake didn't realize the generosity of this girl, which was much like the community baseball, or cat that wondered from house to house looking for food and a pat on the head.

Boom, boom, boom… and no one was banging on the drum set! Oil cans, drumsticks, hammers, screwdrivers, paint brushes, wrenches, you name it, Wavy's dusty tools awoke, and they all started vibrating on their wooden shelves shaking off the dust like an ancient army marching to war, eventually reaching the edge, and plunging to their deaths on the concrete floor. Jake would pick them up later, right now he was busy.

This was an extremely exhausting day so far for Jake, and he knew that he was going to have to see Barbara later on. After Patty hobbled away, he went inside and took a shower, ate a meatloaf sandwich and watched the local and national news on television with the family. Fuzzy images and distorted audio of Vietnam and local protestors flashed on the screen.

At first dark, Jake climbed into Barbara's window and snuck into her closet and into her. Jake had literally turned into a girl crazed beast. Just a couple of weeks earlier he was playing with model rockets and yo-yos.

Barbara felt as though she was in love with Jake, and wanted to announce to the world that they were dating. She and her girlfriends loved the concept of dating because it made them feel like they were cool and pretty... and wanted. Jake was not aware of her feelings, even though he knew he cared deeply for her, but he also liked the others a lot too. Just a few months earlier, neither of them thought that they would be here, let alone with one another, she had never before even noticed him. Jake assumed that she was unreachable, but here they are.

She's sixteen, he's fourteen, what would their parents say, what would Kathy say, and worst yet, what would Kathy do? What about Teresa, Mary, Patty? He enjoyed them all and would miss them; could he still sneak around and keep them? Would the extra time and added stress bring on more habits? But, he just loved the way Barbara looked in her faded, three sizes too small, hip, hugging bell bottoms, with worn knees and seat. He liked the white threads teasingly exposing the smooth tanned skin, combined with her cute bare feet; he was nearly out of control.

Naïve and youthful, Jake had never given much consideration to condoms, pregnancy or disease. So far, he had been extremely fortunate, as he was just following the heat of the moment and strongly giving in. He didn't know about these things and didn't know why no one had filled him in. All he knew was, he loved girls and the more he was with them, the less time he had for his nervous habits, which in his mind, was a very good thing.

Chapter 67

"The sun shines even on the wicked."
~ **Seneca**

Jimmy Willoughby and Grandma rushed to John's Island as soon as they got word about Wavy. Once Jimmy got there and realized that his dad was going to be as good as new, his general mood and demeanor lightened somewhat.

After hearing the facts, his anger lessened, but still he was upset that such a stupid accident could ever have taken place to begin with. On the outside he seemed forgiving; on the inside he was harboring some hatred towards young Jake – big mistake. Everyone was skeptical about Jimmy, just knowing him the little they did, so they kept their eyes on him, especially Ronnie and Kenny, even Uncle Hal scrutinized the stranger.

Jake had that uncomfortable feeling that he was being watched. Not just by Tommy and whatever spirits and ghost that was watching, but a real live flesh and blood half-brother. Even after Ronnie had a conversation with Jake and assured him that things were okay, he was now watching his back more than his soles and elbows. He had them coming at him from every direction now, but he knew his immediate family had his back, and if all else failed, he knew that his mama, no matter what, would protect him.

Meanwhile, Jimmy was falling in love with Charleston. He slept on a foldout cot in Ronnie's room and two nights a week they would hang out and shoot pool together. On one of those nights, after five or six beers, Jimmy's inner feelings about the accident came to surface. After hearing him out, Ronnie put an end to it once and for all by firmly telling Jimmy to drop it.

Ronnie told Jimmy that they are all very fortunate that it was no worse than it was, and that they all would be more careful, and make sure that nothing like that would ever happen again. Ronnie swallowed the last of his beer, put out his half smoked cigarette and looked Jimmy straight in the eyes and said, "You are not the only one that is upset over this, and you would not have been the only one to lose someone."

Jimmy even though he was older, and a little taller, than Ronnie, knew that the Marine meant business and would heed to Ronnie's advice and let it go. The next day Ronnie shared this conversation with Mina and Christine. It wasn't long before the entire neighborhood was watching Jimmy watching Jake ~ ease up Jimbo!

The other girls kept calling Jake, and he was tempted several times, even with Kathy, but his conscious got the better of him. Still, he was afraid that Patty would spill the beans to her best friend, so what? He would just deny it. He then started thinking that all the other girls would become jealous and start blabbering; deny, deny, deny.

Jake had not lived long enough and may never live long enough to learn that women share everything with each other, so be careful dude. A certain paranoia and guilt consumed Jake, and he was constantly telling himself that everything was going to be alright, about two hundred times a day, which made him feel a little better, along with the blowing away of the cooties from his palms.

Ronnie was noticing how all the girls were hovering around Jake and said to him one afternoon, "Take some advice from me, and start using these if you aren't already."

He handed his little brother several packages of condoms. Jake had no clue what they were, as Ronnie suspected. He explained it to him, hoping that it was not too late. At Jake's age, Ronnie himself had ruled the neighborhood with his own skills, and perhaps, he should have thought of this sooner. He realizes now that he should have talked to his little brother earlier, but he had been away, watching his friends, and brothers in arms get blown to smithereens. Then, when he returned, he had to catch up with Christine, unsuspecting that curious Kathy was observing every move.

Wavy recovered quickly and went home and to back to work after only a couple of weeks. Jake and Kenny were back in school, Jimmy returned to Goose Creek, and stayed with his mother, and started to work at the Navy yard, a job he got through some of Wavy's connections.

It seemed that everyone stared at Jake and Barbara as they walked hand in hand through the hallways, playground, and ate lunches together. As a couple, they were so comfortable that they would forget the world around them. Occasionally, they would forget where they were, and kiss on the lips in front of everyone. This drew jeers from several of the witnesses to such affection, especially faculty. After a lengthy lecture from their guidance counselor, they became more conscious of their display of affection. The counselor gave them a quick education on what they had been ignorant to. The young duo became exceptionally worried, especially Barbara, after hearing of all the possibilities.

Then it happened again, when an absolute gorgeous, Italian girl resembling a young Sophia Loren, started flirting with Jake. Maria Lombardi was a seventeen old senior, and Jake's number one weakness; a pretty girl, any pretty girl; he had never seen anyone so absolutely and perfectly gorgeous, she was the complete package, and he just couldn't resist. Jake could not stop thinking about her, and fantasizing about her when he was with Barbara.

After several days of goo-goo eyes, and awkward and silly conversation, they met behind the largest oak tree on the playground, near the back of the fence, and engaged in a slobbering make out session. Jake felt dreadfully guilty afterwards, and nearly confessed to Barbara, but he knew that he would probably lose her and even though he had plenty of backup, he truly cared for her, and enjoyed her company.

He seriously wanted to stay away from Maria, but something compelled him to her, and he wanted her more than anything… Blow away cooties! Blow away cooties! Blow away cooties!

~ Run for cover Jake!

Chapter 68

"The strength of a man's virtue should not be measured by his special exertions, but by his habitual acts."
~ **Blaise Pascal**

To everyone's surprise, including Jake's, he was becoming neater; exceedingly neater, sometimes to the point of nausea. Anything like stacks of magazines, pamphlets or books that seemed out of order or not in a straight line got an adjustment from Jake, even straightening pictures on the walls of neighbors and acquaintances, or while visiting homes of family and offices of doctors and dentist. He also was more organized, painfully organized. Everything had an order, its place, nothing could be upside down, if it was, he would stop whatever he was doing and quickly turn it right side up. Even the bills in his wallet, they had to be in order and right side up and in chronological order, starting left to right, opposite his palm blowing, sole searching and elbow exploring, which was always right to left.

Jake could be leaving a room and notice that something was crooked or upside down or not even within dimensions and return to make it right in order to prevent any sort of disaster from taking place. Some of these peculiarities became noticed by anyone who spent any time with Jake. So much so that Mina and Wavy became increasingly concerned and thus Jake got his very first visit to a psychologist.

Dr. Anthony Sneed seemed to think Jake was nothing more than hyperactive and recommended black coffee to counter-attack the extra energy and offset it. Jake still drinks at least a pot a day of black coffee. Of course Jake was frightened of the consequences of this visit and made the consequential mistake of not telling the good doctor about all of his bad habits because he was afraid of being committed to some mental institution. He also didn't tell the good doctor about his intimate escapades with his girlfriend and the other four girls. Jake was flat out afraid of telling any of this to anyone. Needless to say, he did not tell the good doctor about his death wish to his best friend, and about the blood bath of Johnny Moore and how all of this haunts him, literally.

On numerous occasions at night, while trying to fall sleep, Jake pondered on whether or not to tell Barbara about her brother, but the answer was always the same, "NO!"

Blow away cooties; blow ~ "Lord, please helps me outgrow this problem, PLEASE!"

Jake had the daunting challenge of trying to hide all of his secrets from anyone and everyone, of course over time some of the rituals slipped through the cracks.

The nightmares continued for Jake, as did the odd and bazaar routines, which increased in volume throughout the day and night, in between girls of course. His immediate family had some inkling that something strange was going on, but they really had no clue the extent of it and just chalked it up as hyper activity. No one could imagine what was happening to Jake Willoughby and no one knew the depth, intensity or immensity of all of it. The nervous rituals consumed the majority of his day, unless of course he was with a female. His entire existence was becoming one big fat, vicious nightmare, something had to give…

The only thing that helped Jake was girls, multiple girls…and they came a knockin' and he went to rockin'.

The Space Boy morphed into Rocket Man.

Chapter 69

"Man is a complex, mendacious, artful, and inscrutable animal."
~ **Nietzche**

After an exhausting day, Jake was walking down the hallway, headed to his bedroom when he heard a voice coming from his parent's bedroom. It was his mom, praying to the good Lord for her husband's quick recovery and good health and for all of her children's well-being, especially Jake, *especially me*? Jake had been moved until he heard that so now he was anxious and confused. What had he done to warrant such a special honor, *especially*? Now he was worried. He began thinking back to what his mother could know, and the how's and the when's. *Ugh*, he felt sick. Had Kenny betrayed him? Had his mom seen or heard something? Did one of the girls slip and get had by their parents and then they told Mina? *Ugh, what to do*?

Poor Jake, he just can't relax.

"When can I catch a break" he asked his reflection in the mirror.

Suddenly, he was craving a banana cream pie from The Holly House; only the very best pie known to man or woman. He had no idea why he was suddenly craving pie, because he actually felt nauseated from the anxiety and then boom, he wanted pie, not just any pie, a banana cream pie from The Holly House. He remembered his sister always brought one over about once a month, and it was due.

Then he remembered that it was Tommy's favorite food in the whole wide world. Now he was starting to get scared and he felt like someone was in the room with him. For a split second, he believed he saw Tommy's reflection in the dresser mirror behind his own, a touch on the shoulder, the goosebumps on his arms, and then came the unmistakable stench of pluff mud. The chills went down his neck and arms and rested in the pit of his belly.

"Oh crap!" He yelled at the frightened duplicate.

312

Kenny was watching *Laugh In* when he heard Jake from down the hall and ran to the bedroom.

"What happened, you ok?"

"I don't know. You see anybody in the hall? Do you smell anything?" Jake asked his brother.

"Just your corn chip reeking feet, man, they smell rotten," as Kenny pinched his nose with his thumb and finger. "You need to wash up dude, that's what you smell. Who would be in the hall?"

"Uh, nobody, seriously, that's what you smell?" Jake was now sort of relieved. "Do you see anything odd?"

"Yeah I do actually, that face of yours." Kenny belted out with the belly laugh and all was good again. Kenny went back to the living room to watch more TV.

After a hot shower, Jake lay on his bed in only in his white briefs, and stared in the dark up at his ceiling. He always prayed, but tonight he took a cue from his mom. He closed his eyes, and envisioned Jesus Christ the Lord God Almighty and spoke in a soft whisper. Jake asked the Lord to protect his entire family, but right now, *he especially* and desperately needed help. Jake did not know what was causing his problems, he knew only that sex relieved them, but he knew that had to be a sin, based on what he had learned recently while studying the Bible.

Jake asked for forgiveness, he asked for a new reprieve from his problems other than his current one. He didn't know what the replacement could be but he knew that he trusted the good Lord. Please make things normal again. He was SO sorry for anything and everything that he had done wrong. He has never intentionally did anything wrong, nor has he intentionally hurt anyone. Please help him get on the right track. He needed to know the difference between good and bad, and follow the right path in life and to have some peace of mind. He needed answers; he needed information and resources, he wanted to be wise.

"Please make all the wickedness go away Lord, PLEASE!" Jake was in tears. "I just want to be normal again," he said.

Jake may have been a bumbling idiot at times, but he did believe in Jesus Christ, and he prayed morning and night, and sometimes more. He often wished that they all went to church again, and that he knew more about the Holy Bible, which was so complicated to read and understand. He firmly believes that things would completely turn around and get better for him if he could get back to church.

The door knob slowly turned. Kenny walks in wearing his bathrobe after a shower. He had been watching an old horror movie and eating peanut butter and grape jelly, swirled together in Wavy's favorite beer mug.

"You awake Jake?" he whispered over in his little brother's direction.

"Yeah, yeah I'm awake."

"I thought maybe you were talking in your sleep again," Kenny said.

"No, I was saying my prayers."

"Oh, okay. Well goodnight then."

"Goodnight Kenny."

Chapter 70

"...the eyes that shone, now dimmed and gone,
the cheerful hearts now broken!"
~ Thomas Moore

The room was dark and quiet. Jake's pillow was soft and comfortable. He suddenly felt good again. He drifted off to sleep and to another place. Jake found himself right smack dab in the middle of the Atlantic Boardwalk and Arcade at the end of Center Street on Folly Beach.

The bright sun was centrally located over the jolly, loud, and nearly naked crowd. The pleasing aroma of chili and onions was making everyone hungry. Dozens of seagulls were anxiously awaiting any droppings or crumbs from the clumsy beachgoers. French fries, chunks of hot dog buns and potato chips often missed the intended gaping already full mouths of the rapacious consumers and landed on the ground to be devoured by the fearless and starving shore birds.

Wavy was ordering chili dogs, fries and sodas for himself and his two youngest sons who were obediently standing on either side as of their smiling father as he handed them their lunch. Kenny and Jake quickly ran to the nearest empty picnic table facing the beach and shaded by tall swaying palm trees while Wavy grabbed his own lunch and looked for his boys. He saw the wildly waving hands of Jake and meandered through the crowd of hungry beachgoers and finally sat with his sons as they all three gulped down their meals.

Occasionally, a much needed breeze would rush through their thick hair and across their sweaty foreheads.

Wavy looked out over the ocean and exclaimed; "Now that feels good."

"Uh huh," Kenny said, with a large mouth full.

Jake, choking down the last bite of hot dog agreed with a big nod and an even bigger slurp of cold cola.

Wavy just sat there staring at the ocean. As usual he was wearing his every day attire of a short sleeved white dress shirt accessorized with the pocket protector filled with two Papermate Two heart classic pens, one blue ink, one black ink and the always sharp and ready yellow number two pencil.

Wavy took his last bite in a hurry because he knew his boys were getting restless and ready to ride the rides. Just then a chili covered chunk of onion dropped into his pocket protector without his knowledge and Kenny broke out with laughter as he watched the onion piece disappear into his dad's pocket.

Wavy seemed to not hear a word as he watched the faithful waves rush in. Jake asked Kenny what was so funny, and Kenny explained. Jake failed to see the humor and got his dad's attention and explained to him what had happened. Looking at his dad, he looked like one of the NASA engineers totally out of his element at the amusement park.

Wavy chuckled "How clumsy of me, thanks Jake."

He then pulled the plastic sleeve from his pocket and emptied it of its contents including one small chunk of chili covered onion which he tossed for the birds. Jake felt bad for his dad and felt a little contentment towards his brother for thinking that it was funny.

Jake realized that he loved his father very much. He watched his dad, still smiling, takes his handkerchief and wipe clean the white plastic and the shiny pens and reinserted everything in place except for one piece of Juicy Fruit gum which he handed across the table to Jake who then turned his head towards Kenny with a sly grin as he stuck the flavorful treat into his mouth. Kenny swallowed hard, looked at the ocean for a few seconds and said, "Hey, them bumper cars are waiting!"

"Let's go then," Wavy said with excitement.

They properly placed all of their trash into the large silver trash cans near the entrance to the arcade but Jake had kept the end of his bun and two fries aside which he pitched onto the nearby grass and watched the attack of the greedy shore birds. The boys ran ahead and Wavy walked briskly to keep up, all the while smiling.

A perfect Saturday Jake thought. This is the way everyday should be. Jake really enjoyed and looked forward to the third Saturday of each month during the summer when they all would make a day of it at the beach. Mina stayed home this Saturday just so the boys could have a day bonding with their dad. She and her brother Hal worked on shelling butter beans and talking old times.

A gaggle of bikini clad young girls clamored in line behind the trio and started giggling when they noticed Jake do a double take when they arrived.

"I love bumper cars, don't you?" The one blonde in the group asked Jake.

Jake was busy looking ahead to which car he wanted to jump in and claim as his very own, so Kenny answered her question.

"Yeah we love 'em too."

"What's your name?" she boldly asked Kenny, as her grinning friends observed her mastery.

"I'm Kenny, this is my brother Jake, this is our dad, and we're the Willoughby's!" Kenny proudly announced.

The girls all giggled in unison at his show business professionalism, as if he were was announcing the talents on the Ed Sullivan show.

With "Great Balls of Fire" by Jerry Lee Lewis blaring just above their heads from a large metal speaker Wavy purchased the tickets and handed his boys one each and for the first time noticed the young girls flirting with his sons. He also noticed that Jake was being very shy.

"Hey Jake, let's show these girls how to drive shall we?" Wavy said, smiling at the young ladies who all squealed with laughter.

Jake chewed and smacked on his gum and nodded.

"Yeah let's show 'em big Daddy," Kenny said, then came more laughter.

The blond was attracted to Jake's hard to get approach and tried even harder to get his attention.

"Hi Jake, I'm Cindy."

"I'm Judy and this is Nancy and that's Cheryl," one of the brunettes said.

"Hey girls," Wavy and Kenny said at the same time.

Jake darted a glance, nodded again, and then quickly looked ahead at the assorted cars while already picking his car out ahead of time while he continued to chomp on his gum.

"I tell ya what Cindy, why don't you take my ticket and ride with the boys?" Wavy said, handing the cute blonde in the emerald green bikini his ticket in hopes of nudging Jake in her direction.

Once the chain was dropped Wavy stepped aside and watched as they all scattered into the rink like a swarm of bees selecting their favorite cars.

Jake grabbed his regular blue number 13. Kenny jumped into the red number 5; they were surrounded by the girls in various colors and numbers. Jake felt like he was Custer in his final minutes at Little Big Horn. He just happened to look over at Cindy when she was climbing into yellow number 7 car and he got an eye full of her cleavage – zoom in!

HELLO CINDY!

Wavy saw his youngest son's eyes widen and he could not help but chuckle. Apparently Jake had swallowed the gum because he was no longer chewing. Did Custer have a cheek full of Juicy Fruit?

And they're off. The chaotic blend of colorful cars, screaming kids, loud music, the constant ding, ding, ding from the arcade next door, and the whirring roar of the large roller coaster all made for a wonderful afternoon. The large palms waving at the sun sparkled sea of diamonds shadowing the flock of seagulls as they explored the dunes and sandy coast for their next meal.

The cars bumped, raced, bumped again, wedged between one another, pried loose by a surely attendant, raced again and bumped some more. Within three minutes it was all over. Jake wasn't even aware of Cindy's friends, his brother or father, he just focused on that lovely young girl with the gorgeous smile and inviting freckle covered cleavage. That vibrant and innocent smile of Cindy's as well as the happy valley on her chest danced and floated again and again in Jake's mind over and over.

Onto the roller coaster, this time Jake sat next to Wavy and Kenny was in front with Cindy who was disappointed that Jake opted to sit with his dad but she enjoyed the ride none the less. The other girls were scattered in front of Kenny and behind Jake. The slow incline had everyone white knuckled with anticipation. Then… the bottom literally dropped out as they plunged at lightning speed to the foot then spun a sharp left on their sides, then up again, then another free fall. On each drop, Kenny raised his arms high above his head, Cindy followed suit, and they both screamed with delightful horror.

Jake was wishing that he was next to Cindy. He looked over at Wavy, who for one split second had a slight look of fright in his eyes. That soon turned into a huge smile as the torture coaster continued at a much slower pace. Jake was busy contracting his bowels. *Darn, again? Be over already ride*; Jake thought. He was ready for it to end NOW. And you want to be an astronaut?

Kenny was having the time of his life and wished it lasted much longer. Jake felt the rise of chili dog in his throat; at least it was no longer about to shoot out of the opposite end. Finally, the screeching halt that Jake so longed for and with it the halt of chili puke and a chunky onion covered lap.

"You ready to go again son?" Wavy gleamed at his pale faced youngest child.

Jake cleared his throat and looked up at his dad in disbelief. He couldn't tell if he was being serious or sarcastic. It wouldn't be like Wavy to make fun of anyone especially his own children. Jake assumed if he backed down from another ride he would be thought of as weak, because everyone else immediately yelled yes in response to Wavy's question. However, he wasn't quite sure he could handle it, he felt quite nauseated and light headed.

Cindy and her grandiose boobs rose from her seat and smiled at Jake and Wavy and said, please let's do it again. The scent of her coconut oil overruled Jake's good sense; he was locked in for the torment.

"Let's do this," Kenny hollered, with a big grin.

Jake assumed if he closed his eyes that would make it more bearable… wrong! He couldn't throw up or crap in front of everyone so he would just die instead. At that second he chose to do what Kenny and Cindy were doing in front of him, raise his arms and enjoy the hell out it, if he was going to die he at least wanted to look brave doing it. Enjoy it he did after that. The chili dog found a neutral zone and Jake savored the cool draught against his freckled cheeks.

After the roller coaster they found corn dogs and cotton candy. Jake declined on both but he did drink some lemonade and off to the giant Ferris wheel he went with the others.

Jake decided he was going force himself next to Cindy on this one and that meant shoving his bigger brother aside. Kenny was about to retaliate when Wavy grabbed his shoulders and guided him into the next car where they sat behind Jake and Cindy. After the next couple of compartments were loaded they slowly drifted along and jerked and pulled so that the remaining compartments could be loaded.

Jake and Cindy just sat there suspended in midair as the merry music and laughter became a distant dwindle. The lingering smells of onion, chili and fries eventually sailed off to sea. The airy scent of sea breeze and the sweet bouquet wandering from Cindy were seizing Jake's world. He was now extremely nervous as he realized he was alone with this beautiful near nude girl that would not take her smiling eyes off of him.

"Hmmm," Jake cleared his throat.

"This is nice isn't it Jake?"

"Um, yes it is."

"Your dad and brother are so nice. You have a good family Jake."

"Thank you. Yes I do. My mom, my other brothers and my sister are great too."

"I bet they are. You have a big family."

Everyone was loaded and the jerking stopped and suddenly they whisked through the enormous blue summer sky.

Jake wanted this moment to never end. He nervously thought of grabbing Cindy's hand but feared more than anything stunning rejection so he scratched the side of head instead and looked over his shoulder at the beautiful aerial view of the park, the many shiny cars, and the people speckled shoreline and all the ant size folks below. Jake looked directly beneath him at the compartment below and there sat just as pretty as you please staring right into his eyes was Tommy Stern. Tommy glared at Jake with an evil shimmer to his dark tormented eyes.

The long forgotten chili dog re-entered the scene, lodged just at the end of Jake's tongue. Jake gasped, his black eyes widened as he grabbed the steel bar in front of him. Horror took form in his handsome face. Jake nearly stood to jump and quickly realized that wouldn't be too bright. He didn't want to upset or embarrass his father or brother. Cindy now scared, slid away from Jake with both hands on her seat.

"What is it Jake?"

Jake didn't speak but fearfully looked around for his dad and brother. He looked at her with pure fright in his eyes. He couldn't speak if he wanted to.

"Oh my God Jake, are you okay?! Are you choking? Did you see something?"

Cindy fearfully peered over and down.

Chapter 71

"For the dream of yesterday is the hope
of today and the reality of tomorrow."
~ Robert H. Goddard

Jake's beautiful dream turned nightmare was brought to an abrupt halt with the slamming of dresser drawers by Kenny who seemed to be in a big fat hurry to get ready and go somewhere. It's very unusual for Kenny to ever be in a rush for anything. With fuzzy brain and blurry vision, Jake was trying to comprehend exactly what was going on. He rose his head, slowly looked around his bedroom and his eyes met the harsh glare of the early morning brightness streaking through the curtains that his mother had custom-made.

Startled, he looked up at the ceiling and glimpses of his dream started coming back into focus and he looked down in hopes of seeing Tommy. No Tommy, no Cindy, no Kenny, no Wavy, no beach, no amusement park, no Ferris wheel. Jake rubbed his eyes with the back of his fingers, and then stretched them wide opened with arms extended to greet the day. He raised his torso and let loose a long and loud yawn.

"Geez was that all a dream?" He said aloud.

Jake realized that he just awoke from the most detailed and realistic dream of his young life. He'd been having a lot dreams, well actually nightmares lately but this one was different; this one was very pleasant aside from see Tommy and very real. Jake had spent many such days at the beach with his loving family. He remembered all the wonderful great feelings of sharing the day with his dad and brother, even the shyness when sitting with Cindy. He very much felt ill when the coaster dropped from the top of the incline. He felt the horror when seeing Tommy. He still feels uneasy about that, like deep despair in his very empty belly.

Jake quickly blew away all the impurities and evil cooties from his palms. He was now craving a chili dog and he actually tasted it in his dream along with the smell of the savory onions. Finally, he looked at the clock; 7:25 am.

"I'm hungry, Mom!"

Hearing Mina's sweet, comforting voice told him that everything was alright.

"Get up and come have breakfast; we're going to bring your dad home today."

Jake suddenly had something real to be excited about. His dad would be back home where he belonged and this thought made Jake feel safe and hopeful. He had feared the worst when the explosion rocked Christmas morning now all was well again in Jakedom if only for a while.

Chapter 72

"The only way to get rid of a temptation is to yield to it."
~ Oscar Wilde

Barbara couldn't help herself and started the talk about Jake months earlier; she just had to brag to make herself popular amongst the girls who had done it, and so was born, the man, the myth, the legend. Little did she know all of the little tramps she babbled to would have to find out for themselves.

Jake was unaware of his reputation but he knew that girls do talk to each other a lot and they hardly ever can keep a secret which meant that they will certainly tell as soon as they hear a dial tone. The word on Jake the snake spread like wildfire. Jake was now "the cool guy" and he didn't even know it. All of the guys at school now looked up to and respected Jake. His muffed up hair, tucked in his oversized clothes and slipped on his shoes, sometimes wearing three pairs of socks at a time to make them fit more snug. His nervous and antsy behavior and his shy demeanor were now looked at as "cool". Even the older guys Jake believed were cool, turned out not to be so cool after all. Those poor slobs were still virgins, hence the mounting of the legend. All the girls would make goo-goo eyes at Jake. There was a lot of eye contact, at first he was naïve, and then, he knew and played coy. Deep inside he couldn't help himself and he wanted them all.

A classic Doo-Wop song belted out of the small plastic radio sitting on the night table as the tanned, well-toned, and very exotic Maria danced in front of her large dresser mirror displaying all of her naked curves and smooth secret valleys in collective gyrations and pulsations while her long beautiful fingers teasingly caressed her ample breast. Maria was probably the only virgin in her senior class and she was preparing for that to end real soon; within a few hours.

Maria is a beautiful girl and has had a couple of dates and a few opportunities but being raised an Italian Catholic wanted to wait…then she heard about Jake. She then set her sights on the Master. After their kiss on the playground she has been frequently fantasizing about Jake. She needed the affection, the attention, and the tenderness no matter how fake it was and Jake ready and willing, he was the man for the task.

Friday at school was no different except that Maria Lombardi made her daring move near the large tree where they had kissed before. Jake and Barbara were usually seen at lunch in the playground holding hands and acting silly to one another but Barbara left school at the beginning of lunch to go take her drivers exam to acquire her permit. Oh how great things were going to be Jake and her both assumed.

On the playground Jake and Maria made eye contact, she motioned with her lovely head to the large oak tree and he discreetly followed along a few seconds later.

"Jake, my parents are going to a party tonight which means they won't be home until late, if at all. I can come by and pick you up and we can finish what we started behind that tree over there." Those dark Italian eyes emitted pure sensuality and her full, plump lips begged for attention.

She twisted her forefinger toying with Jake's sweatshirt and swung her round bottom to one side as her short skirt displayed the lighter complexion of the top of her thighs and Jake nearly melted again. Despite everything he felt for Barbara and despite everything he had said and written he had to have this. The unknown was so intriguing, so inviting, so tempting, and so beautiful. She turned again as to highlight the profile and depth of her springy bosom. She watched in playful desire as Jake's wide eyes were captivated by her enticing body.

"Okay but don't come to my house; pick me up at the side of Staley's Store," he sounded as though he were out of breath.

She smiled and exposed large white teeth and whispered "Don't worry honey, we won't let your sweetie know. This is just between you and me. Do you think you're ready for a senior?"

Jake, already drooling and rigid, wanted it now and actually scouted the area. "Are you kidding, I want you now." He said, but thought he saw people observing them.

"You don't want to take any chances here big boy, do you? Seriously, we can't take that chance; we'd probably get expelled even though I'm pretty darned tempted."

They would just have to wait a few more hours. Tick tock, tick tock…

Patty, Mary, and Teresa, separately all viewed from afar. So too did his buddies Chucky, Stevie, and Billy. Be careful Jake, he knew he was being watched and turned and noticed that every girl on the playground was staring at his awkward conversation. Where is Barbara? His dark eyes fretfully explored the entire schoolyard to see if his main squeeze had busted him. Maybe she didn't leave after all, a trap? That's when he noticed that his buddies were watching. Why is everyone so interested in me? He was sure that from somewhere Tommy was watching him as well. He did not like this feeling at all because Jake relished privacy but that is something he'll never again have.

"What time will I see you later?" he whispered while regarding the onlookers and trying not to move his lips.

"6:30" she giggled, also looking in the opposite direction. The more they tried to hide the more conspicuous they were.

The audience laughed among themselves.

"See you at 6:30," he said quietly and walked swiftly towards his pals at one of the many picnic tables.

Chapter 73

"A fool's paradise is a Wiseman's hell."
~ **Thomas Fuller**

Jake's buddies were all extremely envious because of his relationship with Barbara; she was a sophomore and the most beautiful girl in Charleston as far as they were all concerned. Besides, they didn't get to spend any time at all with him anymore and they really missed that, they were "blood- brothers" after all. So when the opportunity presented itself - pounce!

Billy Burns was a bucktoothed, horned-rimmed wearing homely boy with nothing going for himself except his mathematical aptitude, until now that is. His older brother Bobby, who had been banging Patty, was now mad at her because she wouldn't give him any attention. When asked why, the reply was simple.

"I like Jake Willoughby better."

They both sat on a rickety homemade bench behind the storage shed at the end of the yard smoking *grass*. Bobby didn't understand that comment at all. "Really, Jake is just a kid. What are they doing hanging out with a kid?" He took a long drag on his joint and handed it to Patty.

"Like I said, I like him better." sassed the promiscuous teenager as she inhaled and holding her breath she handed Bobby the joint.

"You're kidding me right?" drawled the stoned dupe.

"Not at all," she said, quickly and with much coolness.

"Freakin' far out man, that little dude?" he began laughing hard, started coughing and nearly choked.

"Not little as you," she beamed through the herbal haze.

"I oughtta go kick his little ass right now," Bobby bayed with heavy eyelids.

"Good luck with that dumbass. You know what Ronnie did to you before when you messed with one of his brothers."

"Screw that little war mongering Marine."

"You've been warned captain."

"Kiss off you little tramp."

"Don't worry fool, I'm leaving and don't dare call me again."

Billy, hiding behind the old, rusty utility shed in the neighbor's backyard was getting ready to fire up his own cigarette that he had earlier stolen from his brother's pack when he accidently overheard their conversation. He decided to use it to his advantage by telling Chucky and Stevie curious what they wanted to do.

Bobby Burns already had his ass kicked once by Ronnie because he was bullying Kenny around and he really didn't want to take that chance again, especially with Ronnie now being a trained and seasoned killer. He had just been boasting his toughness to Patty, not to mention stoned out of his gourd which was the norm for ole Bobby Burns. Besides, there's other fish in the sea and little dude could have this one and he heard that she liked "chocolate boys" so she was probably just messing with him about Jake who was just a scrawny little kid, either way he was done.

Bobby or Booby, as Patty used to call him was about to get his second shock of the day when Ms. Grover the part-time mail lady arrives at his mailbox with a letter from the United States Government. "Surprise-surprise- surprise!"

Patty was a striking and alluring young woman who was obsessed with sex; perhaps, pretty Patty had some demons of her own just like her new partner in crime. She liked what Jake had to offer and she wanted it all the time; stand in line young lady.

Chapter 74

"Great souls endure silently."
~ **J.C.F. Schiller**

Jake was so thankful for his father's recovery. He had prayed diligently every day, several times a day since Christmas for his dad to live and be healthy again. Jake had been missing the fishing outings with his dad. Wavy went back to work in a limited capacity so as to not prolong the healing process. He felt as strong as ever and many co-workers noticed a different Wavy, a more relaxed and easygoing man if that were even possible. Wavy more often than not usually let things roll off of his wide shoulders. He joked, laughed and smiled more often than before. Everything he said was in a slow relaxed manner accompanied with a large grin and reflective eyes; he was a man truly in love with life.

Wavy had always been a quiet man who owned a modest home, new car, a good job and a great wife and family that loved him very much. In the blink of an eye all of this nearly ended. This is the third time in his life that he escaped death and he felt extremely fortunate and blessed. He decided that he was going to enjoy every breath that he took. He was going to start going back to church and becoming more involved in the community. He wanted to spend quality time with his family and start doing more things that he enjoyed instead of merely working and sleeping his life away.

On Christmas Day 1968, Wavy Willoughby's life flashed before his eyes and he knew that it was probably the third and final time; he survived rattlesnakes, a deadly car crash and a shotgun blast to the chest. He was a lucky man and he knew it; he also knew that he was a blessed man, very blessed. No one but Wavy and his Lord knew that he too prayed. He prayed every day of his life since that diamondback stuck his long deadly fangs into young Wavy's ankle. He often had visions of the "ghost lady" who tried to warn him of the impending danger. Wavy's family assumed the ghost story was made up,

330

everyone but Jake, because he believed everything his father told him, as he felt a strong connection to his dad. Jake did not know that his dad was aware that he had been through a lot this past year. The family and friends of Wavy Willoughby often misinterpreted his silence as indifference and disconnect although that was not true at all. Wavy was a very sagacious man who preferred the sidelines and observed and critiqued the world around him. Only when it was necessary would he intervene with soft and prudent words that often were outside the box in complexity yet unveiled the common sense that lay dormant within the commoner waiting to be recognized.

Every word Wavy spoke was always very sharp witted and made people think for a few seconds until they finally caught on; even his tongue in cheek humor, which he always relayed with a straight face. Jake marveled at his dad's intellect and wished to be like him. Jake wondered if his dad had also been a "ladies man" but was too afraid to engage in this type of conversation with the man. Jake never really knew why he was afraid to ask his dad questions about his past and as far as he knew no one else dared asked either.

Wavy was a kind and gentle man who never raised his voice and enjoyed his music, maybe he himself didn't understand why no one ever asked him questions. He was a quiet man for the most part and that had to be why. He certainly was not a mean man nor did he look mean. He never volunteered any information thinking that no one really cared. His blue eyes kept everyone curious but too afraid to ask.

After an unremarkable and rainy Sunday afternoon in March, Wavy broke out "Old Nellie" the guitar from his honky-tonk days and tested the tenderness on his chest and fingertips. He cleared his throat and put his thumb and fingers to work.

"Waterloo, Waterloo, when will you meet your Waterloo?"

Uncle Hal, Uncle Olin and Mina chimed in with the harmony as Jake, Barbara, Kenny, Ronnie, and Christine all watched and listened and softly clapped their hands and stomped their feet to the bluegrass beat. It was a memorable afternoon, one that Jake's heart cries for today.

Uncle Olin and family had come by for supper and to give his brother the keys to his mobile home trailer that sat on the edge of the Edisto River near Givhan's Ferry State Park just outside of Walterboro. Wavy wanted to spend the following weekend on the river with family and do some fishing, or *jugging* for Catfish. Mina was concerned that he wasn't healed enough to actually fish and deal with the rigors that accompany the weekend outing. Wavy said that he was up to it and besides he had his boys by his side.

Chapter 75

*"Nothing out of its place is good
and nothing in its place is bad."*
~ **Walt Whitman**

The cool, foggy river air and the sleeping sun brought out the sweaters. Henry Miller's bonfire helped but you had to stand right next to the fire and then you were too hot and had to remove the sweater and then put it on again if you were ousted from your position at the fire which happened often to the youngest at any gathering. So Jake stood behind his two brothers who seemed to enjoy Mr. Miller's stories about the comings and goings of the river's part time residents.

Jake was bored and got busy drawing circles in the sand with the toe of his shoe when Mr. Miller got his attention when he mentioned The Bear Island Ghost which was just up the river a few miles. According to Mr. Miller, a long time ago, a fisherman was trapped on the island after his wife and her lover stole his boat and left to him to the bears and panthers that lived on the island. To this day, the fisherman's ghost prowls around the island in the form of a mighty black bear that kills anything that comes onto his island.

Ronnie, after taking a couple of gulps of Mr. Miller's half pint bottles of Kentucky whisky that he kept in his back pocket, insisted that they take rifles and hop in the boats and go looking for it now. Mr. Miller said that he used to see the bear walking on the beach when he was cruising by on his way to his secret fishing spot but that he had not seen him lately but often he hears some God awful screams in the middle of the night coming from up river.

Jake immediately got goose bumps, and Kenny turned around suddenly and grabbed Jake's unsuspecting ribs with his long fingers and let out a mischievous "BOO". Everyone laughed except Wavy and Jake.

Mina who was sitting on the screened porch enjoying a cold sweet tea yelled at Kenny, "Stop teasing your brother!"

"Yes ma'am," Kenny politely responded.

"Mr. Henry you don't need to be scaring my boys like that," Mina told the old man.

"Oh cackle, cackle, cackle Ms. Mina. I'm not scarin' 'em I'm preparin 'em," the old man shot back.

"And what on earth does that mean?" she said.

"If you sees em, you believes 'em, cackle, cackle, cackle." Mr. Miller nodded and bobbled at his circle of male comrades.

Mina just shook her lovely head okay. Jake and Kenny gave each other and inquisitive stare while trying to hold back the laughter. Kenny finally whispered in his brother's ear "What the hell is that cackle, cackle crap?" holding his belly as if that would keep the laughter inside.

"I don't know," Jake whispered, trying his best not to laugh out loud.

That's when the old man put a finger to the right nostril of his red, warty nose, closed it shut, took a deep breath and blew launching the contents of the left nostril into the fire. He then did the same thing with the opposite side. Kenny and Jake had never seen such a thing in their lives and that was all she wrote as far holding back the laughter. After their four eyes bugged out at the launching ceremony they looked at each other and simultaneously yelled, "Oh crap," as Kenny grabbed Jake's shoulder and they ran from the man circle laughing like they hadn't laughed in months and to the point of belly cramps.

"Boys, watch your language," Mina shouted.

Jake turned to look at his mom who was only visible through the illumination of a candle sitting on the small picnic table on the porch. Jake thought that the candle gave his mom had an eerie appearance and he was tired of being scared of ghost; hearing of them, dreaming of them and seeing them. He badly needed to blow his palms. He searched for an indiscreet area and wondered off behind a large sweet gum tree and blew each palm three times, looked at the bottom of each foot again three times while also looking to make sure that he wasn't spotted and making sure that no bear crawled out of the woods behind them.

Jake started thinking of Barbara, he was missing her badly. They haven't been apart for very long since they started hanging out together. He was thinking of her beautiful face and lovely smile, and the smell of her hair. He was thinking about the way she would tease him when things didn't go his way, and of course he thought of her big boobs. He needed her right now; he was nervous, cold, and afraid. He caught up with Kenny, and together they walked back to the man circle.

Then suddenly from beyond the tree lined riverbank, across from them in the dark night, there was a ghastly and horrifying scream from up the river and it echoed downstream into their taught ring of ghost stories and noogy blowing. It sounded like something or someone was in severe pain.

"Oh my God," Kenny screamed, and then jumped up against Wavy which made him cringe from the pain in his still tender chest.

Ronnie, the fearsome Marine, screamed in reply hoping to be heard by the bear.

Mina yelled at all of them, "stop it now, what was that?"

Even Mr. Miller looked startled because he had been making up this entire story he had just told.

He blurted out as he turned toward the noise with a half burnt and smoldering Chesterfield dangling from the corner of his crusty and cracked lips, "What the f...hell was that?"

Ronnie quickly said, "Get rifles now- LOCK AND LOAD!"

Jake was nervously thinking what the 'ef is going on and again started blowing his palms as he was very afraid now. Wavy even looked concerned. It was a sound so horrific that no one could describe it or define it, but it was definitely something being brutally tortured. Wavy finally said that a gator must have gotten a large shore bird. The river is certainly abundant with gators.

"Are we still going out there tonight to drop bait?" Kenny asked Wavy very nervously.

"You want to catch a mess of catfish don't you?" Wavy said.

"Hell yeah," the Marine hero screamed.

"Oh crap!" Kenny said, scratching the top of his big head.

"Wavy, I don't think ya'll need to be going out there after that. It's too dark and scary for the boys," suggested the very apprehensive Mina.

"Oh, it is all okay; whatever it was is busy eating his catch. He'll be chillin' in hole when we're out there."

"Cackle, cackle, cackle."

The Jon boat was loaded and ready, the lanterns were handy and the nerves were shattered except for Wavy and Ronnie who sat in the boat with rifles on their laps waiting for Kenny and Jake who were very skeptical about this trip. Mina didn't want the boys to go but they didn't want to appear "chicken" to one another or to the older men.

Mr. Miller hurriedly untied the old aluminum boat and tossed the line inside and said, "I ain't ever had bear meat; sho can't wait to try it tho, cackle, cackle, cackle."

Jake looked at the old man in disbelief as he positioned himself very closely on the bench next to Kenny who looked absolutely horrified. After that horrible noise Mina had again protested their going out and went as far as to grab her two youngest boys by the collar to hold them back. Ronnie and Wavy assured her that there was nothing to worry about and the boys were in good hands. They explained that the noise was just some bird that was caught in a tree or brush although it could have been in a gator jaws but they of course didn't say that to the nervous mom. Jake and Kenny looked at each other as if to say, "Is this the end of Rico?" Neither took a stand and they obediently followed their dad and older brother.

As they were pulling away from the shoreline Kenny hollered out, "Wait a minute; I don't even like catfish. Why am I going out there?" No one answered so he grudgingly went along. The murky river met the shadowy night in perfect harmony; all was quiet except Jake and Kenny's hearts about to burst from their chest. The only light came from their lanterns which were unsteady due to nerves and ripples in the water. A strand of moss rubbed against Kenny's cheek, and he screamed nearly as tortured as the creature from earlier. He jumped and nearly took the entire boat over which brought screams from everyone on board and alerted Mr. Miller who was still standing at the old dock with flash light and rifle.

"What the hell is going on out there?" The old man yelled. "Wavy, ya'll alright?"

Now Mina was horrified from the porch a hundred yards away. "What is it?" she shrieked.

"Just some moss," Wavy and Ronnie replied in unison.

"Jake, Kenny, are you okay?" asked a very uneasy mom.

"They're fine," Wavy said, in that calm voice of his.

"We're okay," Kenny said, finally realizing that a snake, bear nor a ghost had got him and that his mom needed to hear from him that he was okay.

"Jake, are you alright honey?" Mina asked.

"Yes, Mama, I'm fine."

Ronnie took a large gulp from one of the cold Pabst Blue Ribbon beers he had on ice in the cooler that he made sure was on board. He looked around with the eyes of a warrior and rifle at the ready, no doubt having flashbacks from the war, finally burping up malt and barley. Jake just hoped that he did not start shooting unless it was necessary. Jake's stomach was in knots and he started blowing his palms again.

Kenny nudged him and whispered, "Do it for me too," in a serious matter of fact tone that surprised Jake. They slowly coasted to the nearest lagoon where they were greeted by several small red lights glaring from the deep black water. The group seemed barricaded by the dense border of large trees and thick brush.

"What is that?" a frightened Kenny quickly asked while pointing at the red lights.

"Gator eyes," Ronnie said, in a very enthusiastic manner as he finished off his fourth beer.

"Oh God no," cried Kenny, "there must be hundreds out there!"

"Just fifty," chuckled Ronnie.

"Shssh," Wavy said to his son.

Crap, crap, crap this is the worst 'effing thing in the world a pale and horrified Jake mumbled to himself while nearly crushing Kenny's hand with his own as he held on for dear life; he wasn't going alone. Kenny grimaced in pain but did not want to alert the gators or his mom.

Wavy confidently commandeered the small craft and stayed in the middle of the lagoon away from the banks and told everyone to remain quiet and still. Jake was about to totally crap in his jeans and knew that Kenny was probably about to do the same if he hadn't already. If they both crap they would surely sink from the extra weight. They were both shocked that their father did not retreat from the lagoon of doom.

They looked at each other in horror and Kenny quietly said, "Let's get the hell out here; this is not funny at all!"

Ronnie said, "Shssh". "Those are giant gators so we don't stand a chance and if you can't be quiet we'll throw you to them so they'll leave the rest of us alone."

Kenny now had tears welling up in his eyes and Wavy impatiently said to Ronnie, "That's enough, toss out the jugs."

Ronnie tossed the empty gallon milk jugs with line and bait attached into the gator infested waters. The splash stirred the gators curiosity and they slowly swam towards the jugs then Wavy controlled the rudder and eased out of the lagoon.

"The gators will probably eat the bait and hooks and turn this entire misadventure into a waste," Jake whispered to Kenny. "I am not coming back to pull the jugs in because there may be a live gator on the other end. Besides, I don't like catfish that much."

"I'm with you on that, Bubba."

As they slowly turned around to leave the eerie lagoon, the side of the small boat bumped into a log; a long ago fallen pine with the top submerged into the river for the many fish to nest in and the long center section out of the water stretching from the bank of the lagoon that served as a sunning perch for box turtles on bright days.

You only thought that you heard screams before.

A stunned and buzzing war-weary Ronnie couldn't help but shoot out the profanities.

"M. F. S.O.B., what the hell was that?!" Ronnie screamed. "Come get me you slant eyed S.O.B.'s!"

Jake and Kenny in accord ripped out the most feminine scream two young men could possibly muster up. That had to scare away any potential predators.

Even Wavy, whose normal calm was shaken with the heavy bump of the boat and his first instinct, was fright but after a split second the fatherly instinct took control.

"Easy fellas, it's okay. Stay still, be calm, and stay quiet." Wavy instructed his sons in a soft soothing whisper at the same time carefully maneuvering the grip on the trolling motor and keeping his sharp eyes open for any obstacles.

After reaching land Kenny and Jake were nearly too frightened to stand let alone walk. Their legs were rubbery and there rumps cramped from the hard bench. They both swore they would never, ever go out in the boat in the dark again and both franticly ran to the safety of the porch where their mom eagerly awaited and greeted them with smothering hugs.

"Little mama's boys!" Ronnie yelled, as he was tying up the boat and mumbling, no doubt jarheadjunglejive who would never had been so verbally abusive had it been not for the beer, whiskey and war.

"Oh, sorry Mom, oops." Ronnie apologized after seeing Mina come out from the shadow of the porch.

Mina stood there shaking her head. She closely observed her two youngest under the meager porch light. She offered them hot tea when they came in. They said for her to go on in and they would be there in a minute. They really needed to compose themselves first.

Jake and Kenny just stood there both slapping at the onslaught of mosquitoes as the voracious insects hovered over their flesh looking for the opportune time to attack just like the gators.

"Heck, that was supposed to be fun?" Kenny exclaimed, to his younger brother while trying to catch his breath. "I think they have lost their minds!"

Jake couldn't even speak. He just stood there in the cool air shaking, and nodding in agreement at his now very pissed off brother. Jake had never seen Kenny this mad, and he thought he was going to punch someone or something. Some karma for all the abuse Kenny bestowed upon Jake in the past... Just don't say anything that you will regret.

Chapter 76

"It is the dim haze of mystery that adds enchantment to pursuit."
~ **Antoine Rivarol**

Christine and Barbara loaded up Christine's new 1961 Volkswagen Beetle convertible that she bought with the money that she had saved while working at Morrison's Department Store. It was a gorgeous spring Saturday morning which made it an ideal time for a little road trip. The girls were excited to be able to make the trip to surprise their sweeties and to have a fun day at the river after a very cold winter.

They weren't expecting the water to still be ice cold when they packed their bathing suits. Barbara was thrilled to be doing things with her older sister especially since they both were dating Willoughby brothers. This same bonding also meant a lot to Jake, giving him opportunity to share a similar interest in his hero brother who fought and was shot in Vietnam.

Charleston and surrounding areas really come alive in the springtime; the scenic Highway 61 between Charleston and Summerville was no exception. The long, narrow road was once the first railroad track in America. The twelve mile journey through the cool, shady tunnel of live oaks bordering the road on either side is a beautiful ride anytime of the year but as the new green leaves mature and the azaleas bloom and the oleanders and dogwoods blossom so does the human spirit. It rejuvenates with the lively sunshine and longer days as the vibrant and colorful flowers fill us with optimism to greet each new morning and to sustain us throughout the day while euphoric birds croon into each warm evening below the magnificent stars and majestic wonder.

The vivacious girls left John's Island at 7:30 am hoping to get to the river early so that they could spend an entire day with their guys. As the little green beetle turned onto Highway 61 and headed southwest you could hear the feeble radio with its greatest effort giving you The Box Tops singing "The Letter" as the long wavy dirty blonde hair of both girls blew in the wind while they were singing along with the radio.

Meanwhile, Jake and Kenny had slept on the front porch facing the river bundled up in sleeping bags and wool blankets and as close to each other as they possibly could be to receive body heat which was something they did in their subconscious in the middle of the night because they would never show such tenderness in their waking moments.

Wavy and a slightly hung-over Ronnie snuck out the back door just before the sun rose to retrieve the bait jugs that hopefully had attached fish... They took their rifles just in case they had hooked a hungry gator or two. They hopped in the Jon boat and paddled a ways to avoid waking anyone. After several yards they started the small trolling motor which happened to startle the half-awake Jake. Sleepy eyed, he raised his head to recollect his whereabouts and to see what snuggled bundle was next to him. Kenny's entire head was covered by the blanket and tucked inside the sleeping bag like a scared turtle.

Jake exhausted his physical effort to uncover Kenny and finally said, "Hey Kenny, wake up; how the heck are you breathing in there?"

Kenny begrudgingly stirred and whined "Why the heck are you waking me? I did not fall asleep till just a bit ago. Leave me be, please!"

Jake didn't sleep well either but the sun was rising and he didn't want to miss a thing.

"Mom is up, I can smell breakfast."

Kenny looked at him in disbelief "So what?!"

Jake climbed from the warm comfort of blanket and bag, and stood up on the hard floor still dressed in yesterday's attire, though adorning several more wrinkles. He peered over at the mist veiled river and thought, what a beautifully wicked scene, as the bright rays of the morning sun broke through the kaleidoscopic haze of branches, on the huge trees from across the river.

"Man this feels good. Wake up butt head, you're missing the sunrise."

"I guess so; obviously you're not going to leave me alone."

Kenny finally gave up on sleep and decided that the sunrise over the Edisto River may be something to behold. As he cleared his eyes and they stepped out of the screened porch and walked to the sandy banks of the river they took in the morning smells of breakfast cooking nearby that made their stomachs growl. They both laughed and agreed that they were hungry. Still they stood side by side and watched as the beauty of the new day presented itself to their intoxicated eyes.

"Wow, I wish we had a camera," Kenny said.

"I know, isn't it beautiful?" Mina responded from behind.

She stood in the door way and admired the sunrise too but with more heartfelt joy as she looked at her youngest sons becoming young men, all of her children were nearly grown now and a bittersweet emotion overcame her as a lonely tear found its way down her cheek. She just stood there and savored the moment, hoping it would never end.

"Where's the boat?" Jake shouted.

Mina said, "Ronnie and your dad went to get the jugs and hopefully some fish."

Jake and Kenny both were relieved that they didn't have to go along but both were worried about the safety of their dad and brother. They sauntered up river on the root laden bank to see if they could see or hear them.

Mina called out to them, "In case there is no fish, I cooked up some bacon to go with the grits, eggs, and flour bread."

She sipped her coffee and smiled as she watched her boys walk up the river bank.

Mr. Miller stepped out from his small porch and sat his Delta Airlines coffee mug on a stump and started gathering wood in his old wheel barrel for his daily inferno. He smiled, waved and greeted a good morning to everyone. Earlier he saw Ronnie and Wavy leave in the boat so he was not alarmed.

The sound of a small car made its way down the winding sandy road and then the green Beetle revealed itself. Surprised, Mina welcomed some female company as the lovely girls parked and jumped out with huge, happy smiles and ran to the porch and greeted Mina with large bear hugs.

"Where is everyone?" Barbara asked.

Mina told them they went off in search of Jake and Kenny. Mina went back to the kitchen to cook more bacon.

Mr. Miller stopped behind the wheel barrel to admire the giggling, jiggling girls as they bounced down the river bank.

The bank dropped off and was no longer accessible as the boys approached the lagoon. A small creek broke through it and the other side was covered in dark brush, bamboo, long needle pines, colossal river birch, and pin oak trees scattered throughout. They stood on the sandy corner of the bank then slid down to the cold water and stuck out their necks as far as they could to see around the trees.

They recognized the opening of the lagoon just a hundred yards away and then they realized that they could very easily be breakfast for gators so they climbed back up the steep, sandy bank to escape any hungry gators that may be nearby only to have the weak bank collapse and give way under their weight. Frantically, they kept crawling and climbing to no avail, only to slide right back down again.

They both started to panic, "Dad, Ronnie, Dad," they were calling out simultaneously.

Jake couldn't help but think of Tommy's final seconds on earth as he fought for air and life. At that precise instant Tommy's eyes appeared from over the crest of the river bank and looked down into his own eyes. Completely startled, Jake nearly fell into the river then realized that is was Barbara who was looking at him.

"Are you okay? What is it?" Christine asked in a very concerned manner as she looked over.

"Oh my God." Kenny screamed.

"Please help us outta here, there's gators out here."

"What? Well what are two fools doing down there?"

The girls looked around in fright and noticed that upstream was a slight dip on the river's edge with some large, slick roots jutting out of the ground from one of the huge oaks for grabbing onto.

"Over there," pointed Christine. "Go over there quickly."

The two boys ran over to where she was directing. Jake kept looking back for hungry alligators and when they finally reached the spot they pulled themselves to safety with the help of the girls. While they tried to catch their breaths Kenny blurted out, "Thank God you two showed up. I can't believe you're here. It's a miracle, it really is, oh my God," as he brushed away the sand from his crumpled and damp clothing.

"We are very glad we got here when we did." Christine said, while helping Kenny brush the sand off of him.

Barbara was doing the same for Jake. "Where are the alligators, when did you see them, just now?"

"Yes, just a short distance from here, we saw 'em last night when we were out in the boat, there was tons of them." Jake said, indicating to the lagoon. "You wouldn't believe what we've been through the last several hours."

"Oh crap, where's Ronnie?" Christine asked impatiently.

"Ronnie and dad are out there getting the bait jugs." Kenny said, looking towards the lagoon.

"Ronnie, honey, Ronnie, Ronnie!" a frantic Christine yelled out.

Jake finally took his eyes off of Barbara's pink cotton sweater covered breast long enough to look in the direction up river and barked, "Dad, Dad, Ronnie, hey guys where are you?!"

The small boat came buzzing into view within minutes with very mixed expressions from both Wavy and Ronnie looking at the foursome on the bank.

"What in the world is going on? When did you two get here?" a very surprised Ronnie asked.

"We just got here .We wanted to surprise you and we rescued your brothers from hungry alligators while you're out fishing." Christine said. "Good Morning Mr. Willoughby," she added.

"What, where are the gators?!"

Jake quickly responded, "We haven't seen any today, she was just kidding."

"No gators, but plenty of catfish so hope you're hungry." Wavy said.

The small group on land slowly walked parallel with the boaters downstream and they all chit chatted the entire way until Wavy and Ronnie docked and tied off the small craft. Barbara couldn't believe all the fish and the massive size of some of them. Jake never forgot how skillful his dad used pliers to skin the whiskered fish. The large breakfast filled the hungry group as the sun reached the middle of the sky and brightened the day to the delight of all including the cheerful songbirds in the many trees.

Chapter 77

"The magic of first love is our ignorance that it can never end."
~ **Benjamin Disraeli**

Ever since he met her Jake had a small crush on Barbara, but knowing she was older he never gave her too much thought. She usually ignored the younger boys anyway. She had a personality unlike the other girls. She was outspoken, confident, and always upbeat no matter the circumstance. Her mind was sharp and she had a quick wit that Jake admired. Also, she didn't take any crap off of anyone and did not hesitate to speak her mind and Jake admired those qualities as well. Wrapped around all of that was the most perfect body that Jake had ever noticed on a girl or woman for that matter.

Wavy and Mr. Miller who had fierceness in the head which is his description of a hangover were feeding a huge blaze. Nearby Kitty Wells sang "It Wasn't God Who Made Honky-Tonk Angels" from Mr. Miller's small radio that sitting on an old wire milk crate. Mina was cleaning up the breakfast disarray and starting lunch and as usual never complaining.

"Thank you dear," Mina said, as Kenny offered his assistance.

Jake and Barbara felt obligated after Kenny offered; everything was cleaned and put away in a matter of minutes. Kenny was always aware of his mother's never ending chores and tried to pitch in whenever possible. His support was starting to wear off on Jake recently who started to take more notice of his mom's hard work. Ronnie and Christine wondered off in the Jon boat and found a quiet and shady spot about a mile west of the landing.

"Ah, this is nice baby," he said to his girlfriend of many years.

Just months ago he was in the jungles of Vietnam dreaming of this and not knowing if he would survive. He closed his eyes and thanked God for bringing him home. Three Galaxies boomed overhead and he cringed.

…As they walked onto the back porch, Jake grabbed Barbara's butt and squeezed it.

"I know, but where?"

"Well, let's see," he said, with one hand scratching his head and the other one rubbing Barbara's firm bottom.

"Let's go behind one of the other trailers where no one is home."

Barbara's eyes lit up with excitement and said, "Heck yeah, great idea."

They walked behind the trailer looking to see if anyone noticed and then they slipped into the woods that bordered the lot and stayed on the edge of the woods until they got to the Jenson's trailer,

"Oh crap." Jake whispered.

"What?"

"The screen door is open to the back porch." Barbara looked, and indeed the screen door was ajar.

"Maybe someone broke in." she said nervously.

"Let's check it out." Jake said, taking charge as Mr. He-man, but inside he was thinking *what if it's the ghost bear?*

They slowly eased onto the metal steps and pulled back the screen, and of course, it squeaked loud enough to wake the dead. They looked around and gingerly stepped onto the porch, Jake tried the knob to the trailer and thank goodness it was locked. They both wiped their foreheads in relief and looked around, they decided on the pollen coated, wicker loveseat. Jake grabbed Barbara's face and planted the most passionate kiss he had ever delivered to her. She melted right into the loveseat.

"Oh baby, I missed you so much," she whispered into Jake's ear, while pulling on his sweatshirt to get it over his head.

A large, planter holding a beautiful, Boston fern fell to the floor and shattered. Barbara screamed, and Jake jumped back in terror, as a huge possum scampered through the screen door and out into the wild where it belonged.

"Oh man, what the crap was that?"

"I think it was a possum."

"Dang, it was ugly. Someone's going to come running over here, so we better leave," She said, while pulling her sweater back on and completely forgetting her bra.

They quickly hopped out of the porch and ran through the woods, hoping again to find another open porch, or at least wait until who ever investigated the noise will leave so they can return. No luck at the next trailer, or the next, so they headed back to the first one.

The smell of burning wood and leaves floated through the air, causing Jake to look down at his left leg. Peeking from behind a tall pine, they did not any sign of anyone, so they went back to the porch. Barbara felt bad about the beautiful, planter and plant but hey, they should have locked the door.

"Where were we?" she asked.

"Oh man," Jake said, pointing at her bra. "I hope no one saw that."

"Crap! What if they come back? What if they call the owners?"

Jake smiled and said, "So what, we'll be long gone by the time the owners get here."

Chapter 78

"Tapping at my chamber door; darkness there and nothing more."
~ **Edgar Allen Poe**

Mr. Miller was a lonely old man. He had been widowed for several years, so he enjoyed occasional visitors, and recently, he accidently stumbled onto a new hobby; voyeurism, sneaking behind the trees and watching Jake and Barbara.

The sun burned into the quiet river mist, and the smoky smell of frying bacon filled the air, while Mina went about feeding the starving brood. Wavy and Ronnie were first to rise, eat a bite, and hit the beautiful, morning riverside, to enjoy the peacefulness of it all. Both these men only months ago were knocking on heaven's door, yet here they are, alive and well, and enjoying their family, and one of God's many gifts of nature, the Edisto River, and its awesome surroundings.

Wavy quickly noticed something odd when Barney, Mr. Miller's old hound was not sniffing at his heels. Mr. Miller and Barney were always up and inspecting things before the crack of dawn. Wavy looked over at Mr. Miller's trailer and saw the door was still shut and the windows were yet to be opened; he knew something was off kilter.

Wavy eyed the trailer and its surroundings with very fretful eyes then he looked over at Ronnie.

"This is odd; follow me." Wavy said to his son.

The two bullet weary men cautiously approached the ragged, old trailer. Wavy put his feet on the steps and pulled on the loose handle of the torn screen door. It was latched shut. The old man was still inside.

"Mr. Miller, Mr. Miller!" Wavy yelled loudly.

No response. Wavy, now extremely concerned looked at Ronnie and rubbed at his freshly shaven chin.

"Mr. Miller, hey, Mr. Miller you okay?!" Ronnie yelled.

"Let's go around back and yell into the windows," Wavy said.

The men continued calling out for the missing morning greeter and his dog. Mina, Kenny, Jake and the two girls soon came to their screened porch to see what all the commotion was about. Kenny was the first to leave the porch and walk towards the old man's trailer, and was soon joined by Jake. They did not see Wavy or Ronnie, but knew they were on the other side of the trailer and yelled out to them.

"What's wrong?" Kenny asked.

Wavy said, "I'm not sure if anything is wrong, it's just strange that Mr. Miller is not out and about yet."

Mina shrugged it off, and went back inside with the two girls to finish the dishes. Jake followed Kenny to the other side of the trailer, where Wavy and Ronnie strained to peer into a window, still calling out to the old man, when the startled hound started barking and startled all four.

Wavy knew that the dog's barking would alert Mr. Miller and he would come to inspect the commotion. The dog continued to bark and several minutes passed, and still no Mr. Miller. "Peculiar," he said, in a distraught manner, while he looked at his three sons.

The three sons followed their dad back to the front porch, where Wavy decided it was time to take drastic measures by jerking on the screen door hard enough to bust loose the lock and latchet. Wavy and Ronnie entered the porch, and ordered Jake and Kenny to stay behind. Wavy grabbed the door handle, and to his amazement, the door pushed open and out rushed one very frightened hound dog, and a very foul odor, unimaginable to man.

"Oh God," Kenny cried.

"Mother f '…um shucker," Ronnie screamed.

"Whoa," Wavy warned.

The three larger men, cursing and tumbling backward, nearly stampeded Jake, who could not see over the shoulders of his elders, did not know what was going on until the vile odors of human excrement and urine mixed with the same from an old dog and rotten food hit his nostrils.

"Crap," Jake whispered under his breath, while pinching his nostrils with his thumb and forefinger from his right hand, and pushing Kenny away with his left, all the while trying to keep his balance.

Wavy shouted, while puffing for air. "Kenny, Jake, go be with the women; Ronnie follow me."

The boys were happy to oblige, and quickly ran across the sandy earth to their trailer, where Mina and the girls peeped out of the window and door to see what all the cursing was about.

"Well here goes," Wavy told Ronnie. He then entered the dark, smelly confines of the old trailer, while Ronnie stooped over and held Barney by the collar.

The further into the trailer, the more profound the smells. New odors came into the mix, old cigarette smoke, stale beer, liquor emanating from old vomit and a sweaty, old dog. Ronnie had smelled his share of crap in Vietnam, but being hung over on top of this nearly made him vomit. He was trying his best to keep control, after all, he was a Vietnam veteran and U.S. Marine, awarded with two purple hearts.

The dark, trailer was a filthy mess. Wavy was tripping over beer cans, empty and full, filthy bowls and plates, crusty spoons and forks, empty whiskey bottles, crumpled and stained newspaper, and piles of dog feces, and large, copper colored stains of urine… Approaching from down the hall, they were greeted with another very unusual and disagreeable odor - death.

"Mr. Miller!" Wavy yelled out.

Wavy, with Ronnie and Barney right behind him, carefully went down the hall to the master bedroom like he was walking through a minefield. A huge picture hung crookedly on the wall with three faces smiling at Wavy as he stuck his head inside. It was obviously a depiction of happier times, with a barely unrecognizable Mr. Miller grinning at the camera, with his lovely wife and dimwitted son sitting in front of him. Mrs. Miller smiled sheepishly, while the dimwit stared off into space with drool hanging off his very large chin that appeared frozen in an awkward angle. At Wavy's feet was a very dead Mr. Miller. Mouth and eyes open, blank eyes staring into space, and vomit dripping from his very large chin, like father like son. The old man was naked and blue, nauseatingly blue.

"Can you imagine the smell if we had not found him?" Ronnie said with disgust, wrinkling his nose up and grimacing. "It's bad enough now."

Wavy kneeled down at the lifeless form. He put two fingers on the neck just under the stubbly jaw bone. He knew that the old man was dead, but instinct made him inquire, despite not wanting to touch it.

Wavy, holding back his own vomit, shook his head back and forth and said, "Damn, it must have been a heart attack."

"Let's get the hell out of here," Ronnie shouted. He had seen enough dead bodies already; he did not need an old, crap covered man to add to the collection.

"I need a dip in the river to wash this stink off. Jake, go get a bar of soap." Ronnie said, as he ran out into the daylight towards the cool, inviting, black water of the Edisto River.

"Watch out for gators" Jake yelled.

"They better watch out for me."

Jake followed his brother into the river; they were quickly joined by Kenny and Wavy, and finally joined by Barney.

Chapter 79

"The best mirror is a friend's eye."
~ **Gaelic Proverb**

After the past year in its shroud of despair; Jake sees his first corpse. He had no choice; Mina carefully laid out his clothes, a dressy white shirt, new, black slacks and a red, snap on tie, all from Morrison's Department Store. Everything fit, except for Ronnie's scuffed, well-worn penny loafers, which had to be stuffed with old socks in the toes to take up the extra space. Three spit shines later, they looked as good as used.

The small white church outside of Cottageville reminded Jake an awful lot of his and Teresa's discovery in the forest behind her house, except this one is not forgotten. It was spotless white and filled with melancholy organ music. Even the trees appeared to be the same to Jake, with their enormous mass sheltering the modest frame building with the small cross sitting at the top of its unassuming steeple, reaching into the heavens through the eerie moss, sagging from great and powerful branches that sprawled high above the church itself.

Against the edge of the woods in the back of the church, were planted a dozen or so identical old tombstones, inscribed with the names of people that once lived, loved and laughed. Mr. Miller's wife and son awaited his company. Henry Miller was a nice old man Jake believed; he was alive and full of energy just two days ago.

Several cars and trucks were parked along the sandy drive leading to the church, and at the end of the line, in front of the steps leading to the front doors, sat a long black hearse. Apparently the old man had some family and friends left; a descent sendoff was afforded by someone. From inside, the organ music began and "Amazing Grace" rolled out of the open windows and hitched a ride on the wind and wafted across the vacant field across the street, and settled into the forest at the end.

The wooden box sat at the front of the church near the foot of the small altar. Jake and family slowly walked the long row of pews behind others who came to show their respect. Jake stared at the opened box as he sluggishly followed his parents, and then the familiar, yet grotesque face of Mr. Miller appeared inside the box. They all did a quick walk by, but Jake was mesmerized, as he looked down at this cold lifeless body, a wax like face, with a stretched on smile, and stiff fingers ineptly entangled. Jake could see the old man's nose hairs hanging like stalactites in his large nostrils, and he could hear the old man's cackle. He could smell the Canadian Mist on his breath, and he could whiff the remnants of wood and leaves swirling in the air from the red hot embers he carefully manipulated. What a crude and appalling ritual this all is, Jake thought. Jake did not like death, why was it everywhere? *Get me out of here please!* If those palms ever needed blowing, this was the time.

Jake spent the rest of the day blowing away the cooties from his sweaty hands. As soon as he got home, he ran to the shower and lathered up, and let the near scalding water beat down on his tender body for a good ten minutes. Afterwards, he threw ALL of the clothes that he had been wearing into the washer; he tossed the sock stuffed shoes under Ronnie's bed where they belonged and certainly not in his room, for something from the funeral to creep into his bed and cause death and destruction. He really wanted to throw the clothes and shoes in the trash or burn them. He was afraid that any sort of contact would bring death to those he most cared about.

After a shower and fresh attire, he hopped on his bike and pedaled as hard as he could, hopeful that somehow the visions of the morning would disappear completely from his memory banks. Jake needed a diversion, and he thought of all the different girls. He decided it was too stressful to even try and finagle, so he decided instead on hanging with his buddies for a while. He hadn't done much with them lately and he was a little excited about seeing his old pals. He rode into Chucky's yard and saw him and Stevie playing with the yoyo's they received for Christmas.

They had just gotten home from school and were shocked to see Jake. They asked why he missed school today and he told them. They could tell that he was upset and didn't want to talk about it; they did not want to do anything that would make him leave. Finally, for lack of anything else to talk about, a garrulous Stevie broke the news to him about Billy's plan to break up him and Barbara. Jake was stunned at such an idea. After they explained that they were jealous and missed him, he apologized and promised that he would spend more time hanging out with them. He told them that he was kind of tired of "going steady" anyway.

Jake's relationship with Barbara had taken him away from his few remaining pals, but on a positive note it also changed the way he was treated by the rest of the guys at school. They no longer picked on him and made fun of him. The fact that he was "making it" with Barbara, earned him a lot of respect and he relished that. Respect was something he never had before, especially from the cool guys. Before he made any hasty decisions he would have to think on it very wisely. He figured there would be no harm in dangling his pals on a rope for a while, to pacify them while he was in their presence.

Riding back home on his bike, he thought about how he felt when he heard his friends tell him they missed him so much they wanted to break up Barbara and him. At first he was sort of angry, but after studying it a little more, he actually felt really good that his friends cared so much of him. He smiled for the first time in days. Now he was hungry and couldn't wait to get home.

Chapter 80

"One devil often drubs another."
~ Thomas Fuller

Barbara Stern was one of those rare humans that was blessed with total beauty, inside and out, from head to toe. She had the perfect physique that developed early, with the flawless face, soft skin, and raspy voice that Jake loved, and it was all enveloped around a bubbly persona that Jake loved even more. But most importantly, she was good to him, very good to him; she treated him like a prince.

Overall, she was a delightful person with a warm and gentle spirit. He knew that he was very fortunate to have her as his girlfriend and he suddenly felt very foolish for ever having any thoughts whatsoever of dumping her or cheating on her. He also felt very selfish; everything was about poor Jake. So consumed with guilt, he went straight home after visiting his buddies and completely forgot about being hungry. He sat down with a composition notebook, and wrote his very first love letter, he drew a picture of flowers in a pot and highlighted them with coloring pencils. He slipped some of Kenny's candy that was hidden in a drawer, inside an Old Spice box and wrapped it in one of his mother's silk hankies. He combed his thick unruly, hair and went to see his girl.

Jake's heart sank when he saw Patty Singleton leaving the Stern's house from the front door.

"Oh crap!" He uttered, and jumped behind the nearest tree.

This ain't good; they are friends after all, and just maybe, hopefully nothing came of this. Jake took refuge behind the branches of the willow and waited for Patty to walk past; he couldn't help but admire her walk, and felt a certain pride.

"Psst, Patty," he whispered.

She wore a tight sweater that wrapped around her huge breast, and made them look like she was hiding two large, honeydews underneath. Jake was excited, and so was Patty, who came bouncing and licking her lips.

"Is that for me darling," teasingly referring to the candy.

Jake was impatient. "No, it's for Barbara. What were ya 'll talking about?" He demanded.

Patty smiled. She thought about letting him stew for a while, and she thought about lying, but she really liked the boy and didn't want to upset him. She liked Barbara too, but she liked Jake more.

"Don't worry big boy, we never spoke of you."

Jake didn't believe her, "You sure?"

She let out a little hoot "Get real baby, yeah, I thought about it, because I want you all for myself, but I like you both, and you're such a sweet boy bringing her gifts, so I couldn't hurt her like that."

Jake thought to himself, *but you'll bang her boyfriend instead.*

Jake breathed for the first time in minutes. "Thank you," he said, in all earnestness.

"But if you ever change your mind about her, I got first bids okay?" She said, with that naughty banter of hers, that she has mastered so well.

"You got it." Jake said, trying to rush off.

"I just want to give you something to think about" She said, lifting her sweater and exposing her large, bare melons with attached pacifiers. Naturally, Jake wanted to reach out grab a handful of melon, but caught himself.

"Oh go ahead Honey, no one will know." Patty said.

Jake was tempted, but he raised his head, and whispered, "Maybe another time," He then walked assertively over to Barbara's front door.

Patty, surprised at his restraint, watched him stroll off; she wanted him even more now.

When he stepped out of the cover of the long, willow branches, Jake caught the tail end of Bobby Burns' royal blue GTO quickly turn the corner and leaving with fading rumble of the baritone muffler and even noisier stereo, with bold, bass pulsating into the air onto Longleaf Drive. Along with the reverberation, the muscle car also left an unusual and distinct odor of a burning herb of exotic sort, lingering in the air that Jake was not yet aware of. Now he had something else to be concerned with, like he didn't already have enough on his plate.

Jake continued the cocky gait of a rock star, but inside, his stomach and nerves was rolling like thunder, and became tangled like the web he felt his life was becoming. He wanted to check his soles, his elbows and he wanted most of all to blow those palms, which were full of cooties and sweat. He reached the side door of the Stern's house off of the carport, as he did each time he visited there, but, with each visit, he would remember the sorrowful image of Mrs. Stern standing in that same exact spot, when she got news of her only son's death.

Jake heard a car pulling into the gravelly drive, and turned to see Mr. Stern driving up after getting in from work. Jake politely and patiently waited for him to exit the car, and then he spoke. Mr. Stern got out of the car with a brown, paper bag filled with a six pack of his favorite brew from Milwaukee in one hand, patted Jake on the head with his other hand which also contained his car keys, which irritably rubbed against Jake's scalp. Jake tried not to grimace; he liked to think that Mr. Stern didn't realize he had the keys in his hand when he rubbed hard on his head. Maybe it was revenge for the death wish upon his son, or revenge for banging two of his daughters. Jake's belly was knotted and rising. Mr. Stern looked at the boy's treats.

"Awe, is that for me?"

Jake now was even more irritated and embarrassed; he really had to get rid of this candy. What a stupid idea.

Clearing his throat, and quickly coming up with a reply, Jake shyly mumbled "Um, actually the candy is for one of your lovely daughters, but if you'd like a piece, you can certainly have one."

Tommy Sr. popped open an Old Milwaukie and laughed "This is my candy son," he took a large swallow of his cold beverage. "Takes the edge off of a long day, Jake, you want some?" He handed Jake the dripping aluminum can. Jake grabbed the slippery offering, and without hesitation put the can to his mouth and took a large swallow of beer, as Mr. Stern gawked in amazement.

"Jake, I'd swear you were one of my own. You've had this tasty beverage before haven't you?" Jake has been uncomfortable around Mr. Stern ever since Tommy's death, and that awkwardness only multiplied when he started nailing two of his daughters.

"No sir, this is the first," Jake lied. He had sipped on Wavy's beer while sitting in his dads lap," driving" the backroads of the island, when he was about six or seven. He never cared for the flavor and did not understand why people would drink it.

Mr. Stern reached into the bag and ripped another can from the plastic strip and pulled off the tab and flicked it into the yard. All the children had sliced open toes on those things many times over the years.

"Well, since we're practically family, I think we should drink to that."

Jake wasn't quite sure how to toast, he waited to see what Tom Sr. would do, and then he would mimic his actions. He was a nervous wreck. Julie, Kathy, and Barbara all ran out onto the carport when they looked out of the window and saw their dad drinking beer with young Master Jake. *Perfect timing,* Jake said to himself. Mrs. Stern was scrutinizing, through the same window after the girls left.

"Well, well, well, what have we here?" Barbara asked.

Papa Stern proudly announced that his possible, future son-in-law was having his first beer with his possible, future father-in-law. Barbara turned beet red and hid her eyes with one hand. Jake just stared at her, trying to pick up any clues to whether Patty spilled the beans or not. Julie looked confused as usual, and Kathy had steam blasting from her cute little pigtails. Jake looked like the cat that just swallowed the canary. He looked over at his possible, future wife, as his scorned, possible, future sister-in-law shot evil deadly laser beams at him, and he surely feel the heat evaporating his very soul.

Poor Jake, now he felt like the house cat with canary breath, surrounded by several, hungry lions. He hurriedly put the can to his mouth and turned the bottom straight up into the air, his eyes glazed over and his freckled cheeks turned even rosier than before. He didn't know what to do exactly, except hide his face behind the beer can.

If he wasn't humiliated enough, he let out a loud belch that made him want to hide. He thought of literally running away, but he would never be able to show his red face again.

"Wow Jake," Barbara, now a little embarrassed said. "So, what's in your other hand?"

Jake looked up at Mr. Stern, as if looking for approval and support. He let out a another huge belch, which made Mr. Stern laugh out loud and pat Jake on the head, again with his keys. Jake felt that this time Mr. Stern actually tore through his scalp. Jake dared not make a face or sound and he dared not look in Kathy's direction, he could actually feel her eyes burning into his flesh. To avoid Kathy's glare, he even shot a quick nod at little Julie, who happened to be in his line of sight. Interestingly, Julie looked very appealing, the way she stared into Jake's eyes. Jake did a double take at Julie to see what was happening there, he wondered if he had put some sort of trance on these girls.

Jake quickly looked over at Barbara, and he walked over to her and handed her his love letter, art work, and stolen candy. Barbara's eyes widened with pure joy.

"For me?" Barbara was genuinely excited, even though she had been staring at the items for some time.

Jake wanted more than anything in the world to disappear, and again, he wondered if he could just run away? Jake was literally speechless. Nothing could come out of his mouth; his brain was no longer working. In fact, his heart was no longer beating, this is it, and he became flabbergasted by his destiny. He wanted to blow his palms, and felt as if something was on the bottom of his soles. *Was it horse poop, pluff mud or funeral dust? Was ghost's breath sheathing him and stealing his soul?* Barbara noticed the shock on his handsome face and grabbed him and hugged him. She could not help herself.

Jake sniffed her fragranced and silky hair, and closed his eyes. Barbara's sweet perfume was soon replaced by the rancid stench of a long sweaty day as Mr. Stern's damp, pungent armpit was right up against Jake's freckled nose. *Oh crap*, he screamed to himself. "Dang, I gotta get out of this place, if it's the last thing I ever do." In fact, his knees went wobbly. The stinky moisture of armpit juice just swathed his entire nose.

Please, oh Lord, let me have air, Jake cried to his nearly dead self. *Man, what else can happen? Kathy could lunge over like one of those hungry lions and rip off his head. Geeze, I just want to go home. Why did I ever come over here? I should have known better.*

Chapter 81

"Affection bends the judgment to her uses."
~ **Dante**

This has been one of the longest hours of Jake's life, while he waited to get Barbara alone to see what she and Patty had chatted about. Apparently, Patty had told the truth based on the look he just now received .Jake hasn't felt this relieved since his feet touched solid ground that horrible night at Edisto River.

They walked over to the old wooden, bench swing on the far side of the house.

"When are you going to read your note?" He asked.

"Can I read it now?" She beamed those warm, green eyes into his.

"Sure if you want."

She opened the sealed envelope, pulled out the carefully folded paper and read aloud.

"My Dearest Barbara,

I am truly ashamed that it has taken this long to put on paper what I have been feeling. Please know that you are my one true love. I love you with all my heart and always will.

Jake"

On the final sentences, she could no longer hold back the tears she had been struggling with since the first line. Jake had not seen her cry since June; tears came to his eyes as well.

"This is so unbelievable." She sniffed, and carefully wiped her mascara enriched eyes. "When did you write this?"

Caught off guard, "Um, a few days ago, I was afraid to give it to you."

"Why would you be afraid to give it to me?"

"You know, I wasn't really sure how you felt. I guess I was afraid of what you might say."

"I love you."

Jake gently wiped a tear from her soft cheek and looked into her wet, green eyes.

"I love you."

He couldn't believe how good it felt to utter those words, the words that he has no clue as to their true meaning. He felt that he loved her; in fact, he knew that he loved her, just a tad bit more than the others. He pulled her head onto his shoulder and they both smiled and soothingly, swung back and forth as the orange, sleepy sun slipped behind the forest in front of them.

Kathy sat on the edge of the dark carport carefully tucked into the shadows and ruefully took all of this in. For a split second she was almost compassionate then she roused back to the spoiled, selfish little girl that she really was. Thinking to herself, wow he was mine; how did this happen? I want him back and I'm going to get him back, you just watch.

There were five other girls if you include Maria Lombardi just around the block thinking the same thing. My, my Master the way you work your magic.

Chapter 82

"She gave me of the tree and I did eat."
~ Genesis III

"Guess who gets to drive Herbie, the love bug?" Barbara shouted at Jake as she ran towards him with her loving arms, a huge smile and displaying her proudest possession; her new driving permit.

"Oh my God, I'm so proud of you," Jake whisked her up in the air and kissed her lips. She giggled while he was tickling her ribs.

"You want to go for a ride?"

"We can find all kinds of spots now. Isn't Christine or someone over 18 supposed to ride with you?"

She looked at him in disbelief. "Are you kidding me, aren't we the masters of sneak?"

Jake flashbacked to when her little sister first used the word master and he immediately got excited and Barbara felt his excitement against her side.

"Oh my goodness. Just the sight of me gets you eager doesn't it?"

"Huh, oh, I was just thinking of us riding down all the dirt roads in search of some good spots."

She grabbed his hand, "Well, let's go."

Christine was with Ronnie in his gray 1965 Impala while Herbie rested beside the carport. Barbara and Jake jumped in cranked it up and backed out of the drive as "Glad All Over" by The Dave Clark Five came from the small German made speaker.

The days were starting to get a little longer and the sun rested eye-level above the trees and the sand gnats were swarming along the edges of the narrow dirt road several miles south of Bohicket Road.

The great thing about John's Island in the late sixties was the never ending amount of untraveled dirt roads out in the deep woods beyond many, many patches of forest and farms. There were ample fields of tall rows of corn plants hiding the cars and their passengers that were up to "no good", as the locals described them. There were many channels of over grown footpaths sprouting off of these dirt roads that were long and straight and looked like caves with the bordering, large oaks, maples, pines, hemlock, and palm trees, particularly, when the sun was about to turn in for the night.

This was a beautiful start to a Friday night, riding down the dusty roads at 30 mph in a VW Beetle with the top down, the clouds of dust at your back and the March winds in your face with The Temptations singing "My Girl" from the dashboard. Jake chugged one of her dad's lukewarm beers with his right hand and caressed her denim covered thigh with his left hand. He threw his head back and gazed at the passing white clouds as his face radiated a contentment that been hidden for months.

Beans, peppers, tomatoes, corn, and who knows what else were springing to life along the side of the long dirt road. An occasional John Deere tractor sat alone at the edge of a field that it had worked hard all day to cultivate as the hungry gulls feasted on the freshly upturned earthworms. John's Island earthworms had to be the largest in the world Wavy had told Jake a couple of years earlier as they dug them up to threw them in a tin can in order to toss a line. Jake's first assumed they were small snakes when Wavy's old shovel pulled them from the earth so Jake stepped back several feet in disgust and shock that these things were in his backyard. This was before the cootie blowing and sole searching.

This sure beats the heck out of the pear orchard Jake thought, while they barreled down the road in search of a hidden gem of a spot to polish. If he had a watch he would surely have checked it a dozen times during the trip after passing the gated road to Maria's house. He may never get that opportunity again and he sure did want to pop that cherry in a very bad way but there was no way at all of getting out of this situation and he just had to deal with it and see how it unfolded.

They passed three possible side trails before settling on one. They turned right while Barbara was still struggling with the clutch. The car bounced and jumped until she found the proper gear then she went about a quarter mile then turned left onto another narrow trail surrounded by tall pine trees and a barbed wire fence. They rode until they came to a small clearing with a large oak in the middle and a huge pond at the rear. They both looked around for any signs of life as Jake reached in the back for Ronnie's well-worn and stained blanket along with Kenny's transistor that Jake has been stealing from Kenny lately, and down to the pond they went as the sun was giving its last rays on this side of the world.

The scarlet and ginger skyline lent an artistic quality to the open fields, majestic oaks, and quiet ponds. Jake loved the vastness of land that once served as a plantation and home to many. The only thing wrong with this picture was the onslaught of gnats and mosquitos that were about to attack the young lovers. They did not think about the pesky insects and were not prepared. On the blanket with his unleashing all his fury in the wide open world for all to see is when the steadfast parasites attacked.

Barbara and Jake both screamed at exactly the same time. Jake started slapping at his back his legs, and face the best that he could and frightened Barbara who didn't know yet what had happened to him. Franticly he rolled over on his back then the insects attacked her and she started slapping, scratching and screaming. At the same time they swiftly dressed, sprinted to Herbie and took off leaving the blanket and radio behind and half of a warm beer. At least the insects could catch a buzz. They both scratched and laughed the entire trip home. Herbie was parked before anyone noticed him missing and Jake kissed Barbara good night and ran home to shower. Jake thought it was still early enough to call Maria to hook up with her.

Chapter 83

"Misfortunes test friends and detect enemies."
~ **Epictetus**

Awaiting Jake was the wrath of Kenny as he walked into the front door of home. "Some girl has called here three times for you and she sounds an awful lot like Maria who happens to be a senior in my homeroom. She will not leave her name and said she will call back…any minute I'm sure, and where the heck is my radio?"

That last part upset Jake more than anything because he had totally forgot about the radio and he knows how much his brother loves music. Jake was already wondering how he is going get it back. Barbara and he will have to sneak off again tomorrow but earlier in the day to see if they can even find the same spot and would the radio still be there? Then he thought of the blanket; he has grown kind of sentimental to the old wool friend.

"What happened to your face?" Kenny said, as he observed the many insect bites on his brother's face, neck and ears.

"Mosquitos in the woods, I'll get your radio tomorrow, sorry."

Ring… ring… ring… Jake ran to the old avocado shaded rotary phone hanging on the kitchen wall.

"Jake?" Maria asked as she was surprised yet pleased that he had answered the phone.

"Yes, oh, hey, yeah. Well I had to tend to some things, you know what I mean. I will meet you in thirty minutes at the back of Staley's store behind the large oak," he whispered so Kenny couldn't over hear.

Kenny snuck into the den and was listening on the phone from in there and shook his head and grinned.

Shower, alcohol on the bites, fresh clothes, Ronnie's English Leather and out the front door with a red delicious apple stuck in his mouth. He took a giant bite from the apple, grabbed his bike and then he realized that he had never been on Maybank Highway on his bike in the dark and on a Friday night too. Fortunately the store was only 300 yards from the far side of the neighborhood and the street lights in front the last three houses on the side of the highway lit up about half the distance to Staley's Store.

Chucky, Stevie, and Billy all were on the side of their house horsing around when they saw the new Western Flyer and its pilot whisk by in a big hurry.

"Let's follow him," squealed Billy.

They grabbed their bikes and took off behind their target. Jake was on the right side of the store and his followers on the left hiding behind what else but a large live oak. Maria pulled up in a red 1966 Malibu SS convertible.

"Holy crap," Chucky said. "Look at that bad ass ride."

Jake hid his bike in the bushes and jumped in the car.

"I told you, I told you, that's Maria, ha, we got his cheatin' ass now," blubbered Stevie.

"Can you believe this guy?" All three boys shook their dull heads.

"Why is he getting all of the girls and we can't get any?" Stevie asked.

Billy answered that one. "Patty banged him and told Bobby that he was hung like an elephant. Girls love big rocks." They looked at each other as if they were all in a hypnotic trance. Snap out of it boys.

"He nailed Patty too?" Stevie asked as if in complete disbelief.

"Yep and a few times at that," Billy replied.

"That lucky piss ant – damn," Chucky screeched at his comrades.

"Let's see, who all he has banged that we know of?" they started naming their fingers with the girls Jake has snaked and they didn't even know about Kathy, Teresa and Mary.

"Crap, that just ain't fair," Stevie blurted out.

"I think that there's probably at least two or three more that we don't even know about," Billy informed them.

"Dang man, I was trying to get with Kathy and she wouldn't have any part of it and I've noticed how she's all google-eyed when Jake's around. I bet he's banging his girlfriend's sister!"

In commandeering flare Chucky said, "Well, you want to tell Barbara? That will fix his ass; we can bring her right here and show her his bike."

They all thought about it then Billy and Stevie simultaneously chimed in "Nah, that's too mean, man." They all agreed.

"Well, let's steal his bike and hide it, that will burn his hide," Stevie said. They all laughed at that idea.

Main Road turned onto a very black Bohicket Road with no street lights at all. The red Chevy turned left onto a gravelly road about three miles south and Maria hopped out to open the gate. She got back in and asked Jake to go close it and lock it.

After a half mile of a tree lined driveway they came to the house sitting on the edge of the Bohicket Creek. This is the same body of water that his sister lived on and the same one that claimed Tommy's life and forever ruined Jake's. How did such a beautiful place which was once one of Jake's favorite places turn so horrific for him in just the blink of an eye or the opening of a stupid mouth?

The house was huge; one of the biggest that Jake had ever seen. They drove to the side where there was a three car garage with one light on in the center and they rolled into the far left stall. In the pitch black after Maria cut the lights she jumped out and said follow me. They walked to the end of the garage and she opened a door that Jake didn't even notice was there. They walked out of the back of the garage and faced the beautifully moonlit river then walked to the side of the large brick home and went in.

They spoke very few words on the ride there; Jake had to explain his bites, which were lies of course, and mostly admired the car since it was too dark to enjoy the beauty that was driving it. Once inside the house, he just knew that he had never seen a more beautiful girl, she looked like a movie star.

"You want anything?" she whispered "Soda, beer, wine, Scotch?" She asked, offering up her parents favorite beverages.

Jake nodded, and then whispered back in his best, sexy voice, some sort of demonic whisper, "Just you," he said.

Maria beamed and her black eyes sparkled, "Follow me then," as she grabbed his sweaty hand and lead the way up the hardwood stairs.

There was no turning back now Jake supposed, as he walked up the large staircase following this beautiful girl who only had one thing in mind. Jake had been beating himself up the entire bike ride to her house.

Once into the kitchen he was still digging into the back of his brain to think of a way out. He even thought of running wild once he left the garage, and saw the open moon kissed waters. He couldn't get Barbara out of his mind. *I cannot go through with this*, he kept telling himself.

Peppermint incense, soft lights, and soothing classical music awaited them. Unexpectedly, Jake felt like something had grabbed him and encased him in some evil grip as his soul was being squeezed from his body. He became entranced as the olive skinned beauty began to undress. As each piece of her clothing fell to the floor it sounded like the old bell at the top of the small white church near Cottageville. The sound echoed and reverberated into Jake's entire body, then he suddenly felt frozen; in mind, body, and in time.

Instead of Mozart he could hear The Temptations and "My Girl".
Tears came to his eyes as he watched the smooth, tanned nakedness
before him. "What would Ronnie do?" he always asked himself in
tough situations.

Before he had an answer Maria's long fingers grabbed his clammy
face and she planted her perfect lips on his very parched mouth. Jake
was a split second from screaming "I can't do this." ~ *Oh yes you can
my dear boy, yes you can… no one will know but the two of you and
you will enjoy it, that's a promise.*

Outside, the moon satirized itself on the cold river and a fine mist
sparkled on the algae covered roots of the stately oaks standing guard
on the banks of black, rich southern soil. A hungry raccoon playfully
washed his front paws with the incoming current beneath the swaying
moss silhouetted moonlight. The lonely willow whispered in the wind
while the demented howl from a lost tomb broke the serenity of the
quiet star screened night in the woods.

Meanwhile, at the same exact time . . . Barbara soaked in a hot bubble
bath; her happy eyes were closed as she smiled thinking of the
mosquito incident just hours earlier, and drifted off into a deep sleep.

. . . Down the road, an old, drunk driver lost his vision and control.

…Twenty six miles away in Goose Creek, Jake's half-brother, Jimmy,
was also making a terrible mistake; one that would cost him dearly.

Chapter 84

"He that is down need fear no fall."
~ **John Bunyan**

The cold, black night showed no mercy. Alone in a dark corner of the woods, the spot where shines no sun ever, sat the last known Cusabo spirit hiding behind the mask of obscurity, the stream of perilous moon glow.

Barbara awoke abruptly as if someone had nudged her; she was incoherent and forgot that she was in the bathtub. Her first instinct was to call Jake by name but she quickly realized that she was at home in her tub and that Jake was just a couple hundred yards away sleeping. She thought of calling him but did not want to wake Mina and Wavy.

...A thick fog quickly descended in front of Chucky, Stevie, and Billy while they pedaled their bikes back home on the same trek that Johnny and Tommy last pedaled together, which was the stretch of road with no lights. They could not see a thing and neither could the driver of 1959 Ford F-150 flying down Maybank Highway. The driver was exactly 666 yards from where Tommy Stern took his last breath and 666 yards from where Johnny Moore had laid in his tub and sliced opened both of his wrists.

The driver of the truck was the owner of the local horse stables and WWII veteran. Mr. Brown had been at an old Army buddy's house for a pig roast and indulged in way too many frosty beers and Kentucky sour mash when he lost sight of the road as the heavy fog dropped out of nowhere right in front of him. He could not see the lines on the dark highway or the boys on bikes in front of his blue truck that was travelling 75 mph. He did however see a boy and his bicycle come through his windshield just before everything went black.

…Jake watched the flickering shadows of the enchanted candles dance violently on the ceiling and walls. The incense became too intense and so did the guilt. The exaggerated frolic on the walls and ceiling seemed to mimic his actions. Jake was being mocked by shadows of flaming candlelight. What lies therein?

Jake and Maria never heard the sirens from the old, over used ambulance and the over-worked deputy sheriff so by the time they reached Staley's Store at 4:30 in the morning there was absolutely no sign of the crash or of any fog. There were several huge stains on the side of the road and some overlooked shards of glass and a blood stained yoyo in the grass but they did not see any of that from two hundred yards away. They also didn't see Jake's bike where he had hid it. Maria kept her head lights on while they both searched frantically for the red Western Flyer to no avail.

Jake did not want anyone to see him and Maria together so he felt it best if he walked the rest of the way. He would sneak and hide behind trees, fences and cars until he reached home. He was troubled about his bike and felt extremely guilty about Barbara so he assumed the missing bike was his just reward. There was no turning back. Not for Jake, his half-brother Jimmy, and not for the three kids and the old man. In the nearby dense woods whip-poor-will toots the little brown and black bird and Jake realized what a glum and lonely sound it was.

While he walked in the thick grass on the side of the road, the cold early morning air gave Jake the chills and shakes as did the slick stains on his sneakers once discovered. When he reached down to rub off the stain he realized that it was wet and when he stuck his fingers to his nose he knew right away the unmistakable copper odor of blood.

"Oh man," he cried out thinking he had stepped on some road kill.

Jake anxiously looked around and saw nothing but suddenly he caught a glimpse and glimmer of a far off light from a turning car. He then caught sight of a familiar yellow shape resting in the high grass near the edge of the woods.

He carefully walked to it and kneeled down to get a better look. It was a yoyo and it looked just like the one owned by none other than his buddy, Chucky.

"It must have dropped out of his pocket at some point while he had been at Staley's store," Jake whispered to himself.

He had no idea that that his comrades in arm had spied on him earlier in the evening. Jake never thought bad of anyone especially his good friends. He blew his palms three times, always starting with the right because he was sure something would go badly wrong if he ever reversed it. He looked at his soles and realized they were very odd looking. After a closer look he figured out that his shoes were covered in grass which stuck to blood.

"Crap, man what is this?"

With each step, the more the blood covered his sneakers. He was really starting to get distraught now, and then he remembered the yoyo.

"I have to get that yoyo for Chucky, he'll be so excited."

While reaching for the yoyo he noticed another familiar object nearby. It was a pair of glasses just like Billy Burn's thick horned-rimmed glasses except that these were cracked and blood stained. "This is very strange. It must be someone else's; it has to be," He said, to the distant crickets.

After another double take, he focused on what looked like his own white sneakers except these did not have *Barbara* scrawled all over them in ink. Chucky had the same white sneakers. He looked around in the dark and saw only the left shoe and it, like his, was covered in blood. Jake didn't grasp all of this but he now felt very uneasy and his empty stomach felt queasy. He felt like that old familiar friend, giddy, came back for a visit.

"Not here, please." Jake said aloud. He did not want to pass out in the blood and right next to the highway.

While his head and body swirled a set of bright headlights focused on him and he squinted from the harsh glare.

The county sheriff's vehicle pulled off the shoulder of the road; a uniformed deputy jumped out and ran to Jake. The officer did not know what to make of this right now just hours at the scene after the deadliest accident on John's Island since the one five years earlier on what is now known as Dead Man's Curve just four miles up the road; then five lives were taken when a speeding drunk teenage lost control of his vehicle and slammed into one of the imposing oaks.

All sorts of scenarios ran through the deputy's mind; had they overlooked the scene and missed one of the kids who may have been unconscious in the woods? Was this some drunk, a hitchhiker or a lunatic? When he got close enough he recognized his friend Ronnie's little brother.

"Jake, Jake Willoughby, is that you?" Deputy Dean Wagner asked now even more concerned.

"Jake, were you in this accident earlier?"

There could be no other reason for Jake to be out here at this time of the night except that he had been knocked out and thrown into the woods by the speeding drunk and unnoticed by the first responders. This also explained his dizzy state.

"My God Jake, thank goodness I came by. You know how lucky you are, Buddy?"

Jake was dazed but not by any accident and was very confused by what the officer was saying.

"Huh?" Jake mumbled in a very lethargic tone.

Deputy Dean now realized that Jake had no clue as to what had happened here earlier, perhaps due to a head injury. Concerned that Jake had amnesia, the thoughtful deputy drove the teenager to the nearest hospital. During the ride the deputy filled Jake in on the horrible accident hoping to jar the boy's memory.

He just knew that Jake had to have been with the other boys and that he must have been far to the outside or pulling up the rear when the out of control truck plowed into them. But what the heck were they doing on their bikes at this time of night on a main highway?

No one other than Jake and Maria Lombardi knew the real whereabouts of Jake Willoughby that fateful night or so they assumed. Such a perfect alibi he had for Barbara, too. Jake did not know why his buddies were on the road at that hour, nor did he really care to dwell on it. He was just thankful that he was not with them.

Jake often wondered what Janet Stern experienced in her state of shock after she found out about her youngest son. Jake seemed to be in his own state of shock after learning about his friends. His mind did not allow him to think too much about what had happened, like it was protecting him. After what seemed like days, Jake realized that he had NO male friends left. He blew his palms more than ever and was doing all the sickening rituals almost non-stop. He knew of only one thing that would help him. He really, really needed Barbara.

During his recovery in the hospital, Jake was questioned about the accident by several different people, including the authorities and family. Jake played like he had amnesia and knew that Maria was smart enough to keep quiet. Jake and Maria would share this secret for life and never divulge it to anyone.

A week after the accident the schools maintenance man found Jake's bike inside the water pump house in the school yard and of course he didn't know who it belonged to. Eventually, through word of mouth Jake retrieved his bike at the school's lost and found. He wondered if his now dead buddies had followed him, stole his bike and hid it where he often met up with Kathy as their way of telling him that they knew what he had been up to. Jake of course would never know for sure and it would be yet another thing that would always disturb him.

Dang, can I just rewind and start my life all over? he would often ponder in his deepest, loneliest moments. *Why is all this crap happening to me?*

Barbara stayed with Jake the entire two days at Roper Hospital. She kept telling him that she assumed he was home in bed after their outing that Friday. She wanted to know when and why he got together with his friends and why in the world they were out there at that time of the night. Jake continued to play dumb and it continued to work.

The square pink church on Maybank Highway was just a mile from the tragedy and conducted four funerals in three days, including that of Mr. Brown. Poor Reverend Pringle, Jake thought. They all laid to rest behind the original church building that the three boys attended kindergarten together. Jake somehow felt responsible, yet again. This now brought the total of dead boys to five in the past nine months, all from the same neighborhood; incomprehensible.

Thank God Jake did not have to attend any of the funerals. He could not imagine the grief stricken Garners having to bury their twins at the same time; in and out of the world together. Jake wanted to move, he wanted to leave the area, something is terribly wrong here and he had to get away from it. You can run but you can't hide. He could not help but wonder if he was next or if he would be responsible for more death. He did not have any answers and did not know how to find any answers... blow away cooties... blow, blow, and blow. It never occurred to Jake that no matter how often he blew at his palms or recanted his ritual adages, the bad things still happened. ~ Please God help me!!

Shadows were in the foggy, dark night as the frosty wind blew across the long, tortuous, and twisted creek. The haunted song of a long lost tribe echoed through the forest, only to be heard by the spirits in the blackness. The omniscient clouds formed beneath the fullness of the moon and brought a torrential downpour to the blood soaked dead zone, washing away the stains of horror from the road and grass, and inscribing it forever in the passageways of Jake's flummoxed mind and wounded heart.

Chapter 85

"It is very natural for young men to be
vehement, acrimonious, and severe."
~ **Samuel Johnson**

On the night of the gruesome accident, while Jake was getting close to Maria Lombardi, his half-brother Jimmy who lived in Goose Creek was in a musty old pool hall near Saint's Corner drinking a few cold ones and having a blast with several of his workmates. The beer was spilling, the cigarette smoke swirling, the eight ball was getting beat-up and the juke box roared into the early morning hours.

Jimmy already had a famous short fuse but bring alcohol into the mix and you had serious problems. One of his billiard buddies accused Jimmy of cheating and this brought the heavy end of Jimmy's pool cue right against his forehead. Marty Robbins was singing about a girl in El Paso when Lenny Eckert hit the floor like a sack of potatoes. Marty was now the only noise in the place when everyone shut up and stared at Jimmy waiting to see what his next move would be.

Jimmy was raging mad and threw his pool stick across the room with all of his might which caused several people to duck when it shattered the Falstaff sign over the jukebox. The bartender quickly ducked down behind the bar with telephone in hand and dialed the police. Jimmy's three workmates bent down to check on Lenny whose face was covered in blood but was still breathing, thank God. Bernie Hanson, the biggest of the three slowly walked over to Jimmy and told him that he had better hurry up and leave before there was any more trouble.

Jimmy quickly walked to the back door and stood long enough to light a Chesterfield in the corner of his mouth. He opened the door and took his free hand and with his fingers combed back his wavy red hair and walked out of the small, smoke filled tavern into the cold wind fading out the country crooner who continued singing his forlorn ballad.

Meanwhile, on John's Island, sirens were soon abuzz.

Henry "Hank" Stovall inserted the short straw into his nostril and snorted, and then he handed the straw to his mistress. Tomorrow they would take her little brother for an airplane ride.

Chapter 86

"Man as man is averse to what is good and evil."
~ Benjamin Whichcote

Barbara Stern was a fairly normal teenage girl, except for her highly developed figure and dreamy eyes and over the top bubbly personality. She loved Bobby Sherman, David Cassidy, Donnie Osmond and Jake Willoughby. She was crazy about butter pecan ice cream and ketchup smothered scrambled eggs; something Jake detested as he hated ketchup. She also liked a few dill pickle slices with her ketchup between two slices of white bread. Jake would cringe when watching her eat the sandwich with the sweet red stuff oozing out of both corners of her pretty mouth. She acted as though she were eating lobster and filet mignon.

Her sister Kathy loved red, ripe John's Island tomato slices with a sprinkle of salt along with mayonnaise on two slices of white bread. Jake enjoyed that too. With tomato season approaching and Wavy's garden full of the red fruit, Kathy would fix Jake plenty of his favorite sandwiches. The way to a man's heart is through his stomach she always heard.

Once Jake got home from the hospital, Kathy would often visit and promise him the sandwiches once the tomatoes came in.

"I miss you," she said, right out of the blue one afternoon.

With no reply she would entice him more, "You know we were the first for each other…how did you get with my sister anyway?" No answer. I thought you were all mine. That crap still blows my mind because I never saw that coming. What a real pisser man."

Jake just stared at the gray figures on the television.

"I'm not going to stop until I get you back. You know that, right?" She declared, not really expecting an answer. She continued to stare at Jake hoping to get a reaction of some sort. "I know that. I miss you too and

I'll never forget you being my first and I would like to have you again. You think we can?" a cool Jake casually asked. Kathy looked dumbfounded.

"We can what?" She asked in amazement, knowing exactly what he was referring to but still wanted to hear him say it.

"You know, get it on." He said, grinning looking at her for the first time that afternoon.

"Get real! What about Barbara?" She asked not really concerned for her sister but more interested in Jake's response.

"What about her?" "What she doesn't know won't hurt her." Jake said slyly.

"Wow, really?" She said, while rubbing his hands and looking around Jake's bedroom and then at the door to see if anyone may be in the hallway listening. She became warm with excitement.

"Really?"

"Okay, when?" She asked impatiently.

"What about now?" Jake asked.

"Wow, really?" She said again.

"Really?"

Jake was recklessly daring, and taking a fool's chance but looking this girl in the eyes and getting all sentimental got the best of him. He really did miss her and besides the way she looked in those tight jeans and softly propped beside him in bed got him a little aroused.

"Check the hall, then quietly close the door and lock it. This has to be very quick." Jake instructed her.

Kathy jumped her cute little rump to the door and after peeping into the hallway she slowly closed the door and soundlessly locked it.

Water pump house my ass, Jake laughed to himself. We won't be going there anymore Jake said, to his reflection while primping in the mirror winking at his reflection and noticing the change in his features and demeanor. Jake was becoming very handsome and he just now realized it for the first time.

He zipped up and went for lunch. What happened to all this guilt about cheating on Barbara? Jake was a man of variety, yeah, that's it, he would tell himself - *Release the beast!*

Jake had missed an entire week of school but Barbara and Kathy visited often to keep him abreast. Barbara brought him his homework and Kathy filled him in on the gossip. Of course they were both rewarded for each visit. It was a mad dance in a hot air balloon; cautious yet exhilarating and right there under the noses of everyone. Jake continued hammering away the horrors of the past week and eventually returned to normal and completely blocked out the atrocious events of the past Friday night. He had been a spoiled rotten brat getting everything and everyone he wanted and he felt as though he truly deserved it.

…Back in school, a lovely black girl by the name of Ida Simmons had been eyeing Jake for quite some time and vice a versa. Jake loved her voluptuous bottom and she always showed it off with too tight denims and high platform soul shoes. Ida looked like a twenty year old, tall and heavenly blessed with physical perfection and the most perfectly shaped lips Jake had ever seen on a woman. Ida had light brown skin, a large afro and big round black eyes, both of which Jake could get lost in.

After sending messages on the same multiple folded notebook paper back and forth about eight times they decided on a rendezvous in the now defunct love patch behind the pear orchard. This place had not been visited in so long Jake new that it would be safe. They met after school behind Staley's Store and she jumped on her bike and followed Jake who was riding Kenny's bike.

Jake was finally feeling better and overall everything was better and how rare has that been? For some odd reason he felt no shame or guilt about anything, he was just happy to be alive. Within a couple of days he gets to fly in an airplane with his sister and a friend. He really was excited especially since the trip was supposed to take place last week but was postponed due to his latest circumstances. Things were looking up for Master Jake.

Chapter 87

"O time too swift! O swiftness never ceasing!"
~ **George Peele**

"Darn your hide," Wavy would say jokingly to anyone that perturbed him. That's what Kenny overheard his dad say on the phone to his half-brother Jimmy when a collect call came in from the Berkeley County Jail in Saints Corner early Saturday morning after the ill-fated ride home for the neighborhood bike thieves. Don't steal from Jake because it brings bad karma.

Jimmy was arrested soon after walking out of the bar and charge with assault and drunk and disorderly conduct. Wavy was not at all pleased with this situation and had about enough of Jimmy's unruly ways. In order to teach his oldest son a lesson Wavy refused to pay his bond and let him sit in the jail for thirty days hoping that this would help his son. Bad call but who knew.

On the second Sunday of March during Jimmy's incarcerated vacation, Wavy, Mina, Kenny, and Jake hopped into the Biscayne and started out to Saint's Corner for a jail house visit. Jake asked how long it would take to get there and when he found out about the forty five minute drive he said he wasn't interested and had Wavy stop.

Jake jumped out of the car in the middle of the neighborhood and said that he would walk back and hangout with Uncle Hal. His intentions were to meet with Teresa since he was right in front of her house and that earned a wink from Kenny. This would be another of those choices that Jake would spend most of his life regretting.

Jake stood there and watched the gold Chevy disappear while Teresa watched him from her bedroom window. She squirted on a little perfume and ran out of the back door then proceeded around the corner of the house.

"Psst, Jake over here." Jake turned, saw the blond beauty, looked around, and nodded his head towards the woods.

He then proceeded into the forest about a hundred yards to the right of her house and waited. She snuck into the woods a couple of minutes afterwards.

They embraced each other like it was the very first time and kissed for five full minutes. "Let's go see our house," she said excitedly. Jake smiled and bobbed his head then grabbed her hand and they scampered deep into the woodlands.

…Saint's Corner is a small town ten minutes from an even smaller town, Goose Creek. Hidden behind large trees, a quaint red brick two story building located right smack dab in the middle of town served as the jailhouse just off Main Street. The jailer and his wife lived next door and would often leave the inmates unattended for hours at a time to go to church, shopping, or go fishing and what not. Guess the jailer watched too many episodes of *The Andy Griffith Show*.

Wavy pulled into a southern fried chicken restaurant on the corner of Main Street and got his oldest son a two piece dinner, one of his favorites. It consisted of a small breast, a drumstick, coleslaw and a dinner roll. He got him a small soda as well. Kenny's stomach was grumbling so he got the same thing. Wavy and Mina decided to join the party and they could all eat together in the jail house just like another Sunday picnic for the Willoughby family.

On the second floor inside what was known as the bull pen was another cell that housed Jimmy and three others. Jimmy was unaware of the visitors and was thrilled to see them. At first he was bitter about his father's decision to let him sit, but after he sobered up and thought on it for a while, he too hoped that it would be for the best. He gobbled up the chicken like he hadn't eaten in several days which was not far from the truth.

After he told the other inmates to stop cussing in front of his mother he surveyed everyone's plate. Wavy gave his son his breast and roll as did Mina. Kenny, totally unaware what was happening, responded to a hard nudge from his mom and her gesture. Kenny had already devoured the breast and roll but gave his hungry half-brother the remaining drumstick and coleslaw.

As a near famished Jimmy ate, Wavy looked around and observed the padded cells. "If a fire started in here there'd be no escaping that's for sure."

Jimmy drank down the last bit of his soda and crushed ice, borrowed a Lucky Strike from one of his cellmates and stared down and observed the box of matches sitting on the concrete floor. He then slowly struck the side of the box and lit the cigarette. He blew a plume of gray smoke into the air and carefully watched it drift across the ceiling. Jimmy's blue eyes looked just like Wavy's, Kenny observed.

Kenny, like his other siblings had Mina's coal black eyes. Kenny never really got to sit across from his half-brother before so he observed him pretty well and noticed that his resemblance to Wavy was uncanny and noticed that Jimmy was the only son with his father's curly red hair. Wavy had to have looked just like Jimmy when he was that age.

"So, where are Ronnie and Jake?" Jimmy asked between puffs. "Are they doing okay?"

"They're doing fine, thanks for asking. Ronnie is with his girlfriend and Jake's at home with Uncle Hal." Mina said.

Wavy told him that he believed he had been in jail long enough, and on his next day off which was Wednesday, he would speak with his lawyer and get Jimmy out of jail no later than Thursday afternoon. Jimmy seemed very appreciative of that news.

After a while they all stood and Wavy gave his oldest son a tight hug. Jimmy shook Kenny's hand and hugged Mina and said, "I promise dad, I will stop drinking and I will come live with you guys for a while and things will turn around for me in a positive way." Wavy had a tear in his eye as he stared at his son with hope in his heart.

"I'm really excited about this and can't wait to get to John's Island." Jimmy said, clutching the steel bars as he watched his family walk down the stairs and wave goodbye.

Jake and Teresa were making out on the dilapidated front porch of their *new house* as chameleons and carpenter bees scuttled around them. Right behind them was something neither of them knew about. It was something that Jake was supposed to look for with his buddies when he got back from Edisto River but never got the chance because of one episode after another. The dangling moss encompassed several old non-legible tombstones.

The poisonous Star of Bethlehem and the black-eyed-Susan grew around the fractured head stones. On the warm spring afternoon a biting cold fog rose from one of the graves, unheard of. It slowly lifted into the air and mingled amongst the new green leaves of the many dogwood trees that were bordered by the enormous pines, black gum and winged elm trees with the saw palmetto sprinkled within the tangled vines of the arterial mass that held the forest together like a secret society.

A red-tail hawk turned its head and watched in curiosity as the rising mist encircled the timberland, and then the bird of prey lurched from the branch of a colossal pine tree into the blue spring sky, flapping madly to the southern horizon across the zigzagging mystic creek.

Chapter 88

"The imagination of man's heart is evil from his youth."
~ Genesis VIII, 21

Jake was smiling the entire walk home from Teresa's through the thick forest which the two of them had previously been lost. Something compelled him to do so and he felt confident that he could find his way. He wished that Teresa was with him when the woods seem to thicken and enclose him with the hundreds of trees with new emerald green leaves so tall that they blocked out the energies of the sun that left him in a cold, dark and scary clearing.

Unbeknownst to Jake, he stood just to the edge of the meandering creek of horror. Jake was becoming alarmed, looking and turning around in all directions. He started talking aloud to himself. "Please Lord let me get out of here."

In the dense, dark forest with no direct sunlight he started to feel chilly. Then the oddest thing happened. He caught a whiff of the distinct pungent redolence of pluff mud - out here? He thought that very bazaar. He briskly rubbed his shoulders with opposite hands to try and warm up a tad. He could have sworn he saw someone's shadow behind a large black tupelo tree. Jake now started getting goose bumps and a bit edgy.

"Hey, anyone there?" he yelled, hearing his echo bounce back off of the forest walls.

He wondered if Barbara had been spying on him, "Nah, she wouldn't be out here alone, just my imagination I'm sure." He look up and around at the many trees. He missed his buddies, he missed climbing trees, and he took great pride in his tree climbing skills.

"That's it," he thought aloud. "I'll climb to the top of one these trees and hopefully get a good look around and find my way home. "Jake searched for the tallest tree that was possible to climb.

He found a sycamore that had the lowest branches on which to ascend and he jumped up to the nearest branch and lifted himself up and continued to climb until he got nearly to the very top, swaying in the breeze. He enjoyed the challenge and temporarily forgot about being lost and afraid. The open air felt good against his face as he held tightly and adjusted himself so that he could sit comfortably on the branch and look out on the woods below.

Jake felt powerful high above the world. He loved the sense of freedom and serenity that it gave him. He had often wished he could fly and just imagined that there was nothing like the thrill of soaring over majestic mountains, treetops, and mighty rivers. He even dreamed more than once that he soared high like an eagle. He felt so good that he almost forgot why he was up there. He studied his surroundings and all he saw were treetops. He searched high and low, far and near.

A gallery of white clouds in the baby blue sky glided above him and the green forest. He saw no houses; he did not think that he had gone that far from civilization. He was forgetting that these trees were old, therefore tall and wide and covered much of the landscape. There were many pines that were higher than he was and had never before realized just how tall these trees were.

Everywhere that he looked all he saw were green trees or blue sky, no clearings or houses. The only movement was that of the hawk off in the distance. He was praying that the hawk would not attack him. Oh how he wished he could fly right now and he was becoming quite afraid of the deplorable situation that he got into.

Then suddenly he had hope, he heard children playing and dogs barking. He could hear an occasional truck rumble past, and so he knew that he wasn't too far from the neighborhood. He looked in the direction of the comforting clatter but could only see trees. He looked in the direction from which he believed he came from, then he followed it to where he thought the abandoned church should be. It was right under the large hemlock tree which seemed to be the highest concentration of trees, brush and shrubbery.

He noticed a shimmering light just beyond the church so he studied it intensely and saw another glimmer a little farther down below some other trees. It looked to him like a stream. The more he focused the more glimmers he saw and he was convinced that it was a stream or small creek.

He did not see a beginning or end and thought about following it, but knew that it would not be long before dark, and that Uncle Hal would tell his folks that he never saw Jake. Then that would start a scene he could live without, that is, if he made it out of the forest at all. Jake would have to plan a day out here with Teresa or maybe Uncle Hal or Kenny to explore the creek.

Finally, he decided to climb down and head back to where he believed the noise came from, which he assumed had to be near Teresa's backyard. While he carefully climbed down, his left foot lost traction on the slick tree and his normally super-fast reflexes could not save him as the momentum pulled him free of his constricted grip and he fell a good four feet to the next branch beneath him and smashed it with his right knee and knocked him backwards into the large limb behind him causing great pain to his knee, back and ribs.

He painfully reached out his arms only to grab air as he plunged another four feet to an awaiting branch that he straddled with both legs. The impact on his testicles caused him to scream out in severe anguish as his hands grasped the branch on which he was now sitting, by accident, though barely hanging was more like it.

Jake felt sick to his stomach. This is a pain he had known only once before when Kenny accidently kicked him in the groin while they were wrestling on the living room floor. It was something he cared not to ever experience again. Tears flooded his eyes as he held on for dear life to the large branch of the sycamore tree. The very second he thought he would vomit, came a startling laugh. He quickly jerked his head over his left shoulder when he heard Tommy laughing at him. *He actually heard Tommy laughing at him;* he knew that squeaky laugh and it came from right behind him.

Suddenly he got colder and the goosebumps returned. He then knew it was Tommy right there with him.

Frightened, he yelled out "Tommy, Tommy, I know you're there, come out, let me see you!"

The cold swirl of mist in front of Jake resembled a mini tornado, and after a few long seconds it took form on the very branch in which Jake was sitting. Tommy Stern was sitting right in front of Jake.

He stared at him with that mischievous grin of his and then darted his pale arms at Jake's pallid face and squawked.

"BOO!"

Jake jumped and nearly lost his balance and his grip.

Had he hit his head and was hallucinating or was he having another nightmare?

Jake had never been this afraid in his life. This was not one of his nightmares; he felt the clutching pain in his nuts and could smell the pluff mud. Tommy was right before him wearing the same tattered cutoffs and dirty t-shirt that he was wearing when he stole his best friend's baseball and Tommy was laughing his ass off.

"Tommy, is that really you?" Jake faintly whispered to the undead kid in front of him.

"Yes, yes, it's really me Jako." Tommy stared right through Jake's terrified eyes and soul. "Can you believe it?"

Jake looked at him and studied him. He looked like Tommy and sounded real enough then Jake looked around the area the best he could and looked up and down trying to get a better comprehension on what was happening. While his grasp on the branch with the crumbling bark started sliding downward. He knew that he was about to fall and be seriously injured or worst. He was again feeling that miserable and sickening pain in his testicles and his entire groin area all the way up into his belly.

Then, up came the delayed return of breakfast and lunch blasting from his mouth like an industrial pressure washer completely covering his right leg, striped tube sock and soiled his sneakers. His puke was dripping to the limb below and ultimately to ground but somehow he managed to balance himself and not end up on the ground in his own vomit. After nearly three God awful minutes of heaving, Jake raised his head in the direction of Tommy hoping that he was just an apparition and that he would be all alone with his tan and lumpy puke. No such luck. Tommy and Jake sat together on the limb of the tree, reminding Jake of many times when they sat together on the Angel Oak, only this time one of them was supposed to be dead or maybe an angel.

"I thought you were dead. Man, how did you pull this off? Are you living in these woods?" Jake managed to ask.

Tommy leaned inward so that their noses were nearly touching and so that Jake could see that he was real, and the undeniable pungent of pluff mud barreled its way into Jake's nostrils and down his throat and into his lungs. This is real, not a nightmare at all Jake thought, and was frightened nearly to death.

The Tommy thing slowly whispered, "I thought that I was too. Ah ha ha, I am dead!" His empty, soulless eyes drilled right through Jake's own horrified eyes.

"Am I dead too?" Jake asked fretfully.

Tommy chuckled, "No my man, you are not dead, not yet anyway." giving his friend a devious snarl and again his weird laugh.

Tommy looked into the sky as the large red-tailed hawk flapped its massive wings and swiftly floated over. Jake wished that the hawk would swoop down and pluck one them into the sky. He believed he would have a better chance fighting off a hawk than he would a vindictive ghost.

"So Jako, how do you like what's been happening to you and yours?" A sarcastic Tommy asked softly.

Jake's eyes grew three sizes, then he cleared his throat "Crap, crap, crap, I knew it was you, it was ALL you, I knew it man!"

The sinister Tommy grinned at Jake's revelation.

"You are the devil, you are evil man. Holy crap!" Jake screamed.

Tommy just sat there smirking and his eyes were pure satanic, not Tommy's bouncy green eyes. Jake, realizing that this was actually happening decided to plea with the wraith.

"Tommy, Tommy, I didn't mean it. You know I really didn't mean what I said that day. You stole my new baseball and you pissed me off. Look man, please forgive me, I didn't mean it. I will do anything. Please, please, please, stop all of this. Please Tommy stop all of this friggin' crap. I don't even know what made me say that crap man except that I was so mad at you for not giving back my new ball. I just got it and it was mine and I wanted to keep it. Please believe me Tommy, please!"

Tommy's malicious grin turned grim and odious as he studied his shaken friend with his haunting and hollow eyes.

After several seconds of silent contemplation, he spoke. "Look man, I know you say you didn't mean it but at the time you did and *you* did this crap to me."

Tommy looked around again as if looking for someone. He slowly looked back at Jake after he got no response.

"Jake, you gotta pay my man." Jake's eyes were the mirrors of terror and starting to fill with tears.

"Me? How did I do this crap?" Jake could not believe what he was seeing and hearing.

Jake screamed at Tommy, "You did this crap to yourself by stealing my baseball with that piece of crap Johnny Moore, who by the way is dead too and I hope I never see *him* again. Besides, I have paid. I have paid dearly.

Enough is enough. Please stop this crap, please man. I am so friggin' sorry. What can I do to make you stop this? You know I've paid, you know I've paid, you know it man!" Jake cried. "I have been through hell, all the weird habits, that's you too isn't it?"

They just stared at each other for several seconds. Still pleading but nearly out of energy Jake said, "Look Tommy, you know I'm not a bad guy. We've known each other a long time and you know I'm far from it man. YOU stole my baseball and I was upset. I was pissed and I said something I should not have said and I regret it. I will never, ever utter those words again to anyone, I promise."

Tommy again looked up and around and then at Jake. "That won't bring me back to life; it won't bring me back to life again. I can't enjoy the things you can." Tommy grinned.

"You know Jake; I wished I could have some boiled peanuts. You remember the time that we ate so many that we got sick and didn't eat them again for years?"

Jake was out of breath and smelled of vomit. He was still deliberating on how any of this was even possible. All he could think of was the cowardly lion in his favorite movie.

I do believe in ghost, I do believe in ghost, I do, I do, I do I do believe in ghost.

Tommy gave him a half smirk and said, "Jako, I'm not bad either. Heck look what I did to everyone that bothered you. I'm making up to you for stealing your precious baseball. Those guys stole your bike and look at them now, hehehe. Look at Johnny. That moron started the whole thing. Look where his ass is now? Dead, that where, thanks to me.

Unlike me he is really and completely dead, he he. I'm looking out for you kiddo, you're banging all the girls you ever wanted. Hell, your dumbass didn't even know how to make it ~ you're welcome. By the way, how are you enjoying my sisters, slime ball? You're welcome!

Tommy told Jake to listen to him carefully on that situation. You need to make a decision on one or the other and you need to leave those other tramps alone or else you will be sorry Jako. You've had your fun so don't hurt my sisters. Let one of them down easy and make the other one happy."

"You killed Chucky, Stevie and Billy didn't you? And Mr. Brown, what did he ever do to you?"

Tommy slowly lifted his right arm high into the air and whispered "Do that and I will leave you and yours alone."

And just like that Tommy evaporated to the cold swirl of mist and tornadoed through the forest and went right to the creek as old leaves from the past autumn blustered against the bordering trees leaving a very cold and damp path in its wake.

"Tommy, come back, hey, hey Tommy!" Jake screamed, to no one.

"Tommy, Tommy. Why don't you just stay, why be dead?!"

Jake looked in the region where the mini Tommy tornado lingered. He stared blankly and just sat there dumbfounded. He thought long and hard about what just happened. This was a lot to process, and he knew for sure he was not dreaming. He originally believed that Tommy's ghost had made him bang his sisters to begin with since everything had happened the way it did and when it did, so why stop now? He heard it from the ghost' mouth so he better obey.

"Crap, this is unbelievable. This is just the craziest, weirdest thing ever." He painfully and carefully climbed down the large sycamore with the bark sliding off with each movement. And touched the ground with his worn and filthy high top Converse sneakers with Barbara scrawled in black magic marker all over them.

On his journey towards Teresa's backyard, Jake tried to reconstruct everything from the past several months leading up to the last few minutes. His cluttered minds chaotic rush to comprehension, left in its wake, a dizzy tribute to confusion. He slowed down his thoughts and went to the beginning of the mayhem.

Everything started going bad in his life after Tommy's death. The bad habits, the death of Bullet, his friends, Ronnie getting shot, Wavy getting shot, Mr. Miller, the discovery of his carnal prowess and obsession which could not be a good thing down the road and Jake knew it. However, he did love the girls, each one of them in a different way but he truly loved Barbara, she was the one. Jake was not yet aware of what seeds had already been planted or of his ill-fated half-brother. Either Tommy or the damn Cusabo ghosts are vindictive as hell. Maybe they're working through Tommy somehow since he died in their mud and they grabbed his soul and all his secrets and they just felt like screwing up someone's life. Why me?

Poor Jake, by a matter of default and because of his personality along with his accidental usage of words and love for a dumb ball, was their victim. Jake really didn't know the answer; he didn't know what to do. He kneeled down on his one good knee and raised his dirty palms to his face and blew them each three times. He looked into heavens and asked God to help him. He slowly rose up and looked back towards the sycamore. On the very spot where Tommy sat was a huge black bird, not the hawk but a black bird. Who was the hawk he wondered? Who was Tommy looking back to see? Why did he leave so quickly?

Jake could never fully grasp the fact that he sat and talked with Tommy. The same Tommy who had once been his very best friend, the same Tommy that chose to impress the older guy Johnny with the betrayal of the trusting and likable Jake and steal his new ball. The same Tommy who rode off into the sunset and met his untimely demise as the tide made its ritual return to the banks of the Church Creek in the hot afternoon sun while summer entertained the local kids on vacation from school. This was the same Tommy who was dragged by a chain from the depths of the incessant mud hours after he sank into the earth. This was the same Tommy that was buried beneath an ancient oak on a hillside facing one of the most beautiful harbors in America.

Many months and many horrors after his funeral Jake had looked into Tommy's eyes and conversed while sitting on a tree branch. Tommy told Jake that he was responsible for all the recent horror in his life. Tommy felt that Jake was responsible for his life ending that day in June of 1968. Before he zapped away, wherever it is that ghost zap away to, Tommy told Jake to make a decision on which of his sisters he was going to be with or else there would be more horror to deal with.

Jake pinched himself until he was bruised and bleeding. He recalled word for word, second for second, every detail of the moment with Tommy. It was real, as real as anything in Jake's life yet so unreal. He had been hearing and seeing things before in the woods that he was sure was Tommy but now he was convinced. Tommy was a vengeful ghost and would not stop until Jake met the same end as his earthly body. Jake was nervous and afraid. He was blowing his palms and repeating the same thought over and over in his head. He was also angry because he didn't get to have his complete say and did not get all of the answers that he wanted. He knew what to do, he needed Barbara, and she was the one that he chose to remain true to.

Jake finally recognized the area behind Teresa's backyard but he did not want her to see him so he searched for a clearing a couple of yards away from hers and made his march homeward. He was so happy to Uncle Hal sitting in the yard reading the paper, he felt safe.

"Hey Uncle Hal, how are you?" Jake waved as he walked by his uncle.

"Well I'm just fine Jake, how are you?" Hal said, as he looked over the Sunday paper at his nephew.

"I'm fine sir, kinda hungry though."

"You'll find something good in the kitchen, wash up first."

"Yes sir." Jake thought for a minute then stopped in his tracks, turned and looked sincerely at his uncle. "Uncle Hal, do you believe in ghosts?"

Uncle Hal chuckled for a second then thought about the question, and possible answers as he rubbed his dimpled chin, with his long hairy fingers. "You know Jake, that's an interesting question. Actually, I believe that I do, mainly because of an incident or two that I have encountered along the way, along with credible information that I have been given from reliable sources."

Jake was very interested to hear what the wise old man had to say. He promptly sat on the ground in front of his uncle and folded his legs like an Indian brave at a pow-wow. After 45 minutes of ghost stories Jake was convinced. However, he did not share his story with his uncle or anyone else, ever.

What happened next changed everything. Jake stepped onto the front porch to be greeted by Mary. "Hello stranger. I've missed you." She said, as she slowly slid her fingers down the length of his torso.

Run fool run.

Chapter 89

"The wind passeth over it, and it is gone; and
the place there of shall see it no more."
~ Psalms III

"Sounds of Silence" by Simon and Garfunkel was Jimmy Willoughby's favorite song, and he was singing it in his head when the fire broke out.

Early that Wednesday morning Wavy and Mina went into downtown Charleston and met with an attorney who would arrange for Jimmy to be released that afternoon but since the jailer was out in his boat fishing Jimmy had to sit and wait until the jailer returned from his relaxing day on the river. The unguarded inmates waited...

The jailer had gone fishing and his wife was next door in her kitchen baking sugar cookies for the doomed inmates. They were locked up and no one with a key could hear their cries for help as the padded walls engulfed into flames from a lit match. Unable to burn through the concrete and brick, the fire dissipated leaving the impenetrable overpowering smoke with nowhere to go except to entertain its audience. Within seconds the entire second floor was seized by the killer white smoke that overwhelmed all five of the young men as they fought, thrashed, and prayed for air. The inmates all screamed, assuming that someone would come to their aid.

They gasped for air but inhaled only more smoke; they coughed and wheezed while they tried in vain to rip the steel bars from their frames. They threw anything that wasn't tied down at the windows and managed to create a few small cracks here and there but not enough to release the smolder and detain the onslaught of imminent death. Jimmy's knuckles were turning white as he put his last bit of strength into breaking free from the bars that held him prisoner.

With his panic stricken face wedged between the cold bars he hopefully watched in the direction of the entrance for someone to enter. He saw nothing but heavy white smoke and heard the inmates downstairs screaming for help as well.

Mustering up the last bit of air in his lungs, Jimmy yelled toward the smoke filled staircase, "Someone help, we're suffocating up here!" he screamed literally for dear life.

Jimmy watched in terror as one of his cellmates drop to the cold cement floor gasping for breath and saw his frightened eyes bulging in horror and finally succumbing to the smoke. They all knew that they were next.

Teary eyed Jimmy looked up at the gray smoke buffered ceiling and huffed "Please Lord forgive me. I'm so sorry!"

One by one they all fell like dominoes. The last thing Jimmy ever saw was the pale ghost of the old woman with the long gray hair that Wavy spoke of often. She was sitting on the lost tombstone deep in the forest from his father's youth. She glared from behind her cloudy veil at Jimmy with those black bottomless eyes and pointed her long wicked finger at the dying young man and motioned for him to come hither...

Forty five minutes after the fire begun, the Berkeley County Fire Department arrived and could not climb the stairs due to antiquated equipment and inability to fight the dense smoke. They evacuated the inmates on the first floor which saved their lives. They opened all doors to the building and threw rocks and bricks at the top bar covered windows to break the glass. Finally, one hour and twenty minutes after the match met the pad the firemen got to the top floor to find five dead men sprawled out on the concrete floor of their cells. Escape they did.

Chapter 90

"I regret nothing in the past but the dead and the failures."
~ **Robert Toombs**

Jake had spent every possible moment with Barbara since his visit with Tommy's ghost. He easily made up his mind that he would see only her especially after his run in with Mary. He was hoping and praying that Tommy took him at his word and did not follow him and did not catch his immediate mistake. He hoped that Tommy was doing whatever it is those kind of ghosts do but ever since then he avoided the other girls. He did not answer the phone, he never called back and he went the other way when he saw them coming down the hallway.

When he was finally cornered, he simply said he had been busy but he would call soon. He could not allow himself to think of other girls and he would not let Tommy cause any more death and mayhem to anyone. He figured that if he simply ignored them that they would go away, besides he loved Barbara. He loved everything about her from her gorgeous head to her pretty little toes.

Kathy was the hardest to avoid since she lived in the same house as Barbara. Ultimately, Kathy got the hint and gave up and so did the others, for the time being anyway.

A March breeze blew through Jake's unruly hair while he walked from his house to Barbara's after a long, boring day of school. There they would have snacks and do their homework. The large sky was a beautiful powder blue and the air felt crisp and clean; spring was approaching. The school days went well as he hid from the girls and didn't read any of their little folded notes that were passed to him.

He smiled when he thought of his father's daily question, "What did you learn in school today?" He still could not believe that he had actually seen a ghost and talked with him no less. *Ghosts are for real man*! It all finally started making sense.

He knew that he had seen Tommy before with Johnny and Lisa but who was Lisa? Had he made her up? The nervous habits started immediately after Tommy died. All the bad things that had happened to his family were after Tommy died. At least Ronnie and Wavy both survived gunshots and were here to talk about it though they never did and probably never would. Maybe those were warnings. He suddenly felt the urge to spend more time with both those men. What about Kenny? He seems to be the only one unscathed… Kenny was always nice to Tommy.

It was four thirty five pm when his half-brother Jimmy took his last breath and fell to the floor. Jake wouldn't know of this for another couple of hours and he would wonder for years if Tommy did this and why? Poor Jake, what started off as a promising new year just kept unraveling with each new day which turned into a disastrous year. Will it ever end?

With each forthcoming year in his life, whenever the month of March would approach, Jake would say, *March sucks*. His nervous routines would go into overtime to prevent anything bad from happening. He never considered that no matter how many times he blew cooties, checked his feet, repeated phrases and prayers, looked at his elbows or avoided cracks and corners, the bad things continued happening. The routines did not prevent the evil, the bad, the tragic but he kept doing the craziness anyway because it became second nature to him. He had absolutely no control of it. He was puppet to a ghost and he hated it with every ounce of his energy.

Wavy was watering his garden as his youngest son walked by.

Jake smiled and said, "How goes it dad?"

"Fine, everything is just fine. What did you learn in school today?"

"Oh not much, some history and math."

Wavy grinned at the boy as he held the old, green, rubber hose spraying the cool, clear John's Island water onto the young, green tomato plants. "We'll have some nice big reduns before too long."

Jake surveyed all the young green plants and said, "I can't wait. That sure is a nice garden; I wish I could learn to do that."

Wavy looked very proud and said, "Well, you can help me plant for the fall."

Jake looked excited, "Okay, that will be great."

Jake glanced over at Uncle Hal who was sitting in a folding lawn chair beneath the pecan tree reading from the letter G from the World Book Encyclopedia.

"Hey Uncle Hal" Jake said, smiling as he walked to the back door of the house.

Uncle Hal never looked up but he nodded his head and uttered "mmhmm" which was his signature response to just about everything.

Jake entered his mom's kitchen and caught the soulful aroma of turnip greens and pigtails simmering in her own mother's large cast iron pot and crackling cornbread was in the oven in a cast iron skillet; generations of flavor in those pots and pans. Jake noticed a large bowl of chopped green onions marinating in white vinegar sprinkled with black pepper. This would all be served with finely coated fried pork chops and then the leftover grease would be turned into the most spectacular gravy served over white rice.

Wavy would buy a fifty pound bag each month; the man loved his rice. Each month on the way to Grandma's they would stop in Conway to buy freshly ground cornmeal and grits and an entire smoked cured country ham. This was food that Wavy grew up eating and could not get enough of.

Mina learned to cook all his favorites including Grandma's beef stew which became everyone's favorite. Mina would cook the savory stew once a month, usually a couple weeks before the visit to Grandma's because she knew that Grandma would prepare it as well. Jake couldn't wait for the next trip to Nichols because no one made sweet tea, buttermilk biscuits or brown cake like Grandma did. They haven't visited the dear old lady in a while due to Wavy's accident and healing so the next trip had to be soon because the food surplus was running low; everything had to be stone ground for Wavy's palate.

After doing his homework, cleaning up and talking teenage nonsense to Barbara on the phone for a half hour, Jake was called by Mina to come to the table for supper. Wavy, Mina, Uncle Hal, Kenny and Jake lowered their heads while Mina said the blessing then they all started digging in. Jake was extremely hungry for some reason and had his eye on a couple big pork chops but would grab only one at a time and top off with some gravy. He dug out a large spoonful of field peas and poured them over his white rice which he then covered with fresh chopped onion. Kenny had a big bowl of turnips and pigtails and was pouring the vinegar on them when the phone rang. It was the call that would forever change Wavy Willoughby and his youngest son Jake.

Mina answered the phone and said "Hold on, I'll get him," and told Wavy the call was for him as she held the phone in his direction with an extremely alarmed look on her face.

Jake dropped his fork and his heart plummeted to the bottom of his belly as he remembered that same look when news came of Ronnie being shot in Vietnam.

Wavy looked disturbed as well since he rarely got any calls because he just wasn't a phone conversation kind of guy. Wavy stood up from the dinner table and walked to the other side of the kitchen where the phone hung on the wall.

"Hello," Wavy said, his handsome face turned very pale as his eyes widened in disbelief, as everyone watched in sincere curiosity.

"When? How? Why? I'll be there as quickly as I can." He said very slow and softly as his voice cracked.

Jake watched his father transform before his very eyes. Wavy just stared into space as he hung up the phone. Everyone still glaring at him waiting for the news; Jake thought something bad had happened to Grandma.

"Jimmy's dead. He suffocated in a fire at the jail about 4:30 p.m. today." Wavy said, in a very low and flat monotone as if he were a robot. This was the same look that Jake had seen before on Tommy's mother's solemn face when she was told of her son's demise.

"Oh God!" Mina screamed.

…A much shaken Jake sat in the living room at his Uncle Olin's house with his cousins Rhonda and Sheila, while *Medical Center* and *Hawaii Five- O* blurred across small gray screen waiting the adults to return home. Jake was hoping and praying there was a mistake and that Jimmy was alive.

Even though he was surrounded by cousins, and the noise from the television and beautiful Hawaiian women, Jake was alone in his own miserable little world. He was sick at his stomach; he was depressed and so sad that he didn't know what to do. He didn't know Jimmy that well but he knew that he was his brother and he knew that his dad loved him. Jake liked pretty much everything he personally knew about Jimmy, like the fact that he was funny, quick witted, handsome and well-built and seemed to be a nice guy. He was just 22 and this is so unfair, Jake believed.

Jake's mind wandered to Tommy and quickly got to the bathroom and aggressively blew at his palms. Not once, not twice, even three times didn't feel right. He had to do it five times each hand until they felt clean and until he felt that the horror, the evil, the bad, was gone from his hands. Oh my God! Jake mumbled his secretive prayer three times and deliberately washed his hands to the point of pain. His hands may be cleaned but his heart was broken and his soul felt drenched in whatever madness and evil lurked in the woods and seemed to follow him where ever he went; much like his very own shadow.

Jake looked in the mad mirror over the sink as his perception of the reflection was not of this world. He quickly left the small room and found himself in the dark unfamiliar hallway and he felt very unnerved. A cold chill shot threw his body as the unforgettable stench of pluff mud filled the narrow corridor.

"I need air." Jake said, in an unusual voice, trying to clear his throat.

A worried Rhonda, noticing the fear on his face, said "You wanna go outside for a bit?"

"Please."

The alacritous Rhonda could sense from the trembling voice that Jake needed some assistance. She jumped up from her bean bag chair in her bell bottom jeans and bare feet as she walked over to Jake and grabbed his hand.

"I need air too, what a horrible night huh?"

The two walked out onto the front porch through the huge picture window while the images of Jack Lord and his perfect hair filled the television screen. Sheila sat in her dad's recliner mesmerized by the TV while she threw popcorn into her open mouth as fast as she could grab it. Jake looked up into the star dappled early spring sky.

"Let's hope there was a big mistake." Rhonda said, in a consoling and optimistic tone.

Jake didn't hear a word.

"You okay Jake?" with an elbow nudge to Jake's ribcage.

"Huh?" Jake just stared blankly into the night.

"I hope that you're gonna be okay Jake. Let's hope all this was just a big mistake."

"Oh, yes, please be a mistake. I don't know how much more Mom and Dad can take."

A loud frightening moan came from behind the house startling both of the young teens.

"What in the hell was that?!" Rhonda asked not using her usual prim and proper demeanor.

"I think it's my dead best friend," Jake said, in a matter of fact tone.

Chapter 91

"While there's life there's hope."
~ **English Proverb**

A gentle murmur from the early spring breeze tickled the dandy lion and its florets softly sailed in the soundless afternoon sun as they gently dismantled beneath the forgiving blue vista that dreams and hopes parlay into the subsequent verity of an unbounded twilight across the realm of heaven's shadow.

Long rows of moss draped live oaks encircled the land of the dead where the body of James Delano Willoughby would sleep throughout the life of the earth. At the western edge of Saints Corner on the riverside where tree lounging birds forever harmonize and the raging sun dazzles in a perpetual prism of majestic colors as it awakens the other side.

Jake lifts his head towards the cloud sprinkled blue sky and closes his eyes while his half-brother Jimmy is lowered into dark cold earth. Tears began to flow down his father's cheeks which wrenched Jake's heart inside out. Wavy Willoughby sealed his eyes shut while he gripped Mina's hand with his right hand and tightly held Ronnie's hand with his left hand.

Creeping in from a distance was the tune of his favorite song. It started like a whisper, soft and gentle then it picked up volume and tempo until it forged its beautiful melody into Wavy's ears and heart. It sounded just like the exact moment decades ago when he first heard the song "The Wildwood Flower" sung by The Carter Family come across his family's table top, silver tone radio in the large living room. That was the precise moment that Wavy convinced himself that he wanted to play the guitar and sing these beautiful songs.

Wavy could see his mother with her long hair pulled atop of her head into a perfect bun sitting in the corner of the large room sewing old dresses and aprons onto a new quilt. He saw his father relaxing in his oak rocker, smoking his old pipe and tapping his worn leather boot that housed his sore, arthritic foot.

He could see his brothers, Olin and Melvin, on the floor with a deck of cards between them as Wavy shared the large couch with his sister Joyce. He could see vividly, the old Waterbury clock on the wall and he could smell the distinct aroma from the coffee that his mother had brewed, comingling with burning oak from the fireplace as well as the Dunhill tobacco from his father's briar-wood pipe.

Then suddenly, the music was louder with each chord with a distinct high definition without the static of poor reception. The crystal clear C chord, the strum of the G7 and F chords and the pick and pull on the A minor rang with true clarity as his thumb went down on the G string. Instead of Mother May Belle, Wavy could hear himself singing about idols of clay and the pale and neglected wildwood flower accompanied on chorus with the backup harmony from Guy and Spivey, his long dead friends and band members. No one but Wavy could hear the music but it sounded to him like the entire world was enjoying it.

Wavy could see Spivey and Guy smiling, each with that Chesterfield dangling from the corner of their mouths while the smoke stung their squinting eyes as they entertained the merry crowd, bouncing their hat covered heads with the tune. He could see and smell the cigarette smoke whirling in the air rising to large fans on the raised ceiling and circulating across the dim and dingy room.

He could see Jenny Hill pouring the cold draught beer from behind the long mahogany bar and winking at him. He could feel the sweat soaked brim from his wool fedora resting above his shining and honky-tonk reflective forehead. The nostalgic journey mingled with the reality of here and now and rested in the heart of the grieving father.

Wavy opened his eyes to the cool morning wind and looked far left, Jenny's eyes were clinched shut, tears found their way out of the corners and Wavy couldn't help but wonder if she was hearing and seeing the same thing that he was. Sad but strong Wavy had so much to think about and beat himself up for. To the astonishment of everyone present, Wavy dropped to his knees with his hands folded in front his face and cried. He quietly prayed for his lost son's soul.

Jake immediately thought of Mr. Stern, Mr. Moore, and the fathers of all his buddies. A strange and tragic paradigm had unfolded before his eyes. He couldn't connect all the pieces enough to make any sense. He felt giddy and jumbled trying to exemplify the entire matter, perhaps another day, another time.

Down the same two lane road sat the red two story brick building with smoke glazed windows, some of which were broken. All is quiet now, a deathly quiet, other than the hungry sparrows, frenzied cardinals, and voracious squirrels which were fluttering on the long gnarly branches of the sweet gum tree shadowing the busted window sills.

The very same windows that separated the caged and the free; the same windows to the room where within trapped captivity three days prior five young men had smoked, cursed, bragged, lied and played poker up to the moment when they desperately screaming for their lives while in the deepest depths of their lost souls begged a higher power for mercy.

On the small city sidewalk in front of the now eerie, creepy and quiet red brick chamber of death, a young mother pulled a red radio flyer wagon filled with her three year old daughter and next week's meals still confined in brown grocery sacks. The small girl pointed at the squirrels and giggled the innocent and happy laugh of a child with a drippy nose and red cheeks.

Several miles away, in the twisted myriad of shadows and murkiness, deep within the thick forest outlining the long twisting mystic creek, the chilling screeches of creatures and spirits echo from tree to tree and slide across each leaf with deft precision and glide above and beyond the cool darkness. The poor souls who stumbled into its madness will never escape its grasp.

High above in the brave blue sky, three cargo planes heading to support freedom fighters roared through the cotton white cumulus, pulsating eardrums and shaking the cold earth while leaving entrails to mark their endeavor.

Chapter 92

*"It is respectable to have no illusions,
and safe, and profitable - and dull."*
~ **Joseph Conrad**

Tommy Stern sat on a boulder against the creek bank beneath whispering shadows of an ancient oak tree. The ebb and flow of time left him ageless. His dead eyes peered through the dark into wandering waters as they drifted by on their majestic journey to the sea.

There is nothing more miserable than being alone. The spine-chilling quiet of deafness, the black abyss of nothingness; buried into the earth and missing out on life, and the amazing experience of living. The splendor of the spring and its fresh, vivacious colored creation for eyes to adore and the passion to celebrate is not known.

No orchestra or symphony for the ear. Not seeing the squirrels scurrying on top of that lonely forgotten grave beneath the tree. Birds sing but are not heard. Rain falls but is not felt. The sun shines but no healing is available for the gone and forgotten. Sometimes a spirit has to escape. Sometimes a trapped soul finds an opening. Sometimes things just happen.

In a nearby magnolia tree, two cardinals chase each other from branch to branch as Jake watched from the silent surroundings sitting on an element tattered and unsteady bench across from his brother's grave.

How does one execute revenge against a ghost he wondered? He had kept his word and wondered why Tommy had not? Perhaps this was result of Jake's initial slipup after seeing Tommy that he hoped went unnoticed. Enough is enough already. Jake wished that Tommy or whatever would end this needless slaughter of innocent people.

He started to blow his palms and suddenly, on the grass right in front of his eyes, he saw a shadow saunter up beside him. Barbara joined Jake on the bench and rubbed his knee. Jake stood, took her hand and they slowly walked back to Christine who was sitting in "Herbie" waiting for them.

They drove down the long, shady avenue of oaks, Highway 61, taking them home to John's Island. The top 40 hits struggled to be heard from the small AM radio. Christine shook her lovely head in tune to every song that writhed forth.

"Hey, why don't we all go to The Patio Drive Inn tonight for some chow?" The green eyed beauty said.

"Sure," her sister chimed in loudly over the music.

"Is that okay with you Jake?" Christine asked.

"Yeah, that's fine," Jake replied.

"Good, when we get home I'll call Ronnie at work; he has wanted to go there."

"Cool," Jake said solemnly.

"Oh man, I just love their onion rings and milkshakes," declared Barbara.

"Oh, I know, and the cheeseburgers, God, I'm starving." Christine replied. "Aren't you hungry Jake?"

"Uh, um, yeah I guess so. You think that we can take Kenny along with us?"

"Absolutely, the more the merrier," Christine said.

"Let's squeeze Julie in too then." Barbara said. Jake thought, what, no Kathy?

"I can taste those yummy onion rings now," Christine said, and then ran her tongue across her lips.

Jake just stared straight ahead. He looked tired and weak. So many people are missing out on cheeseburgers, onion rings, milkshakes, pretty girls, and music. He mused.

…The baseball, the one that Jake had fantasized about and longed for longer than he actually owned it. The same ball that Johnny and Tommy stole from their friend and the same ball that Tommy went in to the mud for and never returned… as human. The same ball that awoke evil spirits that caused several deaths, ruined many families and produced malady in Jake. That small and forgotten ball now rest in the mud on the edge of the still pond just behind the pear trees. It has nowhere else to go. Its journey has ended, for now. The seed is planted, the clouds darken, the sky rumbles.

In a smoldering and ominous jungle in Southeast Asia, Buddy Barfield takes a bullet between the eyes.

Behind locked doors in his sister's bedroom, Kenny admires himself in the mirror as he adorns a dress and makeup.

In her bathroom, a teenage girl vomits into the toilet

.

The darkness from Jake's old friend has come to visit him once again.

Follow the arduous flight of the haunted raven endlessly searching for its tortured soul, breathlessly riding the intransigent southern tides within the tragic twist and turns of the wicked currents, while resonating with the screams of horror and carving the banks and creeks. Where sits the vindictive tribe of the cursed Cusabo Indian, amongst the anonymities of the forever merciless and doomed. A distant storm is formed and strengthens.

…sanity interrupted, and so flows the mystic creek.

Contributing Artist

Roy Acuff – Walbash Cannonball
The Archie's
The Box Tops – The Letter
The Carter Family – Wildwood Flower and Church in the Wildwood
Gene Chandler – Duke of Earl
Joe Cocker – With A Little Help From My Friends
Creedence Clearwater Revival – Susie Q
Crispian St. Peters – Pied Piper
Bing Crosby – White Christmas
Danny & the Juniors – At the Hop
The Dave Clark Five – Glad All Over
Jimmie Davis- You Are My Sunshine
Deep Purple – Hush
Dixon Brothers – The Intoxicated Rat
The Doors – Light My Fire and Hello, I Love You
Stonewall Jackson - Waterloo
Tommy James – I Think We're Alone
Jerry Lee Lewis – Great Balls of Fire
Glenn Miller – Little Brown Jug
The Monkee's – I'm a Believer
Mozart
Gary Puckett – Young Girl
Jeannie C. Riley- Harper Valley PTA
Marty Robbins – El Paso City
Simon & Garfunkel- Sounds of Silence and Mrs. Robinson
Smiths – Baby It's You
Sons of The Pioneers – Cool, Clear Water
The Stanley Brothers – Lonely Tombs
The Temptations – My Girl
Porter Wagoner - Green, Green Grass of Home
Kitty Wells – It Wasn't God Who Made Honky-Tonk Angels
Hank Williams – Your Cheatin' Heart

Special Thanks

To my adoring wife, Charlotte - for her steadfast love and support along with her tireless work as my editor and publisher; good teamwork, let's do it again.

To my daughter, Mallory, for believing in me and my pen.

To Juanita Dew Patrum, for her wonderful artwork.

To the greatest literary minds of all time, for the numerous quotes.

About the Author

Slade Belgard was born, raised, and educated in the South Carolina low country. He has done everything from bagging groceries, acting, modeling, bartending, and feeding wild animals in a zoo. He is a devoted husband, father, son, brother, uncle, nephew, cousin and friend. He enjoys drawing, photography, guitar, kayaking and camping as well as hikes in the mountains as well as strolls on his beloved Folly Beach, and the beautiful streets of his hometown, Charleston.

Nearly four years ago, he set out to do something that he had always dreamed of doing, write a novel. Through the years he was aware that he had the creativity and capability to do such, but was financially challenged, and never afforded the luxury of time. Determined to fulfill his dreams, and when the opportunity eventually presented itself, his journey as a novelist began.

Though without formal training or higher education, he decided to write what he knew most about and what he was most fervent about, his family and himself. Although displaced from his English teacher by nearly forty years, he worked very diligently to use the skills that were taught to him long ago.

His writing first began as a children's book because he wanted to make it as unpretentious as possible, but as the story advanced, and his confidence grew, the tale became somewhat of an R-rated adult adventure. After realizing that some of the subject matter may prove too offensive for some, especially his older cousins and mother-in-law, he took the necessary steps to tone down the rather risqué elements in the story. This arduous task became a complete overhaul of the story, thus enduring the majority of the stages involved, including the proofreading, editing, and publishing.

As an artist, he continues to work on new projects and challenges. He is currently working on Volume II of the Mystic Creek Trilogy and hopes you will join him as the Willoughby saga continues.

www.ingramcontent.com/pod-product-compliance
Lightning Source LLC
Chambersburg PA
CBHW021351260626
47153CB00024B/2